43 Old Cemetery Road: Book Two

OVER MY DEAD BODY

Kate Klise

Illustrated by

M. Sarah Klise

Harcourt
Houghton Mifflin Harcourt
BOSTON   NEW YORK   2009

Harcourt is an imprint of Houghton Mifflin Harcourt Publishing Company.

www.hmhbooks.com

Library of Congress Cataloging-in-Publication Data
Klise, Kate.
Over my dead body / by Kate Klise ; illustrated by M. Sarah Klise.
p. cm.
Summary: In this story told mostly through letters, busybody Dick Tater tries to ban
Halloween and ghost stories, as well as to break up the popular writing team of I. B.
Grumply, ghost Olive C. Spence, and eleven-year-old illustrator Seymour Hope.
ISBN 978-0-15-205734-3
[1. Authors—Fiction. 2. Books and reading—Fiction. 3. Ghosts—Fiction. 4. Haunted houses—
Fiction. 5. Halloween—Fiction. 6. Letters—Fiction. 7. Humorous stories.] I. Klise, M. Sarah,
ill. II. Title.
PZ7.K684Ove 2009
[Fic]—dc22
2009007979

Designed by M. Sarah Klise

Printed in the United States of America

MP 10 9 8 7 6 5 4 3 2 1

This book is dedicated
to Desmond Moss Augustine
with much 12-15-22-5.

A Warning to Readers!

This book contains material that could be considered objectionable.
Some readers might try to ban this book after turning the last page.
Others might want to ban it without even opening it.

If, while reading this book, you feel
bothered,
bewildered,
insulted,
offended,
outraged,
scandalized,
threatened,
and/or inexplicably itchy,
we apologize for the inconvenience.
Kindly return the book to the nearest bookshelf
so that someone else might enjoy this

TRUE GHOST STORY,

which begins
as soon as you
turn this
page.

Welcome to 43 Old Cemetery Road

If this is the first you've heard of 43 Old Cemetery Road, you should be aware of the following facts:

43 Old Cemetery Road is the address of a 32½-room house in Ghastly, Illinois.

Some people call the house Spence Mansion because it was built in 1874 by Olive C. Spence.

Miss Spence was an elegant woman who spent her life writing and illustrating mysteries.

But no one ever read her mysteries—except the hundreds of publishers who rejected them.

Shortly before her death, Olive C. Spence made a solemn vow to haunt her house and the town of Ghastly, Illinois, forever—or until one of her mysteries was published.

And haunt it she did. From stealing muffins to borrowing library books, Olive made her presence known. From time to time, she even appeared in an old mirror at Ghastly Antiques.

(Attempts to photograph Olive's image were never successful.)

More than 80 years after Spence's death, Les and Diane Hope bought Spence Mansion.

The Hopes were professors of the paranormal. They hoped to document the ghost of Olive C. Spence and make a lot of money off their research.

But Olive refused to cooperate. For 12 long years, she declined to have any contact with Professors Les and Diane Hope.

Why? Because she thought they were greedy.

Olive was right.

But as so often happens with wretched adults, Les and Diane Hope had a perfectly wonderful son named Seymour, who was born at Spence Mansion.

(← That's Seymour's cat. His name is Shadow.)

Seymour Hope and Olive C. Spence quickly became best friends.

Olive and Seymour also (after a somewhat rocky start) became friends with Ignatius B. Grumply, a famous author who rented Spence Mansion during the summer Les and Diane Hope abandoned Seymour.

Together, Ignatius B. Grumply, Olive C. Spence, and Seymour Hope collaborated on the first three chapters of a ghost story, which they called *43 Old Cemetery Road*. Ignatius and Olive wrote the words; Seymour drew the pictures.

They gave away the first three chapters of the book and asked anyone who wanted to read more chapters to kindly send $3 to 43 Old Cemetery Road.

Well, *everyone*, it seemed, wanted to read more. Ignatius, Olive, and Seymour were delighted by the thousands of orders they received from all over the world.

The money was nice, too. Seymour used part of it to buy Spence Mansion from his parents, who preferred living without him in a hotel in Paris. (Yes, some parents *really* are *that* awful.)

And Ignatius and Olive really were much nicer—even though Ignatius did get a bit grumpy now and then when he got writer's block.

And sometimes Olive was cranky, especially when she misplaced her reading glasses.

But other than that, everything at 43 Old Cemetery Road was frighteningly perfect until one day in September, when the following letter arrived . . .

Dick Tater
Director

September 5

Ignatius B. Grumply
43 Old Cemetery Road
Ghastly, Illinois

Dear Mr. Grumply,

It has come to my attention that Seymour Hope is living with you in a domicile without the benefit of his parents.

As director of the International Movement for the Safety & Protection Of Our Kids & Youth (IMSPOOKY), it is my duty to see that every child in the world is protected from dangerous people, circumstances, and ideas.

Please submit a letter explaining by what authority you are caring for Seymour Hope. Are you a relative, the boy's legal guardian, or a hired caregiver?

Also, I understand that Seymour Hope has not yet reported for school this year. Please explain that, too.

Authoritatively,

Dick Tater

Dick Tater

IGNATIUS B. GRUMPLY

A WRITER IN RESIDENCE

43 OLD CEMETERY ROAD   **2ND FLOOR**   **GHASTLY, ILLINOIS**

September 9

Dick Tater
Director, IMSPOOKY
2 Bureaucracy Avenue
Washington, D.C. 20505

Dear Mr. Tater,

I'm neither Seymour's relative nor his legal guardian
nor a hired caregiver. I simply found the boy in Spence
Mansion, an old house I rented for the summer.
Through an odd clause in the lease, I acquired the boy
from his parents, who abandoned him three months ago
when they left on a lecture tour of Europe.

Since then, Seymour has been happily living here with
Olive C. Spence and me. Together we've formed a publishing company. Our specialty? Ghost stories.

I'll admit I had very little experience caring for children
before I moved to Spence Mansion. I'll further admit I
didn't even *like* children. But I'm learning from Olive.
She's a wonderful mother figure for Seymour, who I'm
happy to report is safe and happy at 43 Old Cemetery
Road.

As for school, Seymour has asked to be homeschooled by Olive and me. I can't think of a finer education for an 11-year-old artist than illustrating ghost stories.

If you have any more questions, please don't hesitate to contact me.

Yours in the written word,

Ignatius B. Grumply

Ignatius B. Grumply

Dick Tater
Director

September 12

Ignatius B. Grumply
43 Old Cemetery Road
Ghastly, Illinois

Dear Mr. Grumply,

You cannot legally "acquire" a child through a rental lease. Nor can you possibly be sharing a domicile with Olive C. Spence.

According to our records, Ms. Spence has been dead since 1911.

Given the above information, I have no choice but to begin an investigation **immediately** into the suspicious activities underway at 43 Old Cemetery Road.

Emphatically,

Dick Tater

Dick Tater

THE GHASTLY TIMES

Friday, September 12

Cliff Hanger, Editor

"Your Secrets Are Our Business"

50 cents

Morning Edition

Local Boy Living in Mansion Without Parents Is "Very Grave Matter"

Dick Tater, director of the International Movement for the Safety & Protection Of Our Kids & Youth (IMSPOOKY), has ordered an investigation into the safety of Seymour Hope, 11.

Tater told *The Ghastly Times* the investigation was prompted by an anonymous letter he received.

"Thanks to a concerned citizen I have learned that a young boy is living in a house without parents," said Tater. "Instead he's living with a man named Ignatius B. Grumply, who is filling this poor child's head with ghost stories and calling it an education."

Grumply does not deny that since June he has lived at 43 Old Cemetery Rd. with Seymour Hope and the ghost of Olive C. Spence.

"It's a lovely arrangement," Grumply told *The Ghastly Times*. "I occupy the second floor of the house. Seymour's bedroom and art studio are located on the third floor. Olive spends much of her time in the cupola, though she likes to float around the rest of the house, too."

When asked to describe a typical day at Spence Mansion, Grumply said: "We meet for meals three times a day in the dining room. Olive usually cooks. Seymour sets the table. I'm in charge of dishwashing. We spend one hour a day, usually after lunch, discussing our book. Other than that, we work independently."

Tater said his investigation will begin with a visit to Spence Mansion tomorrow. "I plan to get to the bottom of this very grave matter," Tater stated.

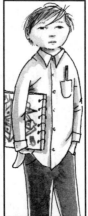

Seymour Hope is living at Spence Mansion without parents.

IMSPOOKY Director Says Halloween Bad for Children

Bad dreams. Head colds. Cavities.

These are just a few of the side effects associated with Halloween, said Dick Tater, director of the International Movement for the Safety & Protection Of Our Kids & Youth (IMSPOOKY).

"It's time we put an end to this dangerous holiday," Tater said at a press conference yesterday in Washington, D.C.

Tater is expected to make an important announcement about Halloween tonight on

(Continued on page 2, column 1)

IMSPOOKY *(Continued from page 1, column 2)*

Tater Tips, the safety news update broadcast weekly on TV and radio.

The IMSPOOKY was established earlier this year by a worldwide committee of concerned parents with children in middle school, often considered the most perilous place for youngsters.

Dick Tater discusses the dangers of Halloween.

Orders for More Chapters Keep Rolling In

Grumply says new chapters will be ready by Halloween.

In just one month, more than 250,000 readers from around the world have sent money requesting three more chapters of *43 Old Cemetery Road*, a work-in-progress ghost story named for the street address of Spence Mansion.

"The response has been overwhelming," coauthor Ignatius B. Grumply said yesterday. "Olive, Seymour and I are delighted and flattered."

Grumply assured readers that the next three chapters of the book would be ready in six weeks. "Just in time for Halloween," Grumply promised, then jumped for joy.

TATER TIPS

DICK TATER: Good evening, and welcome to *Tater Tips*, important safety news from me, your friendly Dick Tater. I'm here tonight with an urgent message.

For the protection of children everywhere, I am canceling Halloween this year and issuing a worldwide ban on all Halloween activities. That includes trick-or-treating, costume parties, bobbing for apples, and especially the telling, writing, and reading of ghost stories.

Ghost stories are bad for children's health. Worse still, ghost stories are a gateway to other dangerous activities and ideas.

As adults, we must protect children from ghost stories and the people who write them.

That's why tomorrow I'm traveling to Ghastly, Illinois, where a man named

Ignatius B. Grumply is living with a young boy and telling him stories about a ghost named Olive C. Spence. Grumply is forcing this child to draw pictures for a book Grumply says he's writing with this ghost.

It's a scam, a hoax, and an outrage! Thank goodness I'm on the case. I'll have more to say about this on the next edition of *Tater Tips*.

Now don't forget: There will be NO Halloween this year. Anyone found wearing a costume, trick-or-treating, bobbing for apples, and/or reading, writing, listening to, or telling a ghost story will be arrested.

Have a safe night. And don't worry about a thing. You can leave the thinking to me, Dick Tater.

VOICEOVER: Tune in next week to *Tater Tips*, brought to you by the International Movement for the Safety & Protection Of Our Kids & Youth.

IGNATIUS B. GRUMPLY

A WRITER IN RESIDENCE

43 OLD CEMETERY ROAD   **2ND FLOOR**   **GHASTLY, ILLINOIS**

September 12

Olive C. Spence
The Cupola
43 Old Cemetery Road
Ghastly, Illinois

Dear Olive,

I know it's late, but I think we should have a meeting as soon as practical to discuss the

I'm right here. What do you want to discuss, dear?

Olive! I wish you wouldn't scare me like that. We need a plan for Seymour. I'm afraid this arrangement we have is not entirely legal.

Legal schmeegal. The boy's parents are weasels. They left him in the middle of the night when they slinked off to Europe on their lecture tour. Who knows what would've happened if I weren't still haunting my house—and if you hadn't rented it for the summer?

14.

I agree. But there's a certain Dick Tater at the

Yes, yes. I know. I read his letter, too. You'll just have to go to Washington, D.C., and explain the situation to him.

I'm afraid it's too late for that. He's coming here.

Dick Tater's coming *here*? Without an invitation? Over my dead body!

I didn't think ghosts *had* bodies.

Don't get sassy with me, Iggy.

I'm sorry, Olive. But Mr. Tater has ordered an investigation. Didn't you read today's newspaper?

I was going to. But then I made a pot of tea and forgot where I put my reading glasses. Ugh. My mind is simply mush these days.

You're just a little forgetful sometimes.

As you will be when you're 190 years old.

I'm sure I will. But back to Dick Tater. Some busybody sent him an anonymous letter informing him of our living situation. What should we do?

Tell him Seymour is happy as a lark here.

I will. But what if Mr. Ta

What if nothing, Iggy. We have three chapters to write before Halloween. You'll just have to convince Mr. Tater Tot that we don't need his assistance.

I'll try, Olive. The only probl

Iggy, I haven't got time for this. I must find something to wear for our visitor tomorrow.

Olive, you're invisible to most people, remember? I've seen you only once, and it was just for a split second.

You've had other chances to see me, but you weren't trying hard enough. Besides, I have my pride. I always dress up for company—even if it is a man named Tater. I'll see you tomorrow, dear.

Good night, Olive.

Good night, Iggy.

O.C.S.

Ghost Writer in Residence
43 Old Cemetery Road, The Cupola
Ghastly, Illinois

September 12

Dearest Seymour,

I don't know why you're still awake at this hour. But since you are, I want to apologize for something.

I've always assumed you wanted to live here with me. We've been friends since you were born. But for all I know, your feelings might have changed. Now that you're almost grown up, you might prefer to live with relatives or friends—or even try to patch things up with your parents.

There are many options that might be more appealing to an 11-year-old boy than living in an old house with a grumpy writer like Iggy and an ancient ghost like me.

If you want to live somewhere else, you must let me know. This is your life and your decision. I will respect whatever choice you make. And I'm sorry that it didn't occur to me to ask you this before now.

With love and respect,

Olive

43 Old Cemetery Road
Third Floor
Ghastly, Illinois

September 12

Dear Olive,

Of <u>course</u> I want to live here with you and Mr. Grumply.
I don't have any other friends or relatives who are
half as cool as you—least of all my crummy parents.

But if you don't want me here anymore, I could run
away. Do you want me to?

—Seymour

Ghost Writer in Residence
43 Old Cemetery Road, The Cupola
Ghastly, Illinois

September 12

Dear Seymour,

Run away? Over my dead body!

Seymour, I adore sharing my mansion with you. I just wanted to make sure that's what you want, too.

Now, a man with a silly name will be here tomorrow. Since Iggy and I haven't given you any new chapters to illustrate yet, why don't you sketch our uninvited visitor? His name is Mr. Tater. I'm guessing he'll make an interesting model.

Good night.

Love,

Olive

43 Old Cemetery Road
Third Floor
Ghastly, Illinois

September 12

Dear Olive,

Will do.

Good night. Rest in peas!

Love,

    —Seymour

September 12

Dear Seymour,

The expression is "Rest in *peace*."

Now go to bed! It's late. And I want you
to be well rested for our visitor tomorrow.

See you in the morning.

Love,

Olive

This is Mr. Tater arriving at 43 Old Cemetery Road.

This is Mr. Grumply trying to explain our publishing company to Mr. Tater.

This is Mr. Tater not understanding.

This is Mr. Tater making phone calls.

This is Mr. Grumply and me being taken away!

ADMISSION TO

ILLINOIS HOME FOR THE DERANGED
Ghastly, Illinois

Patient's name: _Ignatius B. Grumply_

Age: _64_

Voluntary admission (**Involuntary admission**)

Reason for admission: _Patient says he's writing a book with a ghost._

Is this patient considered dangerous? (**Yes**) **No**

Recommended stay: _Forever_

GHASTLY ORPHANAGE

New Resident Form

Name of new resident: <u>Seymour Hope</u>

Age: <u>11</u>

Orphaned _____ Abandoned <u>XX</u> Other _____

Is this child a security risk?   Yes _____ No <u>XX</u>

Does this child suffer from physical or mental illness?
<u>Possible mental illness.</u>

<u>Boy claims his best friend is a ghost.</u>

Length of stay: <u>18th birthday or until his</u>
          parents claim him

Photo:

THE GHASTLY TIMES

Sunday, September 14
Cliff Hanger, Editor

"Your Secrets Are Our Business"

$1.50
Morning Edition

Grumply Deranged, Says IMSPOOKY Director; Hope Placed in Ghastly Orphanage

Ignatius B. Grumply was admitted against his will to the Illinois Home for the Deranged yesterday afternoon while Seymour Hope became the newest resident at Ghastly Orphanage.

These surprising developments came after Dick Tater, director of the International Movement for the Safety & Protection Of Our Kids & Youth (IMSPOOKY), visited Grumply and Hope at 43 Old Cemetery Rd.

"I had no idea how disturbed Ignatius Grumply was," said Tater in a press conference yesterday. "Grumply tried to tell me he was homeschooling the boy with the help of a ghost. Far from it! Spence Mansion is neither a home nor a school, but the former residence of a deranged man and the 11-year-old boy he was holding hostage."

Tater said he plans to reunite Hope with his parents as soon as possible.

"Until then," said Tater, "the boy will be safe in Ghastly Orphanage."

Grumply is taken away by state troopers.

Hope will live at local orphanage until his parents return.

Tater Suggests Burning Books on October 31

From coast to coast, towns and schools are busy canceling Halloween parades, costume balls and neighborhood trick-or-treating activities in response to a ban imposed by IMSPOOKY director Dick Tater.

Halloween has long been a favorite holiday in Ghastly, where generations of children have trick-or-treated at Spence Mansion. Legend has it that anyone brave enough to visit Spence Mansion on Halloween receives a mysterious treat from the ghost of Olive C. Spence.

"See?" said Dick Tater, when told of the Ghastly tradition. "That is precisely the kind of unhealthy practice I'm trying to stamp out."

(Continued on page 2, column 1)

BOOKS *(Continued from page 1, column 2)*

NO parades
NO costumes
NO trick-or-treating

BURN BOOKS!

Dick Tater says bad books make good bonfires.

Tater has suggested a substitute for traditional Halloween activities. "Rather than trick-or-treating, I propose we celebrate October 31 by burning all the ghost stories in the world."

Tater suggests calling the new holiday Dick Tater Appreciation Day.

Was *43 Old Cemetery Road* a Hoax?

Fans of *43 Old Cemetery Road* could be in for a grim disappointment.

The creators promised to deliver three new chapters of the work in progress to subscribers by October 31. But that hardly seems possible now that

Fay Tality admits she fell for scam.

coauthor Ignatius B. Grumply is in custody at the Illinois Home for the Deranged and illustrator Seymour Hope is living at Ghastly Orphanage.

Grumply and Hope were collaborating on the book, along with the ghost of Olive C. Spence—or so they claimed.

But according to Dick Tater, director of IMSPOOKY, the project was a clever hoax designed by Grumply to bilk readers out of their dollars and common sense.

"It's embarrassing that we all fell for it," said Fay Tality, president of the Bank of Ghastly. "I guess I liked believing that Olive C. Spence haunted this town. It made Ghastly feel special. But Dick Tater's probably right. Adults should set a good example for children by rejecting silly ghost stories and the people who tell them."

Tality said she plans to burn her entire collection of ghost stories on October 31, as directed by Tater.

"But before I do, I'm going to reread them all," Tality tattled. "Don't tell Dick Tater, but I've always loved scary stories and the people who write them."

Dick Tater
Director

INTERNATIONAL EXPRESS MAIL

September 18

Professors Les and Diane Hope
Guests, Hôtel de Sens
1, rue du Figuier
75004 Paris
France

Dear Mr. and Mrs. Hope,

It is my duty to inform you that your son, Seymour Hope, has been removed from the domicile located at 43 Old Cemetery Road and placed in Ghastly Orphanage.

The reason is simple: Ignatius B. Grumply is mentally unstable.

An anonymous letter-writer has assured me that you did not know Grumply was deranged when you agreed to let him care for Seymour in your absence. The same anonymous informant claims that you have been *extremely* busy on your lecture tour, titled "Only Fools (and Children) Believe in Ghosts."

Because I know you share my commitment to protecting children everywhere, I am willing to work with you toward the goal of reuniting you with your son.

Please let me know when you plan to return to Ghastly to reclaim him. I will make every effort to ensure that he is safe, healthy, and eager for the reunion, whenever that may be.

Yours officially,

Dick Tater

P.S. If you're wondering how I got your address in France, you can thank the person (or persons) who sent me the anonymous letter.

September 19

Dick Tater
Director, IMSPOOKY
2 Bureaucracy Avenue
Washington, D.C. 20505
USA

Dear Mr. Tater,

We hardly know what to say or write—except
THANK YOU for protecting our beloved son,
Seymour. And thanks, too, to that thoughtful and
anonymous letter-writer, whoever he or she (or
they) might be.

It's true that we have been extraordinarily busy on
our lecture tour. Now we're working on a book
titled <u>Only Fools (and Children) Believe in Ghosts</u>:

30.

<u>The Authoritative Anti-Ghost Story</u>. It's the only way we know to convince the millions of children in the world (including our own son) that there are NO such things as ghosts.

We understand this is a particular concern of yours, so we ask for your patience as we finish this important manifesto. We expect to complete our anti-ghost book by the end of next month.

If it's agreeable to you, we will return to Ghastly on October 31 to pick up Seymour. In the meantime, thank you again for keeping our son away from that <u>horrible</u> Mr. Grumply! We had no idea he was a deranged and dangerous madman!

Gratefully yours,

Les & Diane Hope

Les and Diane Hope

P.S. We are enclosing the cover for our new book. Please let us know if you'd like to order a copy.

Only Fools

(and Children)

Believe in Ghosts

THE
AUTHORITATIVE
ANTI-GHOST
STORY

Professors Les and Diane Hope

"Sure to be a bestseller!" —L.H. and D.H.

2 BUREAUCRACY AVENUE   **WASHINGTON, D.C. 20505**

Dick Tater
Director

September 24

Professors Les and Diane Hope
Guests, Hôtel de Sens
1, rue du Figuier
75004 Paris
France

Dear Mr. and Mrs. Hope,

Thank you for your prompt response. Your new book is *exactly* what children today need.

I would like to order five million copies. My intention is to replace every ghost story on every bookshelf with *Only Fools (and Children) Believe in Ghosts: The Authoritative Anti-Ghost Story*.

Please don't worry about Seymour. He will be safe at Ghastly Orphanage until you return on October 31.

And don't worry about Ignatius B. Grumply, either. Patients at the Illinois Home for the Deranged are kept in solitary confinement. Rest assured that Ignatius B. Grumply is no longer a threat to children or society.

Authoritatively yours,

Dick Tater

Dick Tater

ILLINOIS HOME FOR THE DERANGED

PATIENT REQUEST FORM

NAME OF PATIENT: Ignatius B. Grumply

ITEM(S) REQUESTED: Paper, Pens, Envelopes, Stamps

REASON: Patient says he will become a danger to himself and others if he is unable to write.

APPROVED
SEPT. 27

ILLINOIS HOME FOR THE DERANGED

September 28

1 Cuckoo Lane
Ghastly, Illinois

Olive C. Spence
The Cupola
43 Old Cemetery Road
Ghastly, Illinois

Dear Olive,

Of all the insufferable indignities I've been subjected to in my life, *this* takes the cake.

Just because I mentioned to Mr. Tater that I'd fallen in love with a talented and glamorous writer who happens to be a ghost, I'm locked up in a home for the *deranged*. It's outrageous, and I have every intention of bringing legal action against that petty little Dick Tater—just as soon as I figure out a way to escape.

But enough about me. I'm sick with worry about Seymour. Tater refused to tell me where he was taking him. Do you know? If so, please write back and assure me that Seymour's all right. I worry what might become of that poor child if Tater has anything to say in the matter.

And what about you, Olive? Are you well? Are you still at Spence Mansion? I miss you madly.

Please write back as soon as humanly—or ghostly—possible.

Hopelessly devoted,

Ignatius

Ignatius

September 29

Olive C. Spence
The Cupola
43 Old Cemetery Road
Ghastly, Illinois

Dear Olive,

I finally found some paper so I could write you a letter. I can't believe I didn't even get to say good-bye to you or Shadow.

Dick Tater said there was no competent or legal guardian to take care of me at 43 Old Cemetery Road. The more Mr. Grumply tried to explain it, the worse it got. Were you there? Did you see what happened? Is Mr. Grumply in jail? Is it illegal for us to live together and work on our book?

I hate living here. I've drawn some pictures so you can see for yourself how lousy this place is.

Love,

    —Seymour

The place looks creepy from the outside.

But it's even worse inside.

Dining hall

This is where they feed us.
The food is terrible.

O.C.S.

Ghost Writer in Residence
43 Old Cemetery Road, The Cupola
Ghastly, Illinois

September 30

Ignatius B. Grumply
Patient, Illinois Home for the Deranged
1 Cuckoo Lane
Ghastly, Illinois

Seymour Hope
Resident, Ghastly Orphanage
66 Gruel Drive
Ghastly, Illinois

Dear Iggy and Seymour,

Oh, darlings! I saw the whole shameful showdown with Mr. Tater Tot. I'm sorry that I wasn't able to be more helpful to you in your hour of need. I was foolishly wearing high-heeled boots that were stylish but not

40.

very practical in a crisis—
especially since I haven't
worn heels in 110 years.
Forgiveness, please.

At least now I know
where you are. (You can
see from the addresses
listed on the previous
page where the other is.)
It's all very worrisome,
and I'm afraid the news
here is no better.

Early this morning, I floated over to the
Ghastly Gourmand for tea. I was too distracted to brew my own. While there, I
couldn't help overhear the locals discussing . . .
us!

Kay Daver said: "There's no way on earth
they can continue publishing their book now
that Grumply's in the nut house and the
poor kid's in the orphanage. Olive can't write

the whole thing on her own." To which Fay Tality replied: "Didn't you see Dick Tater on TV the other night? There's no ghost in that mansion. It's a joke. The book was just a scam by Grumply." To which Mac Awbrah added: "Fay's right. It was all a cheap trick." To which Shirley U. Jest said: "I'm canceling my order for the next three chapters of *43 Old Cemetery Road*. I want my money back!" To which they all said in unison: "Me, too!"

Well, of course by that point I had completely lost my appetite for tea, and returned home.

But do you see the problem, boys? Our readers are turning against us. They think we're a joke. A trick! They don't take us the least bit seriously. If our readers all demand refunds, we'll have to sell the house—and then what? Where will we live? What will we do?

We've simply *got* to deliver the next three chapters of our book by Halloween. But how can we do so under our current circumstances? Do either of you have an idea on how we should proceed—other than with caution?

Yours in spirit,

Olive

P.S. Shadow misses you both desperately, but is otherwise fine.

October 1

Ignatius B. Grumply
Patient, Illinois Home for the Deranged
1 Cuckoo Lane
Ghastly, Illinois

Dear Mr. Grumply,

Sorry to hear you're in the asylum. I bet you're already planning your escape. When you're free, can you come get me? Thanks.

I have an idea for the next three chapters of our book. Remember all those mysteries Olive told us she wrote during her life? The ones she could never get anyone to publish? What if she found one of those stories and made copies of it for our customers? She could enclose a letter with the story explaining to readers that she's sending them a special mystery for Halloween. Then, when we're all home again, we can get back to work on <u>43 Old Cemetery Road</u>.

I think people would love to read one of Olive's stories. She's a LEGEND in this town!

If you like this idea, please write to Olive. I get only two stamps every other week.

Miss you lots. Don't forget to come rescue me!

—Seymour

ILLINOIS HOME FOR THE DERANGED

October 2

Olive C. Spence
The Cupola
43 Old Cemetery Road
Ghastly, Illinois

1 Cuckoo Lane
Ghastly, Illinois

Dear Olive,

Seymour has a brilliant idea. (See enclosed letter.)

I'd love to read your old manuscripts, too. But I'd prefer to do so in the comfort of my own reading chair.

Olive, if you'll work on satisfying our customers, I'll devise escape plans for Seymour and me. We'll be back in business at 43 Old Cemetery Road in no time.

Please forward this letter to Seymour, as I haven't the energy to copy it. I hope the food is better where you are, Seymour. On the upside, I seem to be losing a few unwanted pounds.

Till very soon, I hope.

Love,

Ignatius

Ignatius

October 3

Ignatius B. Grumply
Patient, Illinois Home for the Deranged
1 Cuckoo Lane
Ghastly, Illinois

Seymour Hope
Resident, Ghastly Orphanage
66 Gruel Drive
Ghastly, Illinois

Dear Iggy and Seymour,

It's agreed! And I can promise our customers
that more chapters of *43 Old Cemetery
Road* will be forthcoming when the three of
us are reunited.

While I do that, Iggy will escape his handlers and then retrieve Seymour from the orphanage. Also, Iggy, please figure out a way to make our living arrangement legal.

Darling Seymour, may I ask that you continue sketching while you wait for Iggy? Artists must keep their fingers and minds nimble— even in times of adversity.

We have a frightening amount of work ahead of us!

Yours in sensible shoes,

Olive

P.S. I do hope I can find my old manuscripts. I haven't seen them since my death almost a century ago.

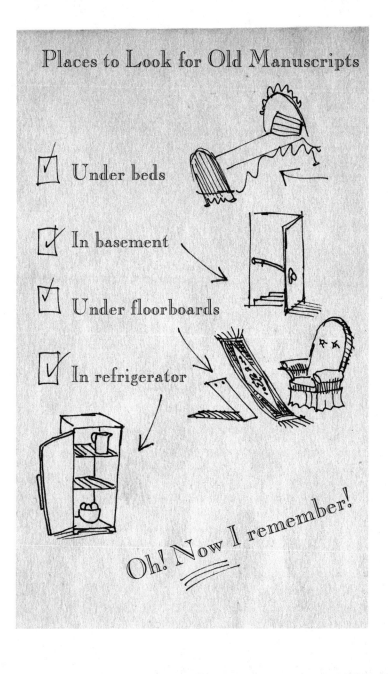

O.C.S.

Ghost Writer in Residence
43 Old Cemetery Road, The Cupola
Ghastly, Illinois

October 4

Ms. Fay Tality
President, Bank of Ghastly
6 Scary Street
Ghastly, Illinois

Dear Ms. Tality,

I couldn't help overhearing you recently at the Ghastly Gourmand. It's a shame you've begun doubting my existence. I was a dear friend of your great-grandfather, who established the Bank of Ghastly in 1904. In fact, I was one of his first customers.

I'm writing to you because I'm in a bit of a pickle. I'm desperately trying to locate my old manuscripts. These were the stories I tried for years to get published and couldn't. My problem is this: I can't for the life—or death—of me remember where I've stored them. But I have a strong hunch they might be in my safe-deposit box at your bank.

I am enclosing my box key. Your great-grandfather was kind enough to give me box 0. Will you please open the box with this key and send me the contents?

I realize that I am probably asking you to violate a bank rule or two. But I hope that you'll agree to do this small favor for me in exchange for all the Halloween treats I left out for you over the years. I watched you every year from my cupola. I especially enjoyed the year you dressed as a pirate. You looked just like your great-grandfather!

With fingers crossed,

Olive C. Spence

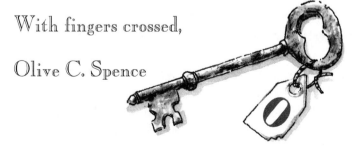

Fay Tality
President

October 6

Wise Guy/Gal
43 Old Cemetery Road
Ghastly, Illinois

Dear Wise Guy or Gal,

Look here, I don't know what kind of joke you're playing, but I'll have you know that I don't believe in ghosts—not anymore, anyway.

Of course as a child I believed in ghosts—or *a* ghost, I should say. Back then everyone in Ghastly believed that Olive C. Spence haunted her old house. And yes, I *did* trick-or-treat one Halloween at Spence Mansion dressed as a pirate. I have no idea how you know this, but it's hardly proof that *you're* the ghost of Olive C. Spence.

I'm assuming your letter has something to do with the hateful little trick Mr. Grumply is playing on our town. Well, you'll not fool me! I plan to burn the first three chapters of "your" book, just as Mr. Tater said we should.

It might interest you to know that I opened safe-deposit box 0—just to satisfy my own curiosity. That box has been something of a mystery to me since the day I started working here 40 years ago.

Of course there were no manuscripts hidden inside the box. The only thing I found was another key—this one considerably rusty—which I am keeping front and center on my desk until I can get to the bottom of this matter.

In the meantime, I am returning your safe-deposit key to you. I hope this will put an end to your silly pranks.

Yours with interest compounded over time,

Fay Tality

P.S. Not that it matters, but since we're on the topic, I will confess that some of my fondest childhood memories are of Halloweens spent trying to muster the courage to walk up the porch steps at 43 Old Cemetery Road. If Dick Tater hadn't canceled Halloween, I'd be tempted to stop by that old house on October 31—just for old times' sake.

P.P.S. Remember the year you gave out licorice jump ropes to all the trick-or-treaters who came to your door? Of course you don't remember, because you don't *exist!*

P.P.P.S. Or do you? And now where is that rusty key I placed on my desk? It was here just a moment ago! This is all very troubling. Please do not write to me again.

O.C.S.

Ghost Writer in Residence
43 Old Cemetery Road, The Cupola
Ghastly, Illinois

October 7

Mr. Ike N. Openitt
Owner, Ghastly Lock & Key
18 Scary Street
Ghastly, Illinois

Dear Mr. Openitt,

I have recently come into possession of an antique key. The problem is, I can't remember what it unlocks. I only know that my most valuable papers are locked behind the door that can be opened with this key.

Will you please examine the key and tell me what kind of door it fits? I will be happy to pay for your time and trouble.

This is not a joke or a prank. If you don't believe me, I will tell your sister about the time you picked the lock to her diary.

Yours in spirit,

Olive C. Spence

Ghastly Lock & Key

18 Scary Street
Ghastly, Illinois

Ike N. Openitt
Locksmith

October 8

Somebody Who's Living at
43 Old Cemetery Road
Ghastly, Illinois

Dear Somebody,

I've got half a mind to forward this letter straight to the police. But then they'd want to know if I really picked the lock to my sister's diary 35 years ago. And I don't really want to get into all that, if you know what I'm saying.

Now, about that rusty key you sent: It isn't a door key. Looks more like a key to an old trunk. Make that a *really* old trunk.

If I were you, I'd ask Mac Awbrah over at Ghastly Antiques to have a look at it. But how could I be you if *you* aren't even you? Now I've got a headache.

I'm returning your key with my invoice.

Sincerely,

Ike N. Openitt

Ike N. Openitt

INVOICE

1807

Ghastly Lock & Key
18 Scary Street
Ghastly, Illinois

DATE: October 8

SERVICE:	FEE:
Key examination	No charge. Just <u>don't</u> talk to my sister.

O.C.S.

Ghost Writer in Residence
43 Old Cemetery Road, The Cupola
Ghastly, Illinois

October 9

Mac Awbrah
Owner, Ghastly Antiques
2 Scary Street
Ghastly, Illinois

Dear Mr. Awbrah,

Do you happen to have an old trunk that can be opened with the enclosed key?

Please respond with alacrity, as some of my most valuable possessions are at stake.

I know over the years you've taken a strange delight in refuting the fact that I haunt Ghastly—despite my frequent appearances in that lovely etched mirror in your shop. If I must take stronger measures to convince you of my existence, I shall.

Yours in spirit,

Olive C. Spence

O.C.S.

43 Old Cemetery Road, The Cupola
Ghastly, Illinois

GHASTLY
ANTIQUES
2 Scary Street
Ghastly, Illinois

October 10

Whoever Is Posing as Olive C. Spence
43 Old Cemetery Road
Ghastly, Illinois

Dear Whoever You Are,

I don't know who you are, but I don't like
people who waste my time. And I especially
don't like being threatened.

But I do like antiques. And if you must
know, the key you sent is from the Victorian era. If I had to guess, I'd say it came
out of Spence Mansion. It probably opens
an old trunk somewhere in the house.

Have you asked Les and Diane Hope about
this key? If you're really Olive C. Spence,
you'd know that the Hopes sold a lot of
things from your house when they bought

it 12 years ago. It's possible they sold the trunk you're looking for. Or maybe they took it with them to France. Just a guess.

I am returning your key with this letter. Now, if you will excuse me, an unusual chill has descended upon my shop. I must find my sweater.

Mac Awbrah

Mac Awbrah

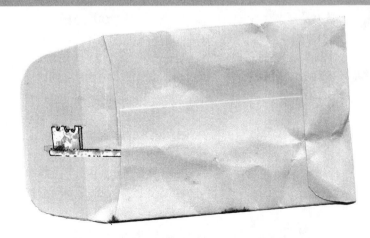

BANNED BOOKS

INTERNATIONAL EXPRESS MAIL

GHASTLY · IL ·
AM
Oct 11

Professors Les and Diane Hope
Guests, Hôtel de Sens
1, rue du Figuier
75004 Paris
France

URGENT

O.C.S.
43 Old Cemetery Road
Ghastly, Illinois
U.S.A.

Ghost Writer in Residence

43 Old Cemetery Road, The Cupola

Ghastly, Illinois

October 11

Professors Les and Diane Hope
Guests, Hôtel de Sens
1, rue du Figuier
75004 Paris
France

You scoundrels.

Until now I've never cared to have any
contact with you. But I have a sneaking
suspicion you stole from my house a trunk
containing priceless manuscripts.

I want the trunk and all of its contents
back <u>immediately.</u>

I am making arrangements with my

colleagues in the ghost network to trans-
port my belongings from Paris to Ghastly.
All I ask is that you leave the trunk in
the lobby of your hotel. My contacts will
take it from there.

Grimly,

Olive C. Spence

P.S. For your information, Seymour, the
son you so heartlessly abandoned in May,
is perfectly happy without you. Or rather,
he *will* be—as soon as Ignatius Grumply
retrieves him from Ghastly Orphanage.

Hôtel de Sens
1, rue du Figuier
75004 Paris
France

October 14

Seymour Hope
43 Old Cemetery Road
Ghastly, Illinois   USA

Dear Seymour,

Still playing your little ghost games, are you?

Look, kid. We don't know how you escaped from
that orphanage, but if you think you can sabotage
our careers again, forget it. Our new book, _Only
Fools (and Children) Believe in Ghosts: The
Authoritative Anti-Ghost Story_, is almost done.
And we've already sold five million copies to Dick
Tater!

We're coming back to Ghastly on October 31 to get
your sorry little self. Then we're going on a book

66.

tour—as a family—and you're going to tell the whole world about your ghost friend, Olive. Why? Because then you'll prove our thesis that only fools and children (and in your case, foolish children) believe in ghosts.

And if you refuse to cooperate? Well, let's just say there are orphanages all over the world that have room for one more little brat like you.

See you soon, kid. Oh, and you can forget about Grumply saving your hide. The geezer's in the loony bin—where he belongs.

Mom + Dad

Ghost Writer in Residence
43 Old Cemetery Road, The Cupola
Ghastly, Illinois

October 20

Professors Les and Diane Hope
Guests, Hôtel de Sens
1, rue du Figuier
75004 Paris
France

Miserable miscreants,

You are truly repellent human beings and deplorable parents. In my younger days, I kept a goodly supply of itching powder on my desk to sprinkle in letters like this. But because I have misplaced my itching powder as well as my manuscripts, my only comfort is knowing that one day you will get exactly what you deserve. Wretched people always do.

Also, I can assure you that Ignatius Grumply is one of the sanest and most capable men I have ever had the pleasure of knowing. By the time you read these words, he and Seymour will almost certainly be back here at Spence Mansion, where they belong.

Confidently,

Olive C. Spence

ILLINOIS HOME FOR THE DERANGED

October 21

1 Cuckoo Lane
Ghastly, Illinois

Seymour Hope
Resident, Ghastly Orphanage
66 Gruel Drive
Ghastly, Illinois

Dear Seymour,

I'd hoped to have flown this cuckoo's nest by now so that I could come rescue you from your captors. I'm sorry to report that escaping is turning out to be more difficult than I'd imagined.

My only contact here is the patient in the next cell. I thought he might be willing to share escape strategies that have worked in the past. So I devised an alphabet of knocks for us to communicate. One knock equals "a," two knocks equal "b," and so forth.

It's working fine, but it's a rare day when we're able to exchange more than a few words. So far my cell neighbor has told me that someone escaped from this miserable place several years ago in the middle of the night using a clever strategy that employed . . .

Well, that's as far as we've gotten.

Please don't give up on me, Seymour. I miss you more than words can express.

Love, and as we say here,

2 knocks 25 knocks 5 knocks-2 knocks 25 knocks 5 knocks!

Ignatius

Ignatius

GHASTLY
PM
Oct 22
5
POST CARD. IL

*Since its founding in 1885, Ghastly
Orphanage has provided a home for
orphaned and abandoned children.*

Mr. Grumply,

I would never give up on you!

12-15-22-5,

—Seymour

Ignatius B. Grumply

Patient

Illinois Home for the Deranged

1 Cuckoo Lane

Ghastly, Illinois

GHASTLY · IL.
PM
Oct 22

Olive C. Spence
The Cupola
43 Old Cemetery Road
Ghastly, Illinois

....

Hi, Olive!

I'm still sketching, like you told me to do. But I'm getting worried about Mr. Grumply. In his last letter, he sounded so lonely and sad.

Hope you're doing okay. Please send news— good or bad. Can you also send me some stamps?

Love,

—Seymour

P.S. Tell Shadow I said HI.

October 23

Seymour Hope
Resident, Ghastly Orphanage
66 Gruel Drive
Ghastly, Illinois

Dearest Seymour,

I have so much to tell you! I shan't waste
time or paper with flowery openings, because
I trust you know how much I miss you.

First the good news: I know where my old
manuscripts are! They're in a trunk. I even
have the key.

The bad news is, I don't know where the
blasted trunk is. I've looked everywhere on
earth.

I'm so sorry, dear. Our deadline is just eight

days away. I've failed miserably in my only assignment. I don't know what to do—except tremble with rage whenever I hear that meddlesome Dick Tater. None of this would've happened if he weren't such a wretched man.

Now I'm getting myself all worked up. I'll write again when I'm in a better mood and have more hopeful news to share.

Almost forgot your stamps! Here they are.

Please think of a way to rescue Iggy from the asylum.

I'm afraid Dick Tater had him committed for life. Stupid man! I'm tempted to pay that ridiculous potato head a visit. I think I shall!

Immortal love,

Olive

TATER TIPS

TRANSCRIPT FOR OCTOBER 24

DICK TATER: Good evening, and welcome to *Tater Tips,* important safety news from me, your friendly Dick Tater. I'm here tonight to remind you that there will be no Halloween this year. Instead, we'll celebrate October 31 with Dick Tater Appreciation Day, when we'll burn all of the ghost stories in the world. I invite everyone listening tonight to round up your dangerous books and take them to your local library or bookmobile. Earlier today I ordered librarians everywhere to prepare giant bonfires so that we can

Oh, for pity's sake.

I . . . I . . . (ahem) Forgive me, viewers. I seem to have lost my place in the *Tater Tips* script. As I was saying, I

You, sir, are a fool.

What's happening here? I'm trying

to read my *Tater Tips* script.

What makes you think you have the right to tell people what they can and cannot read?

This is a live broadcast. Who are you? Where is this coming from? If someone has broken into the secret IMSPOOKY TV studio, there will be a stiff penalty, I can assure you! We have armed guards on duty at every door to prevent trespassers!

I don't need doors. I'm a ghost from Ghastly, Illinois. I can travel through the airwaves if I so choose.

Oh, so that's what this is all about: the legend of Ghastly. Well, that little myth has gone on long enough. I'm putting an end to all that because I am

A bore.

Who is this? I demand to know!

I'm Olive C. Spence.

You are not! Olive C. Spence is dead. She died in 1911.

Yes, but I had unfinished business.

No one is allowed to interrupt my *Tater Tips* broadcast—especially not ghosts.

Normally I don't interrupt. Or at least I try not to. But I have a book to write, Mr. Tater Tot, and I need my coauthor and illustrator to help me. Now listen closely. I will give you ten minutes to release Ignatius Grumply from the Illinois Home for the Deranged and Seymour Hope from Ghastly Orphanage.

This is some kind of trick or black magic. Ghosts don't exist!

Why do you insist on telling people I don't exist? I don't tell people you don't exist— even though there are moments I wish you didn't.

You are a very dangerous person, whoever you are. And I intend to expose you as the safety threat you are.

Blah blah blah.

I will get to the bottom of this, even if it requires an exhumation.

Over my dead body.

Exactly!

THE GHASTLY TIMES

Saturday, October 25
Cliff Hanger, Editor

"Your Secrets Are Our Business"

50 cents
Morning Edition

Tater Plans to Exhume Spence's Body:
"Give up the ghost, Ghastly," says Tater

In an effort to put to rest rumors that the ghost of Olive C. Spence is haunting Ghastly, the director of the International Movement for the Safety & Protection Of Our Kids & Youth (IMSPOOKY) announced plans to exhume Spence's body next week.

"It's time to give up the ghost, Ghastly," Tater said in an emergency press conference held last night.

Tater said he plans to dig up Spence's coffin and put the open casket on display. "That way, everyone can see with their own eyes that this woman is dead and gone," Tater explained.

Spence died in 1911. Her obituary is reprinted below.

Tater ended the press conference by apologizing for his odd performance on *Tater Tips* last night, in which he appeared to be engaged in a heated debate with an unseen opponent.

"I've been working around the clock preparing for Dick Tater Appreciation Day," said Tater, who blamed his bizarre behavior on lack of sleep.

Tater will dig up Spence's coffin on Wednesday.

Olive C. Spence Is Dead; Ghastly's Original Free Spirit Passes Away

No funeral is planned for Spence.

Olive C. Spence, 93, died last night in the home she built on Old Cemetery Road.

Sources say the cause of Spence's death was a heart broken by publishers' continued rejection of her books.

Shortly before her death, Spence vowed to haunt her house and hometown until one of her manuscripts was published. "I shall either publish or never truly perish," Spence told this newspaper last year.

No funeral service is planned for Spence, who left specific instructions for the burial with Kerry N. Barry at Barry Bros. Funeral Parlor.

Balm Refuses to Cooperate in Book Burning

"Over my dead body!"

That's how M. Balm described his reaction to news that he must use the Ghastly bookmobile to collect all the ghost stories in town for a mandatory book burning on October 31.

"I will go to my grave defending a person's right to read ghost stories and other so-called bad books," said Balm. "Mr. Tater thinks they're dangerous. But to my mind, there's nothing more dangerous than a person who tries to dictate what books people can read. It's as offensive as telling people what they can think!"

M. Balm defends the right to read ghost stories.

Readers Demand Refunds

Readers who sent $3 to Spence Mansion, located at 43 Old Cemetery Rd., are now sending requests for refunds to the same address.

"If we're not going to get more chapters of the book, we deserve to get our money back," said Shirley U. Jest, owner of the Ghastly Gourmand and a subscriber to the ghost story in progress.

"Of course I don't know who's going to send us a refund now," Jest continued. "Shadow, Seymour's cat, is the only one left at the house. Well, Shadow and the ghost of Olive C. Spence, if you believe in ghosts."

Jest said she plans to burn the first three chapters of *43 Old Cemetery Road* on October 31.

Jest says readers have right to refund.

"It's the law, so we have to do it," Jest said. "But I'm going to reread the first three chapters before I burn them. Don't tell Dick Tater, but I really do love ghost stories."

October 25

Olive C. Spence
The Cupola
43 Old Cemetery Road
Ghastly, Illinois

Dear Olive,

I just got your letter. Don't worry! I'll help you look for your old manuscripts. I've thought of an escape plan.

The bookmobile from the Ghastly Public Library comes here every Wednesday afternoon. If you can board the bookmobile in the morning before Mr. Balm leaves the library, I'll hide in it when he gets here. Together, we'll take the bookmobile to the Illinois Home for the Deranged, where we'll rescue Mr. Grumply.

What do you think?

Love,

—Seymour

October 27

Seymour Hope
Resident, Ghastly Orphanage
66 Gruel Drive
Ghastly, Illinois

Dear Seymour,

I think it's the perfect plan. You deserve a medal for cleverness!

I'm sure M. Balm won't mind if we borrow his bookmobile for just a little while. We'll make it up to him somehow.

I'll meet you in the bookmobile. Can you bring a sketchpad and pencil? Iggy will want to see how we pulled this one off.

There are some grave developments here at home, dear. I'll explain in more detail when I see you.

Forever yours,

Olive

This is the bookmobile arriving at Ghastly Orphanage.

This is Olive and me in the bookmobile.

This is Olive driving the bookmobile.

This is M. Balm freaking out.

This is us arriving at the Illinois Home for the Deranged.

ILLINOIS HOME FOR THE DERANGED

October 29

Olive C. Spence
The Cupola
43 Old Cemetery Road
Ghastly, Illinois

1 Cuckoo Lane
Ghastly, Illinois

My darling Olive (or as I've grown accustomed to thinking: 13-25 4-1-18-12-9-14-7 15-12-9-22-5),

Your silence suggests that you've lost faith in me. I don't blame you. I promised to escape from this hideous place weeks ago so that I could rescue Seymour. Meanwhile, here I sit, counting out letters on my fingers, knocking on walls, and slowly going craz

Hello, darling.

Olive! You frightened me. Is that really you?

Of course it's me. And Seymour's waiting out in the bookmobile with M. Balm.

Bookmobile? Is Seymour all right? Are you okay?

90.

Calm down, darling. I'll explain everything later. We have to hurry home. Mr. Tater is making preparations to have my body exhumed tonight.

Exhumed?

Yes, dear. Now follow my glasses. We're breaking out of here.

TATER TIPS

DICK TATER: Good evening, and welcome to *Tater Tips,* important safety news from me, your friendly Dick Tater. Tonight we're broadcasting live from the gravesite of Olive C. Spence in Ghastly, Illinois. I have a crew hard at work, digging up one of Ghastly's oldest and cruelest jokes. That's right. I'm talking about the legend of Olive C. Spence, the woman who is believed by many to haunt her old house and town. How are we doing, boys?

UNNAMED DIGGER #1: Almost there, boss.

DICK TATER: Good. Because I want to show all the people watching *Tater Tips* tonight the truth, which isn't always pretty. In fact, folks, I should warn you that what we're about to see will be shocking to behold. When we open Spence's coffin, we're going to find a woman who died 97 years ago. Who can predict what the ravages of time and nature have done to her body?

UNNAMED DIGGER #2: We're bringing her up, boss.

[Enter *Ignatius Grumply and Seymour Hope*]

IGNATIUS GRUMPLY: How dare you dig up Olive's coffin!

DICK TATER: What are you doing here? You're supposed to be in the nut house.

SEYMOUR HOPE: He escaped, just like I did.

DICK TATER: Why you little . . . but perhaps it's for the best. This might be exactly the shock therapy you need, young man, to set your mind straight about ghosts and other such nonsense. Open the coffin, boys!

UNNAMED DIGGER #3: Uh, we can't, sir. It's locked.

Oh, I just remembered something!

DICK TATER: I don't care if it is locked. Open it!

UNNAMED DIGGER #1: Wait. Something's happening with the lock.

Of course something's happening, you mule. I'm using my key to unlock my coffin.

UNNAMED DIGGER #2: Will ya look at that? A rusty old key is opening the coffin. And look what's inside.

SEYMOUR HOPE: Olive! Your manuscripts!

IGNATIUS GRUMPLY: You hid them in your coffin! Brilliant!

Thank you, dear. I only wish I'd remembered before now.

DICK TATER: What is the meaning of this? I demand an explanation. How did—who did—hee-hee-hee!

[Tater begins jumping around and scratching himself uncontrollably]

UNNAMED DIGGER #3: You okay, boss?

DICK TATER *[continues frenetic jumping and scratching]*: Haw, hee, ho-ho-ho! Hee-hee, haw-haw, ho!

UNNAMED DIGGER #1: Um, boss?

DICK TATER: Hiya, waa-waa! Hiya-hiya, ho-ho-ho!

IGNATIUS GRUMPLY *[laughing]*: Olive, what on earth are you doing to him?

I found my stash of itching powder in my coffin, too. I knew I put it somewhere! I just sprinkled a little down Mr. Tater's pants.

DICK TATER *[more jumping and scratching]*: Hi-ho, hee-hee-hee, gimme gummy goomy! Gimme goomy gummy gummy!

[Sound of sirens in distance]

THE GHASTLY TIMES

Thursday, October 30
Cliff Hanger, Editor

"Your Secrets Are Our Business"

50 cents
Morning Edition

Grave Surprise!
Tater taken away after bizarre outburst

Spence's coffin contains her unpublished works.

It was a scene straight out of the movies.

Last night as onlookers gasped at the discovery of unpublished manuscripts in the coffin of Olive C. Spence, Dick Tater was taken away in a straitjacket to the Illinois Home for the Deranged.

Tater, director of the International Movement for the Safety & Protection Of Our Kids & Youth (IMSPOOKY), reportedly suffered a nervous breakdown due to the stress of the Spence exhumation and the long hours devoted to abolishing Halloween.

The discovery of Spence's manuscripts in her coffin prompted funeral director Kerry N. Barry IV, the great-grandson of the founder of Barry Bros. Funeral Parlor, to do a little digging of his own.

"I found the instructions Miss Spence left for my great-grandfather," Barry told *The Ghastly Times*. "She wrote him a letter shortly before her death and told him she wanted all of her manuscripts buried in the coffin."

But what about her body?

"I'm not sure what became of that," Barry said with a shrug. "And I'm not sure I want to know. There's no evidence Miss Spence spent any time at all in that coffin."

Grumply and Hope Reunited—for Now

Grumply and Hope return to Spence Mansion.

Ignatius B. Grumply and Seymour Hope have returned to 43 Old Cemetery Rd. to live together—for now, anyway.

The 64-year-old author and the 11-year-old illustrator escaped yesterday from the Illinois Home for the Deranged and Ghastly Orphanage, respectively. It is unclear whether Grumply and Hope are still considered wards of the state.

The Ghastly Times has learned that Professors Les and Diane Hope are scheduled to arrive in Ghastly tomorrow to pick up their son. The couple has been in Europe working on their book.

Balm the Opposite of Calm

M. Balm, chief librarian at the Ghastly Public Library, is recovering from a high-speed bookmobile ride yesterday that nearly claimed his life.

According to Balm, he and Seymour Hope were transported by an invisible driver from Ghastly Orphanage to the Illinois Home for the Deranged, where Ignatius B. Grumply joined them.

"Then the three of us were driven to Spence Mansion at 150 miles an hour by a phantom driver who almost killed us," said Balm.

Balm refused to speculate whether the bookmobile is haunted.

"If you're asking whether or not I believe in ghosts, the answer is I don't know," said Balm. "All I know is I believe in the right to read ghost stories."

Last week Balm promised to go to his grave defending the right to read ghost stories.

"And it looks like I almost just did," added Balm.

M. Balm says bookmobile ride nearly killed him.

IGNATIUS B. GRUMPLY

A WRITER IN RESIDENCE

43 OLD CEMETERY ROAD **2ND FLOOR** **GHASTLY, ILLINOIS**

October 30

Olive C. Spence
The Cupola
43 Old Cemetery Road
Ghastly, Illinois

Dear Olive,

Thank goodness you found your manuscripts. Now we have something to send our readers. Please choose one story for us to publish. I'll ask Seymour to begi

I'm afraid I have some bad news.

Olive! How many times do I have to ask you not to sneak up on me like that?

Sorry, dear. But I really do have some unfortunate news.

You lost your manuscripts again?

No, I have them. I reread them all last night.

So what's the bad news?

They're not the least bit frightening.

Your manuscripts? Olive, I don't believe you.

98.

Oh, they're perfectly fine as far as mysteries go. But a ghost story should be scary, don't you think? And what we've been through these past two months with Dick Tater is much more frightening than anything I could possibly make up. What do you say we publish *that* story instead?

I say you're brilliant, as always. And Seymour already has a good start on the illustrations.

Perfect. Now, what about the other matter?

What other matter?

Our living arrangement. Don't you remember that I asked you to think of a way for Seymour, you, and me to live here together legally? Les and Diane Hope will arrive in Ghastly tomorrow to pick up Seymour. What can we do to stop them?

I have an idea. Please review the paperwork on the dining room table. I'll ask Seymour to do the same. If you both agree to the terms, we'll go to the courthouse tomorrow morning at 10 o'clock.

PETITION TO ADOPT

GHASTLY COUNTY COURTHOUSE

I, <u>Ignatius B. Grumply</u>, a single person, and I, <u>Olive C. Spence, a free spirit</u>, request permission to adopt <u>Seymour Hope.</u>

We are submitting to the Court a letter from Les and Diane Hope dated October 14. This letter proves that their desire to reclaim Seymour is based not on their love for him but on his potential usefulness in marketing their new book.

We respectfully ask the Court to let Seymour decide with whom he wants to live, and advise the Court that if Seymour wishes to live with us, we would be honored to call him our son.

Olive C. Spence

Olive C. Spence

Ignatius B. Grumply

Ignatius B. Grumply

ADOPTION APPROVED

OCTOBER 31

Judge Claire Voyant

Judge Claire Voyant
Ghastly Circuit Court

Filed in the
Circuit Court
of
Ghastly County

THE GHASTLY TIMES

Saturday, November 1
Cliff Hanger, Editor

"Your Secrets Are Our Business"

50 cents
Afternoon Edition

Seymour Hope Adopted by Grumply, Spence

Seymour Hope is now the legal son of Ignatius B. Grumply and Olive C. Spence.

So ruled Ghastly Circuit Court Judge Claire Voyant yesterday morning after reviewing the evidence. Judge Voyant said the testimonies by Grumply and Spence were especially convincing.

"Ms. Spence communicated with me by writing messages on my computer," said Voyant. "She testified that Seymour is a wonderful boy who deserves to be raised by parents who love him."

Grumply presented Judge Voyant with a letter written by Les and Diane Hope to Seymour Hope, who the couple thought was posing as Spence. After reviewing the letter, Judge Voyant terminated the parental rights of Les and Diane Hope and charged the couple with criminal child negligence.

"But we love our son," said Diane Hope.

"Even if we didn't, we have the right to use him to promote our new book," added Les Hope.

"Over my dead body!" said Judge Voyant, pounding her gavel. Voyant then asked Seymour Hope if he wished to be adopted by Spence and Grumply.

"Of course!" replied Hope. "They practically saved my life."

Grumply told Voyant that, in fact, Hope was largely responsible for rescuing him from the asylum.

"Seymour's plan saved my life and my

Seymour Hope exits courthouse with his new parents.

sanity," explained Grumply.

"I couldn't have done it without Olive's help," Hope corrected.

"And Seymour and Iggy saved me from a deathly boring afterlife," Spence wrote on the judge's computer. "Isn't it crystal clear that we three belong together?"

Judge Voyant agreed. In her ruling she also approved Seymour Hope's home-schooling arrangement with Grumply and Spence.

Minutes later the happy trio emerged arm in arm in invisible arm from the courthouse.

"This is the coolest day of my life!" said Hope.

Ghastly Celebrates Halloween with Tricks, Treats and a Ghostlike Ghost Story

Forget burning books. Residents of Ghastly celebrated Halloween with a much hotter event: three new chapters from the serialized ghost story titled *43 Old Cemetery Road,* handed out by two of the creators at the Victorian mansion where they first met.

Coauthor Ignatius B. Grumply and his son, illustrator Seymour Hope, distributed copies of the new chapters from the front porch. Asked if Ms. Spence was available for comment, Grumply said: "Sorry, but it's been a long day for Olive. She wanted to enjoy watching the trick-or-treaters from her cupola, as she's done for decades."

The Halloween edition of *43 Old Cemetery Road* included both tricks and treats.

"We printed these new chapters in invisible ink," explained Grumply. "We also attached a small envelope containing itching powder to the page where Olive meets Dick Tater at her gravesite."

"Olive found a bunch of tricks in her coffin that we couldn't resist using," added a giggling Hope, who passed out invisible-ink decoder pens to readers, along with anti-itch cream to use as needed.

As for treats, last night's visitors to 43 Old Cemetery Rd. were invited inside the mansion, where the opulent dining room was outfitted with a Halloween buffet that

Trick-or-treaters pick up new chapters of a true ghost story.

included marshmallow soufflés, a chocolate fountain and a dip-your-own-caramel-apple station.

"I grew up trick-or-treating at Spence Mansion," said Fay Tality, president of the Bank of Ghastly. "But this is definitely the best Halloween ever!"

Like most guests Tality stayed at Spence Mansion until well after midnight. Before departing Tality yelled in the direction of the cupola: "Thank you, Olive! I can't wait to go home and read the new chapters! Oh, and I'm sorry I doubted you even for a moment!"

Kid Committee Convened to Abolish IMSPOOKY

A committee of middle grade students has convened to begin proceedings aimed at dismantling the International Movement for the Safety & Protection Of Our Kids & Youth (IMSPOOKY).

Called the Worldwide Committee of Kids Who Wish Their Parents Would Lighten Up a Bit & Quit Worrying So Much About Every Little Thing (WCK-WWTPWLUBQWSMAELT), the group urges children to help their parents relax by providing them with kind words, unasked-for favors and regular doses of chocolate.

A Message to Our Readers

Thank you for supporting our work at 43 Old Cemetery Road. We plan to keep writing, illustrating and publishing new chapters for as long as readers are interested, which we hope will be a very, very long time.

Olive C. Spence
Coauthor

Ignatius B. Grumply
Coauthor

Seymour Hope
Illustrator

Tater Confined Indefinitely

Tater is living at the Illinois Home for the Deranged.

Until further notice Dick Tater will remain at the Illinois Home for the Deranged.

If and when Tater is released from the facility, he won't return to Washington, D.C., as director of the International Movement for the Safety & Protection Of Our Kids & Youth. Tater was fired for using public funds to order five million copies of the now discredited book *Only Fools (and Children)*

Believe in Ghosts: The Authoritative Anti-Ghost Story by Les and Diane Hope.

The professors are being held in the Ghastly County Jail, pending their trials on charges of criminal child negligence.

Les and Diane Hope are behind bars in the Ghastly County Jail.

And so, in a sense, we end where we began . . .

in a 32½-room house
built by a woman who,
in her lifetime, never married
or had children . . .

and rented by a man
who never married
and always thought he
disliked children . . .

and purchased by
a boy whose parents
abandoned him.

Except that now this house is the legal domicile of a new family, whose love for one another has been tested and proven . . .

Ghastly Courthouse

and whose legitimacy has been recognized by a court of law.

And so, even though one member of the family might still get grumpy now and then . . .

and another might become cranky when she misplaces her glasses . . .

neither would ever, could ever,

abandon Hope.

And that is why this 32½-room house at 43 Old Cemetery Road is now, once again . . .

a home.

The End

November 1

Dear Olive,

I like the ending. But I think we forgot something.

Aren't readers going to wonder what happened to your old manuscripts?

Love,

—Seymour

O.C.S.

Ghost Writer in Residence
43 Old Cemetery Road, The Cupola
Ghastly, Illinois

November 1

Dear Seymour,

You're absolutely right, dear. My mind is so full of cobwebs these days. I forgot something else, too.

I'll take care of both matters immediately.

Love,

Olive

THE GHASTLY TIMES

Sunday, November 2
Cliff Hanger, Editor

"Your Secrets Are Our Business"

$1.50
Morning Edition

Ghastly Public Library Receives Original Spence Manuscripts

The Ghastly Public Library received a unique donation yesterday: the unpublished manuscripts of Olive C. Spence.

The original manuscripts, which were delivered to the library in a coffin, were accompanied by a letter from Spence to chief librarian M. Balm.

"I never thanked you properly for the use of your bookmobile last week," wrote Spence. "I apologize for the inconvenience and my somewhat reckless driving. I hope you can understand why we were in such a hurry. I also want to thank you for refusing to burn books. You are a true friend to readers and writers everywhere."

According to Balm, the donation includes more than 200 unpublished mysteries.

"I'm dying to read them all," said Balm, "starting with *Mystery of the Missing Manuscripts*."

Balm sorts library's new collection.

Balm plans to display all of the manuscripts in the library, along with the letter from Spence.

"I wish I could thank Miss Spence for her generous donation," said Balm. "Olive, if you're reading this, please know how truly grateful I am. And don't worry about borrowing the bookmobile. I was happy to be of assistance!"

Anonymous Letter to be Investigated

Judge Voyant examines anonymous letter.

The anonymous letter that launched Dick Tater's investigation of 43 Old Cemetery Rd. is now in court custody.

"People have the right to send anonymous letters," said Ghastly Circuit Court Judge Claire Voyant. "But I want our prosecutor to investigate this letter to make sure no foul play was involved."

According to Voyant, the anonymous letter-writer used a rare font not found on modern computers.

IGNATIUS B. GRUMPLY

A WRITER IN RESIDENCE

43 OLD CEMETERY ROAD   2ND FLOOR   GHASTLY, ILLINOIS

November 2

Olive C. Spence
The Cupola
43 Old Cemetery Road
Ghastly, Illinois

Dear Olive,

You wrote that anonymous letter to Dick Tater, didn't you? I know because only you use a font that

Of course I wrote the letter.

Why?

I wanted to show the world what a relentless busybody Mr. Tater is.

Some people might call *you* a busybody.

How can I be a busybody when I no longer have a body?

113.

I believe I've noted this fact in a previous conversation.

Maybe you have, dear. I'm sorry. I've been terribly distracted by all this Tater turmoil. I never intended for things to get so out of hand. I only wanted to put Tater in his place and bring Les and Diane Hope to justice. Please believe me when I tell you that I had *no* idea you and Seymour would be taken away in the process.

I do believe you, Olive.

Thank goodness. Now, Iggy, dare I mention there's another reason I wrote that letter to Tater?

I think I know, but tell me anyway.

I wanted Seymour to live with parents who love him.

And you thought it wouldn't occur to me to try to adopt him?

Well, Iggy, you *can* be a little slow sometimes.

Would it surprise you to know that I was working on the adoption papers the day Dick Tater's first letter arrived?

Oh, Iggy! You are a treasure. You'll make a wonderful father to Seymour.

Thank you. But sometimes I fear I really am deranged. Falling in love with a ghost? Adopting a child—at my age? The whole thing feels a bit crazy.

The best things in life usually do, dear. Now go to bed. It's late.

I know. See you tomorrow. (I wish.)

You really *do* wish you could see me, don't you?

Yes, Olive, I *do*. I've seen you only once in my life, and it was just a glance.

All right, all right. But make it quick. I'm in my robe and slippers, and my hair is in rollers. This is *not* my best look. But here you go. What? What?! Iggy, say something. *Write* something. You're making me nervous with that silly look on your face. Are you just going to sit there with your mouth hanging open and *stare* at me? Very well, then. The show's over. Are you happy now?

Olive . . . you're beautiful.

Yes I am, darling. I'm also dead tired. Good night, Iggy.

Good night, Olive.

Good night, reader.

The *Real* End

(for now, anyway)

**Other books written by Kate Klise
and illustrated by M. Sarah Klise:**

Dying to Meet You: 43 Old Cemetery Road

*Regarding the Fountain
Regarding the Sink
Regarding the Trees
Regarding the Bathrooms
Regarding the Bees*

*Letters from Camp
Trial by Journal*

*Shall I Knit You a Hat?
Why Do You Cry?
Imagine Harry
Little Rabbit and the Night Mare*

⟨✦⟩

Also written by Kate Klise:

*Deliver Us from Normal
Far from Normal*

A Very Ghastly Halloween

Ignatius B. Grumply
as a
Work in Progress

Seymour Hope
as a
Famous Artist

Shadow
as
Puss 'n Boots

Judge Claire Voyant
as the
Statue of Liberty

Fay Tality
as a
Grown-up Pirate

OXFORD ENGLISH MONOGRAPHS

General Editors

A Critical Difference

T. S. ELIOT AND JOHN MIDDLETON
MURRY IN ENGLISH LITERARY
CRITICISM, 1919–1928

DAVID GOLDIE

CLARENDON PRESS · OXFORD
1998

Oxford University Press, Great Clarendon Street, Oxford OX2 6DP

Oxford New York
Athens Auckland Bangkok Bogotá Buenos Aires Calcutta
Cape Town Chennai Dar es Salaam Delhi Florence Hong Kong Istanbul
Karachi Kuala Lumpur Madrid Melbourne Mexico City Mumbai
Nairobi Paris São Paolo Singapore Taipei Tokyo Toronto Warsaw

and associated companies in
Berlin Ibadan

Oxford is a registered trade mark of Oxford University Press

Published in the United States
by Oxford University Press Inc., New York

British Library Cataloguing in Publication Data
Data available

12|8|00
Library of Congress Cataloging in Publication Data
Data available
ISBN 0 19 812379 5

1 3 5 7 9 10 8 6 4 2

Typeset by Jayvee, Trivandrum, India
Printed in Great Britain
on acid-free paper by
Biddles Ltd,
Guildford and King's Lynn

For my parents

Acknowledgements

In the course of writing this book I've had the good fortune to meet a number of people whose help, both academic and personal, I am very pleased to be able to acknowledge. Jon Stallworthy, David Bradshaw, and Jon Mee in Oxford, and Stephen Baker and Andrew Noble in Glasgow, have been extremely generous with their time and ideas, and have influenced this work in ways they might not even realize. Bernard Bergonzi, Howard Brown, Robert Crawford, Denis Flannery, Saul Frampton, Donald Fraser, Lyndall Gordon, Menno Lievers, Mark Sims, and Marcus and Sarah Wood have at various stages provided vital assistance and support. The staff of a number of libraries are also due my sincere thanks, in particular Mr J. V. Howard, Librarian, Special Collections, Edinburgh University Library; Sandra Bailey, Librarian, Wadham College Library, Oxford; Vera Ryhajlo, Tina King, and Helen Rogers of the Upper Reserve in the Bodleian Library; Eamon Dyas, Group Records Manager at News International; the staff of the Mitchell Library, Glasgow and of the City University Library, London. I am grateful to Mrs Valerie Eliot and Faber & Faber Ltd. for permission to quote from uncollected and unpublished work by T. S. Eliot, and to the Society of Authors, as the Literary Representative of the Estate of John Middleton Murry, to quote from published and unpublished material by John Middleton Murry. I am grateful, too, to the Department of English Studies at the University of Strathclyde for some crucial financial assistance in the latter stages of my research.

The people who deserve the greatest thanks, though, are those who are closest. My parents, Jean and David Goldie, have been unstinting in their support throughout and Christine Green has, in her unfailing and sometimes unappreciated help, disproved all the jokes I have ever heard about mothers-in-law. The person to whom most is owed, however, is Debbie Goldie. She has, along with our daughters Christina Goldie and Katie Goldie, provided the base on which all of what follows has been built.

D.G.

Contents

x *Contents*

Introduction

THE story is a familiar one and has been told many times. The brilliant young man, born towards the end of the 1880s, his philosophical and literary gifts honed by the best education his country can provide, makes his first trip to Europe at the end of 1910. A pretext is attendance at Henri Bergson's celebrated lectures at the Collège de France, the consequence an immersion in Fauvist Paris that will prove pivotal in the development of his literary career. He does not serve with his contemporaries in the First World War, and his twenties are passed, in the time spared by work and marriage, in breaking into a literary world from which his background excludes him: mixing with literary smart society at Garsington, writing poetry, dabbling in verse drama, and gaining a growing reputation as a critic through contributions to small magazines and, eventually, the *Athenaeum* and *Times Literary Supplement*. His development is marred by crises of marital and nervous breakdown in his thirty-fourth year. Yet, out of this breakdown comes a new artistic and critical strength, witnessed, in particular, in the editorship of a magazine within which a distinctive critical practice arises and, slightly later, in an exploration of religious solutions to private and public senses of a contemporary crisis.

This is the story according to which T. S. Eliot arrived at the centre of English literary life, and in whose continuation he won all the accolades of popular and academic recognition that made him one of the last great public men of letters; the beginning of an ascent from obscure and tangled beginnings to the uplands of a singular critical renown. But in its outline and in all its particulars it is also the story of John Middleton Murry. Until his mid-thirties Murry, too, looked to have successfully climbed clear of his obscure beginnings and to promise a great future as a man of letters. Murry's creative writing would never come near the quality of Eliot's. In his critical writing, however, his reputation and prospects were at least as favourable. In the immediate aftermath of the First World War it was to Murry and his *Athenaeum* that many, the massed ranks of Bloomsbury included, looked for the best guarantee of the survival of English literary culture. That they were ultimately disappointed is now a matter of record, as is the fact that it was Eliot rather than Murry who would become the key figure in setting the literary-critical agenda between the wars.

Murry began the post-war period with the critical world at his feet but ended it as something of a doormat. Eliot, who had once been likened by Pound to a stealthy burglar breaking into the backshop of the literary establishment, had, by the 1930s, apparently taken over the store. This book details the relationship between the two writers in the crucial period, the decade after the First World War, during which these changes of fortune were occurring. It traces, in particular, a series of controversies in which both writers participated; controversies that, in fact, acted as defining moments in the development of their critical projects.

As this introduction has already suggested, the two initially had much in common. Their early forays into criticism suggested that they shared a common concern about the need for a revised literary-critical practice adequate to the recent developments of International Modernism and the consequences of the First World War. In the years immediately after the war, when Eliot was contributing to Murry's *Athenaeum*, they appeared to be allied, however uneasily, in a common quest for the restoration of a literary-critical standard. Within that common programme there were already differences of emphasis; while both agreed on the need for a restorative tradition, for example, Murry already saw tradition as little more than a helpful descriptive term for the combined efforts of individual isolated writers, while Eliot emphasized a tradition gently prescriptive in effect, actively shaping individual practice with its powers of suggestion and precedent. The tension between these views was less powerful than the attractive force of the common project, so a form of critical consensus was maintained until the early 1920s. As ties of mutual obligation loosened, these tensions became much more apparent and reached cruxes in two well-publicized disagreements: one subsequent to the setting up of Murry's *Adelphi* in 1923 which hinged on definitions of romanticism and classicism; the other after the relaunch of Eliot's *Criterion* as the *New Criterion* in 1926, which reprised the earlier debate but with the addition of a religious element. By 1928 the stated differences between the two critics were stark. Eliot was clearly on the side of an approach to literature that was temperamentally conservative; that was classical, orthodox, and that stressed the ordered virtues of traditionalism. Murry was now his antipodes, espousing a literary liberalism that was romantic and unorthodox in preferring subjective response to objective evaluation, that was enthusiastic rather than dogmatic, and that hymned the virtues of individualism.

The latter disagreements between the two might be said to have laid bare the latent tensions in the early relationship; to give a chance finally for each man to expose his true orientation. Less crudely, the necessities of debate might be said to have furnished each writer with an opportunity to articulate and make explicit as a critical theory what had up until then only been implicit in a critical practice. The argument put forward here, however, is that substantial parts of each writer's theory of criticism were not so much laid bare by these debates as actively constructed during them. The approach that is followed, then, is one that emphasizes polemic; that suggests that each man's formulation of his critical principles owes as much to the dictates of a particular argument as it does to what might be isolated disinterestedly as the core of his critical practice. There can be no doubt that Eliot appeared to be predisposed towards traditionalism, just as Murry was towards individualism. What is worth noting, however, is that their own statements of these tendencies, as in, for example, Eliot's 'The Perfect Critic' and 'The Function of Criticism' or Murry's 'The "Classical" Revival', were invariably contributions to an ongoing dialogue and, therefore, lacked such objective weight as they might have had had they been uttered gratuitously.

One danger of polemic in dialogue is overstatement; what will be suggested here is that that danger was not entirely avoided in the dialogue between Eliot and Murry, leading them eventually to overstate their dissimilarities in order to emphasize what a contemporary political commentator might describe as the clear blue water between them. The demands of polemic were such, in fact, that their relationship can often be seen to swing as much on differences of emphasis as on clearly substantive issues. This is marked in the paradox that, whereas in the early days of their relationship they stressed common purpose where there was already some dissension, in the latter stages of that relationship they insisted on identifying differences where there was obviously potential for substantial agreement.

In some ways it is difficult to account in rational or objective terms for the latter disagreement between the two. There were certainly substantive issues at stake and clear ideological positions being marked out. But, as Jacques Maritain found out in his *rapprochement* with Henri Bergson, even the most conflicting of opinions can be addressed and acknowledged, if not resolved, where there is goodwill. That there was no such goodwill between Eliot and Murry by the end of their debate, and that in fact Murry exasperated Eliot, will become apparent in following their controversy to its conclusion. To dwell on this point is to note the presence of irrational components in Eliot's formulation of his critical scholasticism, and by extension, his early statements of his critical purpose. He was driven into a dogmatic classicism in the late 1920s for a number of reasons relating to his personal life and the needs of his poetry that have been well accounted for by others. But in his statements of that dogmatic classicism he was also spurred by a hostile personal reaction to Murry (and to people like Murry) into making assertions which proved in the longer term to be unsustainable. This may be an extreme case, but in accepting it we also accept the possibility that all Eliot's critical pronouncements were, to a greater or lesser extent, similarly influenced. The simple point is that not only were Eliot's and Murry's statements of their criticism subject to the normal cultural and ideological inflections that undermine any claim they might have to disinterestedness, they were also the product of an active literary-critical culture in which any such statement was an intervention rather than a spontaneous utterance—an intervention that might be prompted as much by personal animosity as high-minded dialectic. Accordingly, then, this study will explore both the larger cultural contexts within which Eliot and Murry worked as well as the more immediate context of the literary-critical culture within which their debates were framed. It is their response to these contexts and their engagement with the products of these contexts, both as thinkers and as personalities, that is crucial.

In following the relationship between Eliot and Murry two main emphases or arguments (or what Christopher Ricks might call prejudices) will become apparent. The first concerns the relative merits of their criticism. As historiography is the prerogative of the victor, the literary-critical academy has tended to place the higher valuation on Eliot's criticism. There have been notable attempts at a rehabilitation of Murry's work in the past, and there are signs of a more recent revaluation.[1] But even as Eliot's direct influence as a critic wanes, a residual academic–industrial complex dedicated to him lingers on, and he remains the pre-eminent critic in accounts of the period. While few would seriously deny his work this place in terms of its historical impact and its quality, there is a case that his contemporaries tend to suffer neglect in the shadow of that achievement, and that as a consequence we have only a partial understanding of the critical undergrowth out of which Eliot sprang. An attempt such as the one made here to restore balance to this picture need not privilege a writer like Murry over Eliot, but should certainly treat them, as they were treated by their contemporaries, as equals worthy of being taking seriously on their own merits. Likewise, an account of their relationship should not try to suggest that Murry be given priority as the major source or the informing background of Eliot's criticism, or vice versa; however, neither should it suggest what is sometimes implied, that Murry is like the dupe of a Socratic dialogue, the innocent empiricist exposed by the interrogative casuistry of a master theorist. What it is proper to suggest is that Murry, perhaps more than most, played an important part in the development of Eliot's criticism at a time when it was still very much in flux, and that Eliot's work fulfilled a similar function with regard to Murry.

Both men emerged from the First World War with only a partial idea of the place of literature in the larger processes of cultural reconstruction. In each other they found, at first, a mutual ground on which their independent revaluative schemes could build. When co-operation turned into conflict, that mutuality transformed into a fruitful antagonism, as each offered the other a heated cross-examination in which critical ideas could be forged and tempered. Murry was not unique in offering such a stimulus to Eliot, nor was Eliot unique to Murry in this respect. What does remain is the

[1] See Derek Stanford, 'Middleton Murry as Literary Critic', *EIC* 8/1 (Jan. 1958), 60–7; Richard Harter Fogle, 'Beauty and Truth: John Middleton Murry on Keats', *D. H. Lawrence Review*, 2/1 (Spring 1969), 68–75; Ernest G. Griffin, *John Middleton Murry* (New York, 1969); Sharron Greer Cassavant, *John Middleton Murry: The Critic as Moralist* (University of Alabama, 1982); René Wellek, 'John Middleton Murry', in his *A History of Modern Criticism: 1750–1950*, v: *English Criticism, 1900–1950* (London, 1986), 92–116; and Chris Baldick, *Criticism and Literary Theory: 1890 to the Present* (London, 1996), 69–77.

importance of the exchange, which at least one commentator has described as 'probably the most serious intellectual controversy in England during the period'.[2]

The book's second emphasis, argument, or prejudice is related to this and concerns Eliot's relationship to his context. Often his work is contextualized either in terms of a narrative of its own development or as a part of a longer narrative concerned with the development of literary-critical thought. Murry's work is rarely troubled by this contextualization as it is characteristically thought of as sporadic and one-off, developing out of no consistent tradition and founding no recognizable school. Eliot's insistence within his own work upon tradition and its development has undoubtedly assisted traditionalizing and, perhaps, homogenizing interpretations of his critical work. His editing of that criticism into a volume of selected essays helped to prepare this work for canonization and to invest it with a sense of internal coherence. There is nothing sinister in this; it is a typical and sensible case of the construction of an *œuvre*. But it does tend to offer a misrepresentative picture of the processes through which that criticism came about, tempting commentators to treat the work as though it were a form of developing monologue. The picture of Eliot that is often conjured is one, fostered by his tone and by his later occasional criticism, of a man standing on a podium or in a pulpit delivering a subtle, disinterested, unambiguously authoritative pronouncement. But to treat the earlier criticism in this fashion is to miss significant elements in it of confusion, doubt, and, most importantly, polemic. To read Eliot's criticism entirely in the spirit of the *Selected Essays* is like listening to one side of a telephone conversation: a clear and articulate argument can be discerned but its full significance cannot.

There has been some outstanding work carried out on Eliot's intellectual and literary development in recent years.[3] Much of this has properly stressed his connections with and debts to a range of contemporary sources, placing his work in a cultural and literary nexus within which it is seen reflexively to undergo subtle alteration. The necessary tendency of such an approach, focused as it is on an

---

[2] Sir Richard Rees, *A Theory of My Time: An Essay in Didactic Reminiscence* (London, 1963), 44.

[3] See especially John D. Margolis, *T. S. Eliot's Intellectual Development, 1922–1939* (London, 1972), and Piers Gray, *T. S. Eliot's Intellectual and Poetic Development, 1909–1922* (Brighton, 1982).

evolving subject, is to see Eliot and his project as more or less mono-lithic—to consist of a core which, however far it is modified by its environment, remains homogeneous. That homogeneity, tagged with the name Eliot, has been a useful device for commentators to pin down an area of literary-critical coherence. As such, it is no more bogus than the single identity within which we all conventionally cir-cumscribe a range of conflicting and potentially incompatible per-sonal components. But while it constructs a convincing narrative of development it often fails to account adequately for the inconsisten-cies—the changes of opinion, for example, over Milton, or Dryden, or the differing definitions of a literary-critical 'intelligence'. Such inconsistencies arise, not necessarily because Eliot failed adequately to assimilate and unify his sources, but rather more simply because he was a man with his own tastes and prejudices, preoccupations and moods; a man with a highly developed sense of his own variousness who was engaged for much of his early career, and not always entirely happily, in the attempt to build a personal integrity out of the frag-ments that American and European cultures had put in his way. That he argued for an authorizing tradition within which individual iden-tity could be valorized and made coherent, and that he latterly achieved a satisfactory personal resolution along those lines, does not mean he had resolved its complexities from the start.

The comparative approach to his and Murry's work that is engaged in here makes no attempt to challenge or overthrow this sense of reading for coherence. What it does at its simplest is restress an obvious point: Eliot, like Murry, manifestly changed in the ten years after the First World War. The young Eliot who rather enjoyed the reputation of having been described, however wrong-headedly, as a 'drunken helot' or as a 'wild man', cuts a very different figure from the austere cleric *manqué* of the late 1920s.[4] While it is clear that there are continuities between these two figures, obvious differences are also manifest. To say, as many have, that the religious Eliot of the late 1920s is continuous with the Laforguian ironist of ten years earlier is only half the story. The other half of that story is one of

[4] The first description is attributed to Arthur Waugh, although the phrase is actually Ezra Pound's. See Arthur Waugh, 'The New Poetry', *Quarterly Review*, 226/449 (Oct. 1916), 365–86 (p. 386), and Ezra Pound, 'Drunken Helots and Mr Eliot', *Egoist*, 4/5 (June 1917), 72–4. The second was made by Holbrook Jackson; see Richard Aldington, *Life for Life's Sake: A Book of Reminiscences* (New York, 1941), 219: it is particularly ironic, given that Jackson had been an influential popularizer of Nietzsche—a much wilder man than Eliot; see David S. Thatcher, *Nietzsche in England, 1890–1914* (Toronto, 1970), 226–7.

discontinuity, of indecisions and revisions, which underscore both the life and the work. The creator of the multifaceted, indecisive J. Alfred Prufrock, the man whom Pound called a possum and Murry a chameleon, might well see the justification in positing not one Eliot, but several.

The point of this is not to demolish Eliot's reputation or to deconstruct it in some way by pointing to crucial inconsistencies or aporia in the criticism. Rather it is to suggest the pitfalls of attempting to distil a consistent theory from his dispersed statements. The young Eliot once flippantly claimed that 'one must have theories, but one need not believe in them!'[5] While the mature Eliot downplayed such an extreme pragmatism, he was consistent in asserting his work's status as a critical practice rather than the expression of a systematic critical theory. In 1934 he wrote privately to Paul Elmer More, acknowledging 'some skill in the barren game of controversy' but professing 'little capacity for sustained, exact, and closely knit argument and reasoning'.[6] This early rejection of theory had been emphasized with a public exclamation of an 'incapacity for abstruse reasoning', and a statement that 'I have no general theory of my own', in *The Use of Poetry and the Use of Criticism* in 1933, and would be re-emphasized by the retrospective essay 'To Criticize the Critic', in which Eliot chose to align himself not with the theoretical critics described but rather with those writers whose criticism was a by-product of their creative work, describing his own theorizing as 'epiphenomenal' to his tastes.[7]

To add to this, Eliot maintained a sophisticated sense of his work's historicity and its polemicism. In 'To Criticize the Critic', an essay in which his late, benign persona is apparent, Eliot resisted the attempts of commentators to create an overarching and timeless system out of his critical writing, professing himself, on the contrary, to be rather 'struck by the degree to which it was conditioned by the state of literature at the time at which it was written, as well as by the stage of maturity at which I had arrived, by the influences to which I had been exposed, and by the occasion of each essay'.[8] In acknowledging that

[5] To Eleanor Hinkley, 27 Nov. 1914, *The Letters of T. S. Eliot*, i: *1898–1922*, ed. Valerie Eliot (London, 1988), 73. Cited hereafter as *Letters*.

[6] 20 June 1934, quoted in Margolis, *T. S. Eliot's Intellectual Development*, p. xv.

[7] *The Use of Poetry and the Use of Criticism: Studies in the Relation of Criticism to Poetry in England* (London, 1933), 143; *To Criticize the Critic* (London, 1965), 20.

[8] *To Criticize the Critic*, 16–17.

his work developed out of specific contexts or moments, he also had occasion to admit its status as polemic. His disclaimers to facility with propositional thought seem disingenuous when his authorship of a highly regarded doctoral thesis in philosophy is taken into account. Yet he was consistent throughout in admitting rhetorical and stylistic, rather than purely philosophical, debts to the subject of that thesis, F. H. Bradley. On Bradley's death he wrote that his was 'the finest philosophical style in our language', and in 'To Criticize the Critic', in answer to the rhetorical question: what remained of his three years of philosophical studies? he replied: 'the style of three philosophers: Bradley's English, Spinoza's Latin and Plato's Greek'.[9] What this style entailed he had described in 1918, writing that Bradley's philosophical prose attained a perfection that is 'emphatic-ally a perfection of destruction'. His greatness, according to Eliot, 'is due rather to a consummation of dialectical technique than to a single vision'.[10]

And this, perhaps ironically, is where Murry returns. No one has ever taken or mistaken Murry for a theorist. He never pretended towards a system and so no one has found it either necessary or pos-sible to produce on Murry's behalf an *œuvre* comparable to Eliot's *Selected Essays*. Selections of Murry's criticism have been published, but the essays have tended to be regarded as individual *tours de force* rather than planks in a larger platform.[11] Where commentary on Eliot's critical work has tended to exert a centripetal force, driving a sometimes disparate content into a solid theoretical core, that on Murry has worked centrifugally, emphasizing not so much a corpus of work as a constellation of diffused arguments. Murry is, in no small measure, responsible for this himself. He worked at a ferocious rate throughout his life, outproducing Eliot in literary criticism by a ratio of more than three to one.[12] A resultant unevenness in quality

---

[9] 'Francis Herbert Bradley', *Criterion*, 3/9 (Oct. 1924), 1–2 (p. 2); *To Criticize the Critic*, 21.

[10] 'Style and Thought', *Nation*, 22/25 (23 Mar. 1918), 768–70 (p. 770).

[11] See *John Middleton Murry: Selected Criticism, 1916–1957* (1960), ed. Richard Rees, and *Poets, Critics, Mystics*, ed. Richard Rees (London, 1970). Malcolm Woodfield has, however, attempted to find continuities in Murry's criticism in his collection, *Defending Romanticism: Selected Criticism of John Middleton Murry* (Bristol, 1989).

[12] According to information in Donald Gallup's *T. S. Eliot: A Bibliography* (London, 1969), George P. Lilley's *A Bibliography of John Middleton Murry, 1889–1957* (London, 1974), and David Bradshaw's 'John Middleton Murry and the "Times Literary Supple-ment": The Importance and Usage of a Modern Literary Archive', *Bulletin of Bibliog-raphy*, 48/4 (Dec. 1991), 199–212, and id., 'Eleven Reviews by T. S. Eliot Hitherto

was exacerbated by his tendency to allow himself to be led into paradox by the temptations of emotional over-indulgence.

A short account of his political affiliations offers an illustration of
his variousness. Murry saw the First World War out in the post of
Chief Censor at the War Office, a distinguished service for which he
won the OBE at the age of 31. Yet in 1917, while employed by Military Intelligence, he had privately helped formulate for publication
Siegfried Sassoon's insubordinatory protest against the war.[13] By the
1930s he was a prominent member of the Independent Labour Party
and the Peace Pledge Union, remaining pacifist throughout the
Second World War. Pacificist against Hitler, he was less temperate
with the relatively innocuous Colonel Nasser during the Suez Crisis
in 1956, describing Britain's dubious adventure as the 'one just war'.[14]
The combination of intelligence and ability, engagement, energy,
naïvety, and waywardness exhibited here is characteristic of his
literary-critical work. In this, as in his political affiliations, he could
swoop easily from sublime heights to ridiculous depths. He was
acquainted with writers as various as Thomas Hardy and George
Orwell, had exerted an influence on, among others Katherine Mansfield, D. H. Lawrence, and Paul Valéry, yet he could also enthusiastic-
ally endorse Frank Harris as 'the greatest creative critic whom the
world has known'.[15] Commentators who are broadly sympathetic to
his criticism have, on occasion, found themselves having to apologize
for his excesses: one suggested that 'his fine insights are liable to be
lost in their own profusion, and drowned in the rush of his eloquence'; another, prompted to Ruskinesque exasperation, that he
'frequently prefers, in a frenzy of insincere sincerity, to spray a pot of
ink in the public's face'.[16] Even Murry's staunchest defender, Richard
Rees, has described his *God* as reading like the work of a man 'on the
verge of insanity'.[17] But to reject his output as a whole for such lapses
is to miss the other occasions on which that enthusiasm found its
proper subject in the penetrating insights into the work of writers for

Unnoted, from the *Times Literary Supplement*: A Conspectus', *Notes and Queries*,
NS 42/2 (June 1995), 212–15, Murry had by 1929 contributed almost 1,000 articles to
periodicals, while Eliot had published around 300.

[13] See Siegfried Sassoon, *Siegfried's Journey, 1916–1920* (London, 1945), 52.
[14] Quoted in F. A. Lea, *The Life of John Middleton Murry* (London, 1959), 350.
[15] 'Who is the Man?', *Rhythm*, 2/2 (July 1912), 37–9 (p. 38).
[16] Fogle, 'Beauty and Truth', 68; J. S. Collis, *Farewell to Argument* (London, 1935),
203.
[17] *A Theory of My Time*, 59.

whom he felt a particular sympathy. Although his method is perhaps at the lowest ebb of fashion today, his writing on Keats, Shakespeare, Hardy, Dostoevsky, and Chekhov has an undeniable emotional power and at its best can appear, as Stephen Spender observed, 'uncannily perceptive'.[18]

To place Eliot alongside Murry and view his work in the same terms is not to diminish Eliot, but rather to learn something from the way Murry's criticism has been read. Principally, it is to suggest that there is no direct correlation in the practice of criticism between quality and consistency; that a theoretical consistency is by no means a prerequisite for critical writing of the highest quality. This is especially pertinent to Eliot in the 1920s, as there is a strong case to be made that his criticism in that period declined in quality as it increased in internal consistency. The Anglo-Catholicism that he espoused after 1927 brought Eliot peace of mind, but it also brought, for a time at least, a Thomism that turned his criticism from enquiry to denunciation, from disquisition to inquisition. Eliot often spoke of the necessity and desirability of doubt. It may be overstating the case to suggest that his most valuable work arises from doubt and his least valuable from certainty, but that is a possibility that must be entertained. It is raised here because Murry for some time offered Eliot a serious critical challenge, and a pretext for believing his doubts to be justified. In some ways he was a Francis Newman to Eliot's Arnold, in others an Arnold to Eliot's Bradley, but whatever the relationship, he offered Eliot the opportunity to engage in a dialectic out of which some of his best, most probing criticism resulted.

Louis Menand has shrewdly noted the extent to which Eliot was a creature of context.[19] This book attempts to furnish some details of that context, both in the immediate circumstances of the relationship between the two men and in the wider climate of literary-critical culture in the ten years after the First World War. In doing so it will point to inconsistencies in the work of both men, to infelicities, and moments at which they oversold their ideas in the heat of argument. But it does so with a prejudice that these are the circumstances out of which some of the finest critical essays of this century emerged.

---

[18] Stephen Spender, *The Struggle of the Modern* (Berkeley, Calif., 1965), 36.
[19] Louis Menand, *Discovering Modernism: T. S. Eliot and his Context* (Oxford, 1987), 53.

Reconstruction: Murry, Eliot, and the *Athenaeum*, 1919–1921

ELIOT and Murry were peculiarly insulated from the First World War. Murry had been declared unfit for military service, and only in the latter part of the war did he take up an administrative post in the War Office. Indeed, his only spell in France during the war years was in 1916, when he had an idyllic holiday with Katherine Mansfield in Bandol in the south of the country. Eliot had arrived in Britain in 1914, and although he volunteered for military service towards its end, he passed the war firstly in education and then in banking. Although neither was directly involved in it, however, the war and its aftermath would prove of lasting consequence to their criticism.

Their very remoteness from the war would, perhaps ironically, give them a particular advantage over those among their literary contemporaries who had experienced it more directly. For while many of these contemporaries would undergo a kind of literary paralysis, and would only be able to come to terms with the war towards the end of the 1920s (when most of the classic war memoirs were written), Murry and Eliot were able to recognize the war's devastating consequences for intellectual culture without having undergone the kind of experience that might make them despair of a cultural remedy for that devastation.

Murry, in particular, had felt the immediate effects of the war as a cultural and intellectual crisis in this way, and had incorporated that sense of crisis into his criticism. While at Bandol he had been working on his first critical monograph, *Fyodor Dostoevsky*, in which he proclaimed the necessity of the 'dawn of a new consciousness' that he purported to find in the works of Dostoevsky. Those works, Murry suggested, are of especial value for their record of Dostoevsky's own spiritual progress: providing an example to the modern consciousness in their movement from the despair of the early writing to the ecstatic transcendence of *The Brothers Karamazov*. The book's slightly hysterical tone can perhaps be put down to the urgency with which Murry felt the new world must be wrenched free from the old; and his description of this process, in the creation of the character of Alyosha Karamazov, matches Dostoevsky in both its fevered optimism and its anxious tone:

The consummation of belief and full acceptance could come only with a new birth. The life and death of a Stavrogin or a Svidrigailov is the labour pangs of the mind of the world; the pain and the chaos of the mighty blind Karamazov spirit strives towards creation by patterns which the human consciousness, though working in the light of its extreme incandescence, cannot discover. The force which by its own inward contradiction drives the men of this world to self-annihilation and the void, in another world evolves a mighty youth, from whose open eyes no secrets are hid. From the womb of lust and destruction leaps forth the child of life.[1]

This highly wrought desire to bring about a new consciousness would become Murry's rallying cry in the immediate post-war period, and would form the continuous thread through the essays of his first collection, *The Evolution of an Intellectual* (1920). However, as those essays show, Murry's new dispensation would not come without a huge reconstructive effort. The work of the French war writers Pierre Hamp and Georges Duhamel, described in *The Evolution of an Intellectual*, revealed to Murry the full horror of the war, and in so doing stripped away the accreted falsehoods of pre-war culture, exposing the full extent of the crisis over which the Dostoevskian new consciousness must prevail.

It is much harder to locate Eliot's sense of crisis in the public events of wartime. Eliot was ostensibly much less affected by the war, or was much more guarded than Murry about projecting personal anxieties onto public events. For him, wartime was the period in which he was confirming his exile from America and consolidating his new identities as an Englishman, as a poet and critic, and as a married man. Indeed, in one sense it would be from these personal areas that his subsequent anxieties could be seen to spring. But while he concerned himself little with the public pressures of wartime, especially their

---

[1] *Fyodor Dostoevsky: A Critical Study* (London, 1916), 246–7.

more overt manifestations after 1916, the incipient crises of his private life and the concerns of his intellectual formation had imbued in him an outlook that found an immediate correlative in the mood of disenchantment that took hold of his generation in the aftermath of war.

Much has been written about the personal and intellectual sources of Eliot's discontent in the post-war years, but less has been written about the public and literary contexts in which such discontent was articulated and to which it was so conducive. In order fully to comprehend, then, both the vehemence with which Murry insisted upon the need for a new consciousness and the extent to which Eliot found a public discourse that mirrored his own views on the state of civilization, it is necessary to form a clear picture of the intellectual and literary environments of the post-war English world. In particular, it is necessary to understand the ways in which the hopeful mood of a wartime reconstruction movement, which saw war as an unprecedented opportunity for social reform, turned rapidly into the pessimism of post-war disenchantment. In broad terms, this shift engendered the sense of a desperate need for what F. R. Leavis would later characterize as new bearings, or new beginnings, to which the revaluative ideas of young men like Eliot and Murry were particularly welcome; in more narrow ways it helped form a particular literary disenchantment, associated initially with the *Athenaeum*, in which the contributions of the whole machinery of literature—its writers, its editors, its academics—to a compromised war effort were exposed and employed as arguments for the necessity of immediate literary change. War had subjected political and literary values to an examination that many young people felt they had failed. Eliot and Murry, especially in their work on the *Athenaeum*, were ideally situated to expose those failures in the literary arena and to promote alternatives.

In understanding these contexts—the contexts that were crucial in making the *Athenaeum* for a short time the pre-eminent literary journal in England—one can gain a sense of the reasons why the work of Eliot and Murry seemed so appropriate to its times. But one can also gain a sense of why that criticism was itself so unstable and contingent, so prone to rapid revision and internal contradiction. While both writers proclaimed the need for new critical certainties they fell short of such standards in their own practices. This fluidity and openness to change brought occasionally unpredictable results.

Not the least among these was that Eliot and Murry, temperamentally antipathetic from the start and later to become sometimes bitter rivals, frequently found themselves in substantial agreement on literary matters—making common cause in the attempt to reconstitute a sense of tradition by which a literary consensus or Arnoldian 'current of ideas' might be restored. It has been suggested that the two 'disagreed only within the framework of a similar commitment'.[2] A study of the *Athenaeum* and of the underlying circumstances that helped to make the paper so influential furnishes an opportunity to explore the nature and the extent of that common commitment.

RECONSTRUCTION AND 'IMPROPERGANDA'

In March 1917 in an address to the Labour Party leaders the prime minister, David Lloyd George, had expressed a belief

that the present war . . . presents an opportunity for reconstruction of industrial and economic conditions of this country such as has never been presented in the life of, probably, the world. The whole state of society is more or less molten and you can stamp upon that molten mass almost anything so long as you do it with firmness and determination.[3]

With regard to this opportunity, and as a response to increasing domestic tension, Lloyd George attempted to set his stamp on the flux of public opinion by establishing, in July 1917, the Ministry of Reconstruction under Christopher Addison, replacing a smaller Reconstruction Committee of the War Office set up by Asquith. In one sense this new ministry was borne of political expediency in an attempt to defuse popular discontent. Recent events, including the Somme debacle, the introduction of conscription, food shortages, and unofficial strikes at home, combined with the examples of the February Revolution in Russia and the French military mutiny in May 1917 had led to what *The Times* described as a 'Ferment of Revolution' within Britain.[4] The creation of a ministry designed to address or avert such a threat—perhaps in an attempt to offer jam

---

[2] Griffin, *John Middleton Murry*, 43.
[3] Quoted in M. B. Hammond, *British Labour Conditions and Legislation During the War* (London, 1919), 270.
[4] *The Times* began a series with that title on 25 Sept. 1917.

tomorrow in exchange for peace today—has led to subsequent descriptions of it as 'a slightly bogus ministry' or as mere 'window-dressing, to allay labour discontent'.[5]

But there was also a more visionary and genuinely ameliorative aspect to the ministry. Its plans to abolish the poor law and to universalize unemployment insurance, and its schemes for post-war land settlement and new house-building, all based on detailed surveys of existing conditions, bespoke a radical reappraisal of the state's part in social provision and testified to the growing credibility of collectivism in economic and social planning. This sense in which reconstruction could be seen as 'an augury of great promise' or 'the supreme indication of the new constructive mood of wartime' was emphasized by the growth of a wider culture of reconstruction for which the ministry served as a focus.[6] This culture was largely propagated through the written word: in the ministry's own 'Problems of Reconstruction' pamphlets, thirty-eight of which appeared in 1918 and 1919; in newspaper series like *The Times*'s 'Elements of Reconstruction' in 1916; through the growth of periodicals dedicated to reconstruction, the *Athenaeum* and the *Contemporary Review*, and for a short time the literary magazine *New Paths*; and by the publication of numerous books on reconstructive topics such as Bertrand Russell's *Principles of Reconstruction* (1916), W. H. Dawson's *After War Problems* (1917), H. G. Wells's *The Elements of Reconstruction* (1918), and *The Meaning of Reconstruction* (1918) by the *Athenaeum*'s 'Demos', Arthur Greenwood. As a result of these efforts reconstruction gained a popular credibility that saw it become something of 'a magic word'.[7] Advertisers attempted to harness the term's implied promise, labelling products as diverse as patent medicines and the Church of England with the reconstruction tag.[8]

---

[5] Bentley B. Gilbert, *British Social Policy, 1914–1939* (London, 1970), 7; A. J. P. Taylor, *English History, 1914–1945*, corrected repr. (Oxford, 1976), 93. See also Arthur Marwick, *The Deluge: British Society and the First World War* (1965; repr. London, 1973), 189–225.

[6] Paul Barton Johnson, *Land Fit for Heroes: The Planning of British Reconstruction, 1916–1919* (London, 1968), 221; Kenneth O. Morgan, *Consensus and Disunity: The Lloyd George Coalition Government, 1918–1922* (Oxford, 1979), 24.

[7] Charles Loch Mowat, *Britain Between the Wars, 1918–1940*, corrected repr. (London, 1956), 28.

[8] See Samuel Hynes, *A War Imagined: The First World War and English Culture* (London, 1990), 264, and the advertisement 'The Church and National Reconstruction', *Contemporary Review*, 635 (Nov. 1918), 7. The Church had engaged in its own reconstructive 'National Mission of Repentance and Hope' in the autumn of 1916.

Largely through the energetic efforts of its editor Arthur Greenwood, who would later become Minister of Health and deputy
leader of the Labour Party, the wartime *Athenaeum* was an important centre for this revaluative optimism. The paper had a venerable
history as a literary review dating back to 1828, but in an age impervious to its still largely Victorian sensibilities had been remodelled by
Greenwood early in 1917 as 'A Journal of Politics, Literature, Science
and the Arts'. Greenwood aimed at promoting and directing what he
saw as a ground swell of popular demand; the audience he envisaged
was a reconstructive movement growing from a war-weary population that had begun to unite in a clamour for change: 'Amongst
groups of people in civil life, amongst soldiers in hospitals and
camps, discussion is simmering, and the demand for knowledge
increasing. This is all to the good, and every effort should be made to
extend the area and scope of discussion by means of lectures, confer-
ences, classes, and literature.'⁹ At a crucial period in the course of the
war, then, reconstruction furnished a positive sense that some progressive, even radical, social policy could be salvaged from the wreck-
age of wartime. But in the event most of these hopes were
confounded. The Ministry of Reconstruction, along with much of
the apparatus of 'war socialism', was scrapped amid the post-war
cynicism of the Coupon Election and the Peace Conference. But
while the political means disappeared, the mood for change to which
the *Athenaeum* had addressed itself lingered on. Less optimistic,
more overtly cynical, the reconstructive 'turn' now found itself
directed less towards a utopian future than to scathing reappraisals
of the present. Reconstruction had always based its prognostications
on a close analysis of prevailing conditions. Now the recognition of
continuing inequities, coupled with the absence of a political will for
radical solutions, meant that this thwarted progressivism found itself
in step with the less hopeful culture of disenchantment.

Reconstruction had been predicated on the recognition of faults
within the *status quo* exposed by wartime. Disenchantment amplified these faults and added to that recognition a despair that nothing
could be done to amend them. Both attitudes found a literary outlet
in the immediate post-war period: in the work of writers and
critics like Eliot and Murry can be found traces both of the cynical
attitudes of disenchantment, in which all the values and practices of

---

⁹ [Arthur Greenwood], 'Comments', *Athenaeum*, 4625 (Jan. 1918), 7–8 (p. 7).

Edwardian England were to be rejected, and the more positive recon-
structional attitudes, in which some way forward had to be found.
Before moving on to this, however, it is worth considering the *literary*
cost of the war.

In cultural and literary terms, what made the need for reconstruction so pressing was the perceptible breakdown in standards of intellectual and literary probity during wartime. It struck many
commentators that the written word, in all its forms, had not come
out of the war entirely untarnished; that, in fact, the written word,
like the truth it purported to convey, had become one of the prime
casualties of total war.

The press was adduced as the chief culprit, and there were a number of ways in which that institution had been seen to bring discredit
upon itself. Some wartime restrictions that militated against press
integrity, like the repressive Defence of the Realm Act and the official
censorship of the Press Bureau in Whitehall, were of the government's
devising and as such could not be blamed on the newspapers. But
where blame could be apportioned was in the way newspaper editors
and proprietors had appeared willingly to forgo their traditional
independence and acquiesce in the dissemination of state propaganda; propaganda aimed at leading both foreign and domestic opinion through the systematic distortion and suppression of the facts.[10]
This willingness to toe the official line went so far as to prompt
Sir Edward Cook, co-director of the Press Bureau, to comment subsequently that newspapers became 'the *avant-couriers* of necessary
policy' for the government.[11] Indeed, Lloyd George placed such a
value on a supportive press that he described it as having 'performed
the function which should have been performed by Parliament'.[12]

Although there were notable exceptions, such as the *Manchester
Guardian* and the *Nation* (to which Murry contributed on European
matters and in which Wilfred Owen was first published), a range of
newspapers willingly enlisted in the national service.[13] At one end of

[10] For a full account of newspaper involvement in government propaganda see Cate
Haste, *Keep the Home Fires Burning: Propaganda in the First World War* (London, 1977);
Gary S. Messinger, *British Propaganda and the State in the First World War* (Manchester,
1992); M. L. Sanders and Philip M. Taylor, *British Propaganda during the First World
War, 1914–18* (London, 1982).
[11] *The Press in War-Time: With Some Account of the Official Press Bureau: An Essay*
(London, 1920), 5.
[12] Quoted in Taylor, *English History*, 26.
[13] For the high regard in which Murry held H. W. Massingham, the *Nation*'s editor, see
Between Two Worlds: An Autobiography (London, 1935), 431–2.

the range was the self-styled 'Tommy's Bible' *John Bull*, edited by the charismatic charlatan Horatio Bottomley, a weekly newspaper that traded in the vulgar sensationalism and casual xenophobia of modern tabloid journalism, in whose vocabulary the enemy were 'Germ-huns', and which described their leader as the 'Butcher of Berlin' or 'The Potty Potentate of Potsdam'. At the other was the august *Times* newspaper, owned by Lord Northcliffe. Separated by the huge class divide of Edwardian culture these two papers none the less shared a wide range of opinions, from simple chauvinism and an uncritical attitude towards British military and civil policy, through to their unscrupulous campaigns to excise German influences and root out German aliens resident in Britain.

Bottomley had pretensions to high office which, in spite of his election to Parliament in 1918, were never achieved. Northcliffe, in contrast, like his brother Lord Rothermere and competitor Lord Beaverbrook, found his way to governmental power smoothed by the prime minister. Under Lloyd George all three achieved high office: Northcliffe becoming Director of Enemy Propaganda, Rothermere heading the Air Ministry, and Beaverbrook becoming Minister of Information. Greenwood spoke for many when he expressed concern in the *Athenaeum* that such links between press and government were corrosive of public confidence.[14] Lloyd George came under attack from Asquith and other disaffected Liberals who saw in this relationship a threat to the sovereignty of Parliament. One MP, A. F. Whyte, spoke of 'an all but universal feeling in this House and throughout the country that the government is engaging unworthy servants to carry out its services', and he warned that the more the government relied upon 'the unseen influence of the press the less it will be able to rely upon the open confidence of the country and the House of Commons'. Another MP, the Scottish radical William Pringle, put it even more succinctly, accusing Lloyd George and the press barons of engaging in what he described as extensive 'improperganda'.[15]

The deployment of newspapers and newspapermen in the war effort showed the way the press could be manipulated as an arm of government; representing, as John Stevenson has written, 'yet one more ratchet on the wheel whereby the state took greater control over

---

[14] [Arthur Greenwood], 'Comments', *Athenaeum*, 4627 (Mar. 1918), 129–30.
[15] Messinger, *British Propaganda*, 132–3.

peoples' lives'.[16] But as Lloyd George himself realized as his always fraught relations with Northcliffe began to deteriorate towards the close of the war, the relationship cut both ways. By the end of the war, and particularly in the conduct of the post-war General Election, it quickly became obvious that the press had the crucial power not just to disseminate government policy but to influence and substantially shape it; that, as Norman Angell rather ruefully pointed out, a handful of newspaper proprietors 'come nearer, at just those junctures which are crucial, really to governing England and "making it what it is" than Commons or Cabinet, Church or Trade Union'.[17] In the course of the Coupon Election Lloyd George's initial intention to fight on issues of domestic reconstruction, insisting on a just peace with Germany and on building 'Homes fit for heroes to live in', was quickly curbed in a public atmosphere of hostility and recrimination to which *John Bull*, with its desire to 'Destroy the Blond Beast', and the Northcliffe press eagerly contributed. Contemporary commentators were in no doubt that the press had contributed substantially to the political cynicism displayed during the election and in the subsequent Peace Conference. H. M. Tomlinson, the former war correspondent of the *Daily News*, laid the blame for the devastation caused by the peace treaty at Northcliffe's door, describing the treaty as 'ultimately the work of the *Daily Mail*', and suggesting that 'the chaos in the country ever since is as much a monument to the morals and statecraft of Northcliffe and Bottomley as ever was Ypres to the German guns'.[18] Murry joined in the widespread denunciation of the newspapers' conduct in this affair, expressing a vigorous disgust at the 'vile agitations of the Press' and accusing Lloyd George of throwing 'the English Constitution on to the refuse heap to be torn, like so much offal, by the pariah Press'.[19] He criticized the newspapers' advocacy of a recriminatory peace settlement, and predicted the dangers to democracy of a modern press that is 'not merely non-moral, but for the most part deliberately and necessarily immoral'.[20]

The press, then, was perceptibly tainted on two counts. The first concerned its enormous and unconstitutional power over national

[16] *British Society, 1914–45*, Pelican Social History of Britain (Harmondsworth, 1984), 77.

[17] *The Press and the Organisation of Society* (London, 1922), 25.

[18] 'War and Politics', *Adelphi*, 1/10 (Mar. 1924), 906–12 (pp. 908–9). See also John Maynard Keynes, *The Economic Consequences of the Peace* (London, 1919), 127–8.

[19] 'The Problem of the Intelligentsia', *Nation*, 24/9 (30 Nov. 1918), 245–6 (p. 245).

[20] 'Democracy and Patriotism', *Nation*, 24/17 (25 Jan. 1919), 483–4 (p. 484).

and international affairs; the second the ease with which it could gen-
erate and sustain misleading accounts of events, simplifying political
and social complexities into headlines and slogans, reducing public
debate to the exchange of vague emotive counters. For a civilian like
D. H. Lawrence this was the essence of 'the genuine debasement' that
crept into public life in the war, 'the unspeakable baseness of the
press and the public voice, the reign of that bloated ignominy, *John
Bull*'.[21] Those who served in the forces witnessed the simplifications
and distortions of the press even more starkly, finding themselves
unable to communicate the realities of war to a home population fed
on the comforting patriotic myths of popular journalism. Soldiers
found, as Robert Graves and Alan Hodge put it, their 'simple faith in
the printed word' undermined by 'dishonest war-communiques and
over-cheerful despatches'.[22] Barred from reading papers like the
Nation but allowed *John Bull*, servicemen created their own alternative to the press in a flourishing subculture of trench newspapers that
parodied Fleet Street's patriotic posturings and wilful ignorance of
conditions at the front.[23] Just as they turned their backs on popular
journalism, soldiers also found themselves rejecting the official, hieratic language of war as practised by the military authorities. The bur-
geoning of official military euphemism, brilliantly exposed by Paul
Fussell in *The Great War and Modern Memory* and perhaps best
characterized by the Field Service Postcard in which the grisly realities of woundings and injuries were blandly translated into the neat
categories of a polite form letter, was countered in the trenches by a
subversive, carnivalized oral culture. This bound servicemen
together in an ironic confraternity and, in Murry's view at least, represented 'the protest made by the soldiers against the inventions of
the arm-chair journalists'.[24] These subversive activities reinforced a

[21] *Kangaroo* (1923; Phoenix edn. London, 1955), 220.
[22] *The Long Weekend: A Social History of Great Britain, 1918–1939* (London, 1941), 14.
[23] See Richard Aldington, *Death of a Hero* (London, 1929), 293. For a full account of
trench newspapers, see J. G. Fuller, *Troop Morale and Popular Culture in the British and
Dominion Armies, 1914–1918* (Oxford, 1990).
[24] Paul Fussell, *The Great War and Modern Memory* (London, 1975), 169–90; John
Middleton Murry, 'L'Argot Poilu', *TLS* 866 (22 Aug. 1918), 390. Murry had written an
earlier review article on French wartime slang, in which he recognized the importance of
the trench newspapers, and which generated much correspondence: 'L'Argot Poilu', *TLS*
758 (27 July 1916), 354. Wartime slang also provided the *Athenaeum* with one of its most
popular correspondence topics: see Ernest A. Baker, 'Slang in War-time', *Athenaeum*,
4654 (11 July 1919), 582–3, and subsequent issues. See also Sir Edward Cook, 'Words and
the War', *Literary Recreations* (London, 1918), 142–75.

sense of scepticism about the ability of language, and especially institutional language, to render adequately the hard facts of wartime
experience. The net effect of this perceived linguistic slippage, the
loosening of words from their referents, was the widespread feeling
of a general devaluation of language and a sense that, as Charles E.
Montague famously put it, 'you can't believe a word you read'.[25] For
J. S. Collis, 'most of the important words were killed in the War', a
conceit that was shared by Ernest Baker, who described the common
perception that 'the war has mangled and distorted English, as the
German guns mangled North-East France'.[26]

LITERATURE AND THE WAR

As many commentators have pointed out, the advances of the late
nineteenth century in the areas of education and communications
were to have an unprecedented effect on the First World War. The
advent of universal literacy, with its attendant phenomena of mass-
circulation newspapers and a flourishing market in popular fiction,
meant that the war's participants not only engaged with it experien-
tially, but read and wrote about it. As Samuel Hynes has shown in
A War Imagined, the war was subject to a constant reimagining and
reconstruction in language. To that extent, then, it can be described as
one of the first literary wars in history. Literature and literary institutions served a number of functions in the war, interpretative, consolatory, and propagandistic. But as with the newspapers, the functions to
which literature and littérateurs were put in supporting the war
ensured that they would not come out of it with credibility intact.

Paul Fussell has written of the importance of literature to servicemen during the war in providing both a refuge from, and a means of,
contextualizing their experiences, describing the 'oasis of reasonableness and normality' proffered by the poets of the *Oxford Book of
English Verse* and the sympathetic anguish of the 'dark and formal
irony' of Conrad and Hardy. Fussell outlines the literary culture that
existed in the trenches, but he also describes the ultimate failure of
that literary culture to be fully adequate to the representation of the

---

[25] *Disenchantment* (London, 1922), 98.
[26] Collis, *Farewell to Argument*, 118; Ernest A. Baker, 'English in War-time',
Athenaeum, 4647 (23 May 1919), 359–60 (p. 360). See also John Whichelow, 'Jumboism',
Adelphi, 1/8 (Jan. 1924), 735–9 (p. 736).

war: 'the presumed inadequacy of language itself to convey the facts about trench warfare is one of the motifs of all who write about the war'.[27] This reading is supported by Alan Wilkinson, who has written that 'much of the best poetry of the war arose from the gap between war as actually experienced and the romantic, religious, and chivalric images which dominated the imaginations of the conventional'. Wilkinson describes a 'theological gap', like the literary one formulated by Fussell, characterized by 'the failure of ethics and theology to find a new language'.[28]

Many established writers found themselves echoing this frustration and sharing in the wider concern at the apparent failure of language to grasp the new reality. Edith Wharton, in her novel *A Son at the Front*, had one of her characters describe 'how the meaning had evaporated out of lots of our old words as if the general smash-up had broken their stoppers'. Her compatriot Henry James made a similar claim when he wrote that 'the war has used up words; they have weakened, they have deteriorated like motor car tires; they have, like millions of other things, been more overstrained and knocked about and voided of the happy semblance during the last six months than in all the long ages before'—a formulation which so impressed Ernest Hemingway that he wrote it into the manuscript of *A Farewell to Arms*.[29] This sense that literature was itself a casualty of war was allied, then, to the wider sense of the devaluation of language. But it could also be ascribed to the part that literature had played in the cultural war that had accompanied the other hostilities.

When Holbrook Jackson wrote in 1914 that 'there are two wars going on at present. A war of arms and a war of ideas', he was expressing a common assumption, the assumption that the war had a cultural as well as a political basis. At around the same time H. G. Wells was similarly describing the conflict as 'A War of the Mind', in which 'our business is to kill ideas. The ultimate purpose of this war', added Wells, 'is propaganda, the destruction of certain beliefs and the creation of others.'[30] The ideas to which their arguments were

[27] Fussell, *The Great War,* 162–3, 170.

[28] *The Church of England in the First World War* (London, 1978), 235.

[29] Edith Wharton, *A Son at the Front* (New York, 1923), 187–8; Henry James, *New York Times* (21 Mar. 1915), 3–4. Both are cited by Peter Buitenhuis in *The Great War of Words: Literature as Propaganda, 1914–18 and After* (London, 1989), 152, 61.

[30] Holbrook Jackson, 'The Truth about Nietzsche', *T. P.'s Weekly,* 24/625 (31 Oct. 1914), 475–6 (p. 475); H. G. Wells, 'The War of the Mind', in his *The War that Will End War* (London, 1914), 90–9 (p. 91).

addressed were principally those associated with German *Kultur*, the assertive cultural nationalism interpreted by the British as a diabolical admixture of the military, the artistic, and the academic.

Germany, in common with other emergent nation-states, placed a high political value on culture. The new nation profited from the fact that its constituent states had been united linguistically long before they were federated politically. By the cultivation, and occasionally fabrication, of 'national' folk and aesthetic traditions the German state was able to play on linguistic and cultural similarities to procure itself a past apparently common to its people; forging a cultural identity that belied its novel political identity.[31] With the establishment of bodies like the Verein für das Deutschtum im Ausland, culture could act both as a social cement and as a branch of foreign policy, projecting for both external and internal use an image of national coherence and self-confidence. What concerned British commentators at the outbreak of war was the extent to which, as they saw it, discourses of art and literature had been assimilated into this rhetoric of national assertiveness: the way that 'the German mind had been "trained to arms" ' by the sinister figure of the 'Herr Professor', and how 'Goethe, Wagner, and everyone else in the pantheon of German culture had become a war lord'.[32]

The British response to this perceived threat of cultural imperialism was twofold. On the one hand there was a widespread denigration of German pretensions to a superior culture, and on the other was a corresponding inflation of the claims for British culture. Both were to have lasting ramifications in post-war British intellectual life. According to the first response, Germany's was a parvenu culture whose traditions of academicism only served to disguise a profound lack of sensibility. The MP Sir James Yoxall described the product of this callow culture: 'Learned but obtuse—bookish but dull of mind—he, the German, the hobbledehoy and lout of Europe, he the undergraduate of culture, he the 'prentice of art and literature and the card-indexer of science, comprehends nothing *au fond*'.[33] Yoxall's added gibe, that Germany was only 'three generations

[31] See Eric Hobsbawm, 'Mass-Producing Traditions: Europe, 1870–1914', in Eric Hobsbawm and Terence Ranger (eds.), *The Invention of Tradition* (Cambridge, 1983), 263–307.

[32] Cecil Chisolm, 'The Apostle of War: How Prussia Fulminates her Bruiser Philosophy', *T. P.'s Weekly*, 24/616 (29 Aug. 1914), 261; Modris Eksteins, *Rites of Spring: The Great War and the Birth of the Modern Age* (London, 1990), 116–40, 270.

[33] 'Herr Professor Revealed', *T. P.'s Weekly*, 26/661 (10 July 1915), 29.

removed from serfdom', exhibited a common development of this theme in its suggestion that the new Germany's pretensions to culture were a mere overlay, a patina of abstract and technical knowledge disguising what was at bottom a disturbing want of civilization. It was this combination of technical efficiency and cultural deficiency that horrified Arnold Bennett in its addition of, as he put it, 'all the resources of science to the thievishness and sanguinary cruelty of primeval man'.[34] The inflammatory reports of German atrocities in Belgium and their firing of the medieval library at Louvain further stamped in the public mind the idea of the Germans' 'Hunnish' mentality. J. H. Morgan, Professor of Constitutional Law at University College, London, put the notion forward bluntly in his popularized version of the Bryce Report into the Belgian atrocities, *German Atrocities: An Official Investigation* (1916), in which he described Germany as a 'hybrid nation' whose acquired civilization hid the 'instincts . . . of some pre-Asiatic horde': an 'intellectual savage', it nurtured 'dark atavisms and murderous impulses' beneath a civilized veneer.[35]

The second response, the inflation of the claims of British culture, took a number of forms. But perhaps the most interesting was the enlistment of the cultural establishment in aiding and abetting the propaganda war. British academics proved very willing to counter the efforts of their German colleagues, contributing articles and monographs in support of the allied war effort to publications set up specifically for the purpose, like the Oxford University Press's wartime Oxford Pamphlets series. All too frequently these attempts at addressing current events fell short of the necessary academic disinterestedness. Whether by intention or not, most so-called academic dissertations on the war revealed levels of prejudice and tendentiousness that undermined their purported validity as scholarship, making them at best a superior form of special pleading, and at worst simple propaganda.

The academic study of literature did not escape this tendentiousness, with many literary academics engaging in forms of propaganda. Indeed, several, including the professors of English at Oxford and Cambridge, found in war the opportunity to bolster their own

---

[34] *Liberty: A Statement of the British Case* (London, 1914). Quoted by Peter Buitenhuis in *The Great War of Words*, 40.

[35] Quoted in Stuart Wallace, *War and the Image of Germany: British Academics, 1914–1918* (Edinburgh, 1988), 183.

and their profession's prestige by wresting the study of the national literature from the hands of the Herr Professor. For Sir Arthur Quiller-Couch the war was an opportunity to revivify the English language by removing the deadening influence of German scholarship. This was a matter of immediate national concern, for in appropriating the study of the national literature and in organizing and classifying it like a dead classical literature, the German academic had sapped its spontaneity and failed to recognize its creative idiosyncrasy, usurping the Englishman's 'birthright of understanding' and undermining the national culture.[36] In a similar manner, Sir Walter Raleigh attempted to equate what he interpreted as the libertarian ideals of Britain's war aims with 'the illimitable freedom of our English speech':

> It may be objected that literature and art are ornamental affairs, which count for little in the deadly strife of nations. But that is not so: our language cannot go anywhere without taking our ideals and our creed with it, not to mention our institutions and our games. If the Germans could understand what Chaucer means when he says of his Knight that
>
> > he loved chivalry,
> > Truth and honour, freedom and courtesy,
>
> then indeed we might be near to an understanding.[37]

Setting aside the irony that this 'illimitable freedom' had been severely curtailed by the covert censorship of the press and the War Office, Raleigh's casual conscription of literature to the war effort showed the extent to which literature had become enmeshed in a war not just of competing nations but of competing cultures.

This academic intervention would reinforce several myths of the national character that, though challenged, would occasionally resurface and continue to affect literary study after the war. The most obvious is the insistence on the centrality of voluntarism in the national character; the belief that British literature, like British arms, would always triumph through an inspired individualism that is the antithesis of German-style organization and academicism. The way that Murry could insist that the individual literary response is paramount owes much to this trope, as does his later insistence that such

---

[36] 'Patriotism in Literature II', in Quiller-Couch, *Studies in Literature* (Cambridge, 1918), 307–22 (p. 318). See also Chris Baldick, *The Social Mission of English Criticism, 1848–1932* (Oxford, 1987), 87–92.

[37] *Some Gains of the War* (Oxford, 1918), 24–5.

individualism is itself profoundly traditional. This goes some way to explaining, too, why Eliot would have such difficulty in persuading older readers to favour his attempts at a more scientific, impersonal criticism and his fascination with the coexistence of the primitive and the civilized in the mind of the creative artist.

Like other guardians of British culture Raleigh and Quiller-Couch acquiesced in the immediate political imperatives of wartime, loading English traditions of free speech with an anti-German bias. While the alliance of politics and culture was perhaps beneficial to politics in the short term, in the long term it was detrimental to culture and those who claimed to speak on its behalf. For the cultural establishment had allied itself too closely to a political process that had perceptibly become vitiated in the course of the war. Language had suffered at the hands of propagandists and academics, and it would seem that literature too would become devalued through having been implicated in disingenuous attempts to lead public opinion.

There were two related elements contributory to the ensuing disenchantment: first, the collusion of eminent literary figures in government propaganda, and secondly a widely held perception that literature itself had proved inadequate in some way to the experience of modern warfare: the notion, described by Pierre Hamp and endorsed by Murry, that 'in some indefinable way literature itself has failed'.[38] It was this second view which, arguably, would lead to the greater tolerance of modernist experiment in the immediate postwar period. The first opinion may be seen as a direct result of the collaborations of established authors with the government propaganda machine.

Early in the war Asquith's government had sought to sway public opinion, both at home and in America, by utilizing for propaganda purposes the public standing and persuasive talents of a number of prominent Edwardian 'Men of Letters': those 'intellectuals and literary notables' who, in the words of Arthur Ponsonby, proved themselves 'able to clothe the rough tissue of falsehood with phrases of literary merit and passages of eloquence better than the statesmen'.[39] Co-ordinated by C. F. G. Masterman's War Propaganda Bureau at Wellington House, the great men of Edwardian literature, among them Arnold Bennett, John Galsworthy, H. G. Wells, Thomas Hardy,

---

[38] Murry, 'A French Rebel', *TLS* 836 (24 Jan. 1918), 41.
[39] *Falsehood in Wartime* (London, 1928), 25.

Robert Bridges, John Masefield, Sir Arthur Conan Doyle, J. M. Barrie, G. K. Chesterton, and William Archer, contributed in various ways to the propaganda effort. Wells declared himself, in a series of articles for the *Nation* and the *Daily News*, 'enthusiastic for this war against Prussian militarism' and embraced the opportunity that the war offered for 'setting the world to rights', coining the popular description of it as 'the war that will end war'.[40] Though he qualified that early enthusiasm in *Mr Britling Sees it Through* (1916) and *The War and Socialism* (1918), Wells continued to support the war effort, filling for a part of 1918 the post of Head of the Committee for Propaganda in Enemy Country under his friend Lord Northcliffe. Bennett and Galsworthy showed few reservations: Bennett produced more than 300 propaganda articles and ended the war as the Director of the Ministry of Information, while Galsworthy's conversion to the patriotic cause prompted one contemporary commentator to remark that he had paradoxically become the very type of typical Englishman to whom his writing had formerly offered 'a merciless and persistent challenge'.[41] Conan Doyle, who had been knighted for propagandist service in the Boer War, was one of the most robust defenders of the allied cause, writing an official recruiting pamphlet, *The Causes of the War* (1914), which was published in fifty journals in the United States and translated into Dutch and Danish, producing at the commission of the War Office a six-volume history entitled *The British Campaign in France and Flanders* (1916–19), and visiting the front lines in 1916 in order to contradict what he described as 'those mischievous misunderstandings and mutual bafflements which are eagerly fomented by our cunning enemy'.[42] Another vociferous campaigner was Rudyard Kipling, who had a particularly close relationship with the army and its traditions. At the start of the war his writings had been reissued as The Service Kipling in twenty-six volumes, and his *Barrack-Room Ballads* were to prove a staple in the reading of many soldiers throughout the war. Indeed, for some

[40] H. G. Wells, 'Concerning Mr Maximilian Craft', in his *The War that Will End War*, 29. See Irene Cooper Willis, *How we Came out of the War* (London, 1921), 9. For an account of Wells's and other writers' anticipation of the war see Bernard Bergonzi, 'Before 1914: Writers and the Threat of War', *Critical Quarterly*, 6/2 (Summer 1964), 126–34, and I. F. Clarke, *Voices Prophesying War, 1763–1984* (Oxford, 1966).

[41] S. K. Ratcliffe, 'The English Intellectuals in War-Time', *The Century*, NS 94 (Oct. 1917), 826–33 (p. 828).

[42] Sir Arthur Conan Doyle, *A Visit to Three Fronts: June 1916* (London, 1916), 6. See also his *To Arms!* (London, 1914) and *The German War* (London, 1914), 1–31.

Kipling was uniquely responsible for creating the very model of the modern soldier, the plucky, resourceful, and good-humoured 'Tommy': a figure instrumental in improving military morale and in effecting the self-improvement of the troops.[43] In spite of the death of his son in 1915, which led to private misgivings, Kipling remained vocal in his support for the war: as late as 1918 he was still dealing in the unsubstantiated atrocity stories of four years earlier, claiming, preposterously, that 'nine-tenths of the atrocities Germany has committed have not been made public'.[44] The Poet Laureate, Robert Bridges, was less vociferous but equally unthinking in his celebration of the casualties of war, writing in the preface to *The Spirit of Man* (1916) that 'we can . . . be happy in our sorrows, happy even in the death of our beloved who fall in the fight, for they die nobly, as heroes and saints die, with hearts and hands unstained by hatred or wrong'.[45]

While they would lose little support among their popular readership after the war, the effect of their collusion in a subsequently unpopular war effort meant that these Edwardian writers lost the confidence of a younger literary generation. Initially, many established writers had welcomed war as an unparalleled opportunity. For Wells war offered the possibility of a fresh start. But for others it offered a chance for retrenchment, an opportunity for English culture to rid itself of its associations with avant-garde European art. For Edmund Gosse the war would be 'the sovereign disinfectant', an antidote to continental decadence; and for Austin Harrison, editor of the *English Review*, the chance to quash the '*nouveau art* business' emanating from German-speaking countries.[46] Instead, the war helped accelerate the next generation's repudiation of its literary

[43] See Fuller, *Troop Morale*, 130–3, and Hynes, *A War Imagined*, 49–51. Robert Nichols, however, gives a contrasting view and claims that 'during my service I never met a Kipling soldier'. Robert Nichols (ed.), *Anthology of War Poetry, 1914–1918* (London, 1943), 83.

[44] In an address delivered at Folkestone on 15 Feb. 1918, repr. as *Kipling's Message* (London, 1918), [4].

[45] *The Spirit of Man: An Anthology in English and French from the Philosophers and Poets* (London, 1916), [p. vii]. Bridges later recanted. Ironically, he blamed the newspapers for leading him into error: 'we were, most of us, the victims of newspaper war-time propaganda'. 'Notes and Comments', *Athenaeum*, 4739 (4 Feb. 1921), 118.

[46] Edmund Gosse, 'War and Literature', *Edinburgh Review*, 220 (Oct. 1914), 313, quoted in Hynes, *A War Imagined*, 12; Austin Harrison, 'World-Power or Downfall', *English Review*, 71 (Oct. 1914), 312–26 (p. 315). See also D. G. Wright, 'The Great War, Government Propaganda and English "Men of Letters", 1914–16', *Literature and History*, 7 (Spring 1978), 70–100.

inheritance, engendering what Thomas Hardy described gloomily as 'the barbarizing of taste in the younger minds by the dark madness of the late war'.[47] Among the young there sprang up, as George Orwell later noted, 'a curious cult of hatred of "old men" '.[48] C. F. G. Masterman, who had co-ordinated the literary propaganda effort during the war, remarked on what he saw as the 'bitterness and cynicism and contempt of human life' that now distinguished young writers from their elders.[49]

Eliot rarely mentioned the war, and when he did he was dismissive of its cultural implications, writing later that 'perhaps the most significant thing about the war is its *insignificance*'.[50] But at the time even he recognized the post-war sense of hiatus, writing in the first of his synoptic 'Letters from England' to the *Nouvelle Revue française* of the sense of abandonment felt by his literary generation: Kipling had become regarded as an archetypically uninspired writer, and Wells, Bennett, Chesterton, and Shaw were 'separated from us by a gulf; we can no longer draw sustenance from their work'.[51] This intergenerational hostility arose in many forms. It is explicit, for example, in Virginia Woolf's attempts to create discrete Edwardian and Georgian periods in *Mr Bennett and Mrs Brown*. And it would receive its most aggressive and resonant airing in the 'Scrutinies' of the *Calendar of Modern Letters* in the mid-1920s, in which individual Edwardian writers were subjected to frequently scathing revaluations. These essays, which set the tone and gave the title to Leavis's revaluative project, were collected by one of the *Calendar*'s editors, Edgell Rickword, in 1928. In his introduction to that collection Rickword likened the pre-war writers to 'an avenue of cyclopean statues leading to a ruined temple', and apologized only that this necessary revaluation of their work was ten years overdue.[52]

Literature might be seen to have failed in the moral collapse of the literary institution, and Murry argued that it had failed also in a

---

[47] *Late Lyrics and Earlier* (London, 1922), p. xiv. Quoted in Daniel Pick, *Faces of Degeneration: A European Disorder, c.1848–c.1918* (Cambridge, 1989), 17.

[48] *The Road to Wigan Pier* (1937; repr. Harmondsworth, 1962), 121.

[49] *England after War: A Study* (London, 1922), 192.

[50] 'A Commentary', *Criterion*, 9/35 (Jan. 1930), 181–4 (p. 183).

[51] 'Nous nous sentons ajourd'hui très abandonnés. Kipling (qui est devenu complètement l'équivalent anglais du *pompier*), Wells, Bennett, Chesterton, Shaw, sont séparés de nous par un gouffre; dans leurs œuvres nous ne pouvons plus puiser de subsistance.' 'Lettre d'Angleterre', *Nouvelle Revue française*, 18/104 (1 May 1922), 617–24 (p. 623).

[52] *Scrutinies* (London, 1928), p. v.

practical, structural sense. A contemporary of Murry's, Gerald Gould, would write of the impact of the war that 'the shock was too great, the shadows too heavy, the horror too vast, for contemporary artists. Their consciousness would not accept it, still less arrange it.'[53] In an essay entitled 'Mr Sassoon's War Verses' Murry adopted a similar argument, taking exception to Sassoon's war poetry not because it could not summon up a language adequate to an experience of war, but rather because the poetic sensibility itself had proved too fragile under wartime stress. Sassoon's verse, argued Murry, was a moving testimony to the pity and stupidity of war, but it could not attain the serenity necessary to poetry achieved by Georges Duhamel. Sassoon had been 'reduced to a condition in which he cannot surmount the disaster of his own experience', and the failure was not his failure alone, but was rather the failure of the English literary tradition.[54]

In retrospect, it may sound fatuous to talk of serenity in the context of what at the time had been the most destructive war in history. But far from belittling the horror of war, Murry was trying to emphasize the way the experience of that horror had far outstripped the literary models through which it might be comprehended and recreated. His is a typical reaction: the reaction outlined by Samuel Hynes in his description of a generation for whom 'the literary tradition is an obstacle'; for whom the tradition is a hindrance rather than a help in coming to terms with their experience.[55] It is this impulse that had prompted Murry, as early as 1916, to suggest, in a phrase that would reverberate throughout his criticism, that 'a ready-made artistic tradition [is] only a thin excuse for not feeling, not striving, not doing'. The tradition can no longer be accepted unquestioningly, and as a result literature can never be the same, it cannot ignore the war: as Murry put it, 'we stand before the need of new artists and the fact of a new world'.[56]

In November 1919 Katherine Mansfield had written to Murry complaining of the 'lie in the soul' perpetrated by Virginia Woolf in

---

[53] *The English Novel of To-Day* (London, 1924), 56. Gould had been engaged in the propaganda war as head of the French Section at the War Propaganda Bureau so, like Murry, he was not entirely innocent in this regard.

[54] 'Mr Sassoon's War Verses', *Nation*, 23/15 (13 July 1918), 398–400 (p. 400). See also Murry's 'War Pictures at the Royal Academy', *Nation*, 26/12 (20 Dec. 1919), 419–20, where he advances a similar argument about the painting of the war.

[55] *A War Imagined*, 422–63 (p. 456).

[56] 'The Sign Seekers' (Oct. 1916), in his *The Evolution of an Intellectual* (London, 1920), 1–15 (pp. 13–14, 8).

attempting to ignore the consequences of the war in *Night and Day*: 'the novel can't just leave the war out. There *must* have been a change of heart.'[57] Murry's replies to his wife were characteristically self-dramatizing—'I am convinced that you and I have suffered the war more than anyone'—but are valuable in describing the extent to which the war had shaped his aesthetic thinking.[58]

For Murry, the war, and especially the war described by the French writers Barbusse, Duhamel, Benjamin, and Romains, had been a manifestation of the bleak epiphanies he had described in *Fyodor Dosto-evsky* in 1916. For Murry, Dostoevsky's novels were records of the struggle of an ultimately faithless but God-tormented man: 'all that the human soul can suffer is somewhere expressed within his work', Murry wrote. His novels were the heartfelt rendering of the need for a new dispensation, a mode of consciousness that valorizes individual being against the background 'echo of voices calling without sound across the waste and frozen universe'.[59] His works were not consolatory, they were terrifying, but simply by the example of their existential honesty they offered Murry hope of the possibility of this new dispensation. It was this implicit hope, of intellectual honesty tempered in the fires of angst, that Murry found in the work of the French wartime writers. The French tradition, like the English, had, according to Murry, shown itself inadequate to the experiences of war. That tradition had forged for French poetry an instrument 'so subtle that its strings, instead of echoing to the direct experience of war, were shattered by it'.[60] The result of this breach was that French writers were thrown back for better or for worse on to their own individual resources. Georges Duhamel, as an example, had recognized the solipsism of suffering—that a 'human being always suffers alone in his flesh'—but in recompense had made manifest, like Dostoevsky, a 'strange and splendid honesty of soul', in the course of that realization.[61]

---

[57]   10 Nov. 1919, *Katherine Mansfield's Letters to John Middleton Murry, 1913–1922*, ed. John Middleton Murry (London, 1951), 380.

[58]   11 Nov. 1919, *Letters of John Middleton Murry to Katherine Mansfield*, ed. C. A. Hankin (London, 1983), 207. Murry's reactions to the war were also complicated at this time by the onset of Katherine Mansfield's tuberculosis. The extent to which he associated his wife's illness with the wider debilitation of wartime can be seen in *Between Two Worlds*, 491–6. Indeed, F. A. Lea suggests that for Murry Katherine Mansfield's illness came to stand as a particular symbol of national decline. *The Life of John Middleton Murry*, 61–2.

[59]   *Fyodor Dostoevsky*, 47, 33.

[60]   'An Enemy of "La Gloire" ', *TLS* 831 (20 Dec. 1917), 633.

[61]   'The Discovery of Pain', *TLS* 803 (7 June 1917), 270.

What particularly attracted Murry to these writers, then, was the sense their work gave of the survival of personal integrity through devastating experience, or, even more strongly, the sense in which the devastation was a trial through which that integrity would be revealed. This was the quality of self-discovery through suffering that Murry had already found in Keats and had recognized in Rousseau, the idea of life as a 'vale of soul-making' and the sense that in times of trouble the individual response was to be trusted before the traditional: that periods of crisis 'are the times when men have need of the great solitaries'.[62] It was this rejection of tradition in favour of an individual, a personal, response that Murry attempted to adumbrate in the essays collected as *The Evolution of an Intellectual* (1920). In the first essay of that book, written in October 1916, he sought to personalize the conflict, stating that 'there are moments when each man is secretly convinced that in himself he bore the seeds of this great disruption, by reason of his own disharmony'.[63] From this starting-point, the wider task of reconstruction is predicated on the evolution of a new intellectual consciousness: a tearing away of the veils of deceit woven by pre-war culture. Prefiguring the letter from Katherine Mansfield, he had written of the peculiar honesty of the French war writers: that 'in them the war has cauterized the lie in the soul. They have lived out the war, have shrunk from none of its infinite contacts, and, having torn away a web of half-truths and half-honesties, have responded cleanly.'[64]

The war described in Murry's sometimes overheated rhetoric, then, had taken on the qualities of an apocalypse, a scene of revelation. The world after war 'was not really a new world; it was the old one for the first time clearly seen', and its survivors were 'men with the proud privilege of having seen the texture of life stripped of its embroideries'.[65] And this sense is very much to the fore in his reply to Katherine Mansfield's letter: 'The War *is* Life; not a strange aberration of Life, but a revelation of it. It is a test we must apply; it must be allowed for in any truth that is to touch us.'[66] This need to respond

[62] 'The Religion of Rousseau', *TLS* 844 (21 Mar. 1918), 133. Murry's lifelong fascination with Keats, and particularly 'The Fall of Hyperion', had effectively begun in November 1917; see *Between Two Worlds*, 445–8.

[63] 'The Sign Seekers', in *The Evolution of an Intellectual*, 4.

[64] 'The Discovery of Pain'.

[65] 'The Defeat of the Imagination', *Nation*, 24/13 (28 Dec. 1918), 375–6 (p. 376); 'The Disappointed Age', *Athenaeum*, 4641 (11 Apr. 1919), 169–70 (p. 169).

[66] 14 Nov. 1919, *Letters of John Middleton Murry to Katherine Mansfield*, 211.

cleanly, to rediscover a sense of personal integrity on which an aesthetic might be based, free from the vitiated models of pre-war literature, would be a formative influence on the editorial policy of the reconstructed *Athenaeum*. Not only must modern literature take account of the war, it must use the revelation of war as the basis on which to found a new practice.

THE *ATHENAEUM*: 'INWARD ACTS AND ANCESTRAL ATTITUDES'

With the collapse of the reconstruction movement Greenwood relinquished control of the *Athenaeum*. It was bought up in early 1919 by Arthur Rowntree, who intended to restore it to its former role and eminence as a weekly literary journal. As editor he chose Murry, who quickly remodelled the paper under its new masthead, as a 'Journal of English & Foreign Literature, Science, the Fine Arts, Music & the Drama'. Murry acquired promises of contributions from his acquaintances in Bloomsbury and at Garsington: Leonard and Virginia Woolf, E. M. Forster, Bertrand Russell, Lytton and James Strachey, Clive Bell, Roger Fry, and Aldous Huxley; from his erstwhile literary collaborators, Katherine Mansfield, D. H. Lawrence, and S. S. Koteliansky; and from his colleagues at the War Office, J. W. N. Sullivan, D. L. Murray, and J. T. Sheppard. He also secured for publication in early issues two future classic texts: George Santayana's 'Soliloquies in England' and 'La Crise de l'esprit' by Paul Valéry, whom Murry had been responsible for introducing to Britain.[67]

The final issue of Greenwood's *Athenaeum* had expressed the hope 'that its readers will continue to maintain the principles of reconstruction for which the paper has stood'.[68] This appeared to be reinforced by the announcement in the paper's first issue under Murry of an essay competition on the subject of 'Spiritual Regeneration as a Basis of World reconstruction'. But, while this might prove

---

[67] In his review of Valéry's *La Jeune Parque*, *TLS* 814 (23 Aug. 1917), 402. Discussions of Murry's importance in securing Valéry's reputation in Britain can be found in Cyrena N. Pondrom's *The Road from Paris: French Influence on English Poetry, 1900–1920* (Cambridge, 1974), 303, in Charles G. Whiting's *Paul Valéry* (London, 1978), 110, and in Charles du Bos's 'Letters From Paris, V', *Athenaeum*, 4709 (30 July 1920), 158–9. See also Eliot's foreword to Murry's *Katherine Mansfield and other Literary Studies* (London, 1959), pp. ix–xi.

[68] 'The Outlook for Reconstruction', *Athenaeum*, 4639 (Mar. 1919), 87–9 (p. 87).

an unwittingly apt description of Murry's future aspirations, his immediate plans for the *Athenaeum* were of necessity much less ambitious.

One immediate difficulty for Murry's avowed reconstructive purposes, along with the obvious intergenerational literary hostility and the lack of faith in official printed sources generated in wartime, was the coincidental collapse of the popular reconstruction movement. Reconstructive optimism had hit the buffers of a *realpolitik* of national and corporate self-interest at the General Election, and by the time of the demise of the Ministry of Reconstruction in June 1919 there existed a widespread feeling that few positive benefits were going to accrue from the war and that the ostensible ideals for which so many had died had become little more than counters in a cynical political game. The resulting disenchantment, the cynicism derived from thwarted aspiration, is the characteristic mood of the post-war world. This is the world into which Murry's *Athenaeum* was launched, and it is no surprise to see its disillusion seeping into the paper, counteracting the revelatory, reconstructive enthusiasm of its editor. This is clear from as early as Murry's first editorial, where he employs a bold rhetoric to appeal to the qualities of 'spiritual honesty' that will ensure the advent of a 'republic of the spirit' but contrasts this with a singularly disconsolate portrait of the present: 'And who can tell whether it is better that we should continue to inhabit the castle of indolent illusion than that its ruins should fall about our awakened heads? The earthquake has happened and we have to live among the debris. We had better make the most of it.'[69]

In many respects the *Athenaeum* under Murry can be regarded as a particular and identifiable product of a culture of disenchantment. In its early issues it exhibited the hostility to its inheritance characteristic of that mood. Towards the end of the war Murry had welcomed Lytton Strachey's 'patiently cynical showmanship' in wittily undermining Victorian values in *Eminent Victorians*.[70] For his new paper he sought contributions from Strachey in the same vein, and Strachey obliged by providing essays on the eccentric Lady Hester Stanhope and Thomas Creevey. A discernible trend, mildly disparaging to the nineteenth century, soon followed with Virginia Woolf's 'The Eccentrics' and 'The Soul of an Archbishop' and Eliot's various

[69] 'Prologue', *Athenaeum*, 4640 (4 Apr. 1919), 129–30 (p. 129).
[70] 'The Victorian Solitude', *Nation*, 24/5 (2 Nov. 1918), 136–8 (p. 136).

attacks on Victorian sentimentality. Similarly, disenchantment filtered through into accounts of current literary practices. Murry himself took every opportunity to attack Georgianism and its new organ, the *London Mercury*, while Eliot cast a cool eye over other modern coterie poetry. Ivor Brown denounced a modern literary culture dulled by the 'cheap narcotics' of journalistic English and Sullivan, in a review of Sir Charles Walston's *Truth: An Essay in Moral Reconstruction*, outlined the difficulties for a literary reconstruction in attempting to rescue truth from the wilful degradation it had suffered at the hands of politicians and journalists.[71] Murry was quick to point out the analogies between the political and the literary situation as he reviewed the competing post-war poetry anthologies: *Georgian Poetry*, he suggested was like the government, *Wheels* the radical opposition; like their political analogues neither were credible, taken together they were 'remarkable as an index of the complete confusion of aesthetic value that prevails today'.[72]

   This conflation of political and literary disenchantment could also be seen in Paul Valéry's essay 'The Spiritual Crisis' which appeared in the *Athenaeum* in April 1919.[73] The subject of the essay was the by now familiar sense of intellectual abandonment precipitated by 'the extraordinary tremor [that] has run through the spiritual marrow of Europe'. Valéry's is a pointedly bleak description of the post-war world: the war has been a 'demonstration of the impotence of knowledge to save anything whatever', with attempts to rediscover 'refuges, signs, consolations in the whole gamut of memories, of inward acts and ancestral attitudes' proving ultimately fruitless. Bereft of the consolations of science, religion, and 'the lost illusion of a European culture', Valéry describes a post-war Europe ripe not for a literary renaissance but for the ultimately soul-destroying depredations of industrialization and Taylorism. The post-war intellectual he portrays as a Hamlet rendered powerless by the decimation of his critical certainties. His choice of a literary analogy here is telling, for in spite of his professions, Valéry shows that literature still has a continuing value in supplying a culture with analogy and precedent so that, even while attempting the destruction of a lingering belief in the survival

   [71] Ivor Brown, 'The Decay of English', *Athenaeum*, 4655 (18 July 1919), 614–15; [J. W. N. Sullivan], 'Truthfulness', ibid. 621.
   [72] 'Prologue', *Athenaeum*, 4640 (4 Apr. 1919), 129..
   [73] 'Letters from France: 1, The Spiritual Crisis', *Athenaeum*, 4641 (11 Apr. 1919), 182–4.

of an intellectual culture, he subtly confirms that culture's existence and points backward, skipping several generations, to where it may be discovered in a less degraded state.

Valéry talked of the fruitlessness of appealing to 'inward acts and ancestral attitudes', but in fact this is an apt description of the tendencies of the *Athenaeum*, representing the two directions in which contributors attempted to break the circle of disenchantment. For Murry, the lesson of the war had been the need to delve deeper into the self, but Valéry's essay and articles like Eliot's 'The New Elizabethans and the Old' exhibited hints of a different tendency, a looking back to find a new way forward through the past. This second view had already been seen in Greenwood's *Athenaeum*, in John Dover Wilson's description of 'the modern English Muse standing like a broken signpost in the midst of our industrial wilderness, plaintively pointing us backward along the road of history'.[74] In Murry's *Athenaeum* the most coherent statement of this tendency came from Clive Bell. Bell, discussing the contemporary breakdown of values in art, noted that in times of crisis the tendency of great painters had been to 'overhaul the tool chest. Of the traditional instruments some they reshaped and resharpened, some they twisted out of recognition, a few they discarded, many they retained. Above all, they travelled back along the tradition, tapping it and drawing inspiration from it, nearer to the source.'[75] This argument, with its attempt to balance novelty with the reassurance of tradition, can be seen as an anticipation of Eliot's 'Tradition and the Individual Talent'.[76] It can also be seen to be typical of a larger retrospective tendency that was increasingly looking to the past for the consolations of an integrated world-view.

Murry's *Athenaeum*, then, is something of a hybrid. On the surface it maintains the form and the comprehensiveness of the Victorian Review, but in its contents it displays the radical uncertainty of the post-war world. Contributors disagree over the way literature

---

[74] 'Muezzin' [John Dover Wilson], 'Prospects in English Literature, IV: The Great Schism', *Athenaeum*, 4618 (June 1917), 279–83 (p. 279). Interestingly from the point of view of literary reconstruction, Wilson, who would become an eminent Shakespeare scholar and educationalist, sat on Newbolt's post-war committee on the teaching of English and wrote part of its report, *The Teaching of English in England* (London, 1921).

[75] 'Tradition and Movements', *Athenaeum*, 4640 (4 Apr. 1919), 142–4 (p. 143).

[76] James Smith has suggested that Eliot's essay owes a debt to Bell. In particular, Smith suggests that 'Tradition and the Individual Talent' contains many 'echoes' of Bell's *Art* (1914). 'Notes on the Criticism of T. S. Eliot', *EIC* 22/4 (Oct. 1972), 333–61 (p. 352).

and the arts might reconstruct standards, but concur, at least, that the practices they have inherited won't do. This accounts for both the paper's eclecticism and its hostility towards the Victorians and their heirs. Destructiveness, the need to repudiate the immediate past, becomes paradoxically one of the preoccupations of the envisaged literary reconstruction. For this is a destructiveness that predicates reconstruction, it is the clearing of the foundations on which a new literature might be built: as Murry had put it at the war's close, 'the champions of the positive ideal have perished; but the force of the negative ideal might still be drawn upon to shape the world anew'.[77]

It is worth noting the compatibility of Eliot's early criticism with this tendency in the *Athenaeum*. Several critics over the years have remarked on the destructive streak in Eliot's early criticism. Richard Aldington satirized what he described as Eliot's 'oblique method': 'always to create by destruction, to seek truth for oneself by exploiting the errors of others'.[78] In a similar way, I. A. Richards, another contributor to Murry's *Athenaeum*, would write of Eliot's poetry having performed a valuable service to the post-war generation in giving a Conradian voice to their common failure of belief: Eliot 'has shown the way to the only solution of these difficulties. "In the destructive element immerse. That is the way." '[79] More recent commentators have seen this destructiveness as subversive of Murry's editorial line: a 'sort of solemn game or insiders' joke', working in an ironic counterpoint to the critical impressionism of the *Athenaeum*.[80] But this latter impression could hardly be further from the truth. Far from working against the grain of Murry's editorial aims, Eliot can be seen to deploy his ironic style in broad sympathy with them: a contention supported by his own belief that his pieces for the *Athenaeum* were more sustained and better than anything he had contributed to the *Egoist*.[81] This is important, because it

[77] 'The Sorrows of Satan', *Nation*, 24/8 (23 Nov. 1918), 219–20 (p. 219). This idea was still current in the mid-1920s. See e.g. Edgell Rickword's 'The Re-creation of Poetry: The Use of "Negative" Emotions', *Calendar of Modern Letters*, 1/3 (May 1925), 236–41.

[78] Eliot is represented as 'the blessed Jeremy Cibber'. *Stepping Heavenward: A Record* (Florence, 1931), 47.

[79] 'A Background for Contemporary Poetry', *Criterion*, 3/12 (July 1925), 511–28 (p. 520).

[80] Edward Lobb, *T. S. Eliot and the Romantic Critical Tradition* (London, 1981), 96–7. See also Hugh Kenner, *The Invisible Poet: T. S. Eliot* (London, 1960), 85, and Louis B. McKendrick, 'T. S. Eliot and the *Egoist*: The Critical Preparation', *Dalhousie Review*, 55/1 (Spring 1975), 140–54. McKendrick attempts to draw a contrast between the radical *Egoist* and an *Athenaeum* that is 'directed toward the cultural establishment' (p. 143).

[81] 25 May 1919, *Letters*, 296.

emphasizes the accord between Eliot and Murry at this time and serves as a reminder of the importance of the *Athenaeum* in the postwar literary world. The *Athenaeum* may have lacked the modernist fervour of *Blast* and the *Egoist* but it proved none the less to be at least as important in orienting modernist ideas in the mainstream of literary culture. John Carswell, for one, saw it as 'not only distinguished but decisive in forming a new literary taste'.[82] What's more, it offered Eliot a form particularly suited to his developing style. While Ezra Pound and Wyndham Lewis appeared stuck in the strident, sometimes shrill forms of avant-garde coterie journalism, Eliot was able to craft a subtly polemical critical style entirely appropriate to Murry's popular, hybrid review.

To begin with, Eliot had been offered a post as an assistant editor on the *Athenaeum*, an offer which had prompted him to write grandly to his mother, that Murry is 'one of my most cordial admirers', and furthermore that 'there is a small and select public which regards me as the best living critic, as well as the best living poet, in England'.[83] In fact, when Murry made his offer he had never met Eliot nor read any of his criticism; his estimation of Eliot's work had been made solely on the strength of having read *Prufrock* at Garsington some two years earlier.[84] This is perhaps typical of what Eliot would describe as Murry's 'erratic and intuitive nature' in getting the right result for all the wrong reasons.[85] In the event, Eliot did not take up the offer of the assistant editorship.[86] At the time, he wrote to his mother that 'when I declined his offer he decided not to have *any* assistant editor, as, he said, he did not know of anyone else in England whose critical judgement he could trust in matters of the literary policy of the paper'.[87] Again, this was more than a little misleading because Murry already had a first assistant editor in J. W. N. Sullivan

[82] *Lives and Letters: A. R. Orage, Beatrice Hastings, Katherine Mansfield, John Middleton Murry, S. S. Koteliansky, 1906–1957* (London, 1978), 157.

[83] 29 Mar. 1919, *Letters*, 280.

[84] See Eliot's foreword to *Katherine Mansfield and other Literary Studies*, pp. viii–ix.

[85] See Lea, *The Life of John Middleton Murry*, 66.

[86] There is some doubt as to why he didn't. In letters to his family he wrote of his decision not to accept the post for reasons of job security and critical disinterestedness. Peter Ackroyd has accepted this explanation in writing of Eliot's turning down the offer of a putative salary of £500 per annum: *T. S. Eliot* (London, 1984), 96. However, Murry's letters cast a slightly different light on the financial aspects of the matter, in describing Murry's unsuccessful attempts to 'wrestle with Rowntree' to get Eliot an *extra* £500 a year. Quoted in Lea, *The Life of John Middleton Murry*, 66.

[87] 23 Apr. 1919, *Letters*, 286.

and had appointed Aldous Huxley as second assistant editor in Eliot's stead. In spite of this tentative start, however, Eliot's relationship with Murry quickly flourished, and was manifested in a genuine mutual esteem. Once the *Athenaeum* was under way, Eliot wrote of Murry's congeniality, and Murry in turn expressed himself pleased with Eliot's early contributions: 'What a great pleasure it is to have you working with me', wrote Murry, 'I only hope that the collaboration will not be interrupted until we have restored criticism.'[88] Eliot's letters at this time show the extent of his realization of the importance of writing for Murry. The *Athenaeum* brought him a critical notoriety denied him at the *Egoist*; it allowed him greater space resulting in what he considered better work; it procured the cachet of social engagements; and it directly brought him the contact with Sir Algernon Methuen that would lead to the publication of *The Sacred Wood*. However, as well as recognizing the opportunity offered by the *Athenaeum*, Eliot appeared to have a real regard for his editor, writing to Murry: 'You must realise that it has been a great event for me to know you, but you do not know the full meaning of this phrase as I write it.'[89]

This personal congeniality found itself expressed at first in a certain critical congeniality: Murry wrote to Katherine Mansfield describing Eliot as 'the only critic of literature that I think anything of'.[90] And when Eliot was asked by John Quinn to suggest a suitable reviewer for his *Poems*, the first name that Eliot put forward was Murry's.[91] While never being entirely temperamentally compatible, their criticism had enough in common for them to emphasize its convergences and put a gloss over its divergent aspects. Eliot did not share Murry's conclusions concerning the revelatory importance of the war. In fact he rather fitted that 'oppositional' group, made up of the Georgians and certain members of Bloomsbury delineated by Murry, that had sought to ignore the war.[92] Later developments in their criticism would reveal an almost polar opposition, Murry attempting to discover a core of inner authority, innate but ideal,

[88] Quoted in Eliot's *Letters*, 286.

[89] To John Quinn, 9 July 1919, and 25 May 1919, *Letters*, 315 and 296; to Eleanor Hinkley, 17 June 1919, *Letters*, 304; to Henry Eliot, 2 July 1919, *Letters*, 310; and to John Middleton Murry, 29 July 1919, *Letters*, 325.

[90] 30 Mar. 1920, quoted in Lea, *The Life of John Middleton Murry*, 72.

[91] See Eliot's letter to Quinn, 26 Mar. 1920, *Letters*, 377–8.

[92] In a letter to his mother on 14 Oct. 1917 he had described the pleasure of working for the *Egoist* as principally owing to its lack of concern with politics or the war. *Letters*, 199.

while Eliot sought an authority external to the individual, embodied in a culture, a religion, or a tradition. But under the present circumstances their mutual concern at the degeneracy of the prevailing literary tradition, and their insistence on the maintenance of critical standards, was enough to unite them in a common practice. And at this stage the ideas underlying their criticism were not so firmly fixed as to preclude inconsistency, even self-contradiction, in their development, giving their arguments a flexibility that allowed for a genuine exchange of ideas denied their later, more entrenched, criticism.

This exchange of ideas can be seen occurring in several ways: some are merely nuances, others the adoption of one's individual evaluations by the other. For example, Murry's critical estimation of Kipling, his poetry's uncontrolled 'uprush of rhetoric', can be seen to be influenced by Eliot's description of the 'emphatic sound' of Kipling's oratorical style.[93] Similarly, Eliot's acknowledgement of Keats's 'struggle toward a unification of sensibility' in the second *Hyperion*, reproduces the particular emphasis of Murry's argument in 'The Problem of Keats'.[94] Again it can be argued that Murry's rhetorical question—'what right had you to suppose that a man disarmed of tradition is stronger for his nakedness?'—is influenced by Eliot's description two weeks before of Blake as 'The Naked Man': naked because he has not available to him the clothing of a tradition.[95] Perhaps more importantly we can see one source of Eliot's interest in the poetic drama in Murry's earlier championing of the Phoenix Society, and in his ambition 'to restore the poetical drama stage'.[96] Eliot

[93] Murry, 'American Poetry', *Athenaeum*, 4662 (5 Sept. 1919), 840–1; Eliot, 'Kipling Redivivus', *Athenaeum*, 4645 (9 May 1919), 297–8 (p. 297).

[94] Eliot, 'The Metaphysical Poets', *TLS* 1031 (20 Oct. 1921), 669–70 (p. 670). Murry, 'The Problem of Keats', *Athenaeum*, 4656 (25 July 1919), 648–50. Murry's essay itself acknowledges the earlier assessment of the influence of Keats made by Eliot in 'The Romantic Generation if it Existed', *Athenaeum*, 4655 (18 July 1919), 616–17.

[95] Murry, 'The Cry in the Wilderness', *Athenaeum*, 4687 (27 Feb. 1920), 267–8 (p. 267). Eliot, 'The Naked Man', *Athenaeum*, 4685 (13 Feb. 1920), 208–9.

[96] 'The Phoenix and the Pelican', *Athenaeum*, 4669 (24 Oct. 1919), 1057–8. 'Stage Craft', ibid. 1075. The latter essay has not previously been attributed to Murry. However, it closely reflects his interests at this time: it compares a new poetic drama, *Tiger Rose*, with one already reviewed over Murry's name, *Napoleon*; and it is signed M., an abbreviation frequently used by Murry in his dramatic criticism. Concern for the poetic drama was fairly widespread at this time, prompted mainly by the first production of the Phoenix Society, *The Duchess of Malfi*, on 23 Nov. 1919. See e.g. 'The Poetic Drama', *London Mercury*, 1/2 (Dec. 1919), 240–3, in which poetic drama is suggested as a reconstructive antidote to the 'epidemic of materialism' characteristic of wartime.

subsequently signalled his support for the Phoenix Society in a letter to the *Athenaeum*, and took the opportunity in reviewing Murry's verse drama *Cinnamon and Angelica* to point to the necessity of a framework or 'temper of the age' supportive to the production of a modern poetic drama. This review of Murry's play would be restated—in some parts word for word—and developed in the better known 'The Possibility of a Poetic Drama'.[97]

The critical flexibility of both men can be seen in other ways, most notably in their writings on the relationship between the individual writer and the tradition. Eliot, of course, would make the classic formulation of this relationship towards the end of 1919 in 'Tradition and the Individual Talent'. But it is interesting to note the instability of his conception of this relationship before, and even after, that essay was written, an instability that is shared with the work of Murry. A noticeable feature of Eliot's early contributions to the *Athenaeum* is the marked absence of a consistent approach towards the tradition. The key words to denote approval in his critical vocabulary are not 'history' and 'tradition' but 'maturity' and 'rhetoric'; the qualities he derides are 'immaturity' and 'sentimentality'. The poets of the war are immature, bearing the hallmarks of Victorian sentiment rather than the less vitiated rhetoric of the Elizabethans.[98] The Victorians have inherited a debilitated romanticism based on the 'immaturity of genius' of Keats and Shelley, in contrast to Shakespeare who developed a subtly variable, self-conscious 'rhetoric of content not the rhetoric of language'.[99] As the use of these terms implies, Eliot's evaluative standard was still, very much like Murry's, one of personality. Kipling's and Swinburne's verses are 'immature' because 'there is no point of view to hold them together'.[100] Stendhal and Flaubert, in contrast, 'were men of far more than common intensity of feeling, of passion', whose 'discontent with the inevitable inadequacy of actual living to the passionate capacity . . . drove them to art and to analysis'.[101] The 'immaturity' of Henry Adams is felt as 'a lack of personality; an instability'. Again, the criterion for maturity, and hence good art, is the development of the artist's personal

---

[97] 'The Phoenix Society', *Athenaeum*, 4687 (27 Feb. 1920), 285; 'The Poetic Drama', *Athenaeum*, 4698 (14 May 1920), 635–6.
[98] 'The New Elizabethans and the Old', *Athenaeum*, 4640 (4 Apr. 1919), 134–6.
[99] 'The Romantic Generation, if it Existed', 616; 'Whether Rostand had Something about Him', *Athenaeum*, 4656 (25 July 1919), 665–6 (p. 665).
[100] 'Kipling Redivivus', 298.
[101] 'Beyle and Balzac', *Athenaeum*, 4648 (30 May 1919), 392–3 (p. 393).

responsiveness: the development of a sensuous experience that appears as though it has been thought through the body.[102]

Eliot, then, can be seen to share with Murry a concern that artistic value is a direct attribute of the individual qualities of the writer; that, as he put it, the arts 'require that a man be not a member of a family or of a caste or of a party or of a coterie, but simply and solely himself'.[103] Similarly, the writers of the *Wheels* anthology must, for the benefit of their art, shed their familial attributes and 'run the risk of being individuals'; shunning, as the American writers of the nineteenth century did by necessity, the society of the *intelligentsia*.[104] This sense of the primacy of the personal approach applies, too, to the consumption of texts. Eliot rejects academic attempts to form literary taste. Taste, he suggests, is not a correct theory, 'the apprehension of which should supply infallible evidence of values'. Rather, it 'begins and ends in feeling' and depends upon a balance of immediate and acquired reading experiences. The 'test for anything new that appears' is an individual '*Apperzeptionsmass*', a system of feeling, rather than the impersonal stamp of a tradition.[105]

While the notion of an authorizing, structuring tradition is visible in these essays—as the formal requirements of the sermon that inhibited Donne's prose, or the generic rhetoric of the Elizabethans— Eliot's focus is still on the individual. The tradition may help shape the individual, through his reading and in the forms within which he writes, but the final court of appeal, or source of authority, remains the sentient personality. That is not to say, however, that authority is merely subjective; that the individual can simply judge as he sees fit. Instead, this individuality must necessarily be disciplined. Taste, for example, is an 'organization of feeling' that 'cannot be had without great effort'; literary simplicity is 'won by years of intelligent effort'; Sacheverell Sitwell may be 'capable of something exceptional', but this must 'be won by infinite labour'. This emphasis is both that of tradition and reconstruction, balancing a literary liberalism like Murry's against the need for authorizing structures of belief and feeling. It anticipates the assertion of 'Tradition and the Individual Talent' that the tradition may only be obtained 'by great labour', but it

[102] 'A Sceptical Patrician', *Athenaeum*, 4647 (23 May 1919), 361–2 (p. 362).
[103] 'A Romantic Patrician', *Athenaeum*, 4644 (2 May 1919), 265–7 (p. 267).
[104] 'The Post-Georgians', *Athenaeum*, 4641 (11 Apr. 1919), 171–2 (p. 172); 'American Literature', *Athenaeum*, 4643 (25 Apr. 1919), 236–7.
[105] 'The Education of Taste', *Athenaeum*, 4652 (27 June 1919), 520–1.

also resembles the sense in which Murry talks of the 'great labour' that a certain American writer must undertake in his personal journey 'along the road of art'.[106]

The concern with this need to supplement individual qualities with an informing, compensatory tradition had begun to preoccupy Eliot and would lead directly to 'Tradition and the Individual Talent', which would be published in two parts in the *Egoist* towards the end of 1919.[107] Eliot's essays, and particularly those on the verse drama, were increasingly insisting that qualities such as literary 'maturity' had formal as well as personal causes. But the relationship between them was still not clear: a mature artist like Shakespeare had available to him a blank-verse form adequate to the expression of 'more intense art-emotions than it has ever conveyed since'; but his work was still the product of an individuality: his plays are 'all out of the one man'.[108] It was to this problem that 'Tradition and the Individual Talent' was addressed in its attempts to clarify the relationship between the individual artist and the history of his medium and to reformulate the consequent artistic 'maturity' as a quality of craft as much as of personality. Eliot achieved this redefinition by a sleight of hand, most notably by his reformulation of what the tradition actually is. In a later work, *After Strange Gods*, Eliot would describe the tradition in its commonly accepted sense as an *unconscious* transmission of cultural values between generations: 'of the blood, so to speak, rather than . . . the brain'.[109] But in 'Tradition and the Individual Talent' he seeks to bring that tradition directly into the artistic consciousness, describing a 'conscious present' that is 'an awareness of the past in a way and to an extent which the past's awareness of itself cannot show'. By becoming conscious of the tradition the individual writer is less in thrall to it: rather than being its inheritor he becomes instead its mediator and arbiter. This is immediately obvious in the care with which Eliot emphasizes that the central current of tradition 'does not at all flow invariably through the most distinguished reputations'.[110] As soon as this is allowed, if the

---

[106] 'American Poetry', *Athenaeum*, 4662 (5 Sept. 1919), 840–1 (p. 841). He is referring to Conrad Aiken.

[107] *Egoist*, 6/4 (Sept. 1919), 54–5, and 6/5 (Dec. 1919), 72–3.

[108] 'Some Notes on the Blank Verse of Christopher Marlowe', *Art & Letters*, 2/4 (Autumn 1919), 194–9 (p. 194).

[109] *After Strange Gods: A Primer of Modern Heresy* (London, 1934), 30.

[110] *Egoist*, 6/4: 55.

tradition is not a given but a site of contention and reinterpretation, then that tradition becomes the property of the practising artist.

The success of Eliot's argument here depends upon applying the connotative associations of the word 'tradition'—of time-honoured authority deriving from consensual values—to a more contentious denotation, in which tradition becomes simply the uses to which the past may be put by the present. In certain respects this is typical of Eliot's method in the essay in invoking an apparently authoritative standard only to redefine it according to the needs of a contemporary artistic practice. Thus, the impressive-sounding 'historical sense' which the artist must cultivate is not historical at all. It is, rather, a realization of the uses to which the work of the past can be put: 'a perception, not only of the pastness of the past, but of its presence'. Similarly, the 'ideal order' of the existing monuments of the tradition proves to be curiously mutable and unjudgemental. Like the 'mind of Europe' it is eclectic rather than evaluative, abandoning nothing as it develops, and simply getting larger and larger.

As a general statement of the desirability of incorporating a knowledge of the past into a contemporary practice Eliot's essay is irreproachable. It is exactly what a disenchanted post-war literary culture needed, in its ability apparently to reaffirm traditional values while simultaneously condemning the immediate (notably the Victorian and Edwardian) legacy of that tradition. But under the cover of that laudable attempt, Eliot introduced a number of tendentious elements that do not necessarily follow from its initial premiss. Traditionalism need not lead to the distinction that Eliot draws between literary individuality and personality, for example, nor to the separation he attempts between intellect and affect. In many ways the essay's emphasis on the tradition can be seen as little more than a self-serving contribution to the cause of Eliot's own poetry: the writer he envisages, escaping personality and with the whole of European literature 'in his bones', is himself;[111] and the tradition he describes is the one he has found most fruitful in developing his own work and within which he would like that work to be assimilated. As such, Eliot's scheme is too narrowly prescriptive to be, beyond its general encouragement to read dead authors, of much real use to other writers. Ezra Pound, for example, found Eliot's strictures on impersonality

---

[111] Virginia Woolf had written in praise of Eliot some months earlier that 'the poetry of the dead is in his bones'. 'Is This Poetry?', *Athenaeum*, 4651 (20 June 1919), 490.

and submission to the tradition too inhibiting. When Eliot attempted to construe Pound's poetry according to the ideas of 'Tradition and the Individual Talent', seeing it as developing a profound knowledge of the present through 'acquiring the entire past' and suggesting that Pound must hide behind his literary predecessors in order to reveal himself, Pound's reply was just and to the point: Eliot was allowing a '*universitaire* tendency' to creep into his work in regarding literature 'not as something in itself enjoyable, having tang, gusto, aroma; but rather as something which, possibly because of a nonconformist conscience, one *ought* to enjoy because it is literature (infamous doctrine)'.[112]

Eliot's essay, then, must not be seen simply as a disinterested attempt at restoring standards. The restoration of standards is indeed one of his aims, but the standards he wishes to restore are those best suited to the purposes of his poetry. The essay is a polemic, and is a better polemic for being disguised. The tradition he recommends is not a tradition of succession, but of selection, or even of imposition. It is the tradition that is implied in the title of his first collection of essays; a tradition which is not so much inherited as usurped by physical force: the priest of Nemi in Frazer's sacred wood, it will be remembered, occupies his position through having murdered his predecessor rather than through any right of succession.[113] It is fruitless to look to 'Tradition and the Individual Talent' for a definitive statement of Eliot's ideas on tradition because those ideas are still in the process of definition. The tradition he describes is little more than a redefinition of the 'maturity' he had written of earlier. But while the maturity described in his essay on Henry Adams depended upon a ripening of personality that is both 'sensual and intellectual', the maturity of 'Tradition and the Individual Talent' becomes a submission of the affective to the intellective, so that the mature poet is little more than 'a finely perfected medium' whose personality is at one remove from the work which he produces. Maturity is a term that too readily applies to personal qualities for Eliot's purposes. By hypostatizing the attributes of maturity into the substance of tradition, Eliot can mark the qualities he values with the

---

[112] T. S. Eliot, 'The Method of Mr Pound', *Athenaeum*, 4669 (24 Oct. 1919), 1065–6 (p. 1065); Ezra Pound, 'Mr Pound and his Poetry', *Athenaeum*, 4670 (31 Oct. 1919), 1132.

[113] This is pointed out by George Watson in *The Literary Critics: A Study of English Descriptive Criticism* (Harmondsworth, 1964), 187–8, and noted by Chris Baldick in *The Social Mission of English Criticism*, 112.

stamp of an impersonal authority; he can give the qualities he has formerly associated with literary maturity the semblance of an extra-
personal sanction. The tradition he outlines is at bottom a pragmatic
mechanism for holding in check any excesses of individualism that
the deterioration in standards occasioned by the war might throw up.
His essay is embedded in an intellectual culture disenchanted with
the values it has inherited, and in this context it is welcome as much
for its confident, authoritative tone as for anything it has to say about
the specific direction in which literature must proceed.

It might be expected that this insistence on placing writers in the
historical perspective of a tradition, insisting that their work
expresses a medium rather than a personality, would be antipathetic
to Murry. The writers he had previously singled out for special praise
(and for whom he maintained his esteem), Chekhov, Keats, and
Hardy, he prized precisely for their individuality, praising them for
their achievement of a concentrated, individual vision. In the case of
Hardy, Murry had noted 'the manifold and inexhaustible quality of
life . . . focused into a single revelation', a view which can been seen to
continue his post-war revelatory emphasis.[114] But towards the end of
1919, coincidental with Eliot's attempts to articulate a traditional
structure that curbs a merely personal utterance, Murry's work
begins to exhibit an acceptance of the unfeasibility of a literary
reconstruction based on this kind of revelation alone. This perception of the inadequacy of revelation by itself to effect an alteration in
literary practice had been signalled by J. W. N. Sullivan in a perceptive review of Murry's *Evolution of an Intellectual*. Sullivan had
pointed to Murry's failure to explain *why* the new realism fostered by
the Great War should necessarily be any more valid than the literature it replaces: 'we can agree that he has asserted a faith, but not that
he has discovered a truth. Mr Murry believes that what he has
brought is what he has found.'[115]

It can be seen, however, that Murry had already begun to modify
his earlier position in taking account of the arguments, like those of
Eliot, which were attempting to rejuvenate literature through the
rehabilitation of lapsed literary traditions. This can be seen in the
essay he wrote on the death of Auguste Renoir which, like the essay by
Clive Bell quoted earlier, attempts to incorporate modern artistic

[114] 'The Poetry of Mr Hardy', *Athenaeum*, 4671 (7 Nov. 1919), 1147–9.
[115] 'The Dreamer Awakes', *Athenaeum*, 4677 (19 Dec. 1919), 1365.

movements into the tradition of the great masters. Here Murry emphasized both the necessity and the difficulty of incorporating the tradition: 'you have to subdue your own pride, your own desire to be intensely and individually yourself; not till that is forgotten in the eager contemplation of something that is infinitely greater than yourself will you be capable of standing *dans le rang*'. This echoes Eliot with its insistence that 'the tradition is not a thing that can be learned like a manner', but instead requires 'an effort and a submission of self-consciousness to achieve'.[116] This is a long way from Murry's declaration of the previous year that 'without the perspective that comes from intellectual remoteness there can be no order and no art'.[117] Other examples of Murry's new-found interest in tradition can be seen at this time in his articles 'Critical Interest', with its description of tradition as 'a real element of self-submission that is repugnant to an extreme self-consciousness',[118] and 'The Condition of English Literature'. In the latter essay Murry blames the Georgian poets for 'the tinge of complacency in the indulgence of immediate sensation at the present day'. In a manner that is very reminiscent of Eliot, he admonishes the Georgians for the paucity of their literary education and their failure to discover 'that the true artistic individuality comes only after an arduous effort to discipline a merely personal otherness':

A great many of our young men of letters have become public men at a stage of their development when they should have been employing all their energies in the repair of their interrupted education. We doubt whether there has ever been a generation of men so startlingly uneducated as this, so little interested in the study of the great writers before them, so content to handle the English language as though it had been created *de novo* in the middle of the nineteenth century.[119]

What we can observe here, then, is a pronounced shift of emphasis in Murry's approach to literary reconstruction which requires the modification of his radical liberal views. The necessity for this can be seen in the 'continual disintegration of the consciousness' that he describes as 'the most marked characteristic of the present age': a disintegration that has found its way into literature. Tradition is one way by which this disintegrating consciousness may achieve reinte-

[116] 'Auguste Renoir', *Athenaeum*, 4676 (12 Dec. 1919), 1329–30.
[117] 'Mr Sassoon's War Verses', 398.
[118] 'Critical Interest', *Athenaeum*, 4686 (20 Feb. 1920), 233–4 (p. 233).
[119] 'The Condition of English Literature', *Athenaeum*, 4697 (7 May 1920), 597–8 (p. 598).

gration: 'there is, we believe, a genuine desire that a standard should be once more created and applied'.[120]

The sense of a 'disintegrating consciousness' described by Murry may be seen as an analogue and an anticipation of Eliot's theory of the 'dissociation of sensibility', which appeared in 'The Metaphysical Poets' in the *Times Literary Supplement* in October 1921. Subsequent commentators have compared Eliot's formulation with opinions as diverse as those of Matthew Arnold, F. H. Bradley, Remy de Gourmont, and even Horkheimer and Adorno.[121] Frank Kermode has explored the similar theories expounded by Hulme and Yeats; placing their common origin in a wider symbolist concern with the antagonism between image and discourse.[122] But this kind of argument can be expanded beyond symbolism to show that Eliot's theory is also a manifestation of reconstructive disillusion.

The dissociation of sensibility described by Eliot is a psychological rather than a specifically literary event: something that occurred in 'the mind of England' after Donne and Herbert and before Tennyson and Browning.[123] Eliot sites this dislocation specifically in the seventeenth century, predating but then being aggravated by Milton and Dryden. Kermode has remarked on the tendentiousness informing this choice of date and has pointed to similar partiality in Hulme's choice of the Renaissance and Yeats's selection of 1550 as their dates for the schism. For Kermode these various revisions enact a common search for 'some golden age when the prevalent mode of knowing was not positivistic and anti-imaginative'.[124]

This search for a golden age, for an integrated era that predated the present crisis, was not confined in the years after the war to those trawling in the wake of symbolism. Rather, it can be seen as a general

---

[120] 'Poetry and Criticism', *Athenaeum*, 4691 (26 Mar. 1920), 408–9 (p. 408).

[121] J. L. Morse, 'T. S. Eliot in 1921: Toward the Dissociation of Sensibility', *Western Humanities Review*, 30/1 (Winter 1976), 31–40; Eric Thompson, 'Dissociation of Sensibility', *EIC* 2/2 (Apr. 1952), 207–13; F. W. Bateson, 'Dissociation of Sensibility', *EIC* 1/3 (July 1951), 302–12; Jürgen Kramer, 'T. S. Eliot's Concept of Tradition: A Revaluation', *New German Critique*, 6 (Fall 1975), 20–30.

[122] *Romantic Image* (London, 1957; new edn. 1986), 138–61.

[123] 'The Metaphysical Poets', 669.

[124] *Romantic Image*, 143.

concern of a generation traumatized by the disjunctive effects of war. And it can be seen in a number of different forms. One notable example is Leavis's lost 'organic community' which, following the example of D. H. Lawrence's critique of industrialized society, predicates a mental and social equilibrium sited in rural England and destroyed by the Industrial Revolution.[125] Another, more fantastic, was the Atlantean undissociated sensibility posited by Lawrence in *Fantasia of the Unconscious*: a universal science of life predating the golden ages of Egypt and Greece, which was lost as the Atlantic civilizations dispersed in the neolithic and palaeolithic eras.[126] Nearer to home, Richard Aldington contrasted the perfect integration of the Provençal troubadours with the 'arithmetical, thin-lipped pedantry' of the followers of Malherbe, Boileau, and Bayle: laying the blame, as Irving Babbitt did, on the neoclassical movement for the breach in continuity.[127] Ezra Pound similarly praised the troubadour tradition which he saw culminating in Dante and Villon: although for Pound 'the great break in literary history, or in development of the art of literature, came with the fall of inflected language'.[128] For R. G. Collingwood the Middle Ages were a time in which art, religion, and philosophy had uniquely enjoyed a perfect integration: a belief that led him in 1924 to 'demand that the work of the Renaissance shall be undone, and that the middle ages should be brought back'.[129] This had been very much the emphasis of John Dover Wilson who, in a series of articles for Greenwood's *Athenaeum* in the first half of 1917, had apportioned blame to the Renaissance for dissociating the unified medieval qualities of Truth and Beauty.[130] Describing a more

---

[125] F. R. Leavis and Denys Thompson, *Culture and Environment: The Training of Critical Awareness* (London, 1933), 87–98. D. H. Lawrence, 'Nottingham and the Mining Countryside', in *Phoenix: The Posthumous Papers of D. H. Lawrence*, ed. Edward D. McDonald (London, 1936), 133–40.

[126] *Fantasia of the Unconscious* (1923), in *Fantasia of the Unconscious and Psychoanalysis and the Unconscious*, Phoenix edn. (London, 1961), 6–7. Lawrence updated this dissociation later, writing that 'with the Elizabethans the grand rupture had started in the human consciousness, the mental consciousness recoiling in violence away from the physical, instinctive-intuitive'. 'Introduction to these Paintings' (1929), *Phoenix*, 551–84 (p. 552).

[127] 'Pierre de Ronsard', in Richard Aldington, *Literary Studies and Reviews* (London, 1924), 11–31 (p. 23). Babbitt had posited an integration of reason and intuition in classical Greece, lost by the time of Pascal, in his *Rousseau and Romanticism* (Boston, Mass., 1919), 28–9.

[128] 'On Criticism in General', *Criterion*, 1/2 (Jan. 1923), 143–56 (p. 151).

[129] *Speculum Mentis: Or the Map of Knowledge* (Oxford, 1924), 36.

[130] See, 'Muezzin' [John Dover Wilson], 'Pessimism and Prophecy', *Athenaeum*, 4615 (Mar. 1917), 117–19 (p. 119).

modern dissociation, Aldous Huxley wrote of the scientism of the nineteenth century, embodied in Tennyson, having destroyed the emotional assimilation of abstract ideas displayed by Fulke Greville, Donne, and Blake.[131] Even Virginia Woolf had a pet dissociation theory, although with a historically more recent emphasis, expressed famously in her opinion that 'on or about December 1910 human character changed'.[132]

More pertinently for Eliot, Murry had expressed a similar concern, writing of 'the divided being of the present Dispensation' in *Fyodor Dostoevsky*, and of Keats's attempts to reassociate his poetry in 'the calm and various light of united contraries'.[133] In this second example, from 'The Problem of Keats', Murry does not suggest a particular date at which dissociation occurred. Instead, he points to the 'Miltonic manner' as the source of Keats's problems. This, of course, anticipates Eliot's own derogation of Milton's influence in 'The Metaphysical Poets'. Indeed, before Eliot's essay appeared Murry had developed his criticism of Milton further, writing, for example, that 'English blank verse has never recovered from Milton's drastic surgery; he abruptly snapped the true tradition, so that no one, not even Keats, much less Shelley or Swinburne or Browning, has ever been able to pick up the threads again'.[134] The Keats that Murry describes, whose 'decisions were taken not by the intellect, but by the being', is let down both by his Miltonic heritage and by his subsequent Victorian interpretation; and Murry links this reading explicitly to what he describes as a sense abroad 'that the tradition has somehow been snapped, that what has been accepted as the tradition unquestioningly for a hundred years is only a *cul de sac*'.[135]

In retrospect, this anxious concern with psychic integrity and cultural continuity, brought into sharp focus by the effects of war, can be interpreted as an aspect of the larger intellectual revolution

---

[131] 'Poetry and Science', *Athenaeum*, 4660 (22 Aug. 1919), 783.

[132] *Mr Bennett and Mrs Brown* (London, 1924), 4.

[133] *Fyodor Dostoevsky*, 253; 'The Problem of Keats', 648–9.

[134] 'Milton or Shakespeare?', *Nation and Athenaeum*, 28/26 (26 Mar. 1921), 915–17 (p. 916). The similarities between this opinion and that expressed later by Eliot in 'The Metaphysical Poets', which appeared in October 1921, and in 'Andrew Marvell', which was published the week after Murry's second essay, need no pointing up. Ironically, when Eliot came to revise his opinion of Milton, it was not to his own earlier work but rather to Murry's that he looked for 'a statement of the *generalized* belief in the unwholesomeness of Milton's influence'. 'Milton II', in Eliot's *On Poetry and Poets* (London, 1957), 146–61 (p. 149).

[135] 'The Problem of Keats', 648–9.

associated with Nietzsche and Freud. And at this local level Eliot's hypothetical dissociation of sensibility is manifestly typical of a number of evasive strategies in which a wider psychological anxiety is countered with a palliative historical narrative. Kermode has pointed to the ideological reasons why Eliot should want to site his dissociation in the seventeenth century; but there is a larger contemporary discourse, of which Eliot's criticism forms a part, that is eagerly trying to settle on *any* period of the past in which it can find a remedy for the prevailing 'disintegrating consciousness'.[136] As Edmund Blunden put it in 1921: 'it is a curious age that finds so many minds living a century or centuries ago. Research is in the air.'[137]

If questions of individual and national integrity are, as this suggests, perceived to have historical rather than immediately political or epistemological causes then historical research becomes the prime diagnostic and curative activity. Individual and national well-being now depend upon a process of historical revision: the individual must, as Eliot suggests in 'Tradition and the Individual Talent', seek integration in a reconstituted tradition while, analogously, national rejuvenation must become an act of historical recapitulation. This latter aspect is shown up in the various attempts to foster a cultural renaissance in the immediate post-war period. Frequently, as with E. B. Osborn's *The New Elizabethans*, this takes the form of an appeal to precedent, with contemporary actions being valorized in the terms of a triumphalist national history. This is immediately apparent in the confident prognostication made in the *Manchester Guardian* in late 1919 that 'it is already clear that the war is to be followed by a great intellectual renascence in England, comparable with that which arose out of the life-and-death struggle with Spain in the Elizabethan age and with that which sprang from the ferment of the French Revolution and the wars which followed it.'[138] This sense of a national identity wrought out of a revised national history was emphasized by the attempts to revive and create national cultural institutions in the years immediately after the war. William Archer

---

[136] This can be allied to a point made by Michael H. Levenson, that it was only around 1918/19 that Eliot himself began to exhibit a 'historical sense' in his criticism: that his concerns up to that time had encompassed only the 'narrow historical range' of contemporary literature. Levenson, *A Genealogy of Modernism: A Study of English Literary Doctrine 1908–1922* (Cambridge, 1984), 193.

[137] [Edmund Blunden], 'Literary Gossip', *Athenaeum*, 4732 (7 Jan. 1921), 19.

[138] Professor Ramsay Muir, quoted by Murry in 'The False Dawn', *Athenaeum*, 4680 (9 Jan. 1920), 37–8 (p. 38).

sought to revive interest in his plans for a National Theatre drawn up
some fifteen years before; in 1919 Cambridge University Press undertook a new edition of the works of the national poet with its New
Cambridge Shakespeare; a committee was drawn up in the same year
to create a National Opera House that would 'restore to English life
the heritage and beauty of music and of drama that once belonged to
it'.[139] The National Church, too, felt the need to redefine itself
through a revaluation of its working—a need emphasized both by
wartime experience and by the doctrinal challenge of a growing
Modernist movement. This trend was characterized in the first
volume of Bishop Charles Gore's *The Reconstruction of Belief*, with
its early chapters on 'The Breakdown of Tradition' and 'The Conditions of Hopeful Reconstruction', and by the appointment in 1922 of
a Commission on Doctrine in the Church of England.[140] This was
also the year in which the BBC began the regular radio broadcasts
that would play an increasingly important part in reinforcing the
sense of a homogeneous national culture. The publication of
the Newbolt Report in 1921 had a similar impact in the sphere of education, promoting a self-consciously 'national education' through
the medium of English literature.[141]

   To a large extent, then, discussions of culture and literature were
distinctly complected with the overt nationalism manifested in the
Coupon Election. The Edwardian attempts to forge an English literary tradition, to construe literature as a repository of the national
heritage, were re-emphasized in the post-war years.[142] Alongside the
national cultural institutions mentioned above, for example, there
appeared 'heritage groups' such as the Phoenix Society which
attempted to recover the dramatic literature that its founders, quoting Swinburne, considered 'the greatest glory of England'.[143] The

[139] Rutland Boughton and Roger Clark, 'An Appeal for a National Opera-House',
Athenaeum, 4661 (29 Aug. 1919), 824.
[140] Charles Gore, *Belief in God* (London, 1921). This appeared with two subsequent
volumes as *The Reconstruction of Belief* (London, 1926). See also the chapter 'Modernist
Reconstruction', in H. D. A. Major's *English Modernism: Its Origins, Methods, Aims*
(London, 1927), 97–124.
[141] *The Teaching of English in England*. See Baldick's 'Literary-Critical Consequences
of the War', in his *The Social Mission of English Criticism*, 86–108.
[142] See Peter Brooker and Peter Widdowson, 'A Literature for England', in Robert Colls
and Philip Dodd (eds.), *Englishness: Politics and Culture 1880–1920* (London, 1986),
116–63.
[143] W. S. Kennedy *et al.*, 'The Production of Old Plays', *Athenaeum*, 4666 (3 Oct. 1919),
982.

new organ of post-war Georgianism, the *London Mercury*, with its commitment to 'the teaching of English, the fostering of the arts, the preservation of ancient monuments', played a similar role in reasserting the traditional English values that had been threatened in wartime, noting with pleasure a contemporary tendency towards 'poetry of the English landscape and especially the English landscape as a historical thing'.[144] Richard Hannay, the fictional hero of John Buchan's *Thirty-Nine Steps* novels, summed up this retrospective mood well in his first post-war appearance, identifying the nation with its countryside and its literary history: 'I discovered for the first time what pleasure was to be got from old books. They recalled and amplified that vision I had seen from the Cotswold ridge, the revelation of the priceless heritage which is England.'[145] This concern with the centrality of literary history to the national mission was reiterated by Murry in his proclamation that 'the Englishman's most magnificent heritage is English literature'; a belief which had him declaring that 'for our part we can hardly conceive a more valuable work of reconstruction than the issue of a series of complete English texts'.[146]

This concern with the accessibility of the English 'heritage' generated much correspondence in the pages of the *Athenaeum* between July and October 1919, to which J. M. Dent and Eliot amongst others contributed. Dent was widely lauded for the still successful Everyman series, which, along with its old Edwardian rival The World's Classics, was believed to be keeping intact the lifeline to the great cultural triumphs of the past. However, these two series did not confine themselves purely to English literature, and it was Joseph Dent himself who gave the lie to those who would found a renaissance purely on patriotic instincts:

from our experience, we find it easier to sustain interest in classics like Plato, Aristotle, and even the French dramatists, than in our own choice Elizabethan literature, except, of course, in Shakespeare. Even literature which is more familiar to the times, like the work of the eighteenth-century novelists, such as Fielding, Goldsmith, Sterne, etc., hardly has enough buyers to enable us to keep the books in stock.[147]

---

[144] 'Editorial Notes', *London Mercury*, 1/1 (Nov. 1919), 2; 1/3 (Jan. 1920), 260.

[145] *Mr Standfast* (London, 1919), 43. Quoted in Stuart Sillars, *Art and Survival in First World War Britain* (New York, 1987), 134.

[146] 'Our Literary Heritage', *Athenaeum*, 4654 (11 July 1919), 581–2. Eliot had made a similar defence of the Everyman series two weeks earlier in 'The Education of Taste', 521.

[147] 'Our Literary Heritage', *Athenaeum*, 4660 (22 Aug. 1919), 791.

So, very much in the way post-war political nationalism was tempered by reconstructive, internationalist enthusiasm for a League of Nations, literary nationalism found itself challenged from a less parochial direction. The spirit of a supranational literary tradition took a number of forms. One was the return to the classics of ancient and European writers, aided by an upsurge in translations such as the Egoist Press's Poets Translation Series begun in 1915. Others included the work of bodies like the Vasari Society, re-established in 1920 after a wartime hiatus, which began reproducing classic European fine art in the post-war period. A continuing interest in French poetry and criticism was fostered by the *Times Literary Supplement*, the *Egoist*, and the *Athenaeum*. There even appeared an occasional 'Letter from France' in the *London Mercury*. And although academic English was itself attempting to usurp the status of the classics, classical studies were themselves fighting to assert their traditional pre-eminence. Oxford University's attempts to reform its entrance qualification, Responsions, and in particular to abandon the compulsory examination in Greek, early in 1920 met with widespread opposition.[148] J. T. Sheppard continued the *Athenaeum*'s support for classical education, writing of the need to infuse the teaching of modern science with the values of Greek literature: a literature providing models of 'the sort of lives we want our children not only to achieve, but to surpass'.[149] Classical Greece, it was frequently argued, set a range of precedents against which modern events might be gauged. Gilbert Murray, for example, compared the effects of the Great War and the Peloponnesian War in *Aristophanes and the War Party* (1919) and found a new relevance for the statement by Thucydides that 'the dream of a regenerated life for mankind has vanished out of the future, and he rebuilds it in his memory of the past'.[150] Greece also offered the sense of an origin, a solid centre from which the modern age could take its bearings afresh: its culture's particular advantage according to Murray is that it 'starts clean from nature, with almost no entanglements of elaborate creeds and

[148] See e.g. the frequent discussion of this throughout January and February 1920 in the correspondence columns of the *Athenaeum*.

[149] 'Homer and Modern Education', *Athenaeum*, 4663 (12 Sept. 1919), 874–5. This interest in the reconstructive importance of a classical education had been expressed before Murry's period of tenure. See e.g. S. E. Winbolt, 'The Reform of Classical Education', *Athenaeum*, 4625 (Jan. 1918), 25–7.

[150] Quoted in J. T. Sheppard, 'The Greek Anthology', *Athenaeum*, 4655 (18 July 1919), 619–20 (p. 619).

customs and traditions'.[151] It was this sense of a clean break, of a return to a replenishing source, that appealed to Richard Aldington, leading him to a similar return to the classical authors—'to dig into Tacitus'—in a bid at the retrenchment of standards.[152]

In a similar way non-European cultures held out the hope of re-integrating sensibility. One ramification of the pre-war interest in anthropology was the increasing respectability of orientalism: oriental religious philosophy continued to be the subject of the kind of serious academic study typified by Irving Babbitt. The pre-war interest in chinoiserie and all things oriental maintained a popular currency, bolstered by the translations of Arthur Waley, by the huge success of Count Keyserling's *The Travel Diary of a Philosopher*, translated into English in 1925, and by the continuing interest in the theosophical movements of Madam Blavatsky and Gurdjieff, to whom Katherine Mansfield and A. R. Orage, editor of the *New Age*, would be attracted. Primitivism, too, continued to fascinate artists and thinkers. The pre-war fauvism of Matisse, rather like the use of primitive masks by Picasso or the barbarism cultivated by Der Blaue Reiter, and Freud's explorations in *Totem and Taboo*, had been founded on a need to 'go back to the source'.[153] And in the post-war world Eliot's identification of the rhythm of modernity with the vegetation rites of Stravinsky's *Sacre du printemps* implied a continuation of this tendency. Acknowledging that 'the maxim, Return to the sources, is a good one', Eliot explicitly endorsed the study of primitive art and poetry as a means to 'revivify the contemporary activities', and showed triumphantly how this revivification, through the evocation of an experience 'deeper than civilization', might be achieved with *The Waste Land*.[154] The wider revisionary project, to recreate a current of viable ideas or literally to reorient contemporary artistic practice, then, can be seen to split into two separate and potentially antagonistic conceptions. On one side is the idea of a

[151] Gilbert Murray, 'The Value of Greece to the Future of the World', in R. W. Livingstone (ed.), *The Legacy of Greece* (Oxford, 1921), 1–23 (p. 16).

[152] *Life for Life's Sake*, 243.

[153] Jack D. Flam, *Matisse on Art* (Oxford, 1978), 74. Quoted in Christopher Butler, *Early Modernism: Literature, Music, and Painting in Europe, 1900–1916* (Oxford, 1994), 107.

[154] See Eliot's 'London Letter', *Dial*, 71/4 (Oct. 1921), 452–5; 'War-paint and Feathers', *Athenaeum*, 4668 (17 Oct. 1919), 1036; and 'Tarr', *Egoist* (Sept. 1918), 106. See also Robert Crawford, *The Savage and the City in the Works of T. S. Eliot* (Oxford, 1987), 61–102, and Gray, *T. S. Eliot's Intellectual and Poetic Development*, 108–42.

common culture defined nationally, or by language, and on the other an aesthetic or humanistic sensibility that transcends narrow national and historical boundaries. Both notions hold out a sense of community within which a fragmented subjectivity might be reintegrated: each offers a reassuring sense of tradition. There is a difficulty, however, in that these two constructions of tradition are at bottom non-complementary. In the culture of the immediate postwar period problems continually crop up when they are conflated in ways that fail to differentiate between their incommensurable values.

An example of the confusion that results from this conflation of traditions can been seen in Quiller-Couch's two essays on patriotism in English literature originally delivered as lectures in the last year of the war. Quiller-Couch employs a national, linguistic idea of tradition in criticizing German culture's innate inability fully to appreciate English literature, turning its vitality into 'a dead science—a *hortus siccus*'. But in praising the contrasting vitality of English literature, he hails it as the legitimate heir of the classical tradition: so that the patriotism of English writers is a later manifestation of that ideal patriotism set down by Horace.[155] Walter Raleigh, too, used this wider patriotic sense as a stick with which to beat the Germans, when he described the particular character of English patriotism: 'We are patriotic, but our patriotism is often overlaid and infused by a wider thought and a wider sympathy than the Germans have ever known.'[156]

This paradoxical invocation of what amounts to a transcendental, classically based patriotism had also been made on several occasions by Murry. Once, in his description of Edith Cavell as 'that most exquisite product of a true civilisation, the patriot who has passed beyond patriotism', and again, in an essay 'Democracy and Patriotism', where he admits the destructive capacity of an ill-conceived patriotism, but insists on the possibility of an ideal patriotism, capable of being universalized for the general good: 'a lasting patriotism', wrote Murry, 'depends upon the attachment of a moral and ideal significance to the conception of country. If this condition is satisfied, patriotism becomes a completely sufficient motive for mankind.'[157]

---

[155] 'Patriotism in Literature II', in *Studies in Literature*, 307–22 (p. 314); 'Patriotism in Literature I', ibid. 290–306 (pp. 300–2).

[156] *The War and the Press* (Oxford, 1918), 7.

[157] 'Democracy and Patriotism', *Nation*, 24/17 (25 Jan. 1919), 483–4 (p. 484). A notion of patriotism as the 'true internationalism' was also put forward by Murry in 'Internationalism and the International', *Nation*, 24/18 (1 Feb. 1919), 512–13. See also his description of the patriotism of Charles Péguy in 'Péguy and Romain Rolland', *TLS* 879

Implicit in Murry's opinion is the idea, perhaps encouraged by the propagandist literature of the war, that true love for one's country (especially if that country happens to be England) is a straightforward localization of universal love. This clearly runs counter to the lesson on imperialism supposedly taught by the war—the sense in which Germany was seen to be punished for its propagation of a rampant pan-German nationalism—and certainly counter to Murry's avowed intention of making the war the touchstone of his experience.[158] For in making such statements Murry perpetuates a prevalent myth of nineteenth century nationalism: that a modern political state might be interfused with the idealized classical attributes of the patria. Such an idealized nationalism offered Quiller-Couch and Raleigh, among others, a convenient myth according to whose lights a distinct English literary tradition might become established as a central subject for university education. But the way in which English literature became construed as a modern equivalent to the classics only served to confuse its sense of purpose. The Newbolt Report, for example, in a decided echo of Arnold, defined literature as 'an embodiment of the best thoughts of the best minds, the most direct and lasting communication of experience by man to men', but at the same time advocated the study of only one national literature.[159] This paradoxically Hellenized conception of an English national literature was not accepted by all university teachers of English. I. A. Richards, most notably, attempted to put the subject on a scientific footing with his psychological studies of the processes of literary creation in *The Principles of Literary Criticism* (1924) and literary consumption in *Practical Criticism* (1929). But with the provocative and frequently chauvinistic revaluations of Leavis, university English became associated with a particularly insular notion of a literary tradition, which was independent of alien influence, but whose appeal was to the idealized and extra-cultural values of 'life', 'maturity', etc.

These arguments undoubtedly provided a context in which Eliot might advance his own particular conception of tradition. That he was not altogether able to free himself from some of their confusions,

(21 Nov. 1918), 566: 'It was like the Russian patriotism of a Dostoevsky, large and international in scope, drawing its passionate strength from a mystic conviction of his country's spiritual mission in the vast republic of mankind.'

[158] Although Murry was still putting this argument forward as late as 1926. See his 'Patriotism *is* Enough', *Adelphi*, 4/5 (Nov. 1926), 271–8.

[159] *The Teaching of English in England*, 253, cited by Baldick in *The Social Mission of English Criticism*, 96.

however, can be seen in a certain self-contradiction in these attempts. In 'A Foreign Mind' he uses the notion of a national literature to criticize what he sees as the fey crudity of the Irish literary tradition dragging at the heels of Yeats and ultimately tainting his poetry.[160] However, five weeks later he is denying the same individuation to Scottish literature; arguing that it is the continuity of a language that creates a national literary tradition, and as Scotland does not have the continuity of an independent language (he ignores Gaelic) it cannot claim a literary independence from England.[161] This is, however, to conflate a tradition of literature written in English and an English national literary tradition: one having a common language, the other a shared cultural identity. The result of that conflation is that Eliot relegates Scottish literature to the status of a provincial literature—which, if the argument were taken to its logical conclusion, would be the status he would accord Irish, American, and Commonwealth literatures written in English.

In the course of this essay Eliot writes of the national literature as the supposition of 'a mind which is not only the English mind of one period with its prejudices of politics and fashions of taste, but which is a greater, finer, more positive, more comprehensive mind than the mind of any period'; a declaration sounding not unlike that of Murry or Quiller-Couch in positing a transcendent mind that none the less exhibits a set of peculiarly national characteristics. Like Quiller-Couch and Murry, Eliot assumes a fairly crude racial stereotype—the idea of a national character—and attempts to make of it a quality that nears the ideal. This might be just about defensible while it applies to a literary tradition working within a homogeneous, monolingual culture, but in 'Tradition and the Individual Talent' Eliot goes one stage further, positing a 'mind of Europe' which incorporates the national mind of English literature in its trans-historical and transcultural mental equilibrium.[162]

It is possible to discern in both of these positions, the national and the international, responses to the sense of a cultural and psychic crisis of which the war stands as a symbol. Both are manifestly reintegrative strategies aimed at the various narratives of disruption of which Eliot's 'dissociation of sensibility' is one. Eliot and Murry,

---

[160] 'A Foreign Mind', *Athenaeum*, 4653 (4 July 1919), 552–3.
[161] 'Was There a Scottish Literature?', *Athenaeum*, 4657 (1 Aug. 1919), 680–1.
[162] 'Tradition and the Individual Talent', *Egoist*, 6/4: 55.

then, are far from being unusual among their contemporaries in their attempts to forge traditions within which post-war alienation might be comprehended and ameliorated. Indeed, it is possible to see in these two largely undifferentiated notions of tradition the foundation of the notions of romanticism and classicism that would later give Murry and Eliot the conceptual structures in which to frame their opposition. Murry would only require to substitute truth to one's own experience for truth to one's country to achieve his romanticism, while Eliot would replace the European mind with the Catholic, Latin mind in his classicism. But while the seeds of this opposition might be said to have been sown in the disruptive aftermath of wartime, it would be several years before their distinctive germination. Virginia Woolf wrote in 1919 that Murry and Eliot 'have nothing in common save the sincerity of their passion'.[163] While that passion continued to be directed at the immediate problems of art, and while their understanding of tradition remained problematic, their potential antagonism was subsumed within a common concern for the maintenance of 'standards'.

THE PERFECT CRITIC

It is possible to see in the early phase of Murry's and Eliot's collaboration at the *Athenaeum*, in the confused and leaderless post-war atmosphere of reconstructive disillusion, the early outlines of the arguments that would later cause the fissure in their relations as critics. But at this stage the exploitation of shared concerns was more pressing than an examination of mutual differences, and to this extent their common attempts to reorient criticism within a structure supportive to the creative individual led them to a shared commitment. Within this commitment, however, were also shared self-contradictions, most of which hinged on the relations between the creative individual and a formative tradition. Murry's emphasis on the centrality of personal revelation, although still largely unformulated, sits uneasily with any conception of a shaping tradition. But, equally, Eliot's criticism can be seen to be encountering analogous difficulties, along the lines of what he would later describe as 'the old *aporia* of Authority *v.* Individual Judgement'.[164] Having effectively

---

[163] 'Is This Poetry?', 491.
[164] 'The Frontiers of Criticism', in *On Poetry and Poets*, 103–18 (p. 103).

managed to translate judgements of literary maturity into ones of traditionality he was still having difficulty, as evinced by 'Tradition and the Individual Talent', in defining where individual qualities of creative authorship end and the objective standards of an authorizing tradition begin.

To show the difficulties Eliot was still having in 1920 with these problems of definition it is worth considering his essay 'The Perfect Critic', in which a new conception of critical intelligence can be seen to emerge. This notably hinges around a particularly Aristotelian construction of an intelligence according to whose workings the literary object is perceived and articulated into a generalized critical statement. This construction of Aristotelianism, I will suggest, should be read not so much as an integral part of Eliot's critical theory as yet one more temporary resting-place in his search for an impersonal evaluative standard for literature, and that far from being refined through a direct contact with classical thought it is subject to the mediation of Aristotelian (and Gourmontian) thought in a contemporary critical debate. What it shows, among other things, is that rather than being the product of a monolithic critical programme his critical writing is in fact a reflexive and fluid praxis which does not deny to itself the evolutionary virtues of contingency, mutability, and innovation. One advocate of a monolithic reading of Eliot's theory has suggested that Eliot's criticism is an occult transcription of Bradleyan philosophy.[165] This is an argument neatly defused by Eliot himself when he wrote that 'the unity of Bradley's thought is not the unity attained by a man who never changes his mind', and it is with this spirit of reflexivity in mind that the essay should be approached, allowing us to see the way Eliot's critical vocabulary and literary judgements owe at least as much to the demands of a specific argument as to derivation from a general theory.[166]

The argument out of which the essay springs had its beginning in the summer of 1919, with the publication of Irving Babbitt's *Rousseau and Romanticism*. In that book Babbitt had raised the spectre of troubled times to call for a return to Aristotle, from whom the modern spirit might learn 'how to have standards and at the same time not be immured in dogma'.[167] Babbitt's is a book of temperate

---

[165] Lewis Freed, *T. S. Eliot: The Critic as Philosopher* (West Lafayette, Ind., 1979), p. xvii.
[166] 'Francis Herbert Bradley', in *Selected Essays* (London, 1951), 444–55 (p. 453).
[167] *Rousseau and Romanticism*, p. xxii.

classicism, promoting an almost oriental Aristotelianism in preference to the ratiocinative, Christianized Aristotle of neoclassicism or
its distorted mirror image in the vitiating naturalism of Rousseau.
Surprisingly, in view of this emphasis Murry, who had written in
praise of Rousseau in the March issue of the *Athenaeum*, enthusias-
tically endorsed Babbitt's calls for a return to an Aristotelian
standard. Murry's review argued that contemporary trends in appreciative criticism and technical criticism masked a profound aesthetic
nihilism and were the tokens of a moral nihilism that only the re-
imposition of a critical standard could overcome. And he followed
Babbitt in suggesting Aristotle as a model for this 'true law of decorum', writing that 'it is certain that in Aristotle the present generation would find the beginnings of a remedy for that fatal confusion
of categories which has overcome the world'.[168]

Eliot had, of course, been taught by Babbitt at Harvard and still
maintained a correspondence with him. And he was acquainted with
the writings of Aristotle, having studied the *Posterior Analytics* at
Oxford with Harold Joachim. But he had barely written on Aristotle
since, so it is perhaps more than a coincidence that Aristotle crops up
in an essay, 'A Brief Treatise on the Criticism of Poetry', which
appeared only three weeks after Murry's review. In that work Eliot
echoes Murry in denigrating the tendentious criticism that stresses
'appreciative', philosophical, or historical ends, and suggests as a
counterbalance the 'purer' criticism of Aristotle, Boileau, Campion,
and Dryden.[169] But, while Eliot appears to agree with Babbitt and
Murry that Aristotle is valuable, he disagrees as to where that value
lies. For Babbitt and for Murry, the worth of Aristotle's work
depends on its ethical content: Babbitt had written of the 'moral
law' and Murry the 'practical ideal of human life' that informed
Aristotle's aesthetic. But, according to Eliot, Aristotle's worth can be
ascribed less to his humanism than to a practical, almost technical,
quality that Eliot describes as 'poetic criticism'.

The germ of this idea can be seen in Eliot's rejection of biographical, historical, and philosophical approaches to literature in favour of
the technical criticism, or 'workman's notes', sketched in the second
of his 'Studies in Contemporary Criticism' for the *Egoist* in 1918
and, slightly later, in an *Athenaeum* article in which he had opined

---

[168] 'The Cry in the Wilderness', 268.
[169] 'A Brief Treatise on the Criticism of Poetry', *Chapbook*, 2/9 (Mar. 1920), 1–10.

that 'the only valuable criticism is that of the workman'.[170] According to this view the 'purity' of Aristotle's criticism lies in its being geared specifically to the production of poetry: 'the poetic critic is criticizing poetry in order to create poetry'. Eliot eschews idealist and humanist claims on poetry and criticism, referring to poetry's aesthetic function only as 'a means of communicating those direct feelings peculiar to art, which range from amusement to ecstasy'.[171]

Eliot's continued emphasis on the ancillary nature of criticism is understandable from one so obviously concerned with the immediate problems of his own poetic practice. But in stating that the only useful criticism is that carried out by the artist preparatory to his own work, Eliot gets into difficulties with his espousal of Aristotle—a philosopher, critic, and scientist—as the model of 'poetic criticism'. Eliot does not address this difficulty directly. Instead, he advances Dryden, as a model of Aristotelian principles in action, alongside Aristotle in the canon of great poetic critics.

Eliot's difficulties were immediately recognized by Murry, who responded to his essay with a leading article in the *Times Literary Supplement*, 'The Function of Criticism'. Murry returns to his former argument, rejecting Eliot's attempts to draw an absolute division between technique and moral content. Aristotelian criticism is more than merely a poetic or philosophic criticism, Murry argues, because of its implicit ideal of the good life, arrived at through a humanist philosophy. This ideal of the good life, avers Murry, 'if it is to have the internal coherence and the organic force of a true ideal, *must inevitably be aesthetic*'. Therefore, the literary value of Aristotle's criticism comes directly from 'a harmony of the diverse elements of his soul', manifested in 'the standards by which life and art are judged the same'.[172]

Art, argues Murry, 'is the revelation of the ideal in human life', becoming in a sense the consciousness of life. Criticism, likewise, is 'an organic part of the whole activity of art'. Partaking of the same faculty that creates art in the divination of the ideal in life, criticism

---

[170] 'Studies in Contemporary Criticism II', *Egoist*, 5/10 (Nov.–Dec. 1918), 131–3 (p. 132). 'The Local Flavour', *Athenaeum*, 4676 (12 Dec. 1919), 1333: the part quoted here, along with the last five lines of the essay, does not appear in the essay as it is printed in *The Sacred Wood*, an omission that has important consequences for the conclusion of 'The Perfect Critic'.

[171] 'A Brief Treatise', 3–4.

[172] 'The Function of Criticism', *TLS* 956 (13 May 1920), 289–90.

divines the ideal in art: 'as art is the consciousness of life, criticism is the consciousness of art. The essential activity of true criticism is the harmonious control of art by art'. This, Murry argues, is what Eliot should have said when he talked of poets being the only true critics: that 'what distinguishes the true critic of poetry is a truly aesthetic philosophy. In the present state of society it is extremely probable that only the poet or the artist will possess this.'[173] Drawing heavily on Babbitt, then, Murry argues that poetry and criticism are both functions of a larger aesthetic, wedded to an ideal of human action. Where Eliot has ascribed the poet's gift of criticism specifically to his poetic sensibility, Murry ascribes both the poetic and the critical gifts to a larger aesthetic sensibility. Criticism does not 'serve' poetry, rather it is a complementary faculty more likely to be found coexisting with the poetic faculty in a well-developed sensibility.

The impact of this argument is immediately apparent in 'The Perfect Critic' which appeared in the *Athenaeum* two months after Murry's essay, and some four months after Eliot's initial essay. In 'The Perfect Critic' Eliot admits to having changed his view, describing as fatuous the notion 'that criticism is for the sake of "creation" or creation for the sake of criticism'. In place of this he puts forward a formula that sounds very like the one expressed by Murry. 'The two directions of sensibility are complementary', Eliot now writes, 'and as sensibility is rare, unpopular, and desirable, it is to be expected that the critic and the creative artist should frequently be the same person.'[174] With this rejection of the pre-eminence of poetic criticism, Eliot's espousal of Aristotle as a model becomes less theoretically fraught. Aristotle's criticism becomes valuable more for its general sensibility than its contribution to purely poetic ends: its principal quality is the 'universal intelligence' that Aristotle brings to bear.

This new emphasis also leads Eliot to another important revision, in a revaluation of the neoclassical criticism he had praised in his earlier essay. Babbitt and Murry (for whom Eliot had elevated Dryden to a 'purple which he is quite unfitted to wear') had both taken exception to neoclassical distortions of Aristotelian imitation: Babbitt deplored the creation of a secondary imitation which 'does not rest on immediate perception like that of the Greeks but on outer authority', and Murry had similarly described neoclassicism's 'dead

---

[173] 'The Function of Criticism', 290.
[174] 'The Perfect Critic II', *Athenaeum*, 4708 (23 July 1920), 102–4 (p. 104).

mechanical framework of rules about the unities'.[175] Eliot, who two months earlier had written of Boileau's, Dryden's, and Campion's inestimable value to poets, and who had judged Dryden 'a poetic critic of the first rank', now writes of Boileau's precepts as 'merely an unfinished analysis', of Campion as 'a critic in only a narrow sense', and of Dryden's 'tendency to legislate rather than to inquire' where the truly free intelligence of a better critic would be 'wholly devoted to inquiry'.[176]

In two important senses, then, Eliot can be seen to adjust his opinions in the light of Murry's criticism. Indeed, it is perhaps interesting to note how close the whole tenor of 'The Perfect Critic' is to an essay, 'Shakespeare Criticism', written by Murry only two months before. In 'The Perfect Critic' Eliot proceeds from a criticism of the notion that 'poetry is the most highly organized form of intellectual activity'. He dismisses the criticism that attempts to verbalize its impressions of poetry in an 'emotional systematization' that ends only in constructing laws that have little to do with poetry, or in creating something else that is not criticism. Instead, he suggests that criticism's function is solely elucidatory. This elucidation comes directly as a result of an Aristotelian perception in which lies all knowledge and feeling. The clearest elucidation, and hence the best criticism, comes from the most disinterested perception: that which sees 'the object as it really is'. This perception grows into a structure from which the critic can generalize: 'the true generalization is not something superposed upon an accumulation of perceptions; the perceptions do not, in a really appreciative mind, accumulate as a mass, but form themselves as a structure; and criticism is the statement in language of this structure; it is a development of sensibility'.[177] So not only has Eliot altered his evaluation of Boileau, Campion, and Dryden in the four months between 'A Brief Treatise' and 'The Perfect Critic', he has also moved from suggesting that 'the only valuable criticism is that of the workman' to the contention that criticism 'is a development of sensibility'.

Murry's 'Shakespeare Criticism' had similarly been written in reaction to an attempt to apply too rigid a rationality to works of art. In this case it was to Masefield's description of Shakespeare's

---

[175] *Rousseau and Romanticism*, 19. Murry, 'The Function of Criticism', 289.
[176] 'The Perfect Critic II', 103.
[177] Ibid. 104.

King John as 'an intellectual form' which deploys its characters in an illustration of the 'idea' of treachery. Murry regards this as 'an insidious disintegration' of the critical method which can only be remedied by 'keeping our eye upon the object'. He then advances his own prescription for a rigorous criticism whose proper activity is 'the process of the aesthetic ordonnance of impressions':

Poets do not have 'ideas'; they have perceptions. They do not have an 'idea'; they have comprehension. Their creation is aesthetic, and the working of their mind proceeds from the realization of one aesthetic perception to that of another, more comprehensive if they are to be great poets having within them the principle of poetic growth. There is undoubtedly an organic process in the evolution of a great poet, which you may, for convenience of expression, call logical; but if you forget that the use of the word 'logic', in this context, is metaphorical, you are doomed. You can follow out this 'logical process' in a poet only by a kindred creative process of aesthetic perception passing into aesthetic comprehension. The hunt for 'ideas' will only make that process impossible; it prevents the object from ever making its own impression upon the mind. It has to speak with the language of logic, whereas its use and function in the world is to speak with a language not of logic, but of a process of mind which is at least as sovereign in its own right as the discursive reason.[178]

Though these two essays share a number of similarities there is a real difficulty in apportioning direct influence to either writer. For not only are they working in a milieu which encourages the kind of critical dialogue we have seen, they are also subject to the wider influences of the literary culture of their time. They may well be influencing each other directly, but they may equally be deriving their ideas from a common source. There is a range of sources which can be suggested, from the culture of reconstruction and disillusionment through to the more direct literary influence of Babbitt discussed above, and to the work of the French critic Remy de Gourmont. Bernard Bergonzi, for one, has suggested that Eliot's essay represents an illustration of Gourmont's 'ériger en lois' which Eliot had quoted as an epigraph, and Edward J. H. Greene has made a similar observation, reading the passage in question as Eliot's 'correcting and

---

[178] 'Shakespeare Criticism', *Athenaeum*, 4696 (30 Apr. 1920), 568–9 (p. 569). This also anticipates Eliot's statement that 'There is a logic of the imagination as well as a logic of concepts' in the preface to his translation of *Anabasis: A Poem by St-John Perse* (1930; rev. edn. London, 1959), 10. Interestingly, Murry's essay has its own echoes of Eliot's earlier *Chapbook* article in, for example, its description of Coleridge's work as 'a poet's criticism of poetry'.

deepening' Gourmont's formulation in *Le Chemin de velours* that 'aesthetic or moral judgements are only generalized sensations'.[179] In this case there is a further point to be argued: that Eliot, like Murry, is subject to the influence not only of Gourmont, but of a wider Gourmontism common to a number of his contemporaries. Eliot never hid the fact that Gourmont had, to some extent, come to him already mediated through the enthusiasm of Ezra Pound: indeed, his notion of Gourmont's 'intelligence' can be traced directly back to Pound's various accounts of Gourmontian criticism. The similarity between his and Murry's essays shows how much both are part of a contemporary debate taking place, so to speak, on a Gourmontian agenda. This influence will be discussed in the next chapter.

The example of 'The Perfect Critic' has been explored at length not to show that Eliot is directly borrowing from Murry or simply to assert with R. P. Blackmur that 'his second thoughts are often better than his first', but rather as an illustration of the convergence of their opinions at this time and the rootedness of those opinions in a contemporary literary culture.[180] While Murry does not renounce his particular brand of subjectivism, nor Eliot the search for an external poetic authority, it is possible to see a remarkable confluence in their criticism. We can also see a marked fluidity in Eliot's criticism at this time. Far from being the articulation of a more or less fixed philosophical position, as has been suggested by some critics, it is a changeable, at times inconsistent, record of a theory still in the process of definition. In fact, Eliot was unhappy with the essay almost from the outset and was sensitive to hostile criticism of it in the letters pages of the *Athenaeum*.[181] This culminated in a letter to Murry in April 1921, in which he wrote of his decision not to reprint 'The Perfect Critic'.[182] The continuing flexibility of his critical position also goes some way to explaining his almost total neglect of Aristotle subsequently, and the disclaimer he placed in the preface to the 1928 edition of *The Sacred Wood*: 'those were years in which we were struggling to revive old communications and to create new

---

[179] Bergonzi, *T. S. Eliot*, 2nd edn. (London, 1978), 59; Greene, *T. S. Eliot et la France* (Paris, 1951), 151.

[180] R. P. Blackmur, 'In the Hope of Straightening Things Out', in Hugh Kenner (ed.), *T. S. Eliot: A Collection of Critical Essays* (Englewood Cliffs, NJ, 1962), 137.

[181] See the correspondence, 'The Perfect Critic', *Athenaeum*, 4709–10 (30 July–8 Aug. 1920).

[182] 22 Apr. 1921, *Letters*, 447.

ones; and I believe that both Mr Murry and myself are a little more certain of our directions than we were then.'[183]

In fact, 'The Perfect Critic' was the last essay Eliot would write for the *Athenaeum*. While it represents the closest convergence of the critical opinions of the two men, it also marks the point at which they diverge towards their antipodes: the romantic and the classical.

[183]   *The Sacred Wood*, p. viii.

2

The *Criterion* versus the *Adelphi*, 1922–1925

IT was suggested earlier that Eliot's writings at the time of his first contributions to the *Athenaeum* were marked by a number of deep ambiguities concerning the place of personality in creative and critical activity. While his criticism could be seen to be striving to articulate a theory of impersonal literary creation it appeared constantly to be rubbing up against a set of assumptions and a conceptual vocabulary to which it seemed antipathetic, so that, for example, in 'Tradition and the Individual Talent' the poet who is able to synthesize a persona from the materials of the tradition is none the less marked out as recognizably 'mature'. In making these attempts Eliot was intervening in an ongoing debate about the nature of literary style that had roots deep in the nineteenth century. His difficulties in lighting on a critical vocabulary that could convincingly articulate such a theory of impersonality can be seen to derive from the turn that that debate had taken during the previous forty or so years and from its continuing inconclusiveness. For a writer like Eliot English critical writing on style had little to offer, and for a certain time he clearly believed that continental writers—in particular the French poet and critic Remy de Gourmont—marked a way out of a debilitating Anglocentric critical impressionism. It will be seen that Eliot was mistaken in this belief, and that his attribution to Gourmont of a particular form of literary-critical 'intelligence' required him to read that writer increasingly against the grain. What will also be seen is that the dual emphases Eliot's critical writing placed on tradition and impersonality would, in the early 1920s, lead him from Gourmont to a putative classicism which would in its turn, in the later

1920s, become a more rigorously enforced scholasticism. In this movement from Gourmont to Aquinas Murry would have an important part to play, if only because he increasingly became the exemplar of values that Eliot sought to reject: both writers claimed a Gourmontian influence but Murry exhibited what Eliot gradually realized were, for him, the unacceptable aspects of Gourmontism; later, Murry's pressured acceptance of the 'romantic' label would be instrumental in Eliot's declaring on the side of 'classicism'; and later still, it would be Murry—by then in league with the forces of theological Modernism—who would first publicly suggest to Eliot the logical consistency of a religious conversion.

REMY DE GOURMONT AND THE PROBLEM OF STYLE

At the beginning of the 1920s, however, it seemed that both men found in Gourmont's criticism the promise of a way out of a debilitating literary disenchantment. Since around 1913 Gourmont had enjoyed a reputation among the literary avant-garde in England comparable to that achieved by Bergson in the early years of the century. In particular, he had exerted a crucial influence on the Imagists: his emphasis on the poetic revivification of language by, to use his word, 'dissociating' ideas from the vitiating accretions of habit and cliché had underpinned that movement's anti-discursiveness and its search for clarifying visual analogues.[1] Ezra Pound, Richard Aldington, T. E. Hulme, and Amy Lowell all paid homage to him: according to Richard Aldington, 'he was a kind of pattern to us'.[2]

---

[1] See 'La Dissociation des idées' (1899), in his *La Culture des idées*, 15th edn. (Paris, 1916), 69–108.

[2] 'Remy de Gourmont, after the Interim', *The Little Review*, 5/10–11 (Feb.–Mar. 1919), 32–4 (p. 32). For a detailed discussion of Aldington's particular debt to Gourmont see D. Mossop, 'Un disciple de Gourmont: Richard Aldington', *Revue de littérature comparée*, 25/4 (Oct.–Dec. 1951), 403–35. Aldington's essay on Gourmont in *Literary Studies and Reviews*, 164–70, and in his autobiography, *Life for Life's Sake*, 172–5, have further discussions of Gourmont's influence, as does René Taupin's essay 'The Example of Remy de Gourmont', *Criterion*, 10/41 (July 1931), 614–25. Pound also discussed Gourmont in *Fortnightly Review* in 1915 and *Poetry* in 1916, collected as 'Remy de Gourmont' in his *Selected Prose, 1909–1965*, ed. William Cookson (London, 1973), 383–93, and in 'Remy de Gourmont', *Literary Essays of Ezra Pound*, ed. T. S. Eliot (London, 1954), 339–58. See also Amy Lowell's two introductions to *Some Imagist Poets* (Boston, Mass., 1915 and 1916), pp. v–vii, and v–xii respectively, her essay on Gourmont in *Six French Poets* (New York, 1916), and the Remy de Gourmont number of the *Little Review*, 5/10–11 (Feb.–Mar. 1919).

The most visible sign of Gourmont's influence on Eliot and Murry was their common use of one of his phrases as a kind of critical totem: 'to build his personal impressions into laws is the great effort of a man if he is sincere'.[3] This aphorism, actually thrown off casually in a series of public love letters to the American poet Natalie Clifford Barney in the *Mercure de France*, was adopted independently by Eliot and Murry as a general statement of a necessary critical principle, according to which individual judgements might be tempered with a generalizing authoritative sensibility. Eliot used the quotation as an epigraph to 'The Perfect Critic' and Murry would cite it as the measure of his 'critical credo' and discuss it in *The Problem of Style* (1922).[4] But the facility with which Eliot and Murry appeared to assimilate the phrase belied its ambiguity. For, viewed in context, it conveyed not so much a resolution of Gourmont's ideas as its central, and crucially unresolved, problematic.[5]

The phrase had arisen in a discussion of romantic literature (one that, incidentally, anticipates Umberto Eco's famous meditation on the difficulties of expressing love in the age of Barbara Cartland).[6] Gourmont's contention was that far from enhancing the experience of being in love and expressing that love, literature instead vitiates it, degrading an emotional complexity into a series of well-worn formulas through which 'we repeat a mass of ancient or scholastic aphorisms which have no other merit than the oratorical antithesis they contain'.[7] Gourmont's response to this vitiation of experience by literature (somewhat different from that of Eco) is to advocate an empirical 'ingenuousness' that has 'forgotten all literature' as the prerequisite of a truly critical approach to experience. What follows from this is that any attempt to generalize and objectify experience

[3] 'Ériger en lois ses impressions personnelles, c'est le grand effort d'un homme s'il est sincère.' 'Les Deux Sexes', in Gourmont's *Lettres à l'Amazone* (1914; 21st edn. Paris, 1924), 28–36 (p. 32).
[4] 'A Critical Credo', *New Republic* (New York), 28 (26 Oct. 1921), 251–2.
[5] Murry, who had initally been sceptical of Gourmont's liberalism, had been quick to notice this paradox. In 1918 he had written of Gourmont's use of this phrase, that 'no one could have been more scrupulous to insist that each of his personal impressions had nothing in common with a universal law'. 'Remy de Gourmont', *TLS* 841 (28 Feb. 1918), 103.
[6] See Umberto Eco, *Reflections on* The Name of the Rose, trans. William Weaver (London, 1985), 67. Eco prescribes a quite different solution to the Gourmontian problem by suggesting that in a postmodern age romantic sincerity can be achieved only through ironic knowingness.
[7] 'Nous nous repassons, sur l'amour, un tas d'aphorismes antiques ou scolastiques qui n'ont d'autre mérite que l'antithèse oratoire qu'ils contiennent'. *Lettres à l'Amazone*, 33.

into personal 'laws' must be driven not by the canons of literature but by those of individual experience. Such 'laws' must be a systemization of feeling and not learning. In this view, which privileges humanism over formalism, art is neither—as Eliot would later argue—autotelic nor a superior amusement; its end is the mutual improvement of the artist and reader as sentient individuals. From Gourmont's point of view, then, if literature is the record of a number of deeply felt experiences rendered imperfectly in language, then it may only be evaluated empirically and not analytically: it must not be 'read' so much as experienced intuitively through the traces of its imperfect expression. Such interpretation, notwithstanding the codification of personal 'laws', can never pretend to be anything other than subjective.[8]

This goes some way to explaining a paradox implicit in Gourmont's work, and made explicit by Murry, that the writer is not so much working with language as going against its grain—that a work of literature is a victory, as Murry puts it, over the intractability of the everyday words with which the artist must deal: 'Every work of enduring literature is not so much a triumph of language as a victory over language: a sudden injection of life-giving perceptions into a vocabulary that is, but for the energy of the creative writer, perpetually on the verge of exhaustion.'[9] In such a view writing style becomes an aspect of personality rather than of craftsmanship or technique: this is the emphatic argument of *Le Problème du style* (1902), in which Gourmont argued for the pre-eminence of personality in literary style in an extended illustration of Buffon's well-worn phrase that 'style is the man himself'. For Gourmont, style is the unique achievement of personal literary development: it cannot be inherited, nor can it be transmitted; the good writer is one who can distil the essence of his own experience rather than synthesize those of his predecessors. Style is more than an authorial tone or voice, it is the whole sensibility to which that voice gives expression: it may even be said, paradoxically, to exist prior to the written word.

For the Eliot of the early *Athenaeum* and (perhaps appropriately) the *Egoist*, such an emphasis on the personal was still recuperable

---

[8]   Murry came to a very similar conclusion in defending the use of 'sincerity', and particularly its importance in the formation of style, as a literary-critical tool, in a review of Quiller-Couch's *On the Art of Reading*. 'On Reading', *Athenaeum*, 4712 (20 Aug. 1920), 234–5.

[9]   *The Problem of Style* (London, 1922), 94.

within the terms of the 'impersonal' criticism being explored in essays such as 'Tradition and the Individual Talent'. He had some sympathy with Gourmont's and Murry's basically Symbolist belief in literature as a victory over language rather than through it, writing in 1919 of a literary simplicity in which feeling and thought triumphed over 'the natural sin of language'.[10] But there were areas in which his espousal of Gourmont led him into difficulties. These can be seen, for example, in his 'Observations' of May 1918, in which Eliot attempts to incorporate Gourmont into a criticism balanced uneasily between authoritative evaluation and personal response, suggesting that Gourmont makes art from the past relevant to contemporary opinion through the workings of his 'temperament'.[11] The problem here, of arguing for a critical personality vested with the impersonal authority of the tradition, is one that Eliot would later attempt to resolve by recasting Gourmontian 'temperament' into the less subjective quality of 'intelligence'. But for the present this crux remained unresolved, leaving Eliot straddling apparently self-contradictory critical positions. He could, for example, write that 'the poet has, not a "personality" to express, but a particular medium' yet elsewhere argue that great literature is 'the transformation of a personality into a personal work of art'. Or, ignoring his own advice to 'divert interest from the poet to the poetry', he would maintain that Massinger's style would have been conspicuously better had he had as refined a nervous system as Middleton, Tourneur, Webster, or Ford.[12]

These apparent contradictions derive partly from Eliot's attempts to read Gourmont against the grain and partly from the confused definitions of terms like 'personality', 'impersonality', and 'style' that he and Murry had inherited from an earlier generation of critics. The imprecision of the terminology is crucial, for it helps explain both why Murry and Eliot were unable fully to appreciate their crucial differences of emphasis on questions of personality in literature and also why Eliot mistakenly believed that Gourmont's criticism offered an impersonal road out of the swamps of impressionistic criticism.

The relationship between style and personality had been of particular concern to late-Victorian prose writing. Until the end of the nineteenth century dissertations on style tended to be modelled on

[10] 'The Post-Georgians', *Athenaeum*, 4641 (11 Apr. 1919), 171.
[11] 'Observations', *Egoist*, 5/5 (May 1918), 69–70 (p. 70).
[12] See *The Sacred Wood*, 56 and 139, 59 and 128–9.

rhetorical analysis; most followed Richard Whately's seminal *Elements of Rhetoric* (1828) in approaching style as a discipline of persuasion rather than expression.[13] But with the work of T. H. Wright, for whom style was identical 'with character—with unconscious revelations of the hidden self', and John Addington Symonds, for whom style was 'the sign of personal qualities, specific to individuals', this emphasis changed.[14] The extent of the change can be seen in Walter Pater's essay, 'Style' (1889), in which Pater followed the rhetoricians in recognizing the importance of impersonal rhetorical factors in style—such as the matching of form, language, and logical structure to content and the avoidance of 'surplusage'—but qualified this by insisting on the crucial centrality of personality in the selection and deployment of these qualities: style may still be conditional on precision and scholarship but is grounded in personality; its first requirement is 'to know yourself, to have ascertained your own sense exactly'.[15]

This emphasis on the pre-eminence of personality in style was incorporated into the academic study of literature through the work of Sir Walter Raleigh and Sir Arthur Quiller-Couch. Raleigh was quite unequivocal in stating that style 'is the ultimate and enduring revelation of personality'; it was the means by which 'you write yourself down whether you will or no'.[16] Quiller-Couch similarly regarded style as predominantly an attribute of personality, but added a moral dimension to this by insisting upon the centrality of good manners and personal integrity to a fine style. Conflating Buffon's much-quoted dictum that 'style is the man himself' and William of Wykeham's 'manners makyth man' Quiller-Couch had argued that the habits of clear and ordered thought that comprise good style, are, like the classic tenets of rhetoric from which they derive, the 'duties we owe to those who honour us with their attention'.[17]

---

[13] See Patrick Scott (ed.), 'Victorians on Rhetoric and Prose Style', in William B. Thesing (ed.), *Victorian Prose Writers after 1867*, vol. lvii of the *Dictionary of Literary Biography* (Detroit, Mich., 1987).

[14] T. H. Wright, 'Style', *MacMillan's Magazine*, 37 (Nov. 1877), 78–84; John Addington Symonds, 'Notes on Style', in his *Essays Speculative and Suggestive* (1890; 3rd edn. London, 1907), 166–236 (p. 217).

[15] 'Style', in Pater, *Appreciations: With an Essay on Style* (1889; library edn. London, 1910), 5–38 (p. 29).

[16] *Style* (London, 1897), 2, 128.

[17] 'On Style', in Quiller-Couch, *On the Art of Writing* (Cambridge, 1916), 232–48 (p. 245). Quiller-Couch had earlier made clear, in the same series of lectures, that 'manners' might also be taken in their older sense of 'morals'. 'English Literature in our Universities II', in *On the Art of Writing*, 215–31 (p. 225).

By invoking an impersonal standard in judging literature according to moral values, Quiller-Couch found himself exploring a paradox that haunted most studies of style after Flaubert, and which would be revived by Eliot and Murry. Prompted, perhaps, by Flaubert's problematic notion of an author 'présent partout et visible nulle part', Quiller-Couch saw a paradox in the notion that, 'though personality pervades Style and cannot be escaped, the first sin against Style as against good Manners is to obtrude or exploit personality'. While Quiller-Couch accepted Flaubert's judgement that 'great art is scientific and impersonal' he none the less pointed to the importance of the integrity of that writer's personality in making such a statement empirically valid: it was, he argued, a secular analogy to the paradoxical Christian truth, that 'he who would save his soul must first lose it'.[18]

Quiller-Couch's own attempt to resolve this literary paradox, by conflating personal integrity with social manners, was adequate to the social context in which he placed his primarily consensual style. But for artistic liberals like Gourmont and Pater, for whom considerations of morals and manners would only tarnish the amoral aesthetic vision, such a resolution was untenable. Their own attempts to address the problem, however, were little more convincing than Quiller-Couch's. In his own discussion of Flaubert, Pater had come to the confusing conclusion that 'if the style be the man, in all the colour and intensity of a veritable apprehension, it will be in a real sense "impersonal" '.[19] This sense of irresolution would be compounded by Pater's attempts to differentiate between the impersonal style of Flaubert and that of Mérimée on the grounds of its distinctive and individual 'quality of soul'.[20] Gourmont's discussion of the Flaubertian problem in *Le Problème du style* was less metaphysical but no less confusing: here, Flaubert is figured as 'one of the most profoundly personal writers there has ever been', yet his work appears to approach so near to spiritual perfection that 'all Flaubert seems impersonal'.[21] In the end, Gourmont decides the issue on the side of personality, by claiming to find as much personality in the

---

[18] Ibid. 246–7.   [19] 'Style', in *Appreciations*, 37.

[20] 'Prosper Mérimée', in Pater, *Miscellaneous Studies* (1895; library edn. London, 1910), 11–37.

[21] 'Flaubert est l'un des écrivains le plus profondément personnels qui furent jamais'. *Le Problème du style: Questions d'art, de littérature et de grammaire*, 3rd edn. (Paris, 1902), 105. 'Tout Flaubert semble impersonnel. C'est passé en adage.' Ibid. 106.

apparently objective style of science as there is in literature. 'There is not science on one side and literature on the other', he wrote, 'there are minds which function well and minds which function badly.'[22]

It is this formulation that Eliot had found especially pertinent, and which underpinned his attempt in 'The Perfect Critic' to conflate literary and scientific knowledges in the formula that 'there is no method except to be very intelligent'.[23] Indeed, this belief in the importance of a primarily disinterested intelligence, not yet dissociated from a singular personality, can be seen running through much of Eliot's early criticism. An example can be found in his essay on Bertrand Russell's prose style published in 1918, where Eliot suggested that literary methods have a particular validity in discussions of scientific or philosophical styles because 'literary standards help us to perceive just those moments when a writer is scrupulously and sincerely attending to his vision; help us to dissociate the social and the histrionic from the unique'.[24]

There is little doubt about the influence that Gourmont exerted on Eliot at this stage. *The Sacred Wood* has been described as deriving its 'critical idea' from Gourmont; a reading that Eliot did nothing to discourage by proclaiming Gourmont in that book as 'the critical consciousness of a generation'.[25] Later criticism has claimed to find in Gourmont the source of Eliot's 'dissociation of sensibility' and the idea of 'subconscious creation' manifested in 'Tradition and the Individual Talent'.[26] Further influences have been traced in his essays on Massinger and Ben Jonson, as well as the later essays on Middleton and 'The Metaphysical Poets'.[27] A Gourmontian flavour is noticeable in Eliot's emphasis on the pre-eminence of direct perception over theory in 'The Perfect Critic' and 'Dante', in the use of physiological metaphors in 'The Metaphysical Poets' and scientific analogy in 'Tradition and the Individual Talent', and in his description of the

[22] 'Il n'y a pas d'un côté la science et de l'autre la littérature; il y a des cerveaux qui fonctionnent bien et des cerveaux qui fonctionnent mal.' *Problème du style*, 107.

[23] 'The Perfect Critic II', *Athenaeum*, 4708 (23 July 1920), 103.

[24] 'Style and Thought', *Nation*, 22/25 (Mar. 1918), 768–70 (pp. 770, 768).

[25] Graham Hough, *Image and Experience: Studies in a Literary Revolution* (London, 1960), 32; T. S. Eliot, 'The French Intelligence', in *The Sacred Wood*, 44–6 (p. 44).

[26] Bateson, 'Dissociation of Sensibility', 302–12. Bergonzi, *T. S. Eliot*, 66.

[27] Glenn S. Burne, 'T. S. Eliot and Remy de Gourmont', *Bucknell Review*, 8/2 (Feb. 1959), 113–26, and *Remy de Gourmont: His Ideas and Influence in England and America* (Carbondale, Ill., 1963), 131–48. See also John Chalker, 'Authority and Personality in Eliot's Criticism', in Graham Martin (ed.), *Eliot in Perspective: A Symposium* (London, 1970), 194–210 (pp. 199–202).

organic nature of metaphor in 'Studies in Contemporary Criticism'.[28] Even the divisive 'Chinese wall' that Eliot describes Milton erecting in 'Christopher Marlowe' perhaps owes something to the 'walled China' that Gourmont had described in *Le Problème du style*.[29]

But what is at least as telling as this enthusiasm and influence is Eliot's subsequent rejection of Gourmont. Eliot would publicly distance himself from Gourmont's influence in his 1928 introduction to the second edition of *The Sacred Wood*, and would later describe Gourmont's influence on his generation as providing 'types of scepticism for younger men to be attracted by and to repudiate'.[30] These were formal announcements of a difficulty with aspects of Gourmont's writing that is already implicit in Eliot's work from as early as 'Tradition and the Individual Talent' in 1919 and explicit after his dissatisfaction with 'The Perfect Critic'. In the latter essay Eliot had stretched Gourmont almost beyond recognition in attempting to ascribe to his criticism a quality of Aristotelian impersonality: 'a pure contemplation from which all the accidents of personal emotion are removed', in which 'we aim to see the object as it really is'.[31] This rather contrasts with Gourmont's position, as stated in *Promenades littéraires*, that

To be a good critic . . . one must have a strong personality. The critic must impose himself, relying not on the choice of subject but on the quality of his mind. The subject is of little importance in art, or at any rate it is never more than a part of art. It is of no more importance in criticism, where it is never more than a pretext.[32]

Similar discrepancies can be seen in Eliot's essay on Philip Massinger published in the *Athenaeum* in 1920, in which he had attempted to

---

[28] Eliot adverts directly to Gourmont in this latter essay, writing in a footnote that 'all this matter of the cliché and the metaphor has been much more ably put in Remy de Gourmont's *Problème du style*'. 'Studies in Contemporary Criticism', *Egoist*, 5/9 (Oct. 1918), 113–14 (p. 114).

[29] 'La Chine murée n'a que fort peu changé au cours des siècles une fois son ossification achevée.' *Problème du style*, 21.

[30] 'A Commentary', *Criterion*, 8/52 (Apr. 1934), 451–4 (p. 451).

[31] 'The Perfect Critic II', 104.

[32] 'Pour être un bon critique, en effet, il faut avoir une forte personnalité; il faut s'imposer, et compter pur cela, non sur le choix des sujets, mais sur la valeur de son propre esprit. Le sujet importe peu en art, du moins il n'est jamais qu'une des parties de l'art; le sujet n'importe pas davantage en critique: il n'est jamais qu'un prétexte.' 'Renan et l'idée scientifique', *Promenades littéraires I* (1903; 11th edn. Paris, 1922), 13–14.

enlist Gourmont's aid in arguing that personality is important to literature only to the extent that it is incorporated, or more particularly decanted, into the work itself.[33] While this remains more or less true to Gourmont in this particular case, its attendant assumption of a personality created through a prolonged and conscious immersion in the tradition is very much at odds with Gourmont, for whom artistic expression is above all, primary and visceral:[34]

To be a writer, it is enough to have a natural talent for the art, to practise it with perseverance, to learn a little more each morning, and to experience all human sensations. As for the art of 'creating images', it is necessary to believe that this is absolutely independent of all literary culture, since the most beautiful, truest and most daring images are enclosed in our everyday words—the age-old works of instinct; spontaneous blossomings of the intellectual garden.[35]

It is on this matter of tradition that the gulf between Gourmont and Eliot becomes unbridgeable. The idea of a formative literary tradition, for which Eliot was reaching, is untenable for Gourmont, for whom it is axiomatic that what is taught by literature is posterior, and secondary, to what is learned through the senses, and for whom literary history is merely a collection of individual and frequently unrelated utterances of personal feeling collected together and homogenized, as it were, after the fact. Indeed, Gourmont's *Problème du style* was explicitly hostile to such traditionalizing operations, being itself written in an attempt to refute Antoine Albalat's rather Eliot-like arguments for an assimilable literary style in his *De la formation du style par l'assimilation des auteurs* (1901).

---

[33] Eliot quotes Gourmont: 'Flaubert incorporait toute sa sensibilité à ses œuvres . . . Hors de ses livres, où il se transvasait goutte à goutte, jusqu'à la lie, Flaubert est fort peu intéressant.' 'The Old Comedy', *Athenaeum*, 4702 (June 1920), 760–1 (p. 761). The essay was reprinted as part II of 'Philip Massinger' in the *Selected Essays*. Eliot was forced to clarify further this 'decantation of personality', in response to criticism from a reader, in a letter, 'Artists and Men of Genius', *Athenaeum*, 4706 (25 June 1920), 842.

[34] 'Nous écrivons, comme nous sentons, comme nous pensons, avec notre corps tout entier. L'intelligence n'est qu'une des manières d'être de la sensibilité, et non pas la plus stable, encore moins la plus volontaire.' *Problème du style*, 9.

[35] 'Pour être un écrivain, il suffit d'avoir le talent naturel de son métier, d'exercer ce métier avec persévérance, de s'instruire un peu plus chaque matin et de vivre toutes les sensations humaines. Quant à l'art de "créer des images", il faut croire qu'il est absolument indépendant de toute culture littéraire, puisque les plus belles images, les plus vraies et les plus hardies, sont encloses dans nos mots de tous les jours, œuvre séculaire de l'instinct, floraison spontanée du jardin intellectuel.' 'Du Style ou de l'écriture' (1899), in *La Culture des idées*, 3–39 (p. 39).

Garnet Rees has noted Gourmont's lack of a traditionalist perspective, writing that 'in his desire to discover where exactly the individuality of each author lay, Gourmont was apt to suspend his studies in space by not relating them to their literary connections'.[36] Rees regards this as a lamentable failure in Gourmont subsequently made good by Eliot. But this is to misread Gourmont's relation to tradition, for he does not so much fail to incorporate a sense of tradition into his work as reject that sense as being antithetical to his purpose. The kind of tradition advocated by Eliot in 'Tradition and the Individual Talent', which 'abandons nothing *en route*', including Shakespeare, Homer, and primitive cave paintings, is quite contrary to the literary sensibility anatomized in *Le Problème du style*.[37] That sensibility does not develop or grow larger; instead, it mutates according to the changing imperatives of differing eras. As a result, a writer like Homer cannot form part of an unchanging European mind because his 'primitive way of seeing life', free of metaphor, stands in absolute contradiction to the 'synaesthetic' tendencies of modern thought.[38] Gourmont, indeed, goes to considerable lengths to stress his anti-traditionalism, recommending that writers strip away the influence of those who have gone before as Flaubert stripped away the influence of Chateaubriand:[39]

One must occupy oneself neither with Greeks, nor Romans, nor classicists, nor romantics. A writer, when he writes, should never be thinking of his masters or even his style. If he sees, if he feels, he will say something; it may be interesting or not, beautiful or mediocre, the risk must be run . . . style is feeling, seeing, thinking, and nothing more.[40]

For Gourmont, the attempt to read a tradition into these works is a reductive exercise which detracts from each work's individual qualities and imposes unnecessary obligations on subsequent writing. If,

[36] 'A French Influence on T. S. Eliot: Remy de Gourmont', *Revue de littérature comparée*, 16/4 (Oct.–Dec. 1936), 764–7 (pp. 766–7).

[37] 'Tradition and the Individual Talent', in *The Sacred Wood*, 51.

[38] 'Le style homérique, représentatif d'une manière primitive de voir la vie, est en contradiction absolue avec nos tendances "synesthésiques".' *Problème du style*, 91.

[39] See ibid. 104. To complement this 'dépouillement' Gourmont suggested that, 'ce qui est intéressant, ce n'est pas le départ, c'est l'arrivée. La point de départ est commun à tous; les arrivées sont particulières.' *Problème du style*, 102.

[40] 'Et ne s'occuper ni des Grecs, ni des Romains, ni des classiques, ni des romantiques. Un écrivain ne doit songer, quand il écrit, ni à ses maîtres, ni même à son style. S'il voit, s'il sent, il dira quelque chose; cela sera intéressant ou non, beau ou médiocre, chance à courir. . . . Le style, c'est de sentir, de voir, de penser, et rien de plus.' *Problème du style*, 31–2.

as he suggests, 'the true tradition of the French mind is the liberty of
the mind', then 'far from drawing tighter the bonds of tradition we
should release the brains which it binds'.[41] Far from being an aid to
writing, a sense of the tradition is an active hindrance: 'forgetfulness
of the past is a condition of strength, of aptitude for the present. It is
our incapacity to reawaken it completely which urges us to new
experiments.'[42]

These differences help explain Eliot's growing unease with Gourmont, and his increasing need to distance himself from the French
critic. But it is arguable that Eliot's cognizance of these differences
was hastened by the intervention of Murry. Murry's appropriation of
Gourmont's *Problème du style* for critical subjectivism, most notice-
ably in *The Problem of Style*, showed that Gourmont was no longer
an unproblematic source of critical authority. *The Problem of Style*,
first delivered as a series of lectures at Oxford in the spring of 1921,
was Murry's most sustained attempt to define the relations between
authorial personality and literary style. In spite of the book's title
Murry played down the influence of Gourmont, claiming him as only
one among a number of sources.[43] But when he comes to his central
definition of an organic personal style, the similarities are incontrovertible: style, Murry writes, is 'the garment which fits, or rather the
actual skin which covers a fabric of living nerves and tissue, a whole
individual mode of seeing, feeling, thinking; it is no more possible to
imitate a real style than it is to be another man'.[44] This bears immediate comparison to the 'feeling, seeing, thinking' of Gourmont's
definition of style already quoted, as well as the Gourmontian
metaphor of weaving nervous fibres into the garment of style.[45]

This, as has been seen, was still an attractive and convincing model
for Eliot, who would use it to underpin much of the argument of 'The

---

[41] 'Tradition and Other Things', trans. Richard Aldington, *Egoist*, 1/14 (15 July 1914),
261–2 (p. 262).
[42] 'L'oubli du passé est une condition de force, d'aptitude au présent. C'est notre incap-
acité à le réveiller tout à fait qui nous pousse aux nouvelles expériences.' 'Le Souvenir', in
Lettres à l'Amazone, 13–20 (pp. 19–20).
[43] For a discussion of the relationship between Murry's and Gourmont's books see
Burne, *Remy de Gourmont*, 104–7. Garnet Rees has described Murry's work as 'much
stimulated by Gourmont's conclusions', but does not develop this in an argument. See
'The Position of Remy de Gourmont', *French Studies*, 4/4 (Oct. 1950), 289–305 (p. 301).
[44] *Problem of Style*, 117.
[45] 'Ce livre est tellement personnel, tellement tissé comme avec des fibres nerveuses,
qu'on n'a jamais pu y ajouter une page qui ne fit l'effet d'une pièce de drap à une robe de
tulle.' *Problème du style*, 106.

Metaphysical Poets' in the October after Murry's lectures. But, as the essays of *The Sacred Wood* had shown, Eliot was ambivalent as to how far this creative and critical individualism should be allowed to go unhindered. While he recognized the centrality of a writer's individual perception, Eliot seemed also to be prescribing the need for that individualism to be subsumed within a set of impersonal values. What these values were was not always clear: they could be witnessed triumphantly in the work of Dante, and equally by their absence in the less salutary cases of Wordsworth, Blake, and Arnold. Eliot distrusted the 'impersonal ideas' of public opinion that caused Tennyson to squander his talents, or Swinburne's vacuous 'impersonality', yet he celebrated Dante's ability to absorb a whole impersonal belief system and wrote approvingly that 'the emotion of art is impersonal'.[46] Eliot's manifest aim was the tempering of individual artistic and critical excesses by the imposition of a critical standard. That his impressive, apparently formidable criticism failed to sustain a coherent definition of that standard—failing to set out the criteria according to which an emotion might be judged impersonally—was less significant than the aspiration to which it testified.

In *The Problem of Style* Murry came to an analogous recognition of the need for a standard against which an excessively emotional literature might be defined: a need to stress that even the most immediately subjective writing is valuable mainly for its impersonal qualities. Parts of the book come very close to Eliot: Murry's description of Lucretius and Dante employing 'intellectual systems as a scaffolding upon which to build an emotional structure' obviously borrows heavily from Eliot's essay on Dante;[47] similarly Murry's attempts to delineate a style in which form makes a perfect match with content immediately bring to mind the 'objective correlative' of Eliot's 'Hamlet and his Problems'. In this latter case Murry had taken a passage from Katherine Mansfield's short story 'Bliss' as a successful example of the impersonal creative style: 'The sensuous perceptions have aroused an emotional apprehension of the still solitude of the abandoned room; the objects being in an active relation to the emotion, the emotion is crystallized about them.'[48] This similarity with Eliot's celebrated formulation is further emphasized if one compares Murry's favoured formulation of style, taken from Stendhal,

[46] *The Sacred Wood*, 154, 149, 167–71, 59. [47] *Problem of Style*, 29.
[48] Ibid. 104.

with Eliot. Murry quotes Stendhal's description of style as 'adding to a given thought all the circumstances fitted to produce the whole effect that the thought ought to produce'.[49] Eliot had described the objective correlative as 'a set of objects, a situation, a chain of events which shall be the formula of that *particular* emotion; such that when the external facts, which must terminate in sensory experience, are given, the emotion is immediately evoked'.[50]

While a certain yearning for an impersonal standard, or Gourmontian law, is common to both critics, the beginnings of a divergence of opinion as to the source of that authority are also visible. Eliot's work, though not always consistent, was tending towards the placement of contemporary work in the perspective of the past. For Eliot, the tradition offered, if not a set of absolute values, a best practice according to which an artist might be formed and evaluated, and his work becomes impersonal, and hence valuable, according to how near it approaches that practical standard. But for Murry—and this is where he is much closer to Gourmont—the perfection of an adequate style is a human and not merely a formal quality. According to Murry the writer does not merely inherit a praxis from literature, to which he submits and by which he is judged. Instead he inherits the example of a previous writer's individual triumphs over the recalcitrance of the linguistic and literary materials of his day. The achievement of great art is a mastery of technique by a distinctive personality. What the modern writer can learn from great art, like that of Shakespeare, then, is a personal rather than a technical lesson:

> from Shakespeare he can learn in what ways the discrimination of sense-perception is the most active principle at work in refining language, and he can see to what a point of suppleness the stubborn elements of speech can be compelled by the unrelaxing pressure of an overflowing sensuous memory. Studying Shakespeare is studying how to write.[51]

It is the quality of this unique sense-perception that governs the quality of writing, and that perception is refined, not just through literature, but through all sensuous experience of which literature forms only one part: the writer's 'capacity for sensuous experience of every kind should be practically unlimited'.[52] What the writer gleans from

---

[49] 'Ajouter à une pensée donnée toutes les circonstances propres à produire tout l'effet que doit produire cette pensée.' *The Problem of Style*, 79.
[50] 'Hamlet and his Problems', in *The Sacred Wood*, 100.
[51] *Problem of Style*, 116.   [52] Ibid. 93.

literature antecedent to him, then, is not so much a way of writing as a way of feeling, a 'sensuous perception' allied to the writer's individual 'emotional contemplation'.[53] The result of this contemplation is an art, like that described by Gourmont, which actively resists the categorizations of the tradition: the words of 'the magical language of literature . . . are not inherited, neither can they be learnt'.[54]

According to Murry, the great writer, equipped by nature with 'a more than ordinary sensitiveness', accumulates the perceptions of his senses into 'a coherent emotional nucleus'. And it is from this personal 'mode of experience', this 'accumulation of past emotions' that he 'is able to accomplish the miracle of giving to a particular the weight and force of the universal'.[55] In the process of perfecting himself, according to this argument, the writer becomes a microcosm of the wider human values that filter into his work:

Out of the multitude of his vivid perceptions, with their emotional accompaniments, emerges a sense of the quality of life as a whole. It is this sense of, and emphasis upon, a dominant quality pervading the human universe which gives to the work of the great master of literature that unique universality which Matthew Arnold attempted to isolate in his famous criterion of the highest kind of poetry—'criticism of life'.[56]

In emphasizing the quality of being that underlies great writing, Murry is manifestly widening the criteria by which aesthetic value is determined. He is also ignoring the qualities in literature that make it literature and not any other art form or area of human activity. It was exactly this refusal to recognize art's autonomy and literature's specificity that Eliot had objected to throughout *The Sacred Wood* and in his discussion of Arnold in that book's preface. Where Eliot was trying to focus and define, to carve out a critical language particularly applicable to literature, Murry was diffusing and generalizing, absorbing literary values within a wider humanism: it was increasingly looking as though Murry was, in Eliot's eyes, becoming a manifestation not only of the unacceptable side of Gourmont but of Arnold also.

In spite, then, of a common concern with the maintenance of some kind of critical standard, we see arising the outlines of two quite different inflections of artistic impersonality: one that stresses the impersonal checks put on artistic self-indulgence by the discipline of the artistic medium as it has been refined through the tradition; the

[53] Ibid.   [54] Ibid. 93–4.   [55] Ibid. 26–7.   [56] Ibid.

other stressing the personal discipline of the artist in cultivating him-self to the extent to which he can speak meaningfully of the widest possible range of human experience. When Murry writes that in the best style 'we should be able to catch an immediate reference back to a whole mode of feeling that is consistent with itself' and when he singles out 'perception' as the key artistic quality, he is concurring with the conclusions of Eliot's 'Dante'. The difference is that for Murry this comprehensive system of feeling is a particular and indi-vidual construct, while for Eliot it is the result of the poet's own meshing with the larger system of feelings that he has inherited. Far from resolving the issue, however, both accounts do little more than restate the difficulties of discovering an objective set of criteria with which to assess the essential subjectivity of creative authorship—dif-ficulties they have inherited from the discussions of style by Flaubert, Gourmont, Pater, Raleigh, and Quiller-Couch.

Murry began *The Problem of Style* by noting the prevailing vague-ness of critical terminology, a burden later taken up by Eliot, who would write complainingly that 'in literary criticism we are con-stantly using terms which we cannot define, and defining other things by them. We are constantly using terms which have an *in*tension and an *ex*tension which do not quite fit.'[57] The failure of criticism to appropriate for itself a vocabulary worthy of scientific objectivity would be a frequent source of complaint in the 1920s. Percy Lubbock, for example, found his attempts to compile an anatomical, imper-sonal style manual for fiction in *The Craft of Fiction* (1921) frustrated by just such imprecision: 'there are times', he wrote, 'when a critic of literature feels that if only there were one single tangible and measur-able fact about a book—if it could be weighed like a statue, say, or measured like a picture—it would be a support in a world of shadows'.[58] It is arguable that the example described, of the ambi-guous divide between 'personality' and 'impersonality' with which Eliot and Murry had to work, is a case in point. Despite their diver-gent emphases on the desirability of a writer's incorporation into a tradition they share a belief with Gourmont that his personal impres-sions, if they are to be valid at all, must be subject to laws that render them coherent. Eliot describes the need for a writer to be absorbed into an impersonal literary tradition, but recognizes the personal

[57] 'Experiment in Criticism', in *Tradition and Experiment in Present-Day Literature: Addresses Delivered at the City Literary Institute* (London, 1929), 198–215 (p. 214).
[58] *The Craft of Fiction* (London, 1921), 273–4.

contribution that this demands, the 'great labour' with which tradition is acquired. Murry describes great writing as the direct 'communication of individual thought and feeling' but recognizes that, at
its best, such communication approaches the condition of impersonality. But with the imprecise notions of personality bequeathed by literary usage and the pseudo-psychology of Gourmont, neither comes
near an adequate definition of the two terms themselves, never mind
a description of the mechanism by which personality might be transmuted into its nominal opposite.

Eliot would respond to this confusion by expanding the basis of
his search for critical absolutes. This route would lead him to
Aquinas in the late 1920s; in its early stages it would be seen in a
shifting of his critical emphasis from qualities of sensibility to those
of intellect. Murry's search for a critical law would take him in a different direction, sounding out the absolutes in the human personality. But even at this stage, Murry recognized that criticism need not
despair at its lack of an objective vocabulary. The critic, he wrote,
must not forget 'that half the fascination of his task lies in the fact
that the terms he uses are fluid and uncertain, and that his success
depends upon the compulsive vigour with which he impresses upon
them a meaning which shall be exactly fitted to his own intention'.[59]
The irony of subsequent events was that it was not Murry who would
benefit from this recognition of the importance of polemic in criticism, but the objectivity-seeking Eliot.

AFTER THE *ATHENAEUM*

As far as Murry's work was concerned, the difficulties of describing
an aesthetic practice in terms of the inherited antithesis of personality and impersonality continued without sign of resolution for two
years subsequent to the lectures of *The Problem of Style*. His editorship of the *Athenaeum* had terminated early in 1921, when the ailing
journal had been incorporated with the *Nation*. He continued, however, to contribute to the literary section of the new paper. In these
essays Murry was consistent in stressing the importance of personality in the creation of art. His recognition of the need to set external
bounds to the free play of personality, to distinguish egotism from

[59] *Problem of Style*, 1.

individualism, however, saw him moving away from Gourmont's almost asocial liberalism towards the ideas of literary order and personal morality promoted by Raleigh and Quiller-Couch.[60]

In *The Problem of Style* Murry had described the exhilaration a critic feels in the discovery of an 'organically perfect style' as an act of individual appropriation, a sense that finally 'I have my man'.[61] Spurred on by Buffon's dictum that 'style is the man himself', Murry had made free in conflating literary standards with his assessment of the personal qualities of the author: 'Style is organic—not the clothes a man wears, but the flesh, bone, and blood of his body. Therefore it is really impossible to consider styles apart from the whole system of perceptions and feelings and thoughts that animate them.'[62] The result is that discussion of a writer's work slips easily into an appraisal of his life—of the richness of his perception rather than his skill in the manipulation of words.[63] Wordsworth and Balzac are rendered second-rate writers by the poverty of their 'sensuous perception', while Shakespeare's greatness rests on a 'wealth of sensuous perceptions surely unparalleled in human history'.[64] While these are not moral qualities *per se*, Murry makes clear that they are the result of a process of self-perfection that has a strong moral dimension. It is in this way that Chaucer's perfection of style reveals to us 'his mellow, infinitely tolerant humanity'.[65]

Murry's tendency, which he described elsewhere, to 'detect where most the man shows through the texture of his work', and his belief that 'to judge art you must be capable of judging life' developed in the essays collected for publication as *Countries of the Mind* (1922), *Pencillings* (1923), and *Discoveries* (1924).[66] Though the essays were written as occasional pieces and reviews, their subjects are more often than not non-canonical writers or those marginalized by their idiosyncrasy or individualism.[67] In the prefatory note to *Countries of*

---

[60] See, e.g. 'The Personal in Criticism', *Nation and Athenaeum*, 29/8 (21 May 1921), 289–90, and 'A Matter of Form', *Nation and Athenaeum*, 29/9 (28 May 1921), 618–19.

[61] *Problem of Style*, 44.   [62] Ibid. 136.

[63] This is given emphasis in Murry's essay 'Croce and Criticism', where he describes 'the significance of a work of art [as] a quality wholly independent of its artistic perfection.' *Nation and Athenaeum*, 30/9 (26 Nov. 1921), 350–2 (p. 350).

[64] *Problem of Style*, 108.   [65] Ibid. 46.

[66] 'Baudelaire and Decadence', *TLS* 1003 (7 Apr. 1921), 217–18 (p. 217); 'St-Évremond', *Nation and Athenaeum*, 30/23 (4 Mar. 1922), 830–1 (p. 830).

[67] For the interchangeability of these terms in Murry's thought at this time see *The Problem of Style*, 16, 47.

the Mind Murry wrote of a 'theory of the psychology of literary creation' underlying the essays, and it becomes clear that he considers it most fruitful to study this psychology in isolation from a literary tradition. The essays on Burton, Doughty, De La Mare, Baudelaire, Amiel, Clare, and Collins in that volume might each be said to illuminate Murry's thesis, expressed in his essay on Doughty, that 'behind, incessantly lifting and maintaining the book, is the man'.[68] As such, critical judgement becomes more a matter of interpersonal than literary skill:

We like, or do not like, the 'atmosphere' of a book, just as we like, or do not like the 'atmosphere' of a person; and, in fact, we are judging a person through his book. No effort of his towards impersonality can deceive us. On the contrary, a true impersonality, involving, as it does, a closer correspondence between expression and apprehension than is achieved by the writer who permits himself—or a histrionic projection of himself—to appear, provides us with still more certain evidence of the quality of soul. We have, as it were, an essence, from which all superfluous matter has been removed; the last disguise is fallen from the writer's habits of thought and feeling. We may admire his skill and respect his literary ability, but if his quality of soul is mean, or trivial, or repellent, nothing can save him for us.[69]

This sophistic attempt to replace personality with a Paterian 'quality of soul' anticipates the arguments of *Keats and Shakespeare*. In it can be seen the attempt to marry the notion, derived from Gourmont, of a stripping away of the features of literary tradition accidental to the individual expression of the writer, with the notion, espoused by Pater, Raleigh, and Quiller-Couch, of the moral imperative incumbent on the writer. As Murry put it, rather baldly, elsewhere, 'the strength of a truly great writer endures either because he builds upon the foundations of a morality which he accepts, or because he is animated by the intense desire to discover one'.[70]

Murry, then, does not so much clarify the ambiguity of an impersonal personality as transcribe it into a hybrid language of religion and ethics. But while the notion of morality at least implies a consensual criterion by which a writer might be evaluated, Murry comes no nearer an adequate description of a way in which a specifically

---

[68] 'Arabia Deserta', in *Countries of the Mind: Essays in Literary Criticism* (London, 1922), 137–50 (p. 147).
[69] 'Morality Again', *Pencillings: Little Essays on Literature* (London, 1923), 119–27 (pp. 124–5).
[70] 'Henri-Frédéric Amiel, 1821–1881', *TLS* 1028 (29 Sept. 1921), 617–18 (p. 618).

literary consensus might be formed, and so comes no nearer defining the way qualities of literary impersonality might be evaluated. Criticism remains an entirely subjective discipline, varying in its worth according to the sensibility and the intuitive capacities of the critic himself. In his most explicit critical manifesto of this period, Murry expresses this opinion forcefully in an interpretation of Gourmont's maxim that 'the whole effort of a sincere man is to erect his personal impressions into law': 'A law or rule, or rather a system of laws or rules, is necessary to the critic; it is a record of all his past impressions and reactions; but it must be his own law, his own system, refined by his own effort out of his own experience.'[71] Gourmont's law, then, comes to be seen as a peculiarly individual construct, resembling an equally subjective law propounded by another Frenchman, Paul Claudel. On more than one occasion Murry would write approvingly of Claudel's autobiographical couplet:

> J'ai fui partout: partout j'ai retrouvé la loi:
> Quelque chose en moi qui soit plus moi-même que moi.[72]

Murry's critic, then, like the artist of Gourmont and Claudel, appears largely and necessarily independent of literary tradition. His judgement is primarily a product of his personal integrity. And, like the artist, it is the sense of perceptual individuality attendant on that quality that is the guarantee of the value of his work: 'A critic should be conscious of his moral assumptions and take pains to put into them the highest morality of which he is capable. That is only another way of saying that the critic should be conscious of himself as an artist.'[73]

The period in which Murry's criticism was taking this moral turn corresponds with the escalating crises of Eliot's private life, including both his breakdown and the creative effort of *The Waste Land*. Between his final contribution to the *Athenaeum* in 1920 and his founding of the *Criterion* in October 1922, Eliot's critical output was largely restricted to the occasional synoptic 'London Letter' for the *Dial*, which afforded him little scope for the working out of critical ideas. However, he did

---

[71] 'A Critical Credo', in *Countries of the Mind* (1922), 237–46 (pp. 239–40).

[72] 'I fled in all directions: everywhere I rediscovered the law: | Something in me which is more myself than I.', 'Romanticism and the Tradition', *Criterion*, 2/7 (Apr. 1924), 272–95 (p. 275). See also 'English Poetry in the 18th Century', *TLS* 1096 (18 Jan. 1923), 33–4 (p. 34), and 'Newman and Sidgwick: An Essay Towards a New Psychology', *Adelphi*, 2/9 (Feb. 1925), 731–42 (p. 734).

[73] 'A Critical Credo', in *Countries of the Mind* (1922), 246.

manage to write three major essays for the *Times Literary Supplement* in this two-year period which would be collected as *Homage to John Dryden* in October 1924. Each of the essays shows a distinct movement away from the positions of Gourmont and Murry, and a definite qualification of his own 'The Perfect Critic'.

The personal relationship between Eliot and Murry had become strained after Eliot's last contribution to the *Athenaeum*. In January 1921 Eliot complained to his mother of Murry's weakness of character and vanity, and wrote that the two had 'fallen apart completely'.[74] Although that particular rift seemed to have been healed after Murry gave a favourable review to *The Sacred Wood*,[75] it marked the start of a more distant, formal relationship between the two men. In public, Eliot registered dissent but remained magnanimous: Murry was the 'only one of the accredited critics whom I can read at all' and the pre-eminent London editor, even in spite of his 'perverse or exaggerated' opinions.[76] Privately, however, Eliot was less tolerant and forgiving. He had told Virginia Woolf that he and Murry were 'fundamentally antagonistic', and that between them, 'there seemed to be nothing to be said'.[77] This distance seemed to be confirmed when, in October 1921, he described one of Murry's essays as 'a revolting mess of torrid tastelessness and hypocritical insensibility' and when, in January 1922, he suggested ominously that 'something conclusive should be done to Murry'.[78] In fact, the two spent a weekend together shortly after this and apparently achieved some sort of reconciliation. For the rest of 1922, in the lead up to the first issue of the *Criterion*, Eliot became conspicuously friendly towards Murry, dining with him and spending weekends in his company, eliciting Murry's contribution to the *Criterion*, and expressing himself anxious to learn his opinion of *The Waste Land*. Murry seemed eager to reciprocate, writing later in his journal that for one particular day spent with Eliot in late 1922 he had 'come nearer Tom Eliot ... than I had ever been before, or ever was afterwards'.[79] But in spite of this

---

[74] 22 Jan. 1921, *Letters*, 432–4.

[75] 'The Sacred Wood', *New Republic* (New York), 26 (13 Apr. 1921), 194–5. Eliot wrote to Murry that it was 'the best review I have had', 22 Apr. 1921, *Letters*, 447.

[76] 'London Letter', *Dial*, 70/6 (June 1921), 686–91 (pp. 689–90).

[77] *The Diary of Virginia* Woolf, ed. Anne Oliver Bell, vol. ii: *1920–1924* (London, 1978), 124.

[78] To Richard Aldington, 15 Oct. 1921; to Scofield Thayer, 20 Jan. 1922, *Letters*, 479 and 502.

[79] See Lea, *The Life of John Middleton Murry*, 92, and Eliot's letter to Murry, 21 Feb. 1922, *Letters*, 506.

reconciliation, as Murry implies, their work was never again to come near the sense of common purpose achieved at the *Athenaeum*.

A large part of Eliot's disaffection concerned what he saw as Murry's emotional, subjective approach to literature. 'Even when he is right', Eliot had written in a letter to Sidney Schiff, 'he is the victim of an emotion, and the rightness seems an accident.'[80] This distaste for emotional excess had always been a part of Eliot's make-up as a critic, and in the year leading up to his breakdown the three essays he writes on seventeenth-century poetry see an intensification of that concern. When Eliot had figured the tradition in *The Sacred Wood* it had been as the 'Mind of Europe' against which individual emotions must be held in the balance. But with the essays on Marvell, Dryden, and the Metaphysical Poets, all published in 1921, this quality of mind begins to preponderate, turning from a balance into a check. At the time of his breakdown Eliot had ascribed his nervous condition to an *aboulie* or emotional derangement: 'nothing wrong with my mind', he had written to Richard Aldington.[81] It had been the capacity of the mind to shape or place a check on emotional derangement that had been a concern central to the essays of the previous year.

In his essay on Dante in April 1920, Eliot had been explicit in ascribing Dante's strength as a poet to his ability to subsume all experience within a wholly emotional structure, one that is 'complete from the most sensuous to the most intellectual and the most spiritual'.[82] With the essay on Andrew Marvell in the *Times Literary Supplement* in March 1921, Eliot supplemented this emotional conception of poetic creation with a specifically intellectual component: the 'wit' that, as Eliot puts it, is 'probably a literary rather than a personal quality', the 'quality of a civilization, of a traditional habit of life'. This wit is not wholly a quality of intellect, but it is a 'tough reasonableness', an 'impersonal virtue' that in Marvell imparts an emotional precision denied to more emotionally diffuse writers like William Morris.[83]

---

[80] 30 Nov. 1920, *Letters*, 422. Murry himself had long been aware of this aspect of his criticism. In response to Virginia Woolf, who had described him in 1919 as 'the most intellectual of all modern critics', Murry had countered: 'I am an absolutely emotional critic. What may seem intellectual is only my method of explaining the nature of the emotion.' 23 Nov. 1919, *The Letters of John Middleton Murry to Katherine Mansfield*, 223.

[81] 6 Nov. 1921, *Letters*, 486. See also Ackroyd, *T. S. Eliot*, 115.

[82] 'Dante', in *The Sacred Wood*, 169.

[83] 'Andrew Marvell', *TLS* 1002 (31 Mar. 1921), 201–2 (p. 201).

With the publication of 'The Metaphysical Poets' in October 1921 Eliot took this discussion of the emotional precision in poetry further and supplied it with a quasi-historical rationale. In his essay on Marvell, Eliot had referred to an alteration of the 'English mind' at around the time of the Civil War. In 'The Metaphysical Poets' this is worked up into a historical generalization, the theory of the 'dissociation of sensibility' through which the 'mind of England' becomes sundered from its basis in sensation. In the undissociated culture of the early seventeenth century intellect was, as Eliot had written in his essay on Massinger, 'immediately at the tips of the senses'. After Milton, he implied, the absence of that sensuous intellect becomes manifest either in poetry that overvalues ideas or in poetry that fails to keep an adequate check on its emotions. This argument posits an ideal towards which a modern poet may aspire, but also a historical reason why such aspiration, under present conditions, will necessarily fail. It takes the emphasis of poetic creativity away from an unconscious and directly affective response to experience and places it instead in an acquired, conscious, and at least partly intellectual, definition of that immediate response.

The importance of this 'dissociation of sensibility' on Eliot's subsequent criticism is analogous to the realization of original sin in the thought of Hulme, in that both theories remove at a stroke any possibility of verifying authenticity from immediate experience. In accepting what he describes as 'the sane classical dogma of original sin', Hulme assumes the imperfectibility of human action, and the futility of seeking truth in individual inspiration. Rather, the assumption of man's fallibility and limitation requires that he is governed by external sanction, by tradition and by authority: 'A man is essentially bad, he can only accomplish anything of value by discipline—ethical and political. Order is thus not merely negative, but creative and liberating. Institutions are necessary.'[84] While Eliot's is not an original sin but an acquired deficiency, the conclusion of his dissociation argument is similar. As man has lost, perhaps irredeemably, the power to integrate thought and sensibility, he cannot spontaneously fuse the two in poetry. Unable to inherit the complete emotional framework of Dante, he must instead work consciously to school his sensibility, and make it submit to the external authority of tradition and precedent.

---

[84] 'Humanism and the Religious Attitude', in Hulme, *Speculations: Essays on Humanism and the Philosophy of Art*, ed. Herbert Read (London, 1924), 47.

The idea of a kind of post-lapsarian dissociated sensibility, then, like the doctrine of original sin, is the first requirement of what will come to be identified as classicism. Announcing the dethronement of an authority derived from within, it demands in its stead the imposition of an external authority, derived from literary tradition on the one hand and, increasingly, religion on the other.

THE *CRITERION* AND THE *ADELPHI*

Eliot's movement towards classicism would finally become marked in his editorship of the *Criterion*, whose first issue was published in October 1922. It is worth noting that in its early stages the *Criterion* espoused no specific tendency other than a broad eclecticism. Eliot had informed Ezra Pound that he had decided against a manifesto in the first issue, preferring to 'adopt a protective colour for a time, until suspicion is lulled'; to which he added waggishly, 'what do you think of "The Possum" for a title?'[85] Obliged by the conditions of his employment at Lloyds to disguise his editorial function on the periodical, Eliot refrained from editorial commentary and confined himself initially to occasional reviewing.

Although an explicit statement of intent was absent, Eliot's guiding presence can be discerned in the journal's cosmopolitan catholicism: early issues contrasting George Saintsbury and Charles Whibley with Valery Larbaud on Joyce, Julien Benda's 'A Preface', S. S. Koteliansky's translations from Dostoevsky, surveys of foreign periodicals, as well as work by Pirandello, Virginia Woolf, May Sinclair, and the first publication of *The Waste Land*. These issues also carried two essays that might be considered as supports to Eliot's arguments in 'The Metaphysical Poets'. The first was Pound's 'On Criticism in General', which talked in terms of a lineage of European literature from Homer to Dante, broken at the Renaissance. The second, 'The Nature of Metaphysical Poetry', written by Herbert Read with Eliot's assistance, developed and made more explicit some of the implications of Eliot's essay on the Metaphysicals. In particular it emphasized the relative importance of intelligence over the emotions:

it is important beyond everything, in this era of emotional or 'common-sense' philosophies, not to confuse this mental process in which emotion is

[85] To Ezra Pound, 19 July 1922, *Letters*, 548.

the product of thought, with that other vaguer, easier process, which is the emotionalisation of thought, or thought as the product of emotion. Metaphysical poetry is determined logically: its emotion is a joy that comes with the triumph of the reason, and is not a simple instinctive ecstasy.[86]

Such articles in the *Criterion*'s first three issues indicated a tendency, but they still fell short of offering a specific direction. This is not the case with Murry's editorship of the *Adelphi* which was begun in June 1923, some eight months after the inaugural issue of the *Criterion*.

Very much in contrast to the *Criterion*'s editorial reticence, Murry established his periodical with an advertising campaign and an editorial manifesto—attempting in his first editorial to 'justify THE ADELPHI, to write boldly, to unfurl and wave a flag'.[87] What Murry was so eager to impart to the world was a new-found 'belief in life'. This belief, and the zeal with which it was proclaimed, owed much to recent events in Murry's life—especially the events that had surrounded the death of his wife Katherine Mansfield in January 1923. Shortly after her death, Murry had retreated in solitude to a cottage in the forest of Twyford in Sussex where, near to breakdown, he had undergone a mystical experience. This event seemed to confirm Murry in his personal and literary beliefs that extra-human values could be divined in extreme states of individual self-exploration, although it is worth noting how closely this mystical experience, as it was related subsequently by Murry, had been anticipated by descriptions of earlier epiphanies in his work on Dostoevsky in 1916.[88] Though this experience might, in retrospect, be seen to have grown from Murry's existing preoccupations, he interpreted it as a galvanizing new turn. The mystical experience, he later wrote, 'was actual and decisive for me. It impelled me into a course of action which in a sense I still follow; it set my mind upon a chain of thinking which I have never relinquished; it restored me to life of the kind I value; and,

[86] 'The Nature of Metaphysical Poetry', *Criterion*, 1/3 (Apr. 1923), 246–66 (p. 264). Ronald Schuchard has noted Eliot's contribution to the essay in making 'numerous queries and suggestions' on Read's initial two-page draft. *The Varieties of Metaphysical Poetry* (London, 1993), 18.

[87] 'The Cause of It All', *Adelphi*, 1/1 (June 1923), 1–11 (p. 4). For an example of Murry's advance advertising see *TLS* 1115 (31 May 1923), 375. There is also evidence that similarly phrased advertising hand-bills were distributed, though none seem to have survived. See Lea, *The Life of John Middleton Murry*, 106–7.

[88] Compare e.g. 'A Month After', *Adelphi*, 1/2 (July 1923), 89–99, and *Fyodor Dostoevsky*, 34–7.

indeed, it has occupied me ever since.'[89] While in Twyford, Murry had read Lawrence's fevered account of the primary pre-mental consciousness, *Fantasia of the Unconscious*. Inspired by his experience and bolstered by Lawrence's book Murry launched into the espousal of 'life' which would characterize the *Adelphi*. His euphoria gave the paper an attractive proselytizing energy but also led it into a characteristically fervid and ultimately damaging rhetoric. Murry himself summed up this strange mixture of enthusiasm and naïvety in 1929:

> suddenly, I had become a man with a mission, full of energy and conviction. Had I lived in another age, I do not doubt that I should have marched off with staff and scrip to spread the gospel in the highways; being set in the twentieth century, I launched a magazine to carry the good tidings. But what the good tidings were, I found it hard to say. I proclaimed 'a faith in life'. Various people helped me in the magazine. For some strange reason I took it for granted that substantially their faith was the same as my own, which seems, in retrospect, an incredible assumption. But since I did not know what my own faith really was, it was easy to be satisfied. The combination of their good writing and my own enthusiasm made the magazine an alarming success. I was quite incapable of analysing the causes of this success, and I naively took it as a confirmation of my own fundamental rightness.[90]

Employing the editorial pages of the *Adelphi*, as well as regular articles under the thinly veiled disguise of 'The Journeyman', he began to make his experience the foundation of an unembarrassed radical empiricism that applied its tenets to religion and literature alike. The spiritual egotism of which Katherine Mansfield had always been suspicious in Murry's character was now given full rein.

This unashamed foregrounding of his own experience proved an immense and immediate popular success, especially among Methodist and nonconformist communities in the north. The first issue of the *Adelphi* quickly sold out, and three subsequent reprintings brought its circulation figure up to 15,240—more in one issue than the *Criterion* would sell in its first five years.[91] Needless to say, the literary-critical response was at best ambivalent and at worst actively hostile. The *Times Literary Supplement* described the

---

[89]   *God: Being an Introduction to the Science of Metabiology* (London, 1929), 36.
[90]   Ibid. 41.
[91]   Carswell reckons *Adelphi* sales in its first year at around 100,000 copies. *Lives and Letters*, 199. Eliot wrote that 'the *Criterion* had, in its palmiest days, some 800 subscriptions'. 'A Letter from T. S. Eliot, O. M.', *Catacomb*, NS I/I (Summer 1950), 367–8 (p. 367).

journal as 'interesting and vigorous', but considered that 'it does show here and there the tendency to wilful individualism and whimsies'.[92] Desmond MacCarthy, the *New Statesman*'s 'Affable Hawk', noted presciently that 'it would be the greatest pity if Mr Murry threw away his fine gifts as a literary connoisseur because he thought the role of a moral prophet more vital'.[93]

Eliot's *Criterion*, which had up to this point proceeded without editorial commentary, now decided it was time to issue its first direct address to its readers. Appearing in the month after the *Adelphi*'s launch Eliot's first commentary, subtitled 'The Function of a Literary Review', was clearly intended as a riposte to Murry's magazine, and particularly to its advocacy of what Eliot described as the 'insidious catchword: "life" '.[94] It is perhaps characteristic of Eliot that the *Criterion*'s first editorial is less a statement of the journal's principles than a critique of the vitiating qualities of a competitor. As in many later instances, Murry's populism and somewhat glib spirituality brought out a strain of priggishness in Eliot: in a transparent indictment of Murry, he wrote that those 'who affirm an antinomy between "literature", meaning any literature which can appeal only to a small and fastidious public, and "life", are not only flattering the complacency of the half-educated, but asserting a principle of disorder'. Yet in spite of his assumption of the critical high ground, Eliot's attempts at formulating his own paper's critical position were at least as vague as Murry's. Eliot talked of espousing principles that had consequences in politics and morals as well as in literature, but stressed the need not to confuse purely literary values with the ethical and the political.

Eliot and Murry had certainly not set out to antagonize one another. Eliot had stressed in a letter to Richard Aldington that the *Criterion* should not be seen to be being used as a weapon against Murry.[95] He had even written to Murry himself to say he hoped that Murry would be in sympathy with the paper's aims and had included Murry's name on the advertised list of the *Criterion*'s contributors.[96] But after the launch of the *Adelphi* any residue of a mutual sympathy was dissolved as it quickly became apparent that the two men were headed on separate courses. Murry's adoption of an extreme

[92] 'Periodicals', *TLS* 1116 (7 June 1923), 390.
[93] 'Books in General', *New Statesman*, 21/530 (9 June 1923), 270.
[94] 'The Function of a Literary Review', *Criterion*, 1/4 (July 1923), 421.
[95] 30 June 1922, *Letters*, 537.   [96] 13 Oct. 1922, *Letters*, 581.

individualist position, and his attempt to subsume the study of literature into a broader, religiously informed 'criticism of life' was enough to make Eliot drop his earlier reticence and engage in the polemic in which his, and the *Criterion*'s, principles would become articulated. This conflict, begun with such vague definitions, quickly alighted on new terms within which its protagonists might frame their opposition—classicism and romanticism.

ROMANTICISM AND CLASSICISM

When A. R. Orage looked forward in 1914 to 'a classical revival after the war and to the return of the spirit of the masculine eighteenth century' he expressed a hope that would arise frequently in the immediate post-war years.[97] This was one response to reconstruction, discussed above, in which the ordered values of the past were seen as a solid basis upon which new beliefs might be built. A problem with this, however, was how best to define this authoritative and authorizing word. As it stood, the 'classical' retained so many connotations: from ancient Greece, through scholasticism, to the eighteenth century, that its denotation of order and principle had become rather diluted. Gourmont had poured scorn on complementary notions of romanticism and classicism in *Le Problème du style*, considering absurd the attempts to reduce the diversity of individual works to these abstract schemata. He mistrusted classical imitation so far that he believed it to be largely responsible for periods of literary decadence, and that 'classical prejudices are an obstacle to the development of literary history'.[98] Classical writing, he argued, had as much relevance to the modern writer as the vernacular *Chanson de Roland* or even the literature of alien traditions, such as the Zoroastrian Zend-Avesta.[99] Like Gourmont, Pater had shown a disinclination to differentiate between romantic and classical ideas. Discussing the terms in a postscript to his collection *Appreciations*

---

[97] 'Readers and Writers', *New Age*, 15/17 (27 Aug. 1914), 397.

[98] 'Stephan Mallarmé and the Idea of Decadence' (1898), in *Remy de Gourmont: Selected Writings*, trans. and ed. Glenn S. Burne (Ann Arbor, Mich., 1966), 67–76 (p. 74).

[99] See 'La Comparaison et la métaphore: *L'Illiade, Roland, les Védas*, Chateaubriand, Flaubert', in *Problème du style*, 83–107. Gourmont's attitude on this point is described by Murry in ' "Arts-man, Praembula!" ', *Nation and Athenaeum*, 29/17 (23 July 1921), 618–19 (p. 619).

(1889), he had emphasized the resolution of such antinomies in the aesthetic 'House Beautiful', a phrase borrowed from Oscar Wilde, and as such took pains to note both the classical influences on romanticism and the romantic impulse of classical works. 'For an analyst of the romantic principle in art', he wrote, 'no exercise would be more profitable, than to walk through the collection of classical antiquities at the Louvre, or the British Museum, or to examine some representative collection of Greek coins.'[100] For Arthur Symons 'that old antithesis of the classic, the romantic' had, by 1893, become otiose,[101] and some twenty years later Arthur Quiller-Couch was finding similar difficulty in distinguishing between the two apparently dichotomous terms, speaking of their mutual difference as 'notional and vague'. With typical robustness, Quiller-Couch opined that 'the whole pother about their difference amounts to nothing that need trouble a healthy man', and advised that 'it may help our minds to earn an honest living if we dismiss the terms "classical" and "romantic" out of our vocabulary for a while'.[102]

While English critics were prepared to suspend a definition of the two terms, or at least to deny their mutual exclusivity, literary movements in France had for some time been using definitions of romanticism and, particularly, classicism as points of alignment along which their literary debates were oriented. The notion of a classical revival had had currency in France since before the war, having exploded into life with Pierre Lasserre's *Le Romantisme français* (1907). The anti-romantic movement was given a sympathetic hearing in the pages of the *Revue critique des idées et des livres*, *Les Marges*, and in Jacques Rivière's *Nouvelle Revue française*, but was embodied in its most militant aspects in the proto-fascist Action Française movement led by Charles Maurras: a group that had not only an ideological function, but a strong-arm political force in its organized gangs of *camelots du roi*. In a direct contrast to the liberalism of journals such as the *Mercure de France*, jointly founded by Remy de Gourmont, the journals of the neoclassical reaction embodied a militant traditionalism that professed adherence to the triple authority of king, country, and religion. This French classical revival had received sporadic

---

[100] 'Postscript', in Pater, *Appreciations*, 241–61 (p. 259).
[101] Symons, quoted in Holbrook Jackson, *The Eighteen Nineties: A Review of Art and Ideas at the Close of the Nineteenth Century* (1913; repr. London, 1988), 65.
[102] 'On the Terms Classical and Romantic', in *Studies in Literature*, 76–95 (pp. 76, 94, 95).

coverage in the British literary press, partly through the work of Pound and Aldington in the *Egoist* but mainly through Murry in his capacity as French reviewer for the *Times Literary Supplement*. Eliot had made the French classical revival the subject of his extension lectures at Oxford University in 1916: examining the three components of the classical position in politics, religion, and literature in their mutual reaction against the decadent romanticism of Rousseau.[103]

Although the French classical revival was noted in Britain, there was obviously no British counterpart to it. In a review of Maurras's ideas in the *Times Literary Supplement* in September 1920 Basil de Selincourt suggested a number of reasons why this was the case, prime among them being that the 'English mind, with its traditional experience of order as the fruit of character and independence', was temperamentally antipathetic to the ascetic discipline and order of continental classicism. Not only was French-style classicism alien to the romantic tradition of English culture, de Selincourt asserted, but once problems in nomenclature were resolved it turned out that the 'period of classical production in France was . . . a great romantic period'.[104]

Eliot's response to this argument, in the form of a letter to the *Times Literary Supplement*, shows his attitude to the classical revival in 1920. In spite of his continuing adherence to the *Nouvelle Revue française* (he had met several of its leading figures some ten years before and maintained a subscription to the paper),[105] and in spite of his vituperations against romanticism in his extension lectures and in the *Athenaeum* and *The Sacred Wood*, he chose neither to attack this conception of English romanticism nor to defend a classical position. Instead, he noted the failure of an adequate definition of the terms, and argued that, unless they be used 'merely as convenient historical tags' (as Quiller-Couch had suggested), they would be best forgotten.[106]

Murry's relationship with classicism, and with a classical revival, was as ambivalent as Eliot's, having undergone a number of

---

[103] The syllabus of Eliot's six lectures is reprinted in facsimile in A. D. Moody's *Thomas Stearns Eliot: Poet* (Cambridge, 1979), 41–9. It is also reprinted, along with the prospectuses of his other extension lectures, by Ronald Schuchard in 'T. S. Eliot as Extension Lecturer, 1916–1919', *Review of English Studies*, NS 25/98 (May 1974), 163–73; NS 25/99 (Aug. 1974), 292–304.

[104] [Basil de Selincourt], 'A French Romantic', *TLS* 976 (30 Sept. 1920), 625–6 (pp. 625, 626).

[105] Herbert Howarth, *Notes on Some Figures Behind T. S. Eliot* (London, 1965), 175.

[106] 'A French Romantic', *TLS* 980 (20 Oct. 1920), 703.

alterations during the previous ten years. Before the war he had welcomed the French classical renaissance, arguing that 'the time has come for a classical revival after the anarchy and cosmopolitanism of recent years'. But for Murry this classicism was a corrective rather than a replacement for a century and a half of romanticism: 'Romanticism is in the French blood now as it is in ours. A classical revival means putting things in their place.'[107] Murry had initially been enthusiastic towards Maurras, whom he described in 1914 as 'the most brilliant critic of pure letters in France since Sainte-Beuve', but quickly became disillusioned with his political extremism.[108] By the early 1920s Murry apparently shared Eliot's disinclination to draw a distinction between romanticism and classicism. He took exception, for example, to Lascelles Abercrombie's attempts to distinguish between the terms in *An Essay Towards a Theory of Art*, and wrote in the notebook in which he had prepared some definitions for *The Problem of Style* that 'no-one knows what either of these terms mean'.[109] In a note published in that book Murry again chose to commit himself neither to a definition of the terms nor to an expression of preference for one term over the other, referring the reader instead to Irving Babbitt's *The New Laokoon* and *Rousseau and Romanticism* where, as he put it, 'the essence of the matter is admirably expounded from a classical point of view'.[110]

In fact, Babbitt's classicism was not without its own complexities. Although he had given qualified support to the French anti-romantic revival in the conclusion to his *The Masters of Modern French Criticism*, he was less inclined to show favour towards modern classical movements; especially the neoclassicism of the Action Française. In particular, he was suspicious that this neoclassicism was retrogressive in tendency, and as such contradicted the progressive classical humanism of Aristotle and Goethe. 'Though drawing vital nutrient from tradition', he warned, the modern reaction to naturalism 'must not dream of an impossible return to the past. It must not, in short, be reactionary in the French sense.'[111] For Babbitt, classicism and

---

[107] 'French Books: A Classical Revival', *Blue Review*, I/II (June 1913), 134–8 (p. 138).

[108] 'A Young French Critic', *TLS* 642 (7 May 1914), 218. For a more sceptical assessment of Maurras, see Murry's 'The Politics of M. Maurras', *TLS* 781 (4 Jan. 1917), 2, and 'The Lovers of Venice', *TLS* 820 (4 Oct. 1917), 473.

[109] 'What is Art?', *Nation and Athenaeum*, 31/21 (19 Aug. 1922), 684–5; untitled manuscript notebook, Edinburgh, [p. 8].

[110] *Problem of Style*, 146.

[111] *The Masters of Modern French Criticism* (London, 1913), 381.

romanticism in their modern forms were merely the dissociated rem-
nants of Aristotelian humanism: the vitiated products of a false
dichotomy between reason and imagination effected by the Renaissance.[112] As such, classical Greek art exhibited a synthesis of the
elements that had since degraded into romanticism and classicism,
transcending this false dichotomy by showing 'that man may combine an exquisite measure with a perfect spontaneity, that he may be
at once thoroughly disciplined and thoroughly inspired'.[113]

The concepts of romanticism and classicism, then, were markedly
fluid and imprecise by the early 1920s: Babbitt had suggested in *The
New Laokoon* that 'a more searching definition of these words seems
urgently needed'.[114] Under these circumstances it should not be too
much of a surprise to find Eliot being beguiled for a time by the
'romanticism' of Bergson and Gourmont, or Murry espousing Babbitt's classical humanism or employing the word 'romantic' as a
pejorative, criticizing, for example, the 'romanticism' of Sainte-
Beuve, or another writer's inspirational 'romantic conception of
poetry'.[115] As Eliot chose not to embrace 'classicism', Murry refused
to be aligned with a putative 'romanticism': the *Adelphi* was dedicated only to 'life'. T. E. Hulme had written before the war that the
best way of attempting a definition of the terms romanticism and
classicism 'would be to start with a set of people who are prepared to
fight about it'.[116] At first Eliot and Murry were not even inclined to do
this, preferring to use other terms when asked to define their critical
tendencies. But with the launch of the *Adelphi* they found themselves
occupying opposite sides of a romantic *v.* classical argument, and, as
Hulme had anticipated, the terms would come to be defined polemic-
ally, through debate.

The catalyst for this debate was a review of the *Adelphi* in the *New
Statesman* of 21 July 1923, written by Raymond Mortimer, in which

---

[112] See 'The Terms Classical and Romantic', in Babbitt's *Rousseau and Romanticism*,
1–31.
[113] *The New Laokoon: An Essay on the Confusion of the Arts* (London, 1910), 251–2.
[114] Ibid., pp. x–xi.
[115] Murry, 'Sainte-Beuve the Romantic', *Nation and Athenaeum*, 30/14 (31 Dec. 1921),
532–4; 'The Poetic Mind', *Nation and Athenaeum*, 31/24 (9 Sept. 1922), 768–70 (p. 769).
Murry also attacked what he described as the 'sentimental romanticism' of Compton
McKenzie's *Sinister Street*, and criticized Joyce's *Ulysses* as 'the last extravagance of
romanticism'. 'The Future of English Fiction', *Nation and Athenaeum*, 31/1 (1 Apr. 1922),
24–5 (p. 25); 'The Break-up of the Novel', *Yale Review*, (Jan. 1923), repr. in *Discoveries:
Essays in Literary Criticism* (London, 1924), 129–52 (p. 147).
[116] 'Romanticism and Classicism', in Hulme, *Speculations*, 114.

it was claimed that Murry's commitment to 'life' was symptomatic of a romantic decadence and that the *Adelphi* represented a 'last stand' of romanticism.[117] Murry was disinclined to accept the assumptions in Mortimer's argument and at first refused to jump to the defence of romanticism: 'I do not think the opposed forces are Romantic and Classic', he wrote, 'and in any case, I do not see that it is my business to commence hostilities'.[118] His reply to Mortimer, in the essay 'On Fear; And on Romanticism', however, developed into a sustained argument for the centrality of romantic traits in the English character. In an argument reminiscent of de Selincourt's article in the *Times Literary Supplement*, Murry suggested that no antithesis, and hence no confrontation, was possible because classicism, properly understood, cannot exist in English culture. Classicism is superfluous and alien to English literature, he argued, because literature, like the English culture from which it derives, recognizes only precedent and does not submit itself to external authority:

The *decorum* the great English writers naturally observe is one that they fetch out of the depths in themselves. It is not imposed by tradition or authority. There is a tradition in English life and English literature, of course, but it is not on the surface; it is not formulated or formulable, any more than the tradition of English politics is formulated or formulable. It is something you have to sense by intuition, if you are to know it at all. The English writer, the English divine, the English statesman, inherit no rules from their forbears: they inherit only this: a sense that in the last resort they must depend upon the inner voice. If they dig deep enough in their pursuit of self-knowledge—a piece of mining done not with the intellect alone, but with the whole man—they will come upon a self that is universal: in religious terms, the English tradition is that the man who truly interrogates himself will ultimately hear the voice of God, in terms of literary criticism, that the writer achieves impersonality through personality . . . romanticism, as I have tried to describe it, is itself the English tradition. It is national, and it is the secret source of our own peculiar vitality. In England it is the classicist who is the interloper and the alien.[119]

This passionate defence of English liberalism is made particularly telling in its appropriation of the patriotic rhetoric of wartime. This was the rhetoric of an English voluntarism pluckily resisting the blind force of the continental enemy's monstrous and dehumanizing

---

[117] 'New Novels', *New Statesman*, 21/536 (21 July 1923), 448–50 (p. 448).
[118] 'On Fear; And on Romanticism', *Adelphi*, 1/4 (Sept. 1923), 269–77 (p. 273).
[119] Ibid. 274–5.

organization: the rhetoric that had prompted Sir Walter Raleigh to write that 'instead of subduing men to a single pattern', English institutions 'are devised chiefly with the object of saving the rights of the subject and the liberty of the individual' and E. A. Benians to note in his *The British Empire and the War* (1915) that the English 'live by instinct, and advance by experience and their policy seems from hand to mouth, but it is an expression of national character, and is thus a continuous tradition'.[120] At a time when those political traditions seemed themselves to be subject to some threat—with the rise of the Labour Party, a divided Liberal Party in terminal decline, and three general elections between 1922 and 1924—Murry's restatement of an authoritative, self-validating individualism as the foundation of traditional national characteristics is an audacious reconstructive move, with the force of its argument benefiting, like Raleigh's rhetoric, from its place in an increasingly polarized conflict. This new construction of romanticism, espoused at first only hesitantly, would allow Murry to gather his various critical preoccupations (and, perhaps, political anxieties) under one banner, giving his previously dispersed comments on the value of personality, inspiration, and morality in literature the coherence of an apparently unified critical approach. What Eliot had found with 'tradition' in 'Tradition and the Individual Talent' Murry now discovered in 'romanticism': a word that resonated with authority yet was flexible enough to be fitted to the contours of a very personal critical project.[121]

This attempt to forestall an English classicism by identifying an inherent English romantic tradition appeared in the same month as a stinging attack by Murry on the arid intellectualism of *The Waste Land*.[122] The combined effect of the articles prompted Eliot to a swift and wide-ranging reply, 'The Function of Criticism', which was published in the following month and was manifestly an attempt to wrest the mantle of tradition back from Murry's individualism. 'The Function of Criticism' is a key essay in Eliot's *œuvre* for its unprecedentedly clear formulation of the relationship between creativity and

[120] Sir Walter Raleigh, *The War of Ideas* (Oxford, 1917), 13; E. A. Benians, quoted in Wallace, *War and the Image of Germany*, 73.
[121] Murry described the strategic importance of taking up such a position, and also its arbitrary nature, in 'On Fear; And on Romanticism', 274.
[122] 'Son dernier poème *The Waste Land* renferme l'obscure—et quelques-uns disent inintelligible—tragédie de la flétrissure de la force vitale sous la tyrannie de l'intelligence.' 'Angleterre: La Situation politique, la situation morale', *Revue de Genève*, 39 (Sept. 1923), 328–38 (p. 337).

criticism. Eliot's argument, that art is as much a critical as a creative process, resulting from an artist's stringent auto-critique, clears up many of the loose ends left dangling by 'The Perfect Critic' and is a judicious rebuke to some of Murry's less restrained formulations of critical creativity. Equally important is Eliot's response to Murry's evocation of the 'inner voice'. Where Murry had espoused a romanticism that sanctified the workings of this inner voice, Eliot here emphasized the need for what he described as 'Outside Authority' and acquiesced in the description of this as 'classicism'. This was Eliot's first public avowal of classicism and he acknowledged, with some irony, an 'increasing debt of gratitude' to Murry for forcing him into it: Murry had shown him 'that there are at least two attitudes toward literature and toward everything, and that you cannot hold both'. Manœuvred into making what amounted to a manifesto for his new classicism Eliot provided an essay which marked a major shift away from an emphasis on the free, disinterested intelligence of an Aristotle or Gourmont delineated in 'The Perfect Critic', towards an espousal of the Hulmeian belief 'that men cannot get on without giving allegiance to something outside themselves'.[123] The classicist position as it is defined here becomes closely identified with a specifically intellectual formulation of critical practice—the good critic being valued not so much for his sensibility as for the development of what Eliot now isolates as 'his sense of fact'.

F. R. Leavis would describe *Homage to John Dryden* as a continuation of the 'fine intelligence' exhibited in *The Sacred Wood*.[124] Analogously 'The Function of Criticism' seems, superficially, to develop the argument of 'The Perfect Critic', especially with regard to the relationship between criticism and creation. But, viewed closely, the intellectual component of criticism put forward in 'The Function of Criticism' is very different to the notion of intelligence advanced in the earlier work. In 'The Perfect Critic' the intelligence of Aristotle and Gourmont referred, not so much to a 'sense of fact' as to a heightened perception—the perception defined by Aristotle (and promoted by Babbitt) that encompasses both knowledge and feeling. Such an intelligence, Eliot had argued, assumes 'the gift of a superior sensibility' and creates a criticism built upon a perceptive scaffold

[123] 'The Function of Criticism', *Criterion*, 2/5 (Oct. 1923), 31–42 (p. 34).
[124] 'T. S. Eliot as Critic', in Leavis, *Anna Karenina and Other Essays* (London, 1967), 176–96 (p. 178).

that is itself 'a development of sensibility'.[125] This critical quality of perception, constitutive of intelligence, in which knowledge and feeling combine is reduced in the later essay merely to a 'sphere of fact, of knowledge, of control', which reduces 'to a state of fact all the feelings' that readers of Victorian poetry (typified by the Browning Study Circle), 'can only enjoy in the most nebulous form'.[126] In 'The Perfect Critic' Eliot had espoused Gourmont's desire to erect personal impressions into critical laws; here he posits a critic who, like the great artist, owes an allegiance, a devotion even, to 'something outside' himself 'to which he must surrender and sacrifice himself in order to earn and to obtain his unique position'.

Eliot's essay is a model of clarity and critical self-consistency, but it would appear to have achieved these qualities by drastically reducing the scope of legitimate critical enquiry. In forming an articulable classical position Eliot is forced to exclude problematic aesthetic questions that, precisely because they come under the province of aesthetics and not logic, do not lend themselves easily to rational analysis. In spite of the portentous claim that criticism is 'the common pursuit of true judgement' he is actually hesitant to allow the critic a hermeneutic function, and consigns him instead to a factual, elucidatory, non-interpretative role which entails him in the endless deferral of evaluation. Eliot had insisted on a similar deferring, elucidatory criticism in 'The Perfect Critic', but there had allowed the critic a Gourmontian structured sensibility from which he might make generalized statements. In the later essay this function is denied the critic, whose expertise is confined to a comparison and analysis of the facts compounded in a text and the techniques by which they are articulated: '*fact* cannot corrupt taste', Eliot wrote, 'the real corrupters are those who supply opinion or fancy'. In addition to this, Eliot's persistence in arguing for the crucial importance of an alert self-criticism in the creative act, while valuable in debunking the popular myth of the inspirational artist, seems somewhat overplayed in the light of our subsequent knowledge of Ezra Pound's part in the creation of *The Waste Land*. While it accords with Eliot's generous tribute to Pound as the better craftsman, Pound's role as the critical editor of Eliot's diffused creativity takes some of the force from Eliot's argument about the self-criticizing author.

---

[125] 'The Perfect Critic', in *The Sacred Wood*, 11, 14, 15.
[126] 'Function of Criticism', 40.

As an interesting footnote to this argument, Eliot would revise many of the opinions of this essay some thirty years later when the heat generated by his dialogue with Murry had long dissipated. Addressing an American audience in 1956, and returning to the circumstances under which 'The Function of Criticism' had been written, Eliot professed his inability to recall 'a single book or essay, or the name of a single critic, as representative of the kind of impressionistic criticism which aroused my ire thirty-three years ago'. Thus freed from the engagement in polemic, he put forward a prescription of the critical activity much less limited than his own earlier formulation and much more like that suggested by Gourmont and Murry, going as far as to employ the argument of relevance to 'life' which he had found so distasteful in Murry. The literary critic was now described as 'the whole man, a man with convictions and principles, and of knowledge and experience of life'.[127]

MURRY'S ROMANTIC HISTORIOGRAPHY

In 'The Function of Criticism' Eliot, perhaps recalling Bradley's attacks on Arnold, satirized Murry's individualism by describing his notion of an inner voice as like the old principle of 'doing as one likes'. Murry's reaction to this criticism was a more carefully considered, less intemperate definition of romanticism that attempted to answer Eliot by giving this romanticism the legitimacy of its own history. His response took the form of an essay entitled 'More About Romanticism', published in the *Adelphi* in December 1923, some two months after the appearance of 'The Function of Criticism'.

Murry began the essay by restating his earlier assertions: that he himself is a romantic; that romanticism obeys an inner voice while classicism obeys an external spiritual authority; and that the tradition of English literature and spiritual life is romantic. These facts, he argued, can be integrated into an organic whole, mapped out, like Eliot's dissociation of sensibility, on to an interpretation of history: 'the history of the human soul is the story of romanticisms organized into classicisms, and classicisms rebelled against and defeated by romanticisms'.[128] This attempt to use classicism and romanticism as

---

[127] *The Frontiers of Criticism* (Minneapolis, Minn., 1956), in *On Poetry and Poets*, 103–18 (pp. 103, 116).
[128] 'More About Romanticism', *Adelphi*, 1/7 (Dec. 1923), 557–69 (p. 559).

descriptive terms for a pendulum-like dynamic of history was not unique to Murry: J. M. Kennedy had written before the war of recurrent cycles of classical health and romantic decadence, and, contemporaneous with Murry, Herbert Grierson was describing the two terms as 'the systole and diastole of the human heart in history'.[129]

Eliot had recognized the value of appropriating the past, particularly in 'Tradition and the Individual Talent' and in the revisionary literary historiography of 'The Metaphysical Poets': it was now Murry's turn to adopt a similar strategy.[130] Like Eliot's history, the one outlined by Murry in 'More About Romanticism' has its roots in the Renaissance and its ramifications in that movement's English outgrowths. As with Eliot's dissociation theory, its arguments would form the basis for much of what its author would say later on the subject of artistic creation and critical receptivity. In the short term it represented the first coherent description of the pseudo-historical project, the 'history of the human soul', that would inform and underlie what is perhaps Murry's best-known work, *Keats and Shakespeare*.[131]

The Renaissance described by Murry, in 'More About Romanticism', is the paradigmatic romantic act. It is the rejection of external spiritual authority in favour of the individual's 'right to stand or fall by his own experience, to explore the universe for himself'.[132] Murry describes the immediate result of this radical individuation as the paradoxical realization of the gulf between the external realm of

---

[129]   J. M. Kennedy, 'Charles Lamb', *New Age*, NS 4/11 (7 Jan. 1909), 225–7 (p. 226); Herbert J. C. Grierson, 'Classical and Romantic' (1923), in *The Background of English Literature and other Essays* (Harmondsworth, 1962), 221–49 (p. 246). Wolfgang Iser has pointed to Pater's use of a similar argument. According to Iser, Pater transmutes the normative concepts of romanticism and classicism into historical ones in an attempt to ground his aesthetic in an apparently objective dialectical history: Iser writes that 'the successive movements of Classicism and Romanticism are the form in which the historicity of art embodies itself'. *Walter Pater: The Aesthetic Moment*, trans. David Henry Wilson (Cambridge, 1987), 66–9 (p. 68).

[130]   For discussion of Eliot's polemical use of history, see Lobb, *T. S. Eliot and the Romantic Critical Tradition*, 11–59; Gray, *T. S. Eliot's Intellectual and Poetic Development*, 95–102; Grania Jones, 'Eliot and History', *Critical Quarterly*, 18/3 (Autumn 1976), 31–48; Alan Weinblatt, 'T. S. Eliot and the Historical Sense', *South Atlantic Quarterly*, 77/3 (Summer 1978), 282–95. See also the comparisons between Eliot's sense of history and that of his contemporary Walter Benjamin in Kramer, 'T. S. Eliot's Concept of Tradition:', 22–4, and Erik Svarny, *'The Men of 1914': T. S. Eliot and Early Modernism* (Milton Keynes, 1988), 161–4.

[131]   *Keats and Shakespeare: A Study of Keats' Poetic Life from 1816 to 1820* (London, 1925), 1.

[132]   'More About Romanticism', 559.

necessity and the internal world of freedom—with their sheer incommensurability rendering them mutually impenetrable. His description of the romantic approach to this paradox reveals a qualification of his earlier prescriptions of romanticism written soon after his own mystical experience. In those essays Murry had implied that the individual gained a kind of ontological confirmation from the numinous perceptions of mystical experience, perceptions that might be seen to endorse his subjectivism and his right to remodel the world in his own image. However, in this essay he describes such a belief as 'Primary romanticism', that is, a naïve attempt to render the external world of necessity entirely in the terms of the internal world of freedom. The 'Primary Romantic'

retires defiantly into the fortress of his ego, and proclaims that the world wherein his felt sovereignty and freedom no longer hold is a world of illusion. He solves the mystery of the cosmos by an appeal to his immediate experience, and unites by proclamation the kingdom of necessity to his own kingdom of freedom.[133]

This closely resembles the romanticism that Eliot had singled out as the pernicious component in the thought of George Wyndham: the romanticism that is 'a short cut to the strangeness without the reality', that does not penetrate the real world so much as project onto it the world Wyndham had made for himself.[134] Murry's redefinition of his position, and his resulting creation of a *primary* romanticism, allows him to join Eliot in a condemnation of this egotism posing as romanticism. He now describes it as 'dangerous, one-sided and untrue to dismiss the external world as a world of illusion'.[135]

Effectively superseding Eliot's criticism, Murry then goes on to propose a sophisticated 'Secondary Romanticism' that denies absolute truth to mystical perception, but which still recognizes its reality. The moment of mystical perception becomes, instead of divine revelation, an intuitive apprehension of the imperfection of human knowledge. The 'Secondary Romantic' regards these moments of mystical perception as

indications, prophetic monitions, of some as yet undeveloped faculty of apprehension in the human mind, and of some underlying reality with which, lacking that faculty, the human mind cannot establish contact. Thus

---

[133] 'More About Romanticism', 561.
[134] 'A Romantic Aristocrat', in *The Sacred Wood*, 31–2.
[135] 'More About Romanticism', 561.

he comes to regard the fundamental paradox not as an insoluble contradiction in the nature of reality, but as a congenital limitation of human vision.[136]

It is important to note that this takes the emphasis firmly away from the retrogression implicit within the idea of a lapsed tradition. Instead it posits a process of 'becoming' that resembles Bergson's notion of a creative evolution more than it does the return to a central and unchanging truth. It is possible to see in this revision of history, with its attendant rejection of a stable, authoritative centre, the basis for Murry's future political and social orientation. Just as Eliot builds a theory, and then a politics, that is predicated on a historiographical myth of the dissociated sensibility, Murry underwrites the intuitive individualism of his literary, and later political, position with a symbolic post-Reformation romantic history.

Just how symbolic and non-specific these histories are, and how much they are rooted in the individual psychology of their authors, can be seen in the contrasting emphases of their defining characteristics. For Eliot the dissociation of sensibility was an event which occurred in the '*mind* of England' between the seventeenth and nineteenth centuries; for Murry 'Romanticism was something that happened to the European *soul* after the Renaissance'.[137] The difference of emphasis bears an interesting relationship to the similar contrast in their self-diagnoses after their respective breakdowns in 1922 and 1923. As has been mentioned above, Eliot had complained of an emotional *aboulie* and emphasized that there is 'nothing wrong with my mind'. In contrast, Murry wrote: 'I have given up taking important decisions with my head: only disasters came of that, for the head is a good servant, but a bad master; he steers one into agitations and despairs.'[138] One crucial difference between the two histories, apart from this difference, lies in the contrasting natures of their dissociation theories. For while both recognize a dissociation reaching from the past into the present, only Eliot posits a prior undissociated state. Murry's Reformation, aided by his definition of a dynamic secondary romanticism, is described not as the dissociation of a previously integrated age, but rather as a romantic revolution against the

---

[136] 'More About Romanticism', 562.
[137] Eliot, 'The Metaphysical Poets', in *Selected Essays*, 287 (emphasis added); Murry, 'Romanticism and the Tradition', 281 (emphasis added).
[138] 'On Waiting', *Adelphi*, 1/5 (Oct. 1923), 361–7 (p. 365).

sterile classicism of the medieval Catholic Church. That Church, as Murry makes clear, was far from the embodiment of a golden age.[139]

This refusal to posit an undissociated golden age in which religious philosophy, literature, and language achieve an organic interrelation leaves Murry free to emphasize the dynamic aspect of his history—and marks incidentally a return to the ideas of Bergson. By arguing that art is working towards 'a change in the very nature of consciousness' heralded by moments of intense mystical perception, Murry posits a process of continuous becoming that has no need of the kind of tradition advanced by the classicists: for if there has never been a golden age there is no authoritative past, lingering vestigially in institutionalized knowledge, to which appeal might be made. Classicism in its post-war form can be seen to be that part of the reconstructive urge that is nostalgically looking for certainty in 'the ancestral attitudes' described by Valéry. Post-war romanticism seems much more to be looking to Valery's 'inward acts', and in its anti-traditionalism asserting Gourmont's belief that 'the more our present differs from our past, the more our life is multiplied'.[140] The difference is that between a system of belief that works deductively, that derives its values from a priori assumptions, and a system that moves by induction from the particular to the universal, creating consensual values from the agglomerations of empirical evidence. Eliot was not yet a fully paid-up member of the former tendency; Murry was showing signs of a committed adherence to the latter.

HULME AND CLASSICISM

Eliot made no direct response to Murry's 'More About Romanticism', though he did arrange to publish Murry's further thoughts on the romantic/classical question in the *Criterion* of April 1924. He also published attacks on Murry from within his own circle: the same issue saw a satirical swipe at Murry's inspirational style from Vivien Eliot and some gibes from Herbert Read about Murry's views on

---

[139] See his attack on the medieval Church and its doctrine of original sin in 'Keats: the Background', *Adelphi*, 2/7 (Dec. 1924), 553–62 (pp. 561–2).

[140] *Epilogues*, 4th series (1913), in Remy de Gourmont, *Selections*, ed. and trans. Richard Aldington (London, 1932), 149.

Flaubert.[141] Eliot, it seemed, was able to keep sniping at Murry without putting his own head above the parapet. But the extent to which the debate was continuing to help define the contours of Eliot's views can be seen in his reaction in the same issue of the *Criterion* to another event; the posthumous publication of T. E. Hulme's *Speculations*, a selection of dispersed writings that had been collected and edited by Herbert Read. It has been argued that Eliot had come under the influence of Hulme as early as 1916, but it was only now, after he had explicitly adopted classicism and with Hulme's criticism coming back into circulation, that he began directly to address Hulmeian ideas and give them his assent.[142] It was suggested above that Murry had played a part in inflecting Eliot's interpretation of Gourmont, and it is possible to see a similar process at work here. Hulme's work seems to offer Eliot a solid buttress against Murry's romanticism, but looked at more closely it can be seen that this could only be the case if Eliot was to read Hulme selectively, ignoring those aspects of his work that offered support to Murry. What Eliot sought in Hulme was the definition of a solid centre, the statement of a set of values that were fixed and authoritative. Hulme, with his calls to order and his derogation of the relativistic 'canons of satisfaction' of post-Renaissance secularism, offered this. But what he also offered was an interpretation of art, deriving from Bergson, that stressed dynamism and novelty: the sense in which the artist is always struggling against tradition to 'break moulds and make new ones'.[143] The attempt to reconcile the kinetic theories of Bergson with a recognition of the need for an authoritative classical dogma was the contentious and unresolved core of Hulme's critical enterprise.[144] This was a difficulty he shared with other classicists, particularly his contemporaries in France, who were attracted to Bergson's ideas but were anxious of the support they appeared to give to the heterodoxies of the Catholic Modernist movement. Some, including Charles Péguy, Joseph Lotte, and Georges Sorel, attempted, like Hulme, to come to an accommodation with Bergsonian ideas;

---

[141] [Vivien Eliot], 'Letters of the Moment II', *Criterion*, 2/7 (Apr. 1924) 360–4; Herbert Read, 'Foreign Reviews', ibid. 365–8.

[142] See Ronald Schuchard, 'Eliot and Hulme in 1916', *PMLA* 88/5 (Oct. 1973), 1083–94. Eliot never met Hulme, but Murry had known him and had taken part in weekly discussion groups with him before the war. See Michael Roberts, *T. E. Hulme* (1938), repr. with an introduction by Anthony Quinton (Manchester, 1982), 22.

[143] Hume, *Speculations*, 150.

[144] See Murry Krieger, 'The Ambiguous Anti-Romanticism of T. E. Hulme', *ELH* 20 (1953), 300–14.

others, including Jacques Maritain, Jacques Rivière, and Henri Massis, moved from an initial receptivity to outright hostility: their criticism of Bergson, from the orthodox Thomist position favoured by the Catholic intellectual establishment, led directly to his works' inclusion on the Holy Office's Index of Prohibited Books in 1914.[145]

The attempt to work out some kind of an accommodation of the demands of both sides of this argument can be seen running throughout *Speculations*. It can be seen, for example, in the essay 'Romanticism and Classicism', where Hulme rejected romanticism out of hand but argued for a new understanding of classicism as a bipartite category, embodying two distinct qualities: the static and the dynamic. This distinction was designed to clarify what Hulme considered to be the common confusion of restraint with classicism and exuberance with romanticism, and it allowed him to reclaim the latter quality for his own brand of Bergsonian classicism. This discrimination gave him a freer hand in the revaluation of the classical canon, allowing him, for example, to appropriate the more traditionally 'romantic' Shakespeare as 'the classic of motion' while according Racine a complementary position as the classic of stasis.[146] By delineating a bipartite classicism he was able to incorporate the Bergsonian emphasis on fluidity and process with the traditional classical concerns of finiteness and fact.

Bergson's epistemological theory, which emphasized a mechanically distorting intellectual knowledge (described as extensive manifolds) requiring a corrective intuitive knowledge (of the so-called intensive manifolds), had deeply influenced Hulme.[147] Bergson had sketched an aesthetic theory from this model in *Le Rire* (1900) in which he had described art as the attempt to lift the veil of the extensive manifold—the mundanity of a thought and language geared only to utilitarian ends—in order to experience the duration which constitutes reality. This duration, or *durée*, is impervious to rational

---

[145] See A. E. Pilkington, *Bergson and his Influence: A Reassessment* (Cambridge, 1976), 228–32. Thomist critiques of Bergson were also produced in England at this time. See e.g. Thomas J. Gerrard, *Bergson: An Exposition and Criticism from the Point of View of St Thomas Aquinas* (London, 1913).

[146] 'Romanticism and Classicism', in *Speculations*, 111–40 (p. 119). Herbert Read, for one, regarded this attempt to define a dynamic classicism as 'a palpable begging of the question'. 'T. E. Hulme', in *A Coat of Many Colours* (London, 1945), 294–9 (p. 296).

[147] See the two chapters, 'The Philosophy of Intensive Manifolds' and 'Bergson's Theory of Art', in Hulme, *Speculations*, 141–214, and 'Notes on Bergson', in *Further Speculations of T. E. Hulme*, ed. Samuel Hynes (Minneapolis, Minn., 1955), 28–63.

thought, which abstracts at the moment it describes. *Durée*, as a quality of time, may not be quantified like other areas of knowledge; it may only be known through acquaintance, and it is the artist's task to be the exemplar of acquaintance with this reality. He must discover that dynamic reality within himself and establish a rhythm that corresponds with it in his own work. Such an action is supremely individualistic—it is the discovery of an individual rhythm, as Bergson puts it, that compels passers-by to join the dance.[148]

Hulme's broad agreement with Bergson's aesthetic theory is evinced in his essay, 'Bergson's Theory of Art'. Hulme ascribes to the artist the dynamic, flexible quality of a tensioned spring, and describes the 'motive power behind any art' as 'a certain freshness of experience which breeds dissatisfaction with the conventional ways of expression because they leave out the individual quality of this freshness'. The quality of art espoused by Hulme is a Bergsonian 'direct communication', which he summarizes as 'its *life-communicating* quality, as rendered by form and movement', the result of a direct rendering of an intuitive, individual experience.[149]

The Hulme that Eliot describes, however, is denied this Bergsonian influence. Eliot considers only the static side of Hulme's classical dualism—that quality that finds beauty in 'small dry things'.[150] In his homage to Hulme, subtitled 'The Work of T. E. Hulme' and 'Hulme and Classicism', Eliot applauds Hulme as 'the antipodes of the eclectic, tolerant, and democratic mind of the last century' and attempts to use his work as an endorsement of a new classical theory of equilibrium. According to this idea, Eliot opines that the 'classical moment in literature is surely a moment of *stasis*, when the creative impulse finds a form which satisfies the best intellect of the time, a moment when a type is produced'.[151] As is already plain, Eliot here misrepresents a very important part of Hulme's theory; he ignores Hulme's dynamic classicism and the intuitive philosophy that underpins it at every step, and concentrates instead on its static, reactionary component. It is worth noting, too, the way that Eliot

---

[148] *Le Rire* (1900), in *Comedy*, ed. Wylie Sypher, rev. edn. (London, 1980), 162. The sentence from which this comes is translated directly, word for word, in Hulme's essay 'Bergson's Theory of Art', in *Speculations*, 141–69 (p. 156). Indeed much of Hulme's essay follows *Le Rire* very closely, suggesting that it might properly be read as notes on Bergson rather than a finished work.

[149] 'Bergson's Theory of Art', in *Speculations*, 162, 168.

[150] 'Romanticism and Classicism', ibid. 131.

[151] 'A Commentary', *Criterion*, 2/7 (Apr. 1924), 231–2.

subjugates the creative talent to the critical mind here: the developed sensibility called for in 'The Perfect Critic' no longer seems to be a criterion of critical judgement; instead it is the 'best intellect of the time' that must be satisfied.

The reason why he might misappropriate Hulme in this way, apart from an already manifest disinclination towards two of Hulme's sources in Bergson and Gourmont, may be seen in his relationship with Murry. This article was written in the midst of his debate with Murry, and appeared in the *Criterion* alongside Murry's latest contribution to that debate, 'Romanticism and the Tradition', in which Murry adumbrates a religious romanticism that bears many resemblances to Bergsonian ideas. Murry had welcomed *Speculations* on its publication, and although there were many incompatibilities between his and Hulme's ideas there was clearly enough in the book for him to regard Hulme as an ally rather than an enemy.[152] Indeed, Murry's romanticism might be seen to bear a direct, if paradoxical, relation to the dynamic classicism that Hulme had derived from Bergson. Having, in 'More About Romanticism', reclassified romanticism into two stages, primary and secondary, in a way reminiscent of Hulme's bipartite classicism, Murry came very close to the views of that part of Hulme that most resembles Bergson—the part that emphasizes the continuum of reality and the individuality of the effort required by the artist to form a creative sympathy with that dynamic.

This re-emergence of a Bergson-like emphasis on movement corresponds with Murry's profession of a romantic creed, and stands in direct opposition to the stasis called for by Eliot. It surfaces in many of Murry's descriptions of the dynamic qualities necessary to literature that appear at this time:

We cannot *know* a work of literature except as a manifestation of the rhythm of the soul of the man who created it.[153]

My words follow some deeply experienced rhythm of my being, and my aim . . . is to set up a corresponding rhythm in the audience.[154]

---

[152]   Murry had reviewed *Speculations* for the *Algemeen Handelsblad* the previous month and placed two short quotations from Hulme on 'The Weakness of Synthesis' and 'Ritual and Sentiment' in the *Adelphi*, 1/11 (Apr. 1924), 982 and 1027. He would review the book the following year, describing Hulme's definition of 'ordinary Romanticism as "spilt religion" ', as 'simply masterly'. 'T. E. Hulme's *Speculations*', *Adelphi*, 2/10 (Mar. 1925), 848–51 (p. 851).

[153]   'Literature and Religion', in *To the Unknown God: Essays Towards a Religion* (London, 1924), 159–92 (p. 166).

[154]   'What is the Tradition?', unpublished typescript (Edinburgh), 10 pp. [p. 7].

By the fragments of kindred experience we may have, by a complete submission of ourselves to the inward and vital movement of the poet's soul we may come if not to a full, at least to a partial comprehension of his meaning.[155]

This emphasis on an intuitive rather than an intellectual assimilation of artistic experience places Murry much nearer than Eliot to Hulme's 'direct communication', and Eliot is left holding on to those (not inconsiderable) parts of Hulme that are less amenable to Murry's romantic interpretation. Indeed, when it comes to questions of rhythm, especially the rhythm of dance, Eliot stands in direct contradiction to the Bergsonism of Hulme and Murry. Eliot's fascination with the Ballets Russes, for example, is due to his belief in the impersonality achieved by submersion in rhythm. He explained this attitude in the preface to 'Four Elizabethan Dramatists' some two months before, where he had compared the dancer to a vital flame existing only for the duration of the dance, meaningful only within the moment of the performance: 'a conventional being, a being which exists only in and for the work of art which is the ballet.'[156] In spite of Babbitt's warning that neoclassicism, especially in France, had become a 'mixture of Aristotle and the dancing master', Havelock Ellis had suggested a relation between the classical spirit and dance, writing that 'dance is the rule of number and of rhythm and of measure and of order, of the controlling influence of form, of the subordination of the parts to the whole. That is what dance is. And these same properties also make up the classic spirit'.[157] And it is to this more commonly 'classical' approach that Eliot adheres, returning frequently in his criticism to the model of an impersonal rhythm in which the dancer, or the writer, must subsume his individuality, working on the implication of 'Tradition and the Individual Talent' that the writer has 'not a "personality" to express, but a particular medium, which is only a medium and not a personality'.[158]

---

[155] *Keats and Shakespeare*, 176.

[156] 'Four Elizabethan Dramatists: 1, A Preface', *Criterion*, 2/6 (Feb. 1924), 115–23 (p. 119). See also his comparison of dance and ritual in 'The Ballet', *Criterion*, 3/11 (Apr. 1925), 441–3.

[157] Babbitt, *The New Laokoon*, 66; Havelock Ellis, *The Dance of Life* (London, 1923), pp. x–xi. Murry had been highly critical of what he saw as the empty formalism of Diaghilev's company, considering its work to have 'decayed from a revelation into a fashion'. 'The Art of the Russian Ballet', *Nation and Athenaeum*, 29/24 (10 Sept. 1921), 834–6 (p. 836).

[158] *The Sacred Wood*, 56.

This analogy shows graphically the differing approaches adopted by the incipient romanticist and classicist to a common problem. For the classicist, rhythm (or form) is an impersonal force in which the individual is absorbed. Once absorbed he may then express that *form* through his action, much as Eliot describes the dancer expressing not himself, but the dance. Murry's secondary romantic, on the other hand, taking a lead from Bergson, discovers in rhythm the corresponding rhythm of his own soul. This is not so much a submission as a discovery of correspondence. Once that correspondence is made, the romantic artist may then express the knowledge which the rhythm has helped him discover dormant within himself.

While there is much in Hulme to give encouragement to Eliot's classicism—particularly the arguments against humanism that follow from the acceptance of the idea of original sin—there is also much that remains problematic. Eliot had to be selective in what he took from Hulme. Undoubtedly, part of this related to Eliot's critical temperament and to the immediate needs of his critical project. But part also belonged to the negative influence being exercised by Murry. Murry's romanticism had channelled Eliot into a putative classicism defined as much by that opposition as by its own substantive propositions. Any attempt by Eliot to refine or reconstruct this classicism by the appropriation of the work of other writers should, then, be seen not as an innocent attempt at critical self-definition but as a contentious contribution to an ongoing debate. Edwin Muir would later write of Hulme that 'all his public statements implied an invisible contemporary opponent': it was perhaps fitting, then, that Hulme's legacy should be contested and his work reinterpreted according to the needs of argument.[159] The reception of his *Speculations* exhibits signs of a Bakhtinian 'hidden polemic', which is to say that Eliot and Murry were not simply addressing their dialogue directly to one another but continuing it and extending it through third parties.

MURRY AND A ROMANTIC TRADITION

The sense in which this hidden polemic inflected much of Murry's writing can be seen in his continuing attempts to secure for romanticism a history of its own; to continue to claim, indeed, that

---

[159] Edwin Muir, *The Present Age From 1914* (London, 1939), 167.

romanticism was to all intents and purposes the English tradition. In making this attempt, throughout the work of 1924, including the Clark Lectures that would be published as *Keats and Shakespeare* in the following year, Murry worked on the implications of Hulme's and Eliot's historical revisionism and began to devise a history that explained not only literary but also religious change. This translation of a literary into a religious debate will form the subject of the next chapter. It is enough to note at this stage that Murry's attempts to create a romantic tradition are fuelled by Eliot's attempts to claim the tradition for classicism, and that in mounting this justification Murry begins to raise awkward questions about the absence of the spiritual values predicated by Eliot's classicism.

Murry's earlier criticism had hinted at the foundations on which an authoritative romantic tradition would be built, and in the introduction to a collection of essays, *To the Unknown God*, he restated the difference between that tradition and the one invoked by Eliot:

That I am an individualist, I admit: that I am a rebel against authority and a despiser of tradition I emphatically deny. Because I do not accept the same authority and claim the same tradition as they do, it does not follow that I accept no authority and claim no tradition. Far from it. The underlying theme of these essays, the philosophic and religious background implicit in them (and at times, I had believed, explicit also) is that individualism itself is a high tradition, and that in this tradition are contained universal authorities. I sincerely believe that I accept these authorities and follow the tradition which they compose.[160]

The attempt here to invoke universal authorities is notice—if that is needed in a book entitled *To the Unknown God*—that Murry's tradition of individualism is seeking, as it were, to up the stakes on Eliot by appealing not just to an impersonal authority but an absolute one. The thought behind this can be seen in a typescript apparently written at this time but never published.[161] In this paper, entitled 'What is the Tradition?', Murry attempted in a series of notes to work out the distinctions between romantic and classical traditions. In the course of the argument he noted the crisis in literary and cultural values

---

[160]   *To the Unknown God: Essays Towards a Religion* (London, 1924), 8.

[161]   This is in the Murry collection at the University of Edinburgh Library. The script is undated, but a clue to its year of writing can be found on its third page, where Murry's discussion of the historical eruptions of romanticism ends in 1924. Also, the references to Matthew Arnold closely resemble those that appear in an essay on that writer, the typescript of which is also in the Edinburgh collection, dated 29 Nov. 1923.

precipitated by the war. His description of the need for a corrective tradition seems very close to that of Eliot or Bell noted above: 'There is disquiet, dissatisfaction, a sense of isolation, and men look backwards in literature for a period or a person who gave expression to thoughts and feelings like their own. They say: This is the true T[radition]'.[162] But, of course, Murry's analysis of that healing tradition is quite distinct. When Bell and Eliot looked to the past they sought periods of continuous practice in which art was, as Eliot had suggested in the introduction to *The Sacred Wood*, confluent with a 'current of ideas'. In the absence of such a current—in an era of original sin and the dissociated sensibility—traditionalists tended either to become nostalgic about integrated ages like those of Dante or the Troubadours or to emphasize the need for a compensatory order or discipline in the present, like that associated with classicism. In 'What is the Tradition?' Murry noted the need for a traditionalizing current of ideas which he here called 'the common ground'. But for Murry, the common ground is simply that ground shared by all great artists, regardless of the circumstances under which their art was created. Hulme and Gourmont, among many others, had characterized artistic achievement as the triumph over inherited, indurative forms; for Murry it is that achievement, rather than the site from which it springs, that constitutes the common ground. That ground is 'the recurrent embodiment of a mode of thought and feeling in successive generations of writers'[163] and is identified with what Murry describes as a romantic 'creative tradition'. With its emphasis on individual experience this tradition is hostile to a classical 'critical tradition', obviously identifiable with Eliot, that regards 'the whole corpus of previous production as a whole' and in which new work is 'judged and valued according as it can more or less be assimilated to this extant material'.[164] For Murry, the error in this tradition is that its highest court of appeal is 'an audience or society'; its consequence is that 'practically speaking, since the beginning of E[nglish] Literature, the deepest thoughts and feelings of the most gifted individuals have found no outlet in the social or classical literature'.[165] The element that constantly eludes classicism, Murry argues, is spiritual value. Controverting Hulme, who had memorably suggested that romanticism was merely 'spilt religion', Murry suggests strongly

---

[162] 'What is the Tradition?', [p. 1].   [163] Ibid. [p. 6].
[164] Ibid. [p. 1].   [165] Ibid. [p. 6].

that it is spiritual value that ultimately underpins aesthetic value, and that it is this absorption of the spiritual by the literary that constitutes the common ground of the romantic tradition. 'Since the Renaissance', he writes, 'there has been no room for profound (religious) experience in "classical" literature. Since the collapse of the Catholic Church it has never been part of the common ground'.[166] The common ground marked out by the creative tradition is identifiable because in it is enshrined the aesthetic and spiritual value that transcends the mundane 'current of ideas'; *the true tradition is the one which holds the deepest spiritual content. Therefore the true tradition of E[nglish] Literature is Romantic*.[167]

This principled attack on classicism and the classical takes off at a tangent from the hybrid classicism of Hulme. Hulme's argument, one not always held consistently in *Speculations* but one to which Eliot would increasingly subscribe, was that classicism was particularly valuable precisely because it allowed no scope for the discussion of literature in religious terms. Hulme had stressed a discontinuity between the two activities, talking of the need 'to recognise the *gap* between the regions of vital and human things, and that of the *absolute* values of ethics and religion'.[168] To confuse one of these regions with the other was to fall into the cardinal error of humanism, in believing that absolute values could be divined through human experience. As Hulme had made clear, then, religious and ethical values had no place in the aesthetic evaluations of the new classicism.

The extent to which Murry's views differed from this—the extent to which religious and ethical values were actually becoming the central concern of his criticism—could be seen almost immediately in his Clark Lectures, delivered in Cambridge in the summer of 1924 and then published in book form as *Keats and Shakespeare* in August 1925. *Keats and Shakespeare* is arguably one of the great triumphs of Murry's intuitive critical method. Simply as a model of a broad and sympathetic interpretation of Keats it stands as a rebuke to the worst excesses of classical antihumanism. More than this, it marks a sustained attempt to formulate a romanticism that takes account of the recent debate with Eliot, but which advances that argument in a new direction.

---

[166] 'What is the Tradition?', [p. 5].
[167] Ibid. [p. 6].   [168] *Speculations*, 32.

KEATS AND SHAKESPEARE

In a comment appended to his description of the dilemma of post-Renaissance classicism in 'What is the Tradition?' Murry had written cryptically of this dilemma as 'the typical tragedy of Mattthew Arnold'. In an essay on Arnold, Murry explained this 'tragedy' by suggesting that Arnold was 'a man who took refuge from his own romanticism in a reverence for the classical tradition'. Murry's description of Arnold is of a writer riven by the contradictory demands of the two competing traditions. Though romantic by inclination he is drawn, in his insecurity, towards the protective safety of the classical tradition which, argues Murry, is responsible for the destruction of his poetic gift. Murry analyses Arnold's internal division, 'the evidence of the divided soul', in terms of those traditions personified as 'two men, who struggled with one another until they were both exhausted'. He adds, 'we may call one of these Romantic, and the other classical; or we might say that one was the heart and the other the head'.[169]

In this kind of analysis, with its association of competing traditions, classicism and romanticism, rationality and intuition, which become identified with the distinction between head and heart, can be seen the incipient pattern of the argument of *Keats and Shakespeare* as well as the grounds for his future arguments with Eliot. For, having delineated two antithetical traditions associated with classicism and *primary* romanticism, Murry then seeks to argue that the achievement of a truly romantic poetry is the successful synthesis of these competing elements. While Arnold signally failed to synthesize these terms, the Keats of *Keats and Shakespeare* discovers the third term by which the dialectic of classicism and primary romanticism, head and heart, is resolved—a discovery that lifts his poetry clear of concerns for its place in a school or tradition. The term is 'soul', which Murry describes as the end of a vigorous process of self-discovery: 'the final truth . . . the truth of the soul, which comprehends and reconciles the partial truths of the heart and of the mind'.[170]

Keats and Shakespeare may be regarded as an attempt to create a case-history of the ideas of romanticism that Murry had been developing since the war—an endeavour to tie up the various strands

---

[169] 'Matthew Arnold the Poet', in *Discoveries*, 203.
[170] *Keats and Shakespeare*, 26.

running through his earlier criticism. Here his ideas on personality, morality, religion, literary history, and art as a criticism of life are drawn together into a unified argument that directly challenges that view of art which feels able to criticize literature in terms of rational interpretation, and which attempts to articulate traditions through which this rationale is transmitted. In short, a challenge to the barren intellectuality that Murry associates with classicism.

This rebuke to intellectual theories in general, and perhaps to Eliot in particular—reminding him of the heritage he seems to have abandoned—is started even before the book proper begins, in Murry's choice of an epigraph from F. H. Bradley's *Principles of Logic*:

Unless thought stands for something that falls beyond mere intelligence, if 'thinking' is not used with some strange implication that never was part of the meaning of the word, a lingering scruple still forbids us to believe that reality can ever be purely rational. It may come from a failure in my metaphysics, or from a weakness of the flesh which continues to blind me, but the notion that existence should be the same as understanding strikes as cold and ghost-like as the dreariest materialism.[171]

Eliot had written a short piece for the *Criterion* on the occasion of Bradley's death in the autumn of the previous year, in which he had attempted to enlist Bradley among the ranks of the classicists, ascribing to him a 'classic balance' in his style between acute intellect and passionate feeling. Eliot had even gone so far as to suggest an association between Bradley and the sweetness and light of the medieval schoolmen, his remote predecessors at Oxford's Merton College.[172] Murry's use of Bradley might be seen, then, both as a counter to Eliot's tendentious interpretation and an ironic attempt to reclaim Bradleian idealism for a reconstituted romanticism.

From this starting-point of the unsatisfactory nature of rational interpretations of literary art, Murry constructs a theory, based on Keats's letters, of soul-making: the synthetic activity of the intellect and the sensibility in the integration of an undissociated experience. Murry describes the 'vast idea' he sees animating Keats's poetry:

that the rational faculty was impotent to achieve truth, that intuitive apprehension was the sole faculty by which an ultimate truth could be known, that this truth could be recognised for what it was only by its beauty, that

---

[171] Murry quoted this again, expanding on his understanding of it, in 'Poetry, Philosophy, and Religion', *Adelphi*, 2/8 (Jan. 1925), 645–58 (p. 648).

[172] 'A Commentary: Francis Herbert Bradley', *Criterion*, 3/9 (Oct. 1924), 1–2.

perceptions of beauty were premonitions of a reality, that the way towards intuitive knowledge of this reality lay through a reverence for the instinctive impulses, and that somehow in this final knowledge all discords would be reconciled.[173]

Like Eliot, Murry accepts a primary dissociation as the given condition of romantic poetry. But where Eliot would argue that such a dissociation might only be corrected by submission to the authority of a doctrine enshrined in tradition, through which a condition of impersonality may be obtained, Murry suggests that such dissociation requires the artist to dig even deeper into his personal experience, in a process, quite literally, of self-discovery. This returns Murry to a consistently held belief in art, and poetry in particular, as primarily a revelatory activity—the uncovering of a truth latent within the artist.

In his essay 'John Dryden', Eliot had attempted to rehabilitate that writer by emphasizing the technical merit of his work. Eliot had rejected Arnold's criticism that the poetry of Dryden and Pope 'is conceived and composed in their wits', and that 'genuine poetry is conceived in the soul', as a typically misplaced Victorian identification of poetry with sublimity of theme.[174] Instead, he chose to emphasize the poetry that resides in Dryden's technique—the 'wit' with which its fictions are constructed. This emphasis on the fabrication of poetry, the wrighting of the urn that would exercise the American New Critics in Eliot's wake, stands in a complete contrast to Murry's notion of poetic revelation—his belief in poetry as the removal of obscuring veils rather than the construction of clarifying fictions. Bergson had written in *Le Rire* that 'between nature and ourselves, nay, between ourselves and our own consciousness a veil is interposed: a veil that is dense and opaque for the common herd,—thin, almost transparent, for the artist and poet'.[175] Hulme had taken up the same theme, and the same metaphor, in his description of the poetic activity's attempt to break through the obscuring barriers of a speech created by action: 'if we could break through the veil which action interposes, if we could come into direct contact with sense and consciousness, art would be useless and unnecessary'.[176] This notion of art as revelation, as a thinning of the veil of consciousness, was

---

[173] *Keats and Shakespeare*, 32.
[174] 'John Dryden', *TLS* 1012 (9 June 1921), 361–2 (p. 362).   [175] *Comedy*, 158.
[176] 'Bergson's Theory of Art', in *Speculations*, 147. Enid Starkie discusses the transmission of this metaphor into the work of Proust and Gide in 'Bergson and Literature', in Thomas Hanna (ed.), *The Bergsonian Heritage* (New York, 1962), 74–99 (pp. 88–90).

reproduced by Murry in *Keats and Shakespeare*, becoming his central theme in the creation of the poetic persona. It is exemplified in the second 'Hyperion' fragment at the moment in which the poet, in the instant of self-discovery, is vouchsafed a vision of Moneta, the priestess of the temple of Saturn and symbol of worldly consciousness, parting her veil. This vision of a truth behind the veil of consciousness Murry sees as the culmination of Keats's poetic endeavour. It is that moment of perfect knowledge in beauty to which Keats's poetry and his life have aspired, and which is translated automatically, unmediated onto the page.

As I would hardly dare to praise those lines, I hardly dare to try to explain them. They belong, I fear, to that order of poetry, which we either understand intuitively or do not understand at all. They contain a vision of the soul of the world, an apprehension of an ultimate reality. No more perfect or more wonderful symbol of the unspeakable truth has ever been imagined. There is unity, there is calm, there is beauty: it is a vision of a single thing. Yet in that single thing what strange elements are combined? Pain, an eternity of pain; change, an eternity of change; death, an eternity of death; terror, yet no terror; instead, measureless benignity; yet this infinite of love touches no person; it is eternal and impersonal, 'comforting those it sees not'. That, if the word be accepted, is a great poet's vision of God—but of a godhead immanent in the changing and enduring reality of the world. The mortal poet has gained a more perfect vision of that which was revealed to Apollo. Then he had seen through a glass darkly, but now face to face.[177]

Here Murry manages to unite the conventional notion of an epiphany, a moment of insight that reveals a static unified truth, with a Bergsonian revelation achieved through dynamic sympathy with a mutable force. It is important to note here, however, the nature of that revelation. For the vision of reality the romantic artist achieves is far from the static, authoritative truth predicated by Eliot's classicism. Instead it is a 'godhead immanent in the changing and enduring reality of the world', in which a 'measureless benignity' is compounded with 'an eternity of change'. It is also 'eternal and impersonal', but far from being an impersonality from which authority might be derived it is an essentially directionless and changeable impersonality which by its very nature necessitates the mediation of personality—a kind of sublunar idealism whose very mutability precludes interpretation by the received thought of a tradition. Such a

---

[177] *Keats and Shakespeare*, 183.

reality might only be grasped, argues Murry, through the inward exploration of one's personal experience: 'a knowledge and harmony of the universe which can be reached only through the individual's knowledge of unity and harmony in himself'.

By ignoring the technical aspects by which a work of art as artefact is created and instead concentrating on the process of self-possession through which the man predicated by the poetry passes, Murry is able to embody his concerns about the moral, aesthetic, and religious components of literature into the larger concern of an achieved romanticism. The mysticism that underpins this romantic theory is such that tradition as Eliot understands it has no qualification to allow it to take part in the comprehension and assimilation of literary works. Such a tradition is a mere formalism, analogous to the established religion that has fossilized the living romanticism of Christ.[178] This is the tradition, both religious and literary, from which the artist must escape in order to pursue his individual thought-adventure.[179] The only tradition that this position will allow is a romantic one made up of a discontinuous series of individual realizations of a constantly evolving ideal. As such its value is exemplary rather than authoritative, revealing not so much what the truth is as the way in which its variety might be experienced.[180] Murry's emphasis, then, remains on subjective experience—on immediately empirical evaluations of both literature and religion: 'true Romanticism is true individualism—a self-creation of the soul by means of the Mind's faithful interpretation of the Heart'.[181] This true romanticism is anti-traditional and anti-institutional, becoming analogous to the individuation of Murry's religious man who 'takes nothing on trust; he abides by his own experience, and by his own instinctive knowledge of what is truest and most profound in that experience'.[182]

By 1925, and the publication of *Keats and Shakespeare*, the contrasting positions of Murry and Eliot were becoming more marked.

---

[178] 'Nor is it of any avail for the classicist to appeal to the tradition. The tradition is, in the main, the organization and consolidation of many romanticisms, just as the Catholic Church was the organization and consolidation of the great romanticism of Christ.' 'More About Romanticism', 564.

[179] See *Keats and Shakespeare*, 1. The notion of literature as thought-adventure had also been advanced by Lawrence in 'On Being a Man', *Adelphi*, 2/4 (Sept. 1924), 298–306.

[180] 'The deepest things may be revealed, but may not be uttered'. 'The Religion of Mark Rutherford', *Adelphi*, 2/2 (July 1924), 93–104 (p. 96).

[181] *Keats and Shakespeare*, 216.

[182] 'Religion and Faith', *Adelphi*, 1/3 (Aug. 1923), 177–84 (p. 179).

Although they had never been entirely in accord on matters of criticism, the mutual sympathy they had shared at the *Athenaeum* had dissolved with the closing of that paper. Their establishment of competing literary journals, the *Criterion* and the *Adelphi*, helped accelerate an ensuing lack of sympathy into open hostility. The polarization encouraged by this literary-critical competition came to a focus on the question of critical standards. Both writers believed in the need for a standard, or Gourmontian 'law', which might serve as the authoritative centre for their criticism. *Keats and Shakespeare* shows just how far Murry's location of the site of that authority differs from that of Eliot. While Eliot safeguards literature from the artist's 'doing as one likes' by an institutionalized tradition which sanctions the limits within which new works might be accepted, Murry adopts a humanism like that of Babbitt or Arnold whose ultimate appeal is to an 'inner check' or a 'better self'. From this point of view, what Eliot characterized as 'doing as one likes' can actually be construed as a call for discipline as much as a freedom: 'to do what you like may seem rather easy to Mr Eliot. To me, on the contrary, it seems the hardest thing in the world. For to know what you really like means to know what you really are; and that is a matter of painful experience and slow exploration.'[183] So difficult a process is this, the quintessential task of poetry, that only exceptionally—in the cases of Shakespeare and Keats—has it truly been achieved.

While this argument embodies many of Murry's earlier concerns, it can be seen to have been formulated as a response to Eliot's criticism. That criticism had forced Murry into a defence of his intuitive beliefs—a defence that restated those beliefs in the terms of a theory. This new theoretically articulated romanticism, the restatement in a critical language of intuitively derived beliefs, came to be shored up with an associated spiritual and literary history. Out of these elements Murry creates an argument that is irrefutable within its own terms: as he states at the beginning of *Keats and Shakespeare*, it is an argument that must be accepted in its totality or equally wholly rejected. He argues that Keats has achieved a vision, valid within its own terms, which may be grasped only in the kind of intuitive movement of the mind by which Keats first discovered it. Such experience is susceptible neither to negotiation nor qualification; it cannot be achieved in part, but may only be grasped whole: 'I ask this above all

---

[183] 'More About Romanticism', 567.

of my reader that he will not allow his logical mind to obstruct his more immediate understanding, because the things I am trying to investigate—the nature of pure poetry and the character of the pure poet—are not rational at all'.[184]

This outright rejection of rational criticism finally sets Murry outside any possibility of a fruitful dialogue with Eliot. Between the first publication of the *Adelphi* in 1923 and the publication of *Keats and Shakespeare* in 1925 the tendency of Murry's criticism finally becomes fixed in a romanticism that has its own supporting mythical history within which its religion, aesthetics, and ethics can be articulated—as Murry was to write, 'a true romanticism necessitates a new theology, a new ethic, and a new politic'.[185] With his rejection of the authority of institutionalized traditions, religious and literary, and his counter-emphasis on an authoritative Christian individuality, which achieves that authority in the discovery of its soul, Murry begins to set himself beyond the pale of the literary culture of his time. By closing off arguments for the technical importance of language in literature, and ruling out of court criticisms that come from the obstructive 'logical mind', Murry fulfils Hulme's worst prognostications for romanticism, turning the study of literature not so much into a spilt religion as a whole surrogate religion: 'we do need a Church: but we have to insist on founding new ones. We want our Church, not *the* Church'.[186] In common with many religions its articles of faith render its mysteries inaccessible to non-believers, creating an impregnable theology by placing its tenets above those criticisms it regards as otiose or heretical.

The qualification of sensibility that Murry insists upon as a prerequisite of critical ability, then, becomes in its own way just as unresponsive to argument as the more obvious critical dogmatism that Eliot would go on to develop. In this respect, the *Adelphi* movement that grows out of Murry's critical practice can be seen as an anticipation of the equally evangelical *Scrutiny* movement of the next decade. Both movements combine a crusading zeal for openness to experience in literature and education with a dogmatism and exclusivity that demands of their adherents a complete conversion. Like Leavis, Murry builds a theory implicitly upon the foundations of sensibility

---

[184] *Keats and Shakespeare*, 12.
[185] 'More About Romanticism', in *To the Unknown God*, 150. This is a reworking of a similar statement made in the essay's earlier publication in the *Adelphi*.
[186] 'The Two Worlds', *Adelphi*, 1/10 (Mar. 1924), 859–66 (p. 865).

that is tenaciously resistant to criticism; that lays itself open to criticism only according to its own vaguely defined terms of 'life', 'experience', or 'maturity'. As a consequence, critics of Murry and Leavis find themselves arguing not against the theories implicit in their work, but against the often very impressive sensibilities that they can bring to bear upon individual literary works. In this way their defences of their respective movements become a form of self-justification, vouchsafed by their continued ability to produce sensitive and informed readings of the texts in question.

Just as Murry's critical idiosyncrasy begins to place him outside the critical consensus demanded by the increasing respectability of English literature as an academic discipline, so too Eliot's critical ideas start to exhibit an exclusivity and imperviousness to criticism. Although Eliot's criticism is by 1925 not as explicitly worked into a comprehensive theoretical system as Murry's, his work, moving rapidly away from the influence of Gourmont, shows the early signs of a tendency towards the Thomistic interpretation of classicism favoured by Jacques Rivière and Jacques Maritain.

Although his movement towards this position might be construed as an inevitable development of trends already implicit within his critical ideas, it is arguable that his disagreements with Murry at the very least forced the pace of that change—persuading Eliot to become aligned with a classicism defined as much by its opposition to Murry's romanticism as its allegiance to the ideas of the French classicists: a reading further reinforced by Mario Praz's observation that Eliot's 'idea of the essence of classicism is largely a polemical one, as it derives from writers who employed that term in order to contrast it with something against which they fought'.[187] Eliot began the *Criterion* with no immediate desire to espouse a specific programme. Faced with Murry's *Adelphi*, however, the *Criterion* quickly began to align itself, in opposition to the other journal's religious and literary liberalism, with a loosely defined classicism that by 1925 was already showing itself inclined toward a scholastic philosophy—a position it would secure for itself by 1928, when the second and effectively final phase of the dialogue between Eliot and Murry closed.

The arrival at this point is marked by the closing off of all possible communication between what are effectively two discrete doctrines

---

[187] 'T. S. Eliot as a Critic', in Allen Tate (ed.), *T. S. Eliot: The Man and his Work* (London, 1967), 262–77 (p. 269).

based on entirely separate premisses and complete within their own terms. Eliot's insistence that Murry should articulate a theory in support of his romantic individualism—a proof that romantic poets and critics are not merely 'doing as one likes'—combined with Murry's own desire, culled from Gourmont, to 'erect his personal impressions into laws', obliges him to construct a self-consistent theory that becomes less susceptible to external criticism the more complete it becomes. This culminates in a statement of his relation to tradition and authority that, for Eliot at least, must have appeared frustratingly oxymoronic: 'My position is simple. I believe that a man needs both authority and tradition, I also believe that it is best for him to find them out for himself.'[188] In 1924 Murry, called upon to define his beliefs, described them in the terms of an English tradition that is 'romantic through and through: in politics it is a tradition of individualism, in religion of protestantism, and in literature of romanticism'.[189] Some four years later, Eliot would proclaim the dogmas of his classicism in a famous definition, describing himself in terms that could not be more antipodal to those of Murry, as 'classicist in literature, royalist in politics, and anglo-catholic in religion'.[190]

While such conditions prevail the possibilities of a mutually beneficial dialogue become increasingly limited. The competing practices of Murry and Eliot become effectively incommensurable, based as they are on such mutually diverse definitions of common notions of personality, tradition, and the place of religious ideas in literature. There is, then, little overlap between their interpretations that would allow for a common disputed ground. Their argument thus becomes increasingly characterized not by debate but by controversy; a controversy in which dialogue would be increasingly replaced by an overt and sometimes intemperate polemic.

[188] 'Quo Warranto?', *Adelphi*, 2/3 (Aug. 1924), 185–96 (p. 190).
[189] 'In Defence of the "Adelphi" ', *Spectator*, 5003 (17 May 1924), 785–6 (p. 785).
[190] *For Lancelot Andrewes: Essays on Style and Order* (London, 1928), 7.

3
Orthodoxy and Modernism
The Claims of Religion, 1926–1928

THE first phase of the explicit disagreement between Eliot and Murry, framed largely as a contention between classicism and romanticism, had effectively ended by mid-1924. Murry's last contribution to the debate, 'Romanticism and the Tradition', which had been published in April's *Criterion*, elicited only an indirect response from Eliot in the form of an editorial 'Commentary' in the following July. 'Romanticism and the Tradition' had returned Murry to a favourite argument: that 'the tradition of Romanticism is just as lofty and august as the tradition of classicism'.[1] In making this argument Murry had directly confronted those, like Eliot, who criticized his blurring of religious and aesthetic boundaries and who insisted on an absolute separation between the two areas of activity. For Murry, arguments of this kind, relying ultimately for their authority on dogma rather than experience, showed the paucity of both religious and literary traditionalism. The error of assuming no relation between the activities of religion and literature, he had contended, comes from attempting to compare two barren categories devoid of the spiritual content by which they were originally related. Instead of constituting two living and changing areas of experience, the religion described by the Catholic and the literature conceived by the traditionalist persist only as skeletal traces of the living forms that once animated them:

The vital motion of religion becomes petrified into dogmas and ceremonies; the vital motion of literature is ossified into forms and canons; and between

---

[1] 'Romanticism and the Tradition', *Criterion*, 2/7 (Apr. 1924), 272–95 (p. 273).

these empty husks the connection is invisible and non-existent, precisely because it was a connection between the living essences. When literature becomes a parlour-game and religion a Church-mummery, they are alike only in their deadness. But between the literature that is real and the religion that is real the bond is close and unbreakable.[2]

As organized religion has abrogated its right to deal in the deepest individual experiences, and literary classicism has attempted to force such experiences into a formal straitjacket, Murry looks instead to romantic art as the repository of the deepest religious experience. This literature is 'the record of a soul's struggle after life and God',[3] and as such is the direct rendering of an individual experience that is at once greater than the sum of the dogmas of Catholicism and classicism. 'We must', Murry would write in another essay, 'translate all that theology back into the dynamic process of which it is the awkward symbol.'[4]

It was in the same issue of the *Criterion* that Eliot had been reinterpreting Hulme to suggest that the classical moment is, above all, one of stasis.[5] Murry contradicted this absolutely by arguing that the central characteristic of literature, like religion, is the dynamism of its constant process of discovery:

No matter how finally, how beautifully, how profoundly Christ formulated the everlasting truths of religion, in order to know that they are everlasting, in order to know quite simply what they mean, man must rediscover them in himself . . . If we can see that it is inevitable, it is only in so far as we can see that religion is a necessary motion of the human soul, a fundamental rhythm of man's being. Then it is plain that it must be fulfilled in literature which is primarily an expression of that being.[6]

This expression of a necessary link between religious experience and literature, 'the greater the literature is, the more religious it must be',[7] did not go entirely unanswered by Eliot. His 'Commentary' published in the next issue of the *Criterion*, described as 'alarming' what was perceived as a growing tendency to treat literary criticism as 'the expression of an attitude "toward life" or of an attitude toward religion or of an attitude toward society, or of various humanitarian emotions'. Among such heterodoxies Eliot recognized as the most dangerous the

---

[2] Ibid. 276–7.   [3] Ibid. 281.
[4] 'The Need of a New Psychology', *Things to Come: Essays* (London, 1928), 11–33 (p. 24).
[5] 'A Commentary', *Criterion*, 2/7 (Apr. 1924), 231–2 (p. 232).
[6] 'Romanticism and the Tradition', 292.   [7] Ibid. 294.

tendency 'to confuse literature with religion—a tendency which can only have the effect of degrading literature and annihilating religion'. Then, rather than flatter Murry with a direct response or an attempted refutation, Eliot instead invoked a higher authority by referring the reader to the *Nouvelle Revue française*, where, as he put it, 'this particular heresy has lately been dealt with very ably by Monsieur Jacques Rivière'.[8] Eliot's fairly disdainful dismissal of Murry's arguments marked a temporary end to their public dialogue.

Murry, at least, had placed great value on that dialogue. He had written at the end of the first year of the *Adelphi* that although there had been many voices raised for and against the paper, 'the only critic who has made a *criticism* of it is Mr T. S. Eliot'. Although he obviously could not agree with the substance of Eliot's criticism Murry was prepared to admit its integrity and the legitimacy of its motives: anyone who is a 'convinced classicist and Catholic and traditionalist', he stated, 'is rightfully and honourably the opponent of the *Adelphi*'.[9] From the *Adelphi*'s inception Murry had attempted to use the paper to stimulate debate. It had, for example, from its earliest days incorporated a disputative 'Contributors' Club' and, in a similar vein, Murry had gone out of his way to solicit controversy—even to the extent of not only publishing but actually commissioning pieces that were critical responses to his own opinions.[10] With Eliot's withdrawal from a direct dialogue, Murry engaged himself in several controversies with other critics. As with his disagreements with Eliot, such controversies gave a shape and an edge to Murry's critical writing, helping him to refine or to temper his arguments under the close scrutiny of hostile opinion. Many of the most important essays that further defined the religious position outlined in his arguments with Eliot came out of this process, spilling out of his own paper into others like the *Spectator* and the *Guardian*. Essays such as 'Religion and Christianity', 'Quo Warranto?', 'Poetry, Philosophy and Religion', 'Personality and Immortality', 'A Theological Encounter', and the defensive introduction to *To the Unknown God* (1924) all came directly out of controversy, and all were pushing the expression of his religious subjectivism towards what would be its

---

[8] 'A Commentary', *Criterion*, 2/8 (July 1924), 373. See also Vivien Eliot's hostile criticism of Murry's novel, *The Voyage*, in this issue: 'Books of the Quarter', 483–6.

[9] 'In Defence of the "Adelphi" ', *Spectator*, 5003 (17 May 1924), 785–6 (p. 785).

[10] See W. E. Orchard, 'Religion and Christianity: A Reply', *Adelphi*, 1/12 (May 1924), 1074–84.

fullest statement in his *The Life of Jesus* (1926).[11] It was at this time that Murry also fell upon a way of advertising his books that stressed their controversial nature. An advertisement for his novel *The Voyage* cited 'a candid selection of Press opinions' both very good and very bad.[12] Similarly, when he came to advertise publication of *Keats and Shakespeare* in the *Adelphi*, instead of using only the good reviews—of which there were many—he chose to quote the opinion of the *Sunday Times* that the book was 'the work of an exceedingly crude mind . . . written in a correspondingly crude manner' alongside that of the *Manchester Guardian* which had called it 'a great book' and 'a critical study of the very rarest kind'.[13]

Depending on one's view of Murry such attempts to court controversy are either manifestations of a rebarbative egotism or an appealing humility; such a public laundering of private agonies of doubt is either arrogant for assuming that the public might be interested, or brave in its refusal to project a falsely authoritative critical integrity. As the *Adelphi* continued its popular success, it seemed that its many readers adopted the latter view while the professional literary world increasingly adopted the former. Which is to say that Murry, by going over the heads of the littérateurs and appealing directly to common readers—a process described by Eliot as 'flattering the complacency of the half-educated'—was laying himself open to charges of populism and, less forgivably, vulgarity. Even down to its title, the *Adelphi*'s emphasis was on fraternity and consensus: qualities that emphasized the creation and maintenance of common standards and values through open debate. Murry's openness in this regard may have prompted mistrust among his profession, but it was consistent with his literary, and increasingly his religious, views. The basis of such views in a loosely defined humanism—that is, in the placing of a contingent human experience at the centre of a negotiated construction of value—had been manifest in his earlier literary criticism. The extent to which he would broaden this view to incorporate literary into religious value, in a dialogue with other critics and then with Eliot in the second phase of their controversy between 1926 and 1928, will be explored below.

While Murry was continually preaching and practising the

[11] 'Religion and Christianity', *Adelphi*, 1/8 (Jan. 1924), 666–74; 'Quo Warranto', *Adelphi*, 2/3 (Aug. 1924), 185–96; 'Poetry, Philosophy and Religion', *Adelphi*, 2/8 (Jan. 1925), 645–8; 'Personality and Immortality', *Adelphi*, 2/12 (May 1925), 951–8; 'A Theological Encounter', *Adelphi*, 3/2 (July 1925), 77–88.

[12] See the inside front cover, *Adelphi*, 2/3 (Aug. 1924).

[13] See the inside front cover, *Adelphi*, 3/9 (Feb. 1926).

democratic creation of value Eliot was moving in a different direction altogether. Although it had been named—slightly surreally—after a restaurant, his *Criterion* symbolized in its title a different approach: one that stressed the imposition of value; the application rather than the construction of standards; judgement rather than brotherhood. This emphasis was punningly reinforced when, in April 1924, Eliot adopted the pseudonym 'Crites' for his editorial commentaries: a witty adaptation of 'Criton', the name over which Charles Maurras wrote in *L'Action française*. As was the case with Murry, such a symbolism was not accidental to the fundamental purposes of the magazine. Where the *Adelphi* attempted to open itself to a broad swathe of middle-class and working-class experience, risking the offence to literary good manners and taste in the process, the *Criterion* concerned itself more with applying the standards of an élite, and hence appealed to what Eliot implied was 'a small and fastidious public'. Where Murry was democratic, Eliot was hieratic: while Murry came more and more to believe that even religious values were achieved through the workings of consensus and fraternity, Eliot was appropriating a dogma in which all values were already given and required only sensitive adjudication. The impersonal values of the literary tradition were giving way to the more dogmatic values of neo-Thomism, the religious philosophy to which Eliot would subscribe with his conversion in 1927 to Anglo-Catholicism.

When the two men re-established a public debate in 1926, it would start off as a reprise of the romantic-classic exchanges of the first controversy. But it would quickly move on to a dispute about the religious content that was becoming manifest in the work of both men. It is difficult to understand the vehemence of that later debate without understanding the wider context. The key terms of this debate, especially Murry's commitment to a humanistic principle of 'life' grounded in the individual ethical conscience and Eliot's invocation of a dogmatic 'orthodoxy', will be seen to have been shaped by controversies in Roman Catholicism at the turn of the century and by an ongoing controversy within Anglicanism.

MURRY, MORAL RELATIVISM, AND MODERNISM

Murry, as has already been seen, had after the war placed great stress on the ethical value of literature: a stress that led Sharron Greer

Cassavant to describe him, 'in his qualities as a moralist', as 'a link between Matthew Arnold and F. R. Leavis'.[14] The consensual morality assumed by Quiller-Couch and Raleigh, to which Murry apparently subscribed, offered an existing standard against which the value of literature might be ascertained. For Quiller-Couch and Raleigh the relationship was quite unproblematical: literature simply offered a set of ethical values complementary to a more or less traditional Anglican religion. As the 1920s progressed Murry felt less able to invoke a morality so closely interwoven with a religious tradition of which he was increasingly sceptical. In 1921 he had written, of the decline in organized religion, that 'the problem of the nineteenth-century was the problem of morality without institutions'.[15] It was into this institutional void that he had attempted to place an ethical literary romanticism: 'Ethically', he wrote in 1923, 'Romanticism is an attempt to solve the problem of conduct by an exploration of the internal world.'[16] The same impulse which had caused him to return to the testimony of direct experience in the evaluation of literature, then, brought him to a similar revaluation of traditional religious values as they pertained to ethics:

It is no good appealing to a tradition which is not our own, when all sense of a tradition had been lost; it is no good pretending to invoke authority when there is no authority which men will recognise. The system of values on which the spiritual effort of the last century was based has collapsed utterly since the War: we are groping uneasily in a period of moral anarchy and intellectual triviality.[17]

Murry was certainly not alone in recognizing the opportunity for moral revaluation in the decline of organized Christianity. Nietzsche, the self-styled 'first immoralist', had famously identified the death of God in the decline of organized religion and the consequent need for a transvaluation of all values.[18] Remy de Gourmont, lacking Nietzsche's anger and moral earnestness, preferred a passive amorality to Nietzsche's active immorality. His God was not so much dead as posted missing: not known at his last address, as he playfully

[14] *John Middleton Murry*, 129.
[15] 'Henri-Frédéric Amiel, 1821–1881', *TLS* 1028 (29 Sept. 1921), 617–18 (p. 617).
[16] 'More About Romanticism', *Adelphi*, 1/7 (Dec. 1923), 557–69 (p. 568).
[17] 'In Defence of the "Adelphi" ', 786.
[18] See 'Why I am Destiny', in *Ecce Homo: How One Becomes What One Is*, trans. R. J. Hollingdale (London, 1979), 126–34.

suggested in *Promenades philosophiques* in 1909.[19] For Gourmont, the moral implications of the resulting universal transience were outlined in the dialogue of *Une nuit au Luxembourg* (1906) in which an Epicurean divinity uses his role as a 'provisional immortal' to preach the ethics of contingency and chance. For D. H. Lawrence, too, this sense of superlunar mutability had an immediate ethical impact. In a manner reminiscent of Gourmont, Lawrence, in an essay published by Murry in 1924, suggested that 'God doesn't just sit still somewhere in the cosmos', but instead 'wanders His Own strange way down the avenues of time, across the intricacies of space', eventually disappearing below the visible horizon of man.[20] In the absence of a Christian God Lawrence outlined a morality that is not so much handed down in a tradition as constantly created anew in relational experience: morality 'is that delicate, forever trembling and changing *balance* between me and my circumambient universe'.[21]

Nietzsche, Gourmont, and Lawrence, then, used the mutability or absence of God as a basis for the development of an individualist ethic untainted by, and hostile to, what they construed as the *ressentiment* of organized Christianity. While Murry's religious individualism bears a superficial similarity to this position it is, however, subject to a different inflection. Murry was similarly indisposed towards organized religion, but ultimately had a greater belief in the currency of the original Christian message. After his mystical experience in 1923 it was not Christian religious experience he mistrusted but Christian institutions. Rather than throw over Christianity altogether in the manner of Nietzsche, Murry instead attempted to revivify it through his own transvaluation of aesthetic and ethical values.

There were many precedents for Murry's attempts to reintegrate art and morality: G. E. Moore in *Principia Ethica* (1903) had called for a 'direct moral awareness' integral to the artistic vision, akin to what Irving Babbitt would identify in *Rousseau and Romanticism* (1919) as 'the ethical imagination'. In *The Dance of Life* Havelock Ellis had devoted a chapter to reconciling art and morality, and, for Murry at least, Wittgenstein had pressed a similar claim, that 'art and aesthetics are one', in the *Tractatus Logico-philosophicus*

[19] See Gourmont, *Selections*, ed. Aldington, 184.

[20] D. H. Lawrence, 'On Being Religious', *Adelphi*, 1/9 (Feb. 1924), 791–9 (p. 795).

[21] 'Morality and the Novel', *Calendar of Modern Letters*, 2/10 (Dec. 1925), 269–74 (p. 270). See also Lawrence's 'Art and Morality', *Calendar of Modern Letters*, 2/9 (Nov. 1925), 171–7.

(1922).[22] But to these concerns Murry added the extra dimension of religion. If aesthetic and ethical values could be reconciled, then together these could form the basis of a revivified religious practice. Far from complementing the values of a declining religious orthodoxy, then, Murry considered that ethical and aesthetic values might instead subvert that withering orthodoxy. Freed from the shackles of institutionalized religion, the values encapsulated in the best literature might in themselves give the lie to organized religion, leading to a revivified morality grounded in individual experience and not mediated by an ecclesiastical hierarchy.

In this revisionist attempt to reconcile a pragmatic belief in the changeable reality of a mutable God with an otherwise Christian faith and morality, Murry would find his ideas paralleled by the active and influential religious movement of Modernism. Modernism, as it was manifested first within French and Italian Catholicism at the end of the nineteenth century and then within Anglicanism in the early years of the twentieth, represented an attempt to reintroduce a dynamic, empirical component into religious doctrine, and to free it from what one commentator has described as 'the limitations imposed by outdated philosophies, insufficient historical knowledge, and an uncritical acceptance of centuries-old scientific discoveries; and to allow it to take advantage of the discoveries of more modern science and philosophy'.[23] Beginning as an attempt to bring religious doctrine into line with the discoveries of nineteenth-century science and the Higher Criticism, Modernism developed into a fundamental interrogation of religious authority, and particularly the infallibilism of the tradition. In England, the modernization of Christian doctrine had been one of the major controversies in the intellectual culture of the Victorian period. Several controversial works, most notably *Essays and Reviews* (1860) and *Lux Mundi* (1889), had, after much dissension, eventually persuaded majorities in the Church and among the wider public that the Bible could no longer be regarded as wholly divinely inspired and infallible: it was now accepted that '*the word of God is in the Bible*, instead of *the word of God is the Bible*'.[24] Taking advantage of the new

[22] Murry, 'Literary Criticism', unpublished typescript (Edinburgh), 6 pp. [p. 6]. See also Murry's discussion of Wittgenstein in 'English Poetry in the 18th Century', *TLS* 1096 (18 Jan. 1923), 33–4.

[23] Michele Ranchetti, *The Catholic Modernists: A Study of the Religious Reform Movement 1864–1907*, trans. Isabel Quigly (London, 1969), p. vii.

[24] See Owen Chadwick, *The Victorian Church*, vol. ii (London 1970), 111, (italics in original).

consensus on biblical fallibility, the Modernist movement in the twentieth century sought further changes in the liberalization of doctrine, particularly with regard to the Creeds and the institutions of the Church.

From the point of view of this study, one of the most important consequences of this modernization of belief was that stress was taken away from tradition and placed instead on individual experience. It was now acceptable to conceive of a God who derived not from his embodiment in the Bible and the institution of the Church, but who was, rather, immanent in consciousness itself. H. D. A. Major, a leader of the Anglican Modernist movement and editor of its newspaper *The Modern Churchman*, delivered the 1925/6 William Belden Noble Lectures at Harvard which, when published, effectively defined Modernism for his generation. In them he described this change of emphasis:

It is because we are what we are, and are becoming what we are becoming that God can and does unveil Himself to us, that is, *in* us. Hence the Modernist teaches that the Divine method of Revelation is internal—God speaking, not as Traditionalism teaches, in tones of thunder from the sky, but with a still small voice in the human consciousness.[25]

The result was that Modernism construed religious practice ethically as a creative sympathy with Christian experience rather than as obedience to the Church or divine law. For many Modernists the stress this placed on personal experience necessarily downgraded the rational and deductive propositions of dogma, engendering a pragmatic empirical theology that in Antonio Aliotta's description was 'characterised by its decisive opposition to traditional intellectualism', and which opposed traditional authority with a belief in a continually changing God:

Modernism denies to the intellect the capacity of demonstrating and understanding the Absolute, which is the object of religious faith; and it admits a special organ of experience, an experience directed by the Divine, which really reduces itself to moral activity, to the ethical conscience. In this intimate experience, in which we immediately grasp God in his concrete life, lies the essence of piety. God is not an object external to ourselves, an immutable Being, endowed with certain eternal attributes, and who must be respected from without and known in his objective properties, but a living spirit who works eternally through the human spirit and is eternally revealed in it in his profound intimacy.

[25] *English Modernism*, 119.

From this point of view, as divinity is immanent in the ethical conscience, revelation becomes a matter of process: an acquaintance with divine becoming rather than an insight into a fixed and eternal truth:

> Revelation did not happen once and for all at a fixed moment of time, but is eternally taking place in the consciousness of humanity and in its development. There is therefore no fixed body of unchangeable religious dogmas, but a truth which is developed and revealed progressively through the moral experiences of the human spirit.[26]

Modernism, then, to many of its adherents, offered a kind of religious romanticism which, like its literary counterpart, attempted to revivify a practice hardened into a formalism by restoring the claims of personal experience. The extent to which its ideas had seeped into mainstream Anglicanism can be seen in the claim made in 1927 by the Dean of St Paul's, W. R. Inge, that 'it is now generally recognised that the centre of gravity in religion has changed from authority to experience'.[27]

The Modernist debate was continuing in the Church of England as Murry and Eliot were discovering a religious dimension to their own dispute. But while the debate in England provided a context for their disagreement, an earlier controversy provided it with a precedent. Anglicanism managed to contain its Modernist controversy by an invocation of consensus and the workings of a Doctrinal Commission—although the rapid growth of Anglo-Catholicism in the latter half of the 1920s could be seen as a sectarian reaction against Modernism.[28] The Roman Catholic Church, however, had made no attempt to accommodate Modernism and had anathematized it with all the doctrinal machinery at its disposal. Its major support in this effort was Thomism, the reconstituted religious philosophy that Eliot would espouse in the later years of the 1920s, when he would explicitly celebrate its reaction against philosophical Bergsonism, literary romanticism, and political democracy.[29] The debate between Thomism and Modernism in the Roman Catholic Church was long

---

[26] Antonio Aliotta, 'Science and Religion in the Nineteenth Century', in Joseph Needham (ed.), *Science, Religion and Reality* (London, 1925), 149–86 (p. 167). Murry was acquainted with this work, having reviewed it for the *Adelphi* in December 1925.

[27] 'The Condition of the Church of England', in Inge, *The Church in the World* (London, 1927), 1–26 (pp. 9–10).

[28] See W. S. F. Pickering, *Anglo-Catholicism: A Study in Religious Ambiguity* (London, 1989), 30–61.

[29] See e.g. Eliot's 'Three Reformers', *TLS* 1397 (8 Nov. 1928), 818.

and hard fought. As it was expressed in the controversy between Bergson and Jacques Maritain, it offers an insight into the later debate between Murry and Eliot.

Although Bergson would not expressly concern himself with the nature of religious experience until the publication of his *Two Sources of Morality and Religion* in 1932, his work offered particular support to Modernism through its emphasis on a qualitative truth impervious to the quantifying tendencies of intellect—a view that axiomatically denied the validity of dogma and infallibilism. The God described in Bergson's *Creative Evolution* is not a quantifiable entity or force, but is rather what Leszek Kolakowski has described as 'the principle of creativity itself'.[30] 'God', wrote Bergson, 'has nothing of the already made; He is unceasing life, action, freedom. Creation, so conceived, is not a mystery; we experience it ourselves when we act freely.'[31] This challenging of divine authority proved, as has been discussed earlier, too heterodox for official Catholic tastes with the result that, partly due to the intervention of Jacques Maritain, Bergson's works were placed on the Vatican's Index in 1914. This was part of a concerted effort against Modernism that had included the excommunication of two leading Modernists, Édouard Le Roy and George Tyrrell, in 1907 and the imposition of a mandatory oath against Modernism to be sworn by all Catholic clergy.[32]

A papal encyclical of 1879 had effectively made St Thomas 'the official theologian of the whole Roman Catholic Church'.[33] This pre-emptive strike against Modernism had been reinforced in 1914, when twenty-four theses of Thomism were sanctioned as suitable for teaching in Catholic schools. The dogma with which it combated Modernism derived from its originating premiss of the absolute fixedness of the divine. For Thomism the idea of the mutable or dynamic God portrayed by Bergson and Gourmont is absolutely inimical, as the five proofs on which it is founded require God to be the static primary mover; the centre in which all universal activity has its first cause and without which all action would be rendered absurd.[34] Maritain's definition of this originally Aristotelian belief in

[30] *Bergson* (Oxford, 1985), 61.
[31] *Creative Evolution* (1907), trans. Arthur Mitchell (London, 1911), 262.
[32] In the *motu proprio, Sacrorum antistitum* of 1 Sept. 1910.
[33] Anthony Kenny, *Aquinas* (Oxford, 1980), 27.
[34] See Patterson Brown, 'Infinite Causal Regression', in Anthony Kenny (ed.), *Aquinas: A Collection of Critical Essays* (London, 1970), 214–36.

his critique of Bergson, *La Philosophie Bergsonienne* (1913), exemplified the absolute divide between the two schools of thought:

This first mover, this first cause without cause and without any mixture of potentiality, this *pure act* absolutely immobile, not with the immobility of inertia,—far from it,—but with the immobility of pure and supreme activity, which has nothing to acquire and which can become nothing because it has in itself all that can be had and because it is by itself all that one can be, it is this that we call God.[35]

It was on this fundamental difference of interpretation that Maritain grounded his criticism of Bergson. Bergson, Maritain argued, had fallen into a heretical pantheism by his failure to differentiate between the essence of God, which may according to Thomists only be known *analogically*, and the essence of nature known through the existential knowledge of the world. The two types of knowledge, says Maritain, are different in kind and not, as Bergson would seem to imply, merely different in degree. For Bergson's monism, revelation is associated with a dynamic correspondence in which the veil of rationality is momentarily lifted. For Thomist dualism, however, as God may be known only analogically from the data of immediate experience, the possibility of personal revelation is nullified. Instead, knowledge of God (of necessity always imperfect) is inferred from experience only through the intercession of the intellect and is subject to the authority of the intellectual formulation of faith in dogma. Maritain reinforced this point by invoking the dogma that '*reasoning can with certainty demonstrate the existence of God*'.[36] Reason, then, automatically discredits revelation in favour of the claims of tradition. As a property of intellect, religious knowledge may be built up in a process of accretion into the reasonable and coherent doctrine of the Roman Catholic Church. This body of authoritative dogma, in conjunction with the assumption of man's innate imperfectibility asserted by the doctrine of original sin, denies personal revelation. Instead, the individual must submit to the authority of dogma, and follow what Maritain described as the '*via disciplinae* which

[35] Maritain subsequently modified his criticism of Bergson in the light of the latter's *Two Sources of Morality and Religion* (1932). *La Philosophie Bergsonienne* was published with Maritain's conciliatory introduction to the second edition and an 'Essay of Appreciation' as *Bergsonian Philosophy and Thomism*, trans. Mabelle L. Andison (New York, 1955), 183.

[36] According to Maritain, this is 'a proposition imposed by the Congregation of the Index under the signature of the Abbé Bautain in 1840, and of Bonnety in 1855'. *Bergsonian Philosophy and Thomism*, 191.

transmits taught truths to us and enables us to grasp them in their state of fulfilment and objective completion'.[37]

It was precisely this point that had made Thomism unpalatable to Catholic Modernists. In over-emphasizing the positivistic, rational arguments for the existence of God, incorporating a rigid causality that too easily lent itself to a simple quantification of belief, Thomist doctrine was considered by Modernists too crude a systematization to be adequate to the qualitative, empirical nature of their faith. This particularly anti-Thomist thrust of Modernism had been articulated by George Tyrrell, who described his rejection of Thomism in a strikingly Bergsonian way:

I no longer accept as adequate, or as more than ingeniously illustrative, the simple categories of form and matter, purpose, pattern, by which scholasticism seeks a mechanical explanation of things spiritual and celestial, in the terms of the works of men's hands; I see that scholasticism is saturated hopelessly with principles whose development is materialism and rationalism; that the realism it defends plays straight into the hands of idealism; that it really has no room for such conceptions as *spirit* and *life*, since it explains these higher things—thought, will, love, action—mechanically and artificially, in the terms of those that are lower. Hence it is too opaque a medium to admit the full light and beauty of Christianity to shine upon the eyes of those who think and speak in terms of experience higher than those of the workshop or the sculptor's studio.[38]

Eliot, who for a long time had been applying the metaphor of the workshop and its attendant craftsmanship to his own art, had, from his earliest published criticism, been sceptical of Modernism's attempts to facilitate religious belief.[39] If he were looking for a theoretical underpinning for his arguments against Murry's Modernism, then Thomism would appear to be remarkably well fitted. More consistent than Hulme in its rejection of Bergsonian thinking, it offered a structure of authoritative values strikingly appropriate to the tendencies manifested in his work in the early to mid-1920s. From its proofs against humanism, through its deductive rationalism, right down to its emphasis on art as craft rather than mere imitation, scholasticism offered not only an appropriate but an apparently logical next step for the classicist: a move sanctioned by

[37] *Bergsonian Philosophy and Thomism*, 13.
[38] Quoted in Ranchetti, *The Catholic Modernists*, 47–8.
[39] See e.g. his 'Review of *Conscience and Christ* by Hastings Rashdall', *International Journal of Ethics*, 27/1 (Oct. 1916), 111–12.

Maritain himself, who wrote that 'all *the best people*, nowadays, want the classical'.[40]

'LIFE', LIBERALISM, AND ORGANIZED CHRISTIANITY

Tyrrell's criticism of Thomism had proceeded from the recognition that its rationalism and formalism were incapable of comprehending the qualities of 'spirit' and 'life' that animated religious feeling for most people. Murry had, of course, dedicated the *Adelphi* to a 'belief in life' that accorded a similar primacy to direct feeling in aesthetic and religious activity: a quality caught up with the whole being but continually elusive to the mind.[41] In a discussion of D. H. Lawrence he outlined his view of the relationship between 'truth to life' and the religious attitude:

It seems to me that the essence of the truly religious attitude is to be serious about life . . . The man who seeks, with the whole force of his being, a way of life which shall be in harmony with his own deepest experience, is the religious man. It does not matter whether he finds a way of life that is in accord with any known religion. There are two things, and two things alone, which distinguish the truly religious man—the passionate search for a way of life, or the truth, as some may prefer to call it; and the loyalty to his own experience by which that search is governed. The religious man—and perhaps this distinction has become obscured in these Laodicean days—takes nothing on trust; he abides by his own experience, and by his own instinctive knowledge of what is truest and most profound in that experience.[42]

The way in which Murry opposes inherited value on the grounds of a personal experience that is resistant to intellectual apprehension was a common strategy of defenders of the many 'life philosophies' of the time. Frederick Coplestone, for example, has pointed to the similarities between Nietzsche and Bergson in the attempts of each to articulate affirmative philosophies of life in ways that resist the ratiocinative methods of conventional philosophy. The two writers, argues Coplestone, reject positivism and conceptual rationalism and instead utilize the notion of intuition promoted by the current of

[40] Jacques Maritain, *Art and Scholasticism, with Other Essays*, trans. J. F. Scanlan (London, 1933), 55 (italics in original).

[41] See 'A Month After', *Adelphi*, 1/2 (July 1923), 89–99 (p. 90).

[42] 'Religion and Faith', *Adelphi*, 1/3 (Aug. 1923), 177–84 (p. 179).

Lebensphilosophie with which they flow.[43] In Nietzsche's case, this led him to draw an analogous distinction between religious experience and the Church, seeing the latter as a repressive mechanism imposed on the living force of the former. In *The Anti-Christ* he wrote of the God manifested in the Church having 'degenerated to the *contradiction of life*, instead of being its transfiguration and eternal *Yes!*'[44] According to Nietzsche, Christianity is a 'holy lie' that systematically distorts the example of its founder: 'Jesus cares nothing for what is fixed: the word *killeth*, everything fixed *killeth*. The concept, the *experience* "life" in the only form he knows it is opposed to any kind of word, formula, law, faith, dogma.'[45] He defined this explicitly again in *The Will to Power*, writing that 'precisely that which is Christian in the ecclesiastical sense is anti-Christian in essence: things and people instead of symbols; history instead of eternal facts; forms, rites, dogmas instead of a way of life. Utter indifference to dogmas, cults, priests, church, theology is Christian.'[46] This Nietzschean disdain for the life-denying formalism of organized Christianity carried through, albeit moderately, into Edwardian religious Modernism. Roger Lloyd has noted the Edwardian reconstitution of Nietzsche's Superman in 'The Modern Cultivated Man', the opponent of ecclesiolatry and professor of human perfectibility, who was 'fast casting off every garment which traditional and classical religion had taught him to wear'.[47] Richard Ellmann similarly notes a tendency towards what was effectively an attitude of life-worship in the religious humanism in this period when he observes that 'the capitalised word for the Edwardians is not God but life'.[48] This mobilization of religious humanism did much to draw the sting of Nietzsche's indictment of religion in the cause of 'life'. Indeed, the veneration of 'life' offered such scope for quasi-religious sentimentalism that Wyndham Lewis was prompted to Nietzschean anger at the complacency with which the term was being bandied about in the years immediately before the First World War: for Lewis

[43] *Friedrich Nietzsche: Philosopher of Culture* (1942; new edn. London, 1975), 205–13.
[44] *Twilight of the Idols* and *The Anti-Christ*, trans. R. J. Hollingdale (London, 1990), 138.
[45] Ibid. 154.
[46] Aphorism 159, in *The Will to Power*, trans. Walter Kaufmann and R. J. Hollingdale, ed. Walter Kaufmann (New York, 1968), 61.
[47] *The Church of England, 1900–1965* (London, 1966), 61.
[48] 'Two Faces of Edward', in R. Ellmann (ed.), *Edwardians and Late Victorians* (New York, 1960), 186–7, quoted by Eric Svarny in '*The Men of 1914*', 23.

Nietzsche's noble categorization of 'life' had degenerated into 'a hospital for the weak and incompetent'.[49]

Modernism moderated and humanized Nietzsche's rather ascetic notion of 'life', but it held on to the division that he had drawn between the life that had been lived by Christ and its subsequent betrayal by ecclesiastical authority. Even Roman Catholic Modernists accepted this divide and acknowledged that the researches of the Higher Criticism had, as leading Italian Modernists put it, done 'away with the possibility of finding in Christ's teaching even the embryonic form of the Church's later theological teaching'.[50] While the reformed Christianity of Anglicanism rarely fostered such extreme opinions, it did occasionally witness a questioning of the Church's authority in the name of an original Christian experience; as in, for example, the symposium 'Jesus or Christ?', published as a supplement to the *Hibbert Journal* in 1909.

Modernism's key argument in its challenge to the tradition, then, concerned the extent to which that tradition not only denied the value of the religious experience in the lives of its adherents but also consistently failed to apply itself to the spirit of the original Christian experience: from criticizing organized religion for its betrayal of life it was a short step to criticizing its betrayal of the life of Jesus. This attempt to revise Christian institutions by redirecting them to their purest source is curiously typical of the other retrogressive movements of the early years of the twentieth century already discussed; it is also central to Murry's strategy in appropriating religious values for literature. Murry increasingly found the trajectory of his thought following Modernism, especially in its attempts to found an ethical humanism or 'life' on the living example of a historical Jesus. This would become most apparent in his *Life of Jesus* (1926) which would follow earlier Modernist attempts to use that life as a critique of institutional religion. In a later book Murry would talk of 'The Betrayal of Christ by the Churches': the seeds of this argument can be seen germinating before his life of Jesus in the disputatious essays written for the *Adelphi* between 1923 and 1926. In 1925, for example, Murry had

---

[49] [Wyndham Lewis], *Blast*, 1 (20 June 1914), 130. C. K. Stead devotes a chapter to this dichotomy: '1909–16: "POETRY" versus "LIFE" ', in *The New Poetic: Yeats to Eliot* (London, 1964), 67–95. See also a discussion of Orage's adaptation of Nietzsche's attitudes towards 'life' in David S. Thatcher, *Nietzsche in England*, 252–3.

[50] *The Programme of Modernism*, 90, quoted in William Ralph Inge, 'Roman Catholic Modernism' (1909), in *Outspoken Essays* (London, 1919), 137–71 (p. 152).

begun to draw a distinction between what he described as Galilean and Pauline conceptions of Christianity. According to this model the illuminating example of Jesus's life, with its empiricism and its worldliness, had been systematically betrayed by the rationalism and unworldliness of the Pauline Church: a 'condemnation of life in and through the body' that had led the organized Church into a 'grandiose denial of life'.[51] This can be seen as a first step in placing a coherent argument behind his earlier intuitive belief that 'the man who loves Christ passionately will passionately doubt Christianity; by his very love of Christ he will be driven outside the Church'.[52] For Murry, such a questioning of the Church had followed on from his questionings of the literary tradition. In both cases he found a body whose claims to authority were undermined by an inability to apprehend direct experience. For Murry, as ever, authority could only be proved on the pulses:

for me the question of authority and tradition is quite simply resolved. An authority is one which I discover by experience that I cannot help recognizing as an authority—mysterious words spoken in the past which move my depths and claim my allegiance, even though I cannot say clearly why or how; great imaginations which possess and exalt me, so that I feel moving within them the essence of some truth which I cannot wholly grasp; minds that impress me with a certainty that they possess a deeper knowledge of the mystery of life than any I can claim. These are my authorities, and they are very real authorities to me; very real, because they inspire me with a sense of loyalty to the hidden truth which, I am persuaded, they also served as witnesses and instruments. I cannot give a rational account either of the power of these authorities themselves or of my instinctive recognition of them. They exist, they are part of me, and I try not to betray them.[53]

To Murry's way of thinking the minds described here are operative in the spheres of both art and religion—it is the quality of their insight into a truth, whether that is an aesthetic truth or a religious one, that is crucial. This refusal to separate the values of religion from those of art led Murry, in the same essay, into a statement of his 'hero-authorities'—an alternative great tradition drawn from art, philoso-

---

[51] 'Concerning Angels', *Adelphi*, 3/7 (Dec. 1925), 510–16 (pp. 512–13). See also 'Paulines and Galileans', *Adelphi*, 3/9 (Feb. 1926), 630–5.

[52] The Journeyman, 'On Standing Alone', *Adelphi*, 1/8 (Jan. 1924), 749–53 (pp. 751–2). Although this is not in Lilley, the pseudonym, the style, and the critical preoccupations make Murry's authorship almost certain.

[53] 'Quo Warranto?', *Adelphi*, 2/3 (Aug. 1924), 185–96 (p. 190).

phy, and religion, ranging from Aeschylus, Euripides, and Plato, through Jesus Christ, Shakespeare, Keats, and Whitman, to Tolstoy, Dostoevsky, Chekhov, and Hardy. The factor common to these authorities, in Murry's opinion, is the record that has been left of a profound human experience. Qualities of craftsmanship and technical competence are as nothing to the truth of which they are the vehicle, a truth that becomes less literary and more religious the deeper it is plumbed: 'the deeper our own experience of life descends and the more loyally we abide by our experience, the more intimately we understand the words and life of Christ and the more profound is the illumination we receive from them'. This depth of experience becomes both the condition under which great literature must be written and the means by which its greatness is subsequently recognized: 'when great spirits touch a certain depth of knowledge of human life, this is the path they follow,—the path that leads to a new comprehension of the mystery of Christ'.[54]

In forming a canon that places Euripides, Christ, and Hardy side by side, Murry signals an intention to interpret the Gospels according to the standards he had applied to literature. Viewed this way, Christ is less the purveyor of a unique and unrepeatable doctrine than the exemplar of a particular, and repeatable, kind of revelation. Consequently, the heightened form of 'life', for which Christ is advocate is contained as much in the works of Shakespeare as it is in the Gospels:

It is very odd, but people never can remember that Jesus himself was absolutely free of the Christian religion: he knew nothing about it, and if he had, he would have given up the ghost with a more bitter cry than that he uttered. Jesus at one end, Shakespeare at the other, of the Christian epoch— and both free of it. Imagine them thus, as they were, and it is not so hard to understand why they should say the same, and be the same. I know of no two men more profoundly alike than they.[55]

The quality that Christ and Shakespeare hold in common is the principle according to which the *Adelphi* was founded: 'truth to life'. As this 'life' is withered in the empty formalism of organized religion it has come to be enshrined rather in the pages of great literature. According to Murry, it thus 'becomes easier to understand why the religion of Christianity, as such, is dead, and its place long since taken by literature'.

[54] Ibid. 192–3.   [55] 'Truth to Life', *Adelphi*, 3/8 (Jan. 1926), 523–33 (p. 530).

Murry had been working in a piecemeal fashion towards centring the Christian example in his literary criticism: he had made various attempts to 'define more closely than by scattered remarks' his 'attitude to Christianity and to Christ' in, for example, essays like 'Literature and Religion' in *To the Unknown God* (1924) and the three essays of 1925 later collected as 'Christ or Christianity?'[56] It was with the publication in 1926 of his *The Life of Jesus*, however, a book originally contracted in 1924, that he finally made an explicit and exhaustive commitment to the identification of Christian and aesthetic value, and attempted to justify in the boldest possible terms his challenge to authority in the name of experience.

The attempt to recentre Jesus in the Christian tradition, to realize him as an actual historical figure and to distinguish his teachings from those of his followers, had formed an important cornerstone in the revaluative projects of both Anglican and Catholic Modernism. The radical reinvestigations of the authority of the Gospels carried out by the Higher Criticism of nineteenth-century German theologians, notably Schleiermacher, Strauss, and Baur, had led several works to be written in which the story of Jesus was subjected to a radical reappraisal. Taking inspiration from Renan's ground-breaking *La Vie de Jésus* (1863), works such as J. R. Seeley's *Ecce Homo* (1865), Frederick W. Farrar's *The Life of Christ* (1894), and Adolf Von Harnack's *What is Christianity?* (1901) introduced the notion of a historical Jesus to Victorian readers. These were followed by Shirley Case's *The Historicity of Jesus* (1912), B. H. Streeter's 'The Historic Christ' in *Foundations* (1912), and T. R. Glover's *The Jesus of History* (1917), which laid emphasis on portraying Jesus as a real historical figure, promoting the idea of him as a kenotic figure who had voided himself of his divinity in order fully to partake of human experience. Murry's acquaintance with the Modernist reinterpretations of Jesus's experience, as well as the vigorous backlash created by the eschatological Jesus put forward by Albert Schweitzer in *The Quest of the Historical Jesus*, is evident from his oblique references to these

---

[56] 'Christ or Christianity?', *Adelphi*, 3/4 (Sept. 1925), 233–41 (p. 233). The other essays, appearing in the two subsequent issues, were 'From Man to God', *Adelphi*, 3/5 (Oct. 1925), 309–20 and 'A Simple Creed', *Adelphi*, 3/6 (Nov. 1925), 385–94. They are collected in *Things to Come*.

works in his book.[57] And although he is by no means in agreement with all points of the Modernist interpretation, it is their specifically human Jesus that Murry describes. J. F. Bethune-Baker, Professor of Divinity at Cambridge and a Modernist, had written in 1917: 'there is no kind of "evidence" that He [Jesus] ever thought of Himself as God in any sense'.[58] In keeping with this interpretation the Jesus portrayed by Murry does not recognize, and in a sense does not construct, his divinity until the moment of his baptism in the Jordan.

The notion of rebirth had formed an important part of Murry's criticism since his book on Dostoevsky ten years before, in which he had associated his early mystical visions with the 'dawn of a new consciousness' signalled in the Grand Inquisitor's dream in *The Brothers Karamazov*.[59] The reconstructive thrust of the *Athenaeum* had been founded on the 'New Dispensation' born from the death of the old world in the Great War and prefigured in the works of Hamp and Duhamel. The death of Katherine Mansfield and his subsequent mystical experience were made the grounds for a spiritual rebirth on which the *Adelphi* project was founded. Similarly, in *Keats and Shakespeare*, Murry construed Keats's poetic maturity as the result of an intense process of rebirth—the 'dying into life' he saw as the culmination of the second 'Hyperion' fragment. More recently, in essays such as 'The Need for a New Psychology', he had described the 'crucial moment when the man becomes a saint, or the poet a great poet', as 'a veritable death, from which they are as it were reborn'.[60]

The idea of rebirth through a moment of revelation, then, had been a persistent theme in Murry's criticism. The extent to which he saw the Christian revelation in terms of both that aesthetic revelation he had portrayed in *Keats and Shakespeare* and in terms of his own

---

[57] See *The Life of Jesus* (London, 1926), 7–12 and 68–9. Murry describes his acquaintance with Schweitzer's book during the early 1920s in his *The Challenge of Schweitzer* (London, 1948), 5. He made frequent reference in his work to leading Modernists: men such as Bishop Barnes, Canon Streeter, and Dean Inge. That he was a reader of the Modernists' journal, the *Modern Churchman*, is evinced in his 'The "Common-Sense" of Jesus', *St Martin's Review*, 14 July 1927 (this is not in Lilley, but Murry's typescript, with manuscript dating, is in the Edinburgh Murry collection). Eliot, in his review of Murry's book acknowledged the 'evidence of hard labour' in Murry's consultation of 'most of the authorities of the day in New Testament criticism'. 'Recent Books', *Monthly Criterion*, 5/2 (May 1927), 253–9 (p. 255).

[58] Quoted by Alan M. G. Stephenson, in *The Rise and Decline of English Modernism* (London, 1984), 111.

[59] *Fyodor Dostoevsky*, 33–49, 234.

[60] 'The Need of a New Psychology' (1925), in *Things to Come*, 11–33 (pp. 27–8).

experience can be seen in his later description of his preparation for the new book: 'It was already apparent that my method of approach to Jesus would be of the same order as my method of approach to Keats. The mere fact that I had decided to write a life of Jesus meant that to some extent I claimed to understand his experience in virtue of my own.'[61] It is perhaps unsurprising, then, that he describes the baptism of Jesus, rather than his birth, as the cardinal event of Christianity. Murry discounts the story of the virgin birth and the nativity—which he considers the invention of a Pauline repugnance towards Jesus's physicality—describing them elsewhere as 'pious legends' and 'priggish and repulsive dogma'.[62] Instead, he describes a Jesus entirely human from birth to the age of 30, undergoing a metaphorical rebirth into a divinity that depends as much upon his faith in, and indeed construction of, God as it does in God's divine grace. This idea has its germ in the spiritual rebirth of Keats portrayed in *Keats and Shakespeare*, where the poet achieves identity with God in the discovery of his soul: the point at which 'the atom of God comes to self-consciousness of its own divine nature'.[63] In 'Christ or Christianity?' this identification becomes creative responsibility, with Jesus creating a loving God through his suffering: 'what he died for is not a Father that exists but a world that may be; and he has made the coming of that world inevitable'.[64] The idea that God's fatherhood is the product of human desire to stress a common brotherhood had been to the fore in Murry's 'A Simple Creed'. In that essay he had written that 'the existence of God the Father depends absolutely upon the number of his veritable sons'. He added,

I love my fellow-men sufficiently to desire actively that God should be a good deal more like a father than he actually is. So I am prepared to do something towards making God what I want him to be. The method of God-creation is simple: you have only to remember the simple fact that what you do, God does; what you are, God is. Even to the uttermost: if you disbelieve in God, then God *pro tanto* disbelieves in himself. Every man has the responsibility for God upon his shoulders.[65]

In Murry's thinking, as 'God is realised only through man', he becomes paradoxically the creation of reborn man's consensual faith—'I hold that we humans have it in us to make God what we

[61] *God*, 60–1.   [62] 'Concerning Angels', 513.
[63] *Keats and Shakespeare*, 141.   [64] 'Christ or Christianity?', 240.
[65] 'A Simple Creed', 390.

desire. If we truly desire a loving God we can have him.'[66] What he describes in *The Life of Jesus* as 'the secret centre of Jesus' profoundest teaching' is 'no less than that man must *be* God'.[67] The result of this radical reinterpretation, the reinterpretation that Murry insists is Jesus's message, is that God's work is not the product of obedience to his commandment but is rather the action of that which is carried out spontaneously in his name: 'For Jesus, the will of the reborn man was *identical* with the will of God. There was no effort: it was no question of keeping commandments.'[68] The immanentism of this belief leads to a transposition of Christian doctrine into the terms of humanism: 'Not faith in God, but faith in man was necessary. It was enough to believe in Jesus as a reborn man.'[69] This, in turn, leads to a corresponding humanization of Christian ethics. Morality becomes less a matter of obedience to divine authority than 'the spontaneous acts of the reborn man.'[70] In 'Poetry and Religion' Murry had united these major concerns in describing as 'organic' the 'connection between poetry, religion and conduct.'[71] Through the community of reborn men that he considers the Kingdom of Heaven truly to be, these concepts fuse, in *The Life of Jesus*, to form the 'new dispensation' that he has been hailing for the past ten years; manifesting itself now as a new, humanistic, religion. 'Thus', writes Murry, 'the nature of the reign of God was completely changed . . . from the transcendental theocracy established through the stern and awful judgement of God's Messiah into the blessed company of reborn men and reunited sons of God.'[72] This doctrine leads to hard words for those who attempt a purely intellectual knowledge of God:

In Jesus' teaching the rebirth of the individual man was a birth into a knowledge of God as Father. Apart from this rebirth, God could not be known; to know him was to know him as Father. Therefore to assert or deny the Fatherhood of God, without experience of this rebirth, is to utter empty words. Only those who have become God's sons can know him as Father.[73]

In Jesus's lifetime, those who undertook to interpret God's will according to an established tradition were the scribes and the Pharisees, and Murry describes Jesus's scorn for their dogmatism in terms reminiscent of those he himself had used, and would use again, in his

---

[66] *Life of Jesus*, 183; 'A Simple Creed', 390.   [67] *Life of Jesus*, 196.
[68] Ibid. 185.   [69] Ibid. 114.   [70] Ibid. 191
[71] 'Poetry and Religion', *Adelphi*, 3/10 (Mar. 1926), 695–9 (p. 697).
[72] *Life of Jesus*, 197–8.   [73] Ibid. 189.

attacks on the corresponding inflexibility of Eliot's criticism. Murry's Jesus is profoundly anti-traditional, an 'anarchist' who quotes Isaiah in telling the Pharisees, ' "You have let go God's commandment, and taken hold of the 'tradition' of men. How beautifully you make null the commandment of God that you may keep your own 'tradition!' " '[74] When he is asked on whose authority he acts when he allows his disciples to break the Sabbath, or when he cleanses the Temple of Jerusalem, Murry's Jesus stands upon his own authority as the first reborn son of God, in direct opposition to the regulated and traditional authority of the Scriptures. Murry describes this conflict of 'a personal knowledge of God's will set over against an impersonal knowledge of that will as declared ages ago to the men of old', seeing in it, 'the voice of God speaking directly and anew through a living Man against the voice of God graven immutably upon stone: a new revelation against the old'.[75] This direct confrontation between personal revelation and an original revelation subsequently codified into a religious tradition exposes, in Murry's opinion, the inherent contradiction in any organized religion:

the position of organized religion has always been the same. Because it is religion, God has revealed himself directly to men; because it is organized, that direct revelation can never be renewed. A new revelation cannot be suffered, for it strikes direct at the heart of authority. It is, and must be condemned as, subversive and heretical.[76]

As his other writings show, Murry regarded this contradiction—encapsulated in the notion that Jesus was a heretic in terms of the scriptural tradition and the 'Church' of his times—as an insurmountable obstacle to the arguments for any form of religious organization that did not have its primary basis in individual revelatory experience.[77] Even at its height, the Modernist controversy over Jesus's divinity had never gone as far as to suggest that Jesus's example might be inimical to the organization of a Church. But for Murry, as the title of his essay 'Christ or Christianity?' suggests, a choice must be made. In choosing Christ, as Murry does, the believer must necessarily reject the intercession of a religious organization.

---

[74] *Life of Jesus*, 142.   [75] Ibid. 79–80.   [76] Ibid. 53–4.

[77] 'It is because we insist on speaking the ineffable divine, on holding it in the grasp of the intellectual mind, on organizing it into systems and institutions, that troubles and disquiet begin.' 'The Religion of Mark Rutherford', *Adelphi*, 2/2 (July 1924), 93–104 (p. 98).

Murry's opinions seem highly unorthodox, but it is worth noting just how closely his Jesus resembles the historical figure being recreated by Anglican Modernists—and being interpreted by them as the single most important source of religious authority. I have mentioned some of the earlier discussions of the life of Jesus. To these several more had been added in the period under consideration. The most controversial of the new interpretations had been given at the subsequently infamous Conference of Modern Churchmen at Girton College Cambridge in 1921. Two papers in particular had drawn the attention of the popular and ecclesiastical media: Hastings Rashdall's 'Christ as Logos and Son of God' and J. F. Bethune-Baker's 'Jesus as both Human and Divine'. Rashdall had put forward five points that stressed Jesus's humanity, his fallibility, and the wholly natural aspect of his advent. He added further that Jesus's particular value lay in the extent to which he realized the God that is incarnate in every human being—anticipating Murry's suggestion that Jesus's experience was different only in degree and not in kind from ordinary religious experience.[78] Professor Bethune-Baker took this argument further, suggesting that the relationship between man and God that Jesus had exemplified to a high degree was one of mutual definition. Men have their origin in the will and love of God, argued Bethune-Baker, but 'they are the counterparts of that will and love, as necessary to the existence of God as He is to theirs. Neither is complete without the other.'[79] The sense in which the knowledge of God is achieved solely through the intermediation of the specifically human aspect of Jesus's incarnation leads Bethune-Baker to a humanism that directly anticipates Murry:

When our conception of reality has become essentially ethical, spiritual, personal, our faith, our religion, must be expressed in terms of our own relation as persons to it: and when I say that the man Jesus is 'God', I mean that He is for me the index of my conception of God. I say 'He', because I mean not only His teaching, His own ideas about God, but also His life, His personality as a whole, as I can learn it, primarily from the impression He

---

[78] 'Christ as Logos and Son of God', *Modern Churchman*, 11/5 and 11/6 (Sept. 1921), 278–86 (p. 283). The argument, and the outcry against it, are summarized in Stephenson, *Rise and Decline of English Modernism*, ch. 5, 'Men of Girton' (pp. 99–122). 'Echoes of the Cambridge Conference', *The Modern Churchman*, 11/7 (Oct. 1921), 349–72, outlines both the popular and the wider theological responses to the conference papers.

[79] 'Jesus as Both Human and Divine', *Modern Churchman*, 11/5 and 11/6 (Sept. 1921), 287–301 (p. 292).

made, so far as it can be inferred from the Gospels and the early religious experience of which He was the centre.[80]

It is this belief, that God is intuited entirely through the example of a human Jesus—that, as Bethune-Baker puts it, 'Jesus is the creator of my God'[81]—that Murry describes in the paradox of Jesus having 'created the living God for whom he died', and that he made the basis for his *Life of Jesus*.[82]

It is tempting to view *The Life of Jesus* from a modern perspective as an example of the kind of naïve and sentimental religiosity against which Eliot had set his face: the kind of sublimated humanism that Hulme had characterized as 'spilt religion'. But it is important to note the currency of Murry's opinions. Far from representing the musings of an isolated enthusiast, the book had a place in a living radical tradition that had Arnold and the Higher Criticism as forebears and Modernism as its cognate. An advertising insert for the work, distributed inside copies of Murry's next book, *God*, testified to the warm reception accorded the work: quoting several laudatory reviews, including those from the *Times Literary Supplement*, the *Nation*, from Evelyn Underhill in the *Spectator*, and from Dean Inge, who saw the work as 'a sort of *Ecce Homo* for our generation'. Indeed, as a measure of the strength of the book, Murry was given the task of reviewing subsequent lives of Jesus for the *Times Literary Supplement*.[83]

In the preface to *The Life of Jesus* Murry had written that, for the purposes of this book, his credentials as a literary critic were as valid as the more specialized training of a professor of Divinity. His meaning becomes clear later in the book, when he describes the nature of Jesus's experience. For, very much contrary to the beliefs of Hulme discussed earlier, Murry is quite explicit in describing the nature of religious experience as being continuous with aesthetic experience:

although there was in Jesus' experience of God a quality peculiar to himself, an ineffable sweetness of personal reunion, which directly derived from the personal quality of Jesus himself, the *kind* of the experience was not unique: it can be paralleled exactly from the experience of great saints and great poets. Fundamentally, it was an act of profound obeisance to the

---

[80] 'Jesus as Both Human and Divine', 300–1.

[81] Ibid. 301   [82] 'Christ or Christianity?', 239.

[83] See e.g. Murry's 'Christian Origins', *TLS* 1290 (21 Oct. 1926), 714; 'Mr Barbusse's "Jesus" ', *TLS* 1312 (24 Mar. 1927), 214; 'Two Lives of Jesus', *TLS* 1343 (27 Oct. 1927), 754; 'The Historical Jesus', *TLS* 1429 (20 June 1929), 484; and 'Two Lives of Jesus', *TLS* 1439 (29 Aug. 1929), 660.

apprehended wonder and beauty of the universe—a sudden and for ever incontrovertible seeing that all things have their place and purpose in a great harmony.[84]

In an earlier essay Murry had averred that 'the pure poet is a pure poet because he is a pure man'.[85] In *The Life of Jesus* he extended this claim from aesthetics to religion, arguing that 'Jesus was the supreme manifestation of God simply because he was the supreme manifestation of Man'.[86] He would follow this with a definition of Christianity as a belief 'in humanity in its finest manifestations'.[87] The explicit humanism here, which identifies both poetry and divinity as necessary products of a particular intensity of human experience, follows on from 'Romanticism and the Tradition' and 'Truth to Life' in giving Murry's writings on religion an immediate relevance to his literary-critical practice. What he describes in his next book as a realization that 'the mystical experience and the aesthetic experience were indeed the same' leads to a form of criticism in which their terms become interchangeable.[88] Murry's Jesus takes his place with little incongruity alongside the hero-authorities that had been listed in Murry's 'Quo Warranto?', quoted above, because the quality of the experience manifested in his parables, and which inspired the Gospel of Mark, is of the order, if not the intensity, of those that had inspired Keats and Shakespeare: as he had written earlier, 'my scriptures have been books which the mystic would not regard as scriptures at all—Shakespeare supremely, next perhaps Tchehov and Keats, then Dostoevsky, Nietzsche, Tolstoi, Whitman, Melville'.[89] In a similar manner, Jesus's rejection of an inherited, reified authority in favour of one that is revealed in a state of intense being, is, according to Murry, the paradigmatic act of literary creation, the point at which the common inheritance of tradition gives way to the rebirth of the individual through a revelatory experience.

Making the example of Jesus a critique of organized Christianity takes Murry back to the irony expressed in the preface to *The Life of Jesus*. For if organized religion has, as Murry claims, lost sight of the historical Jesus by turning his living example into an empty tradition, then the imaginative reconstructions characteristic of literature have at least as good a chance of rediscovering the essential Jesus as

[84] *Life of Jesus*, 190.
[85] 'A Prologue to Keats', *Adelphi*, 2/6 (Nov. 1924), 461–72 (p. 471).
[86] *Life of Jesus*, 209–10.   [87] *Things to Come*, 5.   [88] *God*, 315.
[89] 'The Unknown Country', *Adelphi*, 2/5 (Oct. 1924), 369–78 (p. 376).

has academic theology: as he wrote in *Keats and Shakespeare,* 'poetry in its highest and purest forms is one of the few roads that remain open to the eternal reality that is less fully expressed in religion. We have lost contact with that reality; and we have to regain it'.[90] Murry reiterated this point early in 1926, in drawing a distinction between poetry written in an age of religious belief and the poetry of an age in which that belief has lapsed. In ages of belief, the religious and aesthetic experience are identical—'the poetic and the religious noêsis in Aeschylus or Plato or Dante are one and the same'—but in ages in which belief has lapsed and in which religion has withered into formalism it is through the agency of a living literature that religion can be resuscitated—'through a loyal obedience to the poetic noêsis the full perfection of religious noêsis—the Word made flesh—is reachieved'.[91] Only through understanding this trenchant anti-traditionalism, expressed in Murry's conflation of aesthetic experience and religious noêsis, is it possible to comprehend his apparently scandalous assertion that 'a modern man will more quickly and more truly find what the Kingdom of Heaven means from Shakespeare than he will from the New Testament itself'.[92]

THE CLASSICAL REVIVAL

Apart from the letter quoted earlier, in which Eliot exhorted Murry not to discard religious dogma but to attempt to change it from within, the two men had little contact from the end of their first debate in the middle of 1924 to the beginning of 1926. In January of that year Eliot relaunched the *Criterion* as the *New Criterion.* The extent to which this pointed to a new direction for Eliot was marked by his authorship of an editorial manifesto for the new journal, 'The Idea of a Literary Review'. The *Criterion* had been launched without an explicit statement of aims, a fact that underpinned its initial claims to critical disinterestedness. The *New Criterion* was launched, however, with a quite explicit agenda. In the editorial

---

[90] *Keats and Shakespeare,* 144.
[91] 'Poetry and Religion', 699. Eliot would never go quite this far in identifying poetry and religion, but he would, as Kristian Smidt has argued, admit 'the possibility of a noetic relation' between the two activities in *The Use of Poetry and the Use of Criticism* and after. See Smidt, *Poetry and Belief in the Work of T. S. Eliot,* rev. edn. (London, 1961), 56–7.
[92] 'Truth to Life', *Adelphi,* 532.

statement of that agenda Eliot's claims for disinterestedness were undercut by his endorsement of what he described as a modern tendency 'toward something which, for want of a better name, we may call classicism'. For Eliot, this classicism is marked by 'a more serene control of the emotions by Reason' and according to its precepts he confidently separated out classical sheep from romantic goats, favouring Sorel, Maurras, Benda, Hulme, Maritain, and Babbitt over Wells, Shaw, and Russell, whose recent works 'all exhibit intelligence at the mercy of emotion'.[93]

In a sense, this appears to be Eliot's first unprovoked exposition of his classicism; the first time he had attached the classical label to himself outside of a controversy. This unusual forthrightness can perhaps be ascribed to several major changes in the circumstances of his personal life. His literary-critical output in 1925 had been at best sporadic, limited first by his wife's severe illness, by a consequent breakdown of his own, and later by his exchanging jobs to join the board of directors at Faber & Gwyer. Both Lyndall Gordon and Peter Ackroyd have described the end of 1925 and the beginning of 1926 as a crucial time for Eliot; marking a clear break between his early career and the middle course of his life.[94] Supporting this contention are Eliot's new employment, the rejuvenation of his magazine, publication of his collected poems to 1925, and the beginning of the severance between himself and his wife. Allied to this is the stirring of a newly invigorated religious belief, prompted in part by his recent readings in the Thomism of Jacques Maritain.

Ackroyd sees this as discontinuity rather than development: pointing to the alterations in Eliot's personal circumstances that help to effect the small discontinuities through which the larger body of his poetic and critical practices undergo a radical change. But it can be argued that, as far as Eliot's criticism is concerned, such small changes take place within an increasingly consistent attitude toward authority: one that is present in his literary criticism and which becomes mapped out, as it were, onto his religious criticism. Lyndall Gordon draws a rather more developmental, and more convincing, picture of the growth of Eliot's religious sensibility. Gordon points to Eliot's early interest in mysticism, and plots the gradual development of his austere religious egotism into what is, initially at least, an

---

[93] 'The Idea of a Literary Review', *New Criterion*, 4/1 (Jan. 1926), 1–6 (pp. 4, 5, 6).
[94] Lyndall Gordon, *Eliot's Early Years* (Oxford, 1977), 127–8; Ackroyd, *T. S. Eliot*, 149–56.

equally austere Christian collectivism. From Gordon's point of view, in the year leading up to his conversion Eliot begins a repudiation of the earlier stages through which his religious sensibility has evolved: a sloughing off of the religious isolationism of St Narcissus and the Desert Fathers and a recognition of the 'possibilities for saintliness within the parish'.[95] While Murry could never quite be considered as a St Narcissus, he arguably represents the kind of religiously inspired egotism that Eliot was in the process of repudiating in his own experience. And just as he had provided an antagonism out of which Eliot's classicism had been defined, Murry's religious liberalism would offer Eliot the kind of opposition—perhaps even a devil's advocacy—against which his religious ideas might be tested. At the very least, Murry offered a contrast to Eliot: an idea of where he did *not* want to go.

Eliot's restatement of his critical principles was followed almost immediately by a riposte from Murry. In February he reviewed Eliot's *Poems, 1909–1925* for the Dutch journal the *Algemeen handelsblad*. But his main interrogation of Eliot came in an article, 'The "Classical" Revival', published in the *Adelphi* in two parts in February and March, and separately in the *Revue de Genève* in March.[96] The article is most remarkable for its anticipation of Eliot's conversion: an act that Murry construes as the only logical resolution to the contradictions he perceives in Eliot's classicism. But it is also of particular interest in highlighting the relationship between the two writers.

Three distinct versions of the article have come to light: the two published versions described above; and a third unpublished typescript. The typescript appears to be an early draft of the article and is almost certainly the text from which the French translation was made for the Genevan journal. Although undated, internal evidence suggests that it was written at around the same time as Eliot's editorial manifesto in December 1925. But while there is a remarkable coincidence in its preoccupation with classicism, Murry's article appears to be written independently of Eliot's.

What makes the typescript particularly remarkable is that it has been heavily annotated by Eliot. There is evidence that Murry was continuing to pass articles to Eliot for his comment before

---

[95] Gordon, *Eliot's Early Years*, 120.

[96] 'The "Classical" Revival', *Adelphi*, 3/9 (Feb. 1926), 585–95, and 3/10 (Mar. 1926), 648–53; 'La Renaissance du classicisme en Angleterre', trans. K. de Watteville, *Bibliothèque universelle et revue de Genève*, 13/3 (Mar. 1926), 356–68.

publication: Eliot had read and commented on Murry's 'Christ or Christianity?' before its publication the previous year. The typescript shows that this practice was continuing and suggests that Eliot may have been prompted into his defence of classicism by a pre-publication reading of Murry's essay. This, however, cannot be proved. What can be proved is that Murry made a number of changes to his *Adelphi* article in the light of Eliot's comments on his draft. The first half of the article was published much as it had been drafted, although there are several instances where Murry defers to Eliot's comments or clarifies his argument in the light of them. For example, two short paragraphs on the second page of the typescript were omitted after Eliot had written of their being 'not necessarily of any significance'. On the third page of the typescript Murry's description of a 'general desire' for a classical revival became a 'universal desire' at Eliot's suggestion. Similarly, Murry refers on the sixth page of the typescript to Strachey's works being 'the most truly *accomplished* writing since the war'. Eliot's general disparagement of Strachey throughout his notes, and his particular description of this claim by Murry as 'bosh', results in Murry dropping the claim. Again, on the twelfth page of the typescript Murry describes the Catholic Church as possessing knowledge derived from a time 'when it was big enough to include all romanticism'. In a longer note Eliot opines that 'it is still big enough, if "bigness" be originality, to include a prodigious amount of romanticism'. Murry defers to this opinion in the *Adelphi* article, writing that the Catholic Church 'has managed to include most romanticisms'.[97] In other instances Murry notes Eliot's criticism but does not alter his opinion. One example is given on the ninth page of the typescript, in which Murry describes the contradiction of a self-proclaimed classicist having written *The Waste Land*, which uses a method that is not itself 'classical in any sense of the word'. Eliot replies to this by writing in the margin that, 'no one ever said it was. "The Waste Land" makes *no attempt whatever* to be "classical".' For the essay's publication in the *Adelphi*, Murry added a short sentence—'Nor can it be supposed that they believe it is'—to register Eliot's point while leaving his own argument substantially intact. This is a strategy Murry uses elsewhere, and is particularly obvious in the footnotes that he added to the *Adelphi* article. Each of the first three footnotes to the *Adelphi* article is a direct, if

[97] 'The "Classical" Revival', 593.

unacknowledged, reply to Eliot's comments. The second and third footnotes,[98] like the opinion on *The Waste Land* mentioned above, merely take account of Eliot's resistance to being incorporated in a classical grouping. The first, and largest, footnote, however, directly addresses the conception of romanticism made by Eliot in his marginal commentary. On the second page of the typescript Murry disassociates himself from Wells, Bennett, Shaw, and Galsworthy, who 'represent an extreme phase of confidence in modern society' that should not be confused with romanticism. Eliot replied in the margin: 'Not, I imagine, according to your conception; but according to the ideas of several reputable writers—esp. Babbitt, Seillière, this "extreme phase" is a phase of romanticism.' Murry responded in his *Adelphi* article, 'I am not unmindful of the fact that critics of repute—Babbitt, Seillière, Lasserre—French, or of French inspiration, maintain that precisely this *is* "romanticism". But romanticism and religious nullity are, in my judgement, mutually exclusive.'[99]

Although the alterations made by Murry to the first part of the article, published in February's *Adelphi*, are not largely substantive they none the less exhibit an openness to criticism, and at least an attempt to confront Eliot's more serious criticisms. The second part of the article, published in the following month, shows evidence of more substantial alteration, becoming a much sharper probing of Eliot's classicism in moving from the generalization, and sometimes verbosity, of the typescript to specific and trenchant *ad hominem* arguments. This may be due, in part, to the increasing asperity manifested in Eliot's comments towards the end of the typescript. Or it may be the result of Murry's having read Eliot's 'The Idea of a Literary Review', in which Murry's religious views are disdainfully dismissed. Whatever the case, the second part of the article as it appears in the *Adelphi* is a more pertinent, and trenchant, assault on Eliot's position, moving from a general discussion of classicism, and the work of Eliot and Woolf, to a more particular exposition of the contradictions that Murry discerns in Eliot's classicism.

Ackroyd has remarked on Murry's prescience in insisting that Eliot's classicism obliges him, if he is to be logically consistent, to espouse a form of Catholic Christianity. This is undoubtedly the strength of Murry's article. But, ironically, it is made more cogent by the opportunity for revision given by Eliot's comments. Murry's is

---

[98] 'The "Classical" Revival', 590, 592.   [99] Ibid. 586.

the first explicit rendering of a charge that would frequently be levelled at Eliot, concerning the impossibility of squaring *The Waste
Land*, and the more recently published 'The Hollow Men', with the
classicism advocated by his criticism. In the *Adelphi* article, Murry
described the double standard involved as Eliot's having 'classicism
for his wife and romanticism for his mistress'.[100] (A later critic would
describe a similar double standard as 'chasing with the hounds of
Modernism while running with the hares of classicism'.[101]) Murry is
in advance of many later commentators, however, in insisting that
the apparent contradiction could be comprehended within a conversion to the Catholic faith. Murry had written earlier that 'the "intellectual" *convert* to Catholicism to-day is a renegade to humanity'.[102]
And in the typescript, and the first part of the *Adelphi* article, he is
unrelenting in his description of the potentially humiliating climb-
down represented by Eliot's projected conversion: 'it is unfortunate
for him that his recantation must be public; but since his profession
was public, it is inevitable'. But by the time he came to revise the second part for publication, that attitude was substantially moderated.

In a note to the typescript Eliot had made quite explicit the source
from which his classicism derived. 'It is not the Catholic Church,' he
wrote, 'but the XII–XIII centuries that were classical. The Church of
the XVII C. was romantic. Jesuism has nothing to do with classicism', an interpretation that formed the basis of the Clark Lectures at
Cambridge which he was in the process of giving, and in which he
publicly adverted to his disagreements with Murry.[103] Murry had
adverted to an analogous separation in the typescript in discriminat-
ing between what he described as the 'Augustanism' of Strachey,
Huxley, and David Garnett and the more 'serious classicism' of Eliot
and Woolf. In that version, however, he had failed to make the
grounds for that distinction clear—a failure Eliot had remarked on at
several points. In the revised article for the *Adelphi* he defined this
Augustanism as 'classicism without belief in God'.[104] This clarifies
the typescript argument substantially, and allows Murry to drop
some of the more obscure arguments about the nature of Eliot's

[100] Ibid. 649.
[101] Eliseo Vivas, 'The Objective Correlative of T. S. Eliot', in Robert Wooster Stallman
(ed.), *Critiques and Essays in Criticism, 1920–1948* (New York, 1949), 389–400 (p. 390).
[102] 'A Simple Creed', 387.
[103] See *The Varieties of Metaphysical Poetry*, ed. and introd. Ronald Schuchard
(London, 1993) 75–6 and 100–4.
[104] 'The "Classical" Revival', 653.

'seriousness', leaving himself free to address himself directly to his perception of Eliot's medievalist classicism. As he shows in the first footnote to the *Adelphi* version, Murry takes this classicism quite seriously. 'Serious classicism' is no longer the 'negation' and 'self-deception' described on the sixteenth page of the typescript. It is, rather, the peculiar characteristic of a spiritual crisis of one whose intelligence is too strong for the cynical formalism of Augustanism, but whose faith is too weak to accede to a simple piety. By addressing himself directly to the form of classicism that Eliot proclaims, Murry is able to get to the heart of Eliot's dilemma. Eliot, Murry believes, yearns for the certainty that was granted to Dante by medieval theology: 'Dante could trust his own intellectualism because he believed in that supra-intellectual reality which he used it to articulate. His theology was, so to speak, a metaphysic *of which he was certain*.' That certainty having been lost, Eliot is left espousing a forlorn theology. The intellectual coherence of that theology derived from a shared belief. Eliot's mistake lies in attempting to reconstruct that belief intellectually:

It is not possible for a man so sensitive and so scrupulous as Mr Eliot to reach a belief in God by the grand old ways. Those grand old ways were not built from man to God, but from God to man. The belief was there, the intellectual explication of it came afterwards. It is easy for a man who inherits a faith to be classical; it is impossible for a man without one to achieve a faith through classicism.[105]

The only remedy for the crisis of 'serious classicism', according to Murry, is the unqualified acceptance of religious belief associated with conversion: as he had written earlier, 'a God whom you have to conceive intellectually is a God of whose existence you are not, never have been, and never will be certain'.[106]

In a sense, Murry's argument—that belief gives substance to dogma, but that dogma cannot itself substantiate belief—echoes Bergson's argument that 'fixed concepts may be extracted by our thought from mobile reality; but there are no means of reconstructing the mobility of the real with fixed concepts'.[107] It also follows a clear strand of Modernist thinking, expressed by T. R. Glover in his *The Jesus of History*: 'We have always to remember that thought

[105] 'The "Classical" Revival', 653.
[106] 'Religion and Christianity', *Adelphi*, 1/8 (Jan. 1924), 666–74 (p. 668).
[107] *Introduction to Metaphysics* (1903), trans. T. E. Hulme (London, 1913), 58.

does not strictly supply its own material, however much it may help us to find it. Philosophy and theology do not give us our facts', a point made by A. N. Whitehead, when he wrote that 'religions commit suicide when they find their inspirations in dogma'.[108] Eliot himself had, some years earlier, made a similar suggestion concerning the status of philosophy, writing in his dissertation that 'a philosophy can and must be worked out with the greatest rigour and discipline in the details, but can ultimately be founded on nothing but faith'.[109] More recently, he had made a similar distinction in his discussion of the relationship between dance and ritual, observing that 'you cannot *revive* a ritual without reviving a faith'.[110] While this seems particularly pertinent to Murry's criticism of him, it was not an argument that Eliot felt applied to his own case. Murry's argument in 'Religion and Christianity', however, has an undeniable pertinence that defies him to make that 'blind act of faith'.

Eliot would begin to undertake this conversion some twelve months later. In the short term, underlining a section of the typescript in which Murry had written of the possibility of his conversion ('it might conceivably be done, by an act of violence, by joining the Catholic Church'), Eliot added the cryptic comment, 'to be proved'.

In his notes to the tenth page of Murry's typescript, Eliot contended that he saw 'no contradiction at all' between his classical principles and the apparent nihilism of 'The Waste Land'. This related to what he recognized as the crux of Murry's argument: Murry's belief that the 'pro-classical velleities' uttered by Eliot and Virginia Woolf are contradicted by the 'disordered, obscure, indecorous' content of their creative writing. Eliot's reply to this shows, arguably, the distance he has yet to travel before conversion, illustrating a distinction that Peter Ackroyd has drawn, between his early religious sensibility and his later religious conviction. For Eliot staunchly refuses to perceive the contradiction, writing in a marginal note to Murry, 'you assume this to be failure. It is merely sincerity.' This prefigures the defence that Eliot would use to the same charge levelled some twelve months later by I. A. Richards. On the later occasion Eliot would

---

[108] T. R. Glover, *The Jesus of History* (London, 1917), 224. A. N. Whitehead, *Religion in the Making* (Cambridge, 1926), p. 144.

[109] *Knowledge and Experience in the Philosophy of F. H. Bradley* (London, 1964), 163. Quoted by Pamela McCallum, in *Literature and Method: Towards a Critique of I. A. Richards, T. S. Eliot and F. R. Leavis* (Dublin, 1983), 103.

[110] 'The Ballet', *Criterion*, 443.

write, 'a "sense of desolation", etc. (if it is there) is not a separation from belief; it is nothing so pleasant. In fact, doubt, uncertainty, futility, etc., would seem to me to prove anything except this agreeable partition; for doubt and uncertainty are merely varieties of belief.'[111] This argument—that doubt is a form of belief—lacks, at the very least, the 'clearer conception of Reason' he advocated as his critical principle in 'The Idea of a Literary Review'. The discrimination he attempts to draw is, I think, similar to that made by Murry in describing him as a 'serious classicist'. Eliot's refusal to acquiesce in the pat certainties of a reconstituted Augustanism, and his insistence instead upon the sincerity of his doubt is what makes him, as Murry had recognized, a special case. But where Murry is more clear than Eliot is in his insistence that this sincere doubt is rather a precondition of belief than, as Eliot would seem to imply, somehow its complement.

In taking Eliot's doubts as an earnest of his religious sincerity, Murry is able to constitute that doubt as a kind of belief without faith. But in imputing an intellectual pride to Eliot he can also isolate the particular barrier erected against this faith. The solace associated with belief will not come to Eliot 'because Mr Eliot will dictate the way it must come. His intellect must be satisfied'.[112] This charge, of a faithless belief predicated on intellectual rather than experiential grounds, would become the mainstay of Murry's critique of organized religion. It would also be the centre of contention in the next phase of their debate.

REASON AND ROMANTICISM

In 1928 Murry described the 'curious and interesting discussion' in which he and Eliot had recently been engaged. 'The essential matter in dispute', wrote Murry, 'might be variously described, for its manifestations are Protean. It appears as a dispute sometimes about religion, sometimes about philosophy, sometimes about poetry. It is, indeed, a dispute about any and all of these.'[113] This description of the second, and effectively last, phase of their dispute sums up Murry's contention in brief: that the values of religion, philosophy,

---

[111] 'A Note on Poetry and Belief', *Enemy*, 1 (Jan. 1927), 15–17 (p. 16).
[112] 'The "Classical" Revival', 653.
[113] 'Poetry and Philosophy', unpublished typescript, Edinburgh, 8 pp. [p. 1].

and poetry are continuous and that therefore their terms are inter-changeable. Thus Shakespeare can be construed as a philosopher (in that word's original connotation), Keats as an exemplar of religious sensibility, and the parables of Jesus as the finest poetry. While Eliot might agree that religion, philosophy, and poetry are constituents of his dispute with Murry, he would hardly concur that the dispute at any time was 'about any and all of these'. For Eliot's concern throughout the later debate with Murry was to distinguish between these various categories in the attempt to construe them as discrete and discontinuous activities. His search for a better-defined literary-critical language and his espousal of neo-Thomism require him to make clear distinctions, much as Maritain would do in *Art and Scholasticism*, in order to keep 'philosophy, religion and poetry each in its proper place'.[114]

The second phase of their disagreement had its ostensible source in their conflicting views of the notion of critical intelligence advanced by Herbert Read in *Reason and Romanticism*, published in 1926. Even in its title, Read's book shows the extent to which the kind of romanticism championed by Murry was back, at least as a recognizable term on the literary-critical agenda. Read, however, sets out to subject this perceived romanticism to what he regards as the necessary corrective of the critical intelligence, or reason. The first essay in the collection, 'The Attributes of Criticism', sets out Read's position explicitly. Interestingly, bearing in mind the dialogical process of the Murry–Eliot debate, Read chose to define his own opinions in opposition to those advanced by Waldo Frank in his essay 'For a Declaration of War', published in *Salvos* (1924). In that essay Frank had put forward an analysis of a decadent Western culture, reminiscent of that advanced by Valéry in 'The Crisis of the Spirit' and characteristic of the whole post-war literature of disenchantment. The gradual degradation of civilized values posited by Frank led him to suggest that the Western intellectual tradition had effectively been over-thrown. This usurpation, characterized by the supersession of religious beliefs by science, was, he suggested, the product of an inflexible and ultimately reductive intellectualism. The only remedy to the consequent sterility (a remedy that had been prefigured in the science of Einstein and Poincaré) would be 'a new synthesis' which

[114] 'Mr Middleton Murry's Synthesis', *Monthly Criterion*, 6/4 (Oct. 1927), 340–7 (p. 344).

would be marked by the recognition of irrational knowledge by scientific reason: what Frank described as the preparation of 'the intellect to receive Mystery'.[115]

As has been seen, such arguments were not uncommon at this time. Read, however, takes great exception to Frank's derogation of intellectual values. What marks out Read's response for special attention, however, is its description not of a single European tradition, but of two discrete but coexistent traditions. This response shows the extent to which the debate between Murry and Eliot had percolated through at least as far as their immediate literary circles—for the traditions Read describes are exactly those delineated by Eliot and Murry during the previous five years. Read agrees with Frank's analysis of a contemporary breakdown in cultural values; he disagrees, however, with Frank's contention that this breakdown threatens the whole European intellectual tradition. Read believes rather that the crisis challenges only one part of that tradition—a pernicious component that was introduced at the Renaissance. Frank's mistake, suggests Read, lies in his failure to differentiate between the continuing vitality of a pre-Renaissance tradition and its moribund post-Renaissance adjuncts:

the first European tradition reached its perfect expression in the thirteenth century. The tradition with which Mr Frank is occupied is quite another tradition; it has its origins in a different emotional attitude, and this attitude has its own expression in art and its own rationalization in philosophy: it has the Renaissance, the Humanists, and the Cartesians, in fact.[116]

Frank is, according to Read, the victim of a subjectivist tradition that sees only itself in the larger European tradition. If he were able he would see that the contemporary crisis does not so much overthrow that tradition as strip away its post-Renaissance accretions to reveal a wholly consistent European tradition drawn on scholastic lines: 'if we were required to point to a philosophy worked out in terms of Western reality and consonant with our deepest instincts, we should turn to mediaeval philosophy and particularly to the thought of St Thomas Aquinas'.[117] The crisis described by Read does not so much challenge the intellectual values implicit in Victorian scientism

---

[115] *Salvos: An Informal Book about Books and Plays* (New York, 1924), 20, 22.
[116] 'The Attributes of Criticism', in *Reason and Romanticism: Essays in Literary Criticism* (London, 1926), 10.
[117] Ibid. 13.

as reveal the importance of the intellect as that term is constituted in Thomist philosophy. It is only through this intellect, enshrined in the critical tradition, that literature might be restored and saved from the chaos of unchecked emotionalism. In his description of the workings of that intelligence, Read articulates the conception of tradition he holds in common with Hulme and Eliot:

intelligence is a growing principle in humanity, and an excellent carapace for tender hearts. It not only shelters the growth of the spirit, but trains it to unexpected fertility. All progress is a question of deliberate preparation: the building of foundations, the accumulation of knowledge, the careful culti-vation of traditions, and the embodiment of these in institutions. And always discipline and order, with utmost clarity of statement and honesty of thought. It would be better to sacrifice art altogether than to make it a mere analogous groping in the void of nescience.[118]

Murry's review of Read's book was written in May and appeared as the leading article of the *Times Literary Supplement* for 8 July 1926. In many respects that article is the complement of an essay he had written for the *New Criterion* of June 1926, 'The Romantic Fallacy'. In that essay he had signalled his dissatisfaction with the dichotomy between romanticism and classicism that had been characteristic of his earlier exchanges with Eliot. The essay itself focuses on two of the central contentions of Tolstoy's 'What is Art?': that the judgement of art is carried out according to the shared religious perceptions of a society; and that the upholders of that religious perception have been, since the Renaissance at least, the disenfranchised and the peasantry. In criticism of this position Murry advanced two argu-ments he had been developing over a period of years. First, that it is not organized religion but rather literature that has been the upholder of religion since the Renaissance: 'not Christianity (Church or Tolstoyan) but post-Renaissance art itself contains and communi-cates the highest life-conception of which Western humanity has so far proved itself capable'.[119] Secondly, that the invocation of a natural truth innate to the peasant is the kind of naïve Rousseauism that the work of Keats had discredited. Both arguments bring Murry back to the example of Keats, and he devotes the rest of the essay to that writer, developing the ideas of *Keats and Shakespeare* as a corrective to the fallacy of Tolstoy's naïve romanticism. The Keats described by

[118] Ibid. 21–2.
[119] 'The Romantic Fallacy', *New Criterion*, 4/3 (June 1926), 521–37 (p. 528).

Murry achieves both the highest religious and aesthetic experience through the activity of possessing his own soul: the soul-making of his famous letter. The grounds of this soul-making had been traversed before by Murry, in his essays on Matthew Arnold discussed earlier, in *Keats and Shakespeare*, and latterly in *The Life of Jesus*. Corresponding to Murry's continuing preoccupation with the notion of rebirth, soul-making as he envisages it is a dialectical process in which the soul of the artist is synthesized from a fusion of head and heart, the properties of intelligence and feeling, which lead him into an art that is beyond the redundant labels of classicism and romanticism.

This 'new synthesis', marking an attempt to get away from the terms of his earlier dispute with Eliot, is what Murry claims to find (albeit malformed) in Read's critique of Frank. In his book, Read had talked of going beyond the head/heart opposition and achieving a synthetic resolution in the Thomist notion of intelligence. In his review of Read's book, Murry recognized this attempt to synthesize what he now describes as 'the old and barren opposition between classicism and romanticism'.[120] The main difference, however, between his and Read's conception of this synthesis lies in the relative importance each places on intelligence: for Read intelligence is the product of synthesis, for Murry it is merely one of the terms of the dialectic through which the synthesis occurs. Intellectual knowledge, for Murry, is too systematic and does not do justice to the effectively organic understanding that great literature achieves:

There is observable in the great province of life to which we human beings belong another kind of order than the geometric or intellectual; there is organic order. And that is the kind of order we should naturally suppose to be appropriate to human experience. That also is the kind of order we find in the highest literature. We cannot say, even in the simplest instance, that we 'understand' an organism; neither ought we to say that we must abjure our understanding . . . to apprehend it; rather, perhaps, that we must transcend our understanding.[121]

Instead, then, of a reductive intellectual knowledge of literature, Murry posits a faculty of 'Reason' in which the conflicting ways of knowing—the emotional and the intellectual, 'the war of the romantic against the classic'—are resolved. His description of this faculty

---

[120] 'Reason and Criticism', *TLS* 1275 (8 July 1926), 453–4 (p. 453).
[121] Ibid. 454.

shows both the development of his literary theory (and particularly his preparedness to find a resolution of the terms of his dispute with Eliot) and of the pantheism of which Eliot had accused him.

Reason is born of the pregnant opposition between intelligence and feeling, Mind and Heart; and they exist no longer in themselves, but in their off-spring. There is a complete interfusion of understanding and emotion, so that both are different in nature from what they were before. This organic evolution of the consciousness which both Goethe and Coleridge strove, not wholly in vain, to describe and to communicate finds its appropriate object of contemplation in an organic universe: to this end indeed was it born, and from the failure of the effort to accommodate emotional experience of the living world, within and without, to intellectual categories, it took its origin. Reason is the understanding of life.[122]

Eliot's own review of Read's book appeared in the *New Criterion* of October 1926—the issue following the one in which was published Murry's 'The Romantic Fallacy'. Eliot's review plays three opinions off against each other: Read's from his recent book; Ramon Fernandez's from his *Messages*; and Murry's *Times Literary Supplement* review of Read's book.[123] In common with the works that his review addresses, Eliot sites his argument in what he perceives to be a crisis of literary value, the *problème de hiérarchie* described by Fernandez. Eliot discerns two contrasting responses to the necessary reconstruction of critical and literary values predicated by the crisis. Read (like Eliot himself) espouses the Thomist solution, characterized by an acceptance of an external 'metaphysical and logical truth'. Fernandez, on the other hand, adopts what Eliot defines as a Cartesian point of view which conversely builds outward from personality. 'The issue', writes Eliot, 'is really between those who, like M. Fernandez, and (if I understand right) Mr Middleton Murry . . . make *man the measure of all things*, and those who would find an extra-human measure'.[124] Descartes had figured earlier in Eliot's demonology, and had similarly been vilified in Read's recent book. Hulme too had viewed Cartesianism as one of the principal errors of

---

[122] Ibid.

[123] Because of the *TLS* policy of anonymous contribution, Eliot was apparently not aware that it was Murry who had reviewed Read's book. Although the review sparked off a dispute between the two men, there is no evidence to show that Eliot ever knew of Murry's instigatory role. Indeed, in his essay 'Towards a Synthesis' Murry, perhaps disingenuously, refers to the author of the earlier essay in the third person, as 'the writer in *The Times*'.

[124] 'Books of the Quarter', *New Criterion*, 4/4 (Oct. 1926), 751–7 (p. 755).

post-Renaissance humanism in its attempts to make man rather than God the central object of philosophical enquiry; promoting a view in which, to use Eliot's description of Fernandez, 'psychology seems to take precedence over ontology'.[125]

Eliot's argument restates the disputes between himself and Murry over the relative importance of personality and impersonality in literature, only this time with a gloss from the history of philosophy. But this divide, between a meaning induced from subjective experience and one deduced from a larger pre-existent truth, now lies also at the root of their conflicting attitudes towards religion. For Murry, and for the Modernism with which he is in broad agreement, the incarnation represents an affirmation that man can indeed be the measure of all things. The delineation of a kenotic Jesus and the description of him as 'the creator of my God' made by Bethune-Baker, quoted earlier, shows the Modernists' readiness to acknowledge the authority of a historical figure, constituted as human, in preference to the traditional authority of the institutions in which his name is enshrined. Dean William Inge had summed up this attitude succinctly at the time of the Girton controversy, quoting Tertullian to the effect that 'our Lord called Himself the Truth; He never called Himself Tradition'.[126]

The relationship between Eliot's notion of an impersonal intelligence and a tradition through which he considered literature to grow had, as I have argued, become closer as the 1920s progressed. With the development of a religiously informed criticism, that tradition now came to be identified with the definition of intelligence given by neo-Thomism. And it is to this intelligence that Eliot returns in the last part of his review; defining it, as often before, in opposition to the arguments of Murry. Eliot recognizes the perspicuity of the *TLS* review, but raises an objection to its dismissal of the principle of intelligence put forward by Read. Murry had written in the *TLS* that 'to a modern mind the word "intelligence" does not connote the faculty or act of "simple apprehension of truth". To a modern mind that act or faculty is "intuition".'[127] Eliot controverted this in a brief argument

---

[125] Hulme, 'Humanism and the Religious Attitude', in *Speculations*, 60; Eliot, 'Books of the Quarter', 755.

[126] See 'Signs of the Times', *Modern Churchman*, 11/7 (Oct. 1921), 353. H. D. A. Major subsequently cited this as one of the 'Six Golden Sayings' of Modernism in *Thirty Years After* (London, 1929), 81–91 (pp. 86–7).

[127] 'Reason and Criticism', 454.

by suggesting that no one familiar with the work of Aquinas or Aristotle would doubt that as a term 'intelligence' was adequate.[128]

Although there is a serious difference between the religious perspectives that inform their criticism, then, this next phase of the debate between Murry and Eliot would seem to hinge on semantics, and more particularly on their interpretations of 'intelligence' and 'reason'. Both words, as we have seen, are construed as the product of a synthesis that goes some way to correcting the dissociations of thought and feeling posited at one time or another by either critic. In one sense, both can be said to be moving towards the same goal; of an aesthetic in which discursive thought becomes reconciled to the nebulous emotions engendered by literary experience, and which, in Murry's opinion, will transcend the hitherto fruitless opposition between romanticism and classicism. By a process of mutual critical repulsion, however, this potential for agreement would again become transmuted into antagonism.

TOWARDS A SYNTHESIS

Murry's essay 'Towards a Synthesis' appeared in June 1927 in response to Eliot's review article. F. A. Lea has pointed to the biographical importance of the essay.[129] It is crucial too in his literary relationship with Eliot, for it offers a conciliation between their opposed views in suggesting an end to the contention between romanticism and classicism. In essays such as 'The Romantic Fallacy' and 'Reason and Criticism'—and 'Romanticism and Christianity', in which he described 'the pure romantic' as 'unintelligible' and the 'pure classicist' as 'not worth the trouble of understanding', and 'The Romantic Mean', in which he would describe romanticism as 'halfway mysticism'—Murry had been qualifying his claims for romanticism.[130] In 'Towards a Synthesis' he described classicism and romanticism as 'those Protean and unsatisfactory words', and began a search to find a common ground with Eliot beyond their terms.[131] In keeping with this conciliatory mood, the sometimes strident tone

---

[128] 'Books of the Quarter', 757.
[129] *The Life of John Middleton Murry*, 150–1.
[130] 'Romanticism and Christianity', *TLS* 1278 (29 July 1926), 506, 'The Romantic Mean', *TLS* 1334 (25 Aug. 1927), 573.
[131] 'Towards a Synthesis', *New Criterion*, 5/3 (June 1927), 294–313 (p. 300).

and *ad hominem* arguments of essays like 'The Classical Revival' give way to what is, by Murry's standards, a cool and often elegantly persuasive essay. Its purpose, as Murry describes it, 'is most emphatically not polemical'.[132]

At the close of his review Eliot had seemed to encourage polemic and partisanship by declaring himself 'on the side of' intelligence.[133] Murry, as the title of his essay suggests, assiduously avoided the implied confrontation, stressing instead the possibilities for agreement. The essay essentially fleshes out the skeletal argument of 'Reason and Criticism': that criticism gains little by striving for the rigour of science, and that instead it should seek to balance a necessary judicial intelligence with an equally important aesthetic intuition. The combination of these two elements, of mutually exclusive knowledges of quantity and quality, creates a *tertium quid*: a criticism analogous to the art on which it operates that is irreducible to the terms of either of its constituent ways of knowing. As such, art embodies an 'objective synthesis' of experience that replicates the 'subjective synthesis' undergone by great writers.

As far as Murry is concerned this is in broad agreement with Eliot's views. His only disagreement with Eliot concerns the latter's stubborn attachment to the word 'intelligence', which Eliot construes as the result, rather than one of the terms, of the synthetic activity of art. As he had done in 'Reason and Criticism', Murry argues that contemporary usage denies such a wide interpretation to intelligence: its connotations extend only to rational ways of knowing. If that common definition is accepted, then the only other way 'intelligence' may be used is in its specifically Thomist sense. But, argues Murry, this usage is legitimate only if one accepts Thomist doctrine in its entirety: 'St Thomas', he warns, 'is not a bird from whom one can safely pluck a single feather'.[134] This, he argues, is where Eliot in particular, and neo-Thomism in general, come unstuck, and he uses Eliot's example to examine what he sees as the paradox of a reconstituted Thomism.

In an argument reminiscent of 'The Classical Revival' Murry

---

[132] 'Towards a Synthesis', 294.

[133] This, perhaps, is in self-conscious imitation of Henri Massis's similarly polemical 'Party of Intelligence', raised during a debate in *Les Cahiers du mois* in February/March 1925. See Germaine Brée, *Twentieth-Century French Literature*, trans. Louise Guiney (London, 1983), 133.

[134] 'Towards a Synthesis', 297.

suggests that Eliot's lack of faith makes an adherence to Thomism untenable. St Thomas's metaphysic, according to Murry, recognizes two legitimate, and mutually exclusive, ways of knowing which unite to form understanding: the 'psychic reality' of the 'one and indivisible *anima*' being the product of 'its two potencies of *intellectus* and *fides*'.[135] As Eliot possesses no faith corresponding to St Thomas's *fides*, he is unable to recreate this synthesis. In the consequent attempt to reconstruct that faith intellectually he goes against Thomism's major premisses:

The Thomist who is not orthodox is bound to make *intellectus* co-extensive with *anima*, 'intelligence' with 'soul': he has no *fides* as a counterpoise and equivalent to *intellectus*. It follows that the 'intellectualism' of St Thomas is of a totally different kind from the 'intellectualism' of a non-believing Thomist of to-day.[136]

In accusing Eliot of being something of a doubting Thomist, Murry, it would appear, did not know of the religious instruction he was undergoing in preparation for conversion. In fact, Eliot was baptized and received into the Church of England in the same month that Murry's essay appeared. This does not render Murry's argument redundant, however. For he had used Eliot only as a starting-point from which to attack the recent growth of neo-Thomism. His argument, in brief, was that the Renaissance had irrevocably altered the nature of belief, reapportioning the relative importance of the two terms of the scholastic synthesis. The knowledge engendered by the new science had encroached so far into the realm reserved by scholasticism for faith, as to make that scholastic sense of faith all but incommensurable with the reformed faith to which modern man is heir. Scholastic faith cannot be reconstituted because the world-view which supported it, and which it in turn buttressed, has been superseded. This leaves the neo-Thomist in a position in which, like Eliot, he is forced to overcompensate for the altered nature of faith with his intellect. Such a disproportion of intelligence and faith militates against a modern Thomist synthesis and renders neo-Thomism, for Murry at least, untenable.

Instead of attempting to accommodate the obsolete terms of an outdated metaphysics, Murry suggests, the desire for synthesis manifested in neo-Thomism would be better served if it addressed the real

---

[135] Ibid. 298.   [136] Ibid.

divide in post-Renaissance knowledge: that between art and science. As suggested in the last chapter Murry, along with many of his contemporaries, construed such a divide as a split between quantitative and qualitative knowledge. Such an assumption is explicit in Bergson's project, and is arguably at the root of most forms of religious Modernism.[137] Murry suggested that these qualitative and quantitative knowledges, which he associates with the workings of intelligence on the one hand and intuition on the other, be synthesized within the workings of 'reason':

Reason as the product of a true and creative fusion of 'intelligence' and 'intuition' would seem to be the sign under which a new synthesis may be achieved; intelligence being intelligent enough to realize its own inadequacy to what Professor Whitehead calls 'the complete concreteness of our intuitive experience', 'intuition' intuitive enough to see that the manipulation and ultimate ordonnance of immediate experience depends upon the help of the intelligence.[138]

According to Murry, the finest example of this reason, partly because it is born at the same time as the divide occurs, is in the work of Shakespeare. Thus it is from literature that the new synthesis must proceed. In scholasticism the philosopher preceded the poet: St Thomas laying down the structure within which Dante might work. In the modern age, suggests Murry, the situation is reversed, and the knowledge achieved through literature in general and Shakespeare in particular gives the lead to philosophy: 'In the modern epoch it is not the poet who must study the philosopher, as Goethe knew when he put Kant aside, but the philosopher the poet'.[139]

Murry might have expected his article to strike a chord with Eliot, for although it is critical of him it concurs at several points with Eliot's published opinions, and offers a debate in which several of his problems might be resolved. Murry, for example, now seems to agree with, and to build on, the arguments of Eliot's first 'Dante' essay. Similarly, his description of the workings of intuition and intelligence, with the latter working consciously to order the former in a critical manner, bears a close methodological resemblance to the argu-

---

[137] See e.g. B. H. Streeter's argument that religious knowledge fuses the quantitative truth of science with the qualitative experience of art, in 'Science, Art and Religion', *Reality: A New Correlation of Science and Religion* (London, 1926), 23–48. Streeter, an ardent Modernist and religious popularizer, was, ironically perhaps, Eliot's godfather.

[138] 'Towards a Synthesis', 307.   [139] Ibid. 312.

ments concerning creativity and criticism put forward by Eliot in 'The Function of Criticism'.[140] Furthermore, Murry's argument is not in itself unreasonable. It is certainly, by his own standards, a temperate and carefully worked essay. He was in the process of defining a respectable lineage for the critical 'reason', claiming to derive it from Coleridge's understanding of the term in *The Friend*, and from the distinction Spengler had borrowed from Goethe between *Vernunft* and *Verstand*, and he could be forgiven for thinking that Eliot and Read might be 'on the side of' this construction of reason.[141] Eliot had, after all, only recently dedicated his *New Criterion* to 'a higher and clearer conception of Reason'.[142] Read, in *Reason and Romanticism*, had recognized the importance of intuition in critical judgement, and had described a reason, like Murry's, which was neither mechanistically logical nor purely rational, but was rather 'the widest evidence of the senses, and of all processes and instincts developed in the long history of man'.[143] Indeed, Read later wrote that the intention behind the book was to effect 'some reconciliation or "synthesis" ' between romanticism and reason.[144] But, though Murry sought no argument with the proponents of Thomism, writers with neo-Thomist inclinations took particular exception to his attempt to expropriate its terms, and the next few issues of Eliot's reconstituted *Monthly Criterion* resonated with controversy.

The September issue contained essays in response to Murry by M. C. D'Arcy and Charles Mauron. D'Arcy's essay, 'The Thomistic Synthesis and Intelligence', was the first, exhibiting an entrenched and dogmatic neo-Thomism that refused to concede any ground to Murry. Recent commentators on medieval philosophy have recognized the importance of sense-perception and intuition in the model

[140] This, in turn, is close to Maritain's formulation of a 'spontaneous gush of images' that 'precedes and feeds the operation of the poet', but that is controlled and ordered by his conscious intelligence. See 'Poetry and Religion', pt. 1, trans. F. S. Flint, *New Criterion*, 5/1 (Jan. 1927), 7–22 (p. 21).

[141] See 'The Romantic Theory of Poetry', *TLS* 1266 (22 Apr. 1926), 298, and 'The Second Religiousness', *Adelphi*, 4/4 (Oct. 1926), 201–9 (pp. 206–9). See also 'Gotthold Ephraim Lessing (1729–1781)', *TLS* 1408 (24 Jan. 1929), 49–50. Murry's difficulties here bear many similarities to Bergson's defence of intuition against the intellectualism of critics like Julien Benda. See H. Stuart Hughes, *Consciousness and Society: The Reorientation of European Social Thought, 1890–1930* (Brighton, 1979), 113–25.

[142] 'The Idea of a Literary Review', 5.

[143] 'The Attributes of Criticism', in *Reason and Romanticism*, 27–9. See also Read's definition of intelligence as 'but one aspect of the single faculty of apprehension': 'Pure Poetry', ibid. 59–66 (p. 66).

[144] 'T. S. E.—A Memoir', in Tate (ed.), *T. S. Eliot: The Man and his Work*, 22.

of the cognitive process outlined by Aquinas. John F. Boler has noted that, 'compared to his Franciscan successors—and to Augustine— Aquinas offered a most unusual picture of radical incompleteness in the intellect's operation within the context of human knowing'.[145] D'Arcy, like several of the commentators on Murry's essay, chooses to neglect this sense of 'radical incompleteness' and instead posits a Thomist 'intelligence' that is both complete and all-comprehending. The argument between Thomism and Murry, he suggests, 'can be argued without any reference to Faith'.[146] Murry had devoted much of his article to discussing non-rational knowledge, of the kind experienced by artists and mystics. Faith, he had suggested, was the product of this non-rational, experiential knowledge. By denying such knowledge, and by invoking the specious neo-Thomist argument that all experience takes place ultimately in mind and must therefore be a function of intelligence, D'Arcy refuses to recognize the grounds of Murry's argument. Almost inevitably, this results in his talking, at some length, at cross-purposes to Murry.

This failure to recognize the grounds of Murry's arguments— Murry attempted to delineate an aesthetic 'reason', D'Arcy only a strictly philosophical 'intellectus'—shows the difficulties Murry faced in attempting dialogue with an entrenched religious philosophy. In line with the doctrine of the obligatory Oath against Modernism sworn by all Catholic clergymen, D'Arcy dogmatically sets aside questions of subjective faith to assert belief as a discipline of intellect. For D'Arcy, it is 'suicidal' to believe that 'no expression of truth has more than a temporal and experimental value'. From Murry's perspective, such an absolute truth is no longer conceivable. Truth is rather an organic correspondence, subject to a Bergsonian creative evolution, which can be more satisfactorily apprehended by the 'reason' of the artist than the 'intelligence' of the philosopher— 'the poet makes contact with the divine reality in its immanence: the reality that is God's garment and is God, he knows immediately, without the intervention of theology and ritual'.[147]

Charles Mauron's 'Concerning "Intuition"' was the second res-

---

[145] 'Intuitive and Abstractive Cognition', in Norman Kretzmann, Anthony Kenny, and Jan Pinborg (eds.), *The Cambridge History of Later Medieval Philosophy* (Cambridge, 1982), 460–78 (p. 475).
[146] 'The Thomistic Synthesis and Intelligence', *Monthly Criterion*, 6/3 (Sept. 1927), 210–28 (p. 216).
[147] 'Poetry, Philosophy, and Religion', *Adelphi*, 2/8 (Jan. 1925), 645–58 (p. 656).

ponse to Murry. Mauron avoided the strident tone and dogmatic assurance of D'Arcy's Thomism, but he shares what might be described as a philosopher's scruples at Murry's necessarily loose definition of 'intuition'.[148] In a cogent argument, Mauron correctly identified what is, from a philosopher's point of view, a crudity in Murry's antinomy between quantitative and qualitative ways of knowing. Employing the perspective of contemporary psychology, he was also critical of Murry's facile acceptance of an undivided soul. On purely pragmatic grounds, Mauron did not attempt to take sides on the 'intelligence versus intuition' debate (as it was rapidly becoming), but rather adjudged such antinomies as next to useless for the practising psychologist or philosopher. Like D'Arcy he had little to say about the aesthetic value of Murry's metaphysical synthesis; and although he put forward a damning case against its worth as science he failed to address its value as a theory of literary criticism.

Murry was immediately deflated by this criticism. On 22 September he wrote to Eliot, 'all my hopeful feeling when I undertook that frightful essay has evaporated'. He added despondently, 'it seems that there really is some sort of abyss between us—not humanly thank goodness—but in respect of our ideas and convictions'.[149] As if to emphasize this divide, two further essays appeared in the following *Monthly Criterion*. The first, by Ramon Fernandez, perhaps came closest to understanding Murry's argument in showing an appreciation of the importance Murry attached to the '*affective* certitude' experienced in reading great poetry.[150] But in spite of a basic sympathy with Murry's conception of intuition, Fernandez insisted that in the last resort 'there can be no genuine knowledge where there can be no verification'. This assumes as axiomatic what Murry would describe as the quantitative nature of all knowledge, and so effectively closed the door on Murry's argument before it could be considered.[151]

[148] 'Concerning "Intuition" ', trans. T. S. Eliot, *Monthly Criterion*, 6/3 (Sept. 1927), 229–35.

[149] Lea, *The Life of John Middleton Murry*, 151–2.

[150] 'A Note on Intelligence', *Monthly Criterion*, 6/4 (Oct. 1927), 332–9 (p. 336).

[151] Murry had addressed this kind of verificationist criticism earlier, in his essay 'Jesus and the Bishop', *Adelphi*, 3/11 (Apr. 1926), 760–7, in which he had questioned the validity of applying verificationist principles to articles of religious faith. Even I. A. Richards would place poetry beyond verificationist criteria, opining that 'the bulk of poetry consists of statements which only the very foolish would think of attempting to verify. They are not the kind of things that can be verified.' *Principles of Literary Criticism* (London, 1924), 272.

The second criticism of Murry's article in the October issue was by Eliot himself. The essay, 'Mr Middleton Murry's Synthesis', is arguably, in the quality of its argument and its tone, one of the poorest and least generous pieces of criticism Eliot would write. Like *After Strange Gods* its polemic is too naked to be veiled by Eliot's customary elegance, and its use of the Bradleyan device of pretended incomprehension of another's argument is stretched to a point that exceeds disingenuity. For example, Eliot combatively denies the instances Murry puts forward of widely accepted poetic 'truths': the moments at which poetry seems to apprehend a truth otherwise inexpressible in prose. Fernandez had, at least, concurred with Murry in recognizing such an example in Dante's lines, 'nessun maggior dolore, che ricordarsi del tempo felice nella miseria'. Fernandez described the emotion that the lines evoke as 'a fact of experience, in the positive and rational sense of the word'. Eliot, in contrast, describes the passage only as a dramatic statement in which Dante would not necessarily have had any belief. Its value, he contends, is solely a matter of characterization; showing how far the character of Francesca is from a state of grace.[152] This is little more than a rhetorical trick that dismisses Murry's example without addressing the argument it exemplifies. What is more, its disingenuousness is made more apparent if it is compared with the opinion expressed in Eliot's *Shakespeare and the Stoicism of Seneca*, published a month earlier. In that essay, originally delivered as a lecture the previous March, Eliot had averred that 'what every poet starts from is his own emotions', and had described 'Dante's railings, his personal spleen' which are manifested in 'his nostalgia, his bitter regrets for past happiness—or for what seems happiness when it is past'.[153] This undoubtedly refers to just that part of *The Divine Comedy* he would censure Murry for taking as an expression of Dante's own opinions: the lines spoken by Francesca in the *Inferno* that express the great weight of sadness felt in remembering happiness in a time of misery.

This kind of posturing is continued throughout the essay: another example comes when Eliot facetiously responds to Murry's attempt to distinguish between intellect and intuition by suggesting that 'to me both intelligence and intuition are mysterious'. Far from being a

---

[152] 'Mr Middleton Murry's Synthesis', 342.
[153] 'Shakespeare and the Stoicism of Seneca', in *Selected Essays*, 137. Eliot had also used these lines in his Clark Lectures of the previous year to illustrate Dante's greatness as a philosophic poet. See *Varieties of Metaphysical Poetry*, 56.

serious point, this appears only to have been said to preface the gibe that 'it is as mysterious and miraculous to watch Mr Murry conducting discursive reasoning as to watch him apprehending his intuitions'.[154] Eliot goes so far in his antagonism to Murry that he apparently suggests that he has only taken sides in the argument out of a spirit of contradiction: 'I mean furthermore that I am "on the side of the intelligence" because I am convinced that Mr Murry, just as roughly and readily as myself, is against it'.[155]

Another aspect of this antagonism manifests itself in Eliot's misrepresentation of Murry's arguments. Perhaps the most glaring is Eliot's insistence, in spite of Murry's disavowals, that this was a controversy between 'intelligence' and 'intuition'. Murry had taken great pains in 'Towards a Synthesis' to make the terms of that synthesis clear. The critical faculty he advocated was a 'reason' synthesized from the dialectic of intelligence and intuition: a position he restated two months later when he wrote that 'I myself make no claim to be "on the side of intuition"—I dislike the word as much as they.'[156] In 'Towards a Synthesis', Murry had noted, in passing, his agreement with Etienne Gilson that Thomism 'is not a physical, or a psychological, but a *metaphysical* theory of knowledge'.[157] Eliot extrapolates a whole epistemological theory from this short paraphrase, contending that Murry 'divides theories of knowledge into three kinds: the physical (I suppose he means physiological?), the psychological, and the *metaphysical*', and then berates him in the names of Meinong, Husserl, and Russell for such a naïve simplification.[158] Again, Eliot feigns incomprehension at a contention made by Murry several months earlier, in an article for the *Hibbert Journal*.[159] Eliot prefers to address himself to a clumsiness in Murry's exposition than to his central argument: that Coleridge, Goethe, and Keats found in poetry rather than discursive prose a more apt medium for the transmission of their apprehended experience. For Eliot, this reasonable proposition only exhibits Murry's 'ineradicable contempt for intelligence'.[160] At another point, Eliot writes that Murry's description of the alteration of faith since St Thomas 'means that there is simply *no* religious faith at all to-day'.[161] Far from saying this

---

[154] 'Mr Middleton Murry's Synthesis', 343.   [155] Ibid. 342–3.
[156] 'Concerning Intelligence', *Monthly Criterion*, 6/6 (Dec. 1927), 524–33 (p. 530).
[157] 'Towards a Synthesis', 279.   [158] 'Mr Middleton Murry's Synthesis', 345.
[159] 'The Metaphysic of Poetry', *Hibbert Journal*, 25 (July 1927), 610–22.
[160] 'Mr Middleton Murry's Synthesis', 343.   [161] Ibid. 345.

at all, Murry had made it quite clear at several points in his essay that it was not faith *per se* that had died with the passing of St Thomas's teaching, but rather the *fides* construed as an integral part of that doctrine. Murry had even gone so far as to append a postscript to his essay reaffirming that argument, and further describing the modern mind as 'certainly "capable of faith" '.[162]

Where Eliot shows most his inability, or unwillingness, to comprehend Murry is in his concluding argument. Here his fundamental disagreement with Murry's apparent relativism in seeking to historicize Thomism leads him to an intemperate distortion of Murry's argument. The recognition of the historicity (and therefore fallibility) of certain aspects of both the Bible and Christian doctrine had been growing for nearly a century, and was widely welcomed by most thinking Christians as an acceptable explanation for the incongruities that had arisen with the findings of modern science. In his own criticism of Murry, Eliot disregards this consensus and, in strictest Anglo-Catholic fashion, portrays any qualification of orthodoxy as the first step on the perilous slope to moral anarchy: 'in Mr Murry's fluid world everything may be admired, because nothing is permanent. There is therefore no place for the human will . . . for a world like Mr Murry's there is no danger, because nothing in it is worthy of preservation'.[163]

Murry had some cause to be dismayed by the polemic his attempt at reconciliation had engendered. After publishing another attack on him in the November *Criterion*, Eliot allowed Murry space to reply to the various criticisms that had been levelled against his article.[164] But, as that reply confirms, any kind of useful debate in these circumstances was virtually impossible. Although Murry addressed the more serious points made by the *Criterion* contributors, he could do little more than restress the problem of critical authority from his own perspective. His only small satisfaction appears to come from responding to Eliot in Eliot's own ironic, polemical manner:

I do not wonder that Mr Eliot finds the world, past and present, distinctly barren if he can admire only that which he believes in. (How much of St Thomas does he believe in?) And since he is pleasantly facetious about my 'world', I may be permitted to commiserate with him on being condemned to live in a world where every advance in present knowledge annihilates

---

[162] 'Towards a Synthesis', 313.   [163] 'Mr Middleton Murry's Synthesis', 346–7.
[164] T. Sturge Moore, 'Towards Simplicity', *Monthly Criterion*, 6/5 (Nov. 1927), 409–17.

some past achievement . . . It must be terribly depressing to live under the perpetual threat of being unable to admire to-morrow what one has admired until to-day.[165]

This was the last sustained debate between Murry and Eliot: their last head-on confrontation. Although they would occasionally express conflicting opinions on public matters, such as the revision of the Book of Common Prayer the following year, and would work together as members of the Moot in the late 1930s, there was no longer a sense of a common commitment, or even of a fruitful antagonism, out of which their critical ideas might come. This refusal to entertain a genuine exchange of opinions had been manifest in Eliot's final contribution to that debate, his essay 'Mr Middleton Murry's Synthesis'. What was perhaps most interesting about this essay was the way Eliot allowed himself to be forced into the kind of unsustainable assertions described above, driven there apparently by the force of his own rhetoric and by his hostility to Murry's ideas. It would be foolish to discount the fundamental differences between their religious ideas, but it is arguable that there remained enough common ground for them to engage in some form of fruitful literary-critical exchange. This had been Murry's hope from the start. His notion of a synthetic 'reason', and particularly his preparedness to accept this as the guiding principle of a 'new classicism' showed a flexibility that at times appeared to come near to appeasement: René Wellek has justly described 'Towards a Synthesis' as 'Murry's rather pathetic attempt to reach a reconciliation'.[166] In a less combative atmosphere the 'reason' described by Murry could have been assimilated with ease to the 'intelligence' outlined by Eliot and Read. As has been argued, Eliot and Read had frequently used the term synonymously with 'intelligence': Murry's 'reason', for example, could easily pass for the 'intelligence' that Eliot discerned in the Gourmont of 'The Perfect Critic'. Furthermore, in November 1927 Eliot published without demur an essay by Ernst Robert Curtius entitled 'Restoration of the Reason', which shared with Murry the opinion that 'neither Thomas Aquinas nor Boileau nor Dryden can give us what we want. Tradition that comes from books can help us no longer.' What is more, Curtius proposed a reconstituted Thomism that sounds remarkably like the one suggested by Murry in 'Towards a Synthesis':

---

[165] 'Concerning Intelligence', 532.
[166] 'John Middleton Murry', in *A History of Modern Criticism*, v. 98.

'our task is not to resuscitate these forms [Thomism and classicism] artificially, but to revive the spirit which created them, and so to create a form of Reason proper to the 20th century'.[167] Similarly, Eliot had shown a sophisticated appreciation of the decline of Thomism in an essay for the *Times Literary Supplement* in December 1926, that belied the crude simplification of his argument with Murry. There, Eliot had come close to restating Murry's argument, in opining that 'it was as much the *emotions* as the *ideas* of Aristotle and St Thomas which went out of favour'.[168] In its narrowing of the notion of intelligence, Eliot's argument could not even be said to be typical of neo-Thomism. Jacques Maritain, for example, had, in *Art et scolastique*, described art as 'an intellectual virtue', but had made the important qualification of distinguishing a separate faculty of knowledge associated with the Fine Arts: 'man can certainly enjoy purely intelligible beauty, but the beautiful which is *connatural* to man is that which comes to delight the mind through their senses and their intuition'.[169] Maritain would come to a full reconciliation with Bergson in the 1930s, but in the preface to the 1929 edition of *La Philosophie Bergsonienne* he exhibited the kind of flexibility about terminology—admitting a certain closeness between his and Bergson's position—from which Eliot's criticism might have prospered.[170] Furthermore, Murry was not alone in finding the idea of intelligence too constricting a criterion for literary criticism. J. F. Holms, reviewing *Reason and Romanticism* in the *Calendar of Modern Letters*, had written that '"intelligence", in the sense in which it is sometimes used by writers of the school to which Mr Read belongs, is by itself an inadequate instrument for criticism'.[171]

There is a certain amount of overkill in Eliot's response to Murry: a wish to be quickly rid of his arguments without necessarily having

---

[167] 'Restoration of the Reason', trans. William Stewart, *Monthly Criterion*, 6/5 (Nov. 1927), 389–97 (pp. 394, 396).

[168] 'Medieval Philosophy', *TLS* 1298 (16 Dec. 1926), 929.

[169] *Art and Scholasticism*, 24.

[170] See *Bergsonian Philosophy and Thomism*, 21–6. Later, in his *Creative Intuition in Art and Poetry* (New York, 1953) he would not only recognize the importance of the intuition, denied by the more zealous neo-Thomists of the 1920s, but would recognize it, and its manifestation in poetry, as a vital source of knowledge through connaturality. It was perhaps for these views that Eliot had written of Maritain in 1928, that 'I have never seen a more romantic classicist, or a Thomist whose methods of thought were less like those of Aquinas'. 'The Idealism of Julien Benda', *New Republic*, 57/732 (pt. 2) (12 Dec. 1928), 105–7 (p. 107).

[171] 'Reason and Romanticism', *Calendar of Modern Letters*, 3/3 (Oct. 1926), 251–4 (p. 251).

to answer them. Having already branded Murry a heretic, Eliot perhaps reasoned that his arguments were to be scorned rather than refuted point by point. Whatever the reason, Eliot's method shows a departure from the subtle ironies customarily exhibited in his criticism. There were, indeed, legitimate grounds why he might want to dissent from Murry's argument. Murry's notion of synthesis, for example, plainly owes more to Hegel than it does to Aquinas, resulting, as Eliot quite rightly pointed out, in Murry's real misapprehension of the centrality of the intelligence in St Thomas's metaphysic. Murry had compounded this error by insisting, in his reply to Eliot, that true Thomism was in fact more Platonic than Aristotelian.[172] Eliot would have been quite justified in correcting Murry's efforts to bend Aquinas too far towards his own purposes. But he went much further and attempted to discredit Murry's arguments altogether. In the past, debate and even polemic had proved useful in helping Eliot define and clarify his own position. But here what sometimes looks like an irrational hostility seems to deflect him into vehemence rather than vigour, and pedantry rather than rigour. This hostility perhaps owes something to a growing revulsion felt towards Murry's ideas and his personality by many of Eliot's peers: the 'sticky sentimentality' of which Leonard Woolf would complain.[173] But it can perhaps also be explained by the way in which Murry, as *démodé* as he was, had frustratingly exposed the weaknesses inherent in Eliot's attempts to render a dogmatic religious orthodoxy compatible with the subtleties of a sophisticated poetic and critical practice.

SOME PROBLEMS OF ORTHODOXY

In response to certain of the comments made by Eliot in his two essays on Seneca and Shakespeare published in September 1927, Murry wrote: 'I disagree with Mr Eliot, but I do not know whether he seriously holds his own views.'[174] This is, perhaps, just another example of the debased rhetoric into which their debate had fallen. But it does point to a real ambiguity in Eliot's criticism. Murry pertinently noted in a summary of their debate for readers of the *New Adelphi* that 'to use the values of Orthodoxy against others without

---

[172] See 'Concerning Intelligence', 529–30.
[173] *An Autobiography*, ii: *1911–1969* (Oxford, 1980), 148.
[174] 'The "Philosophy" of Shakespeare', *New Adelphi*, 1/3 (Mar. 1928), 253–6 (p. 253).

being Orthodox oneself is dishonest'.[175] Although he did not directly impute this kind of bad faith to Eliot, his admonition was clearly aimed at Eliot's party. Eliot's assumption of orthodoxy had been implicit in his earlier description of Murry as that 'very rare bird . . . the genuine heretic'.[176] Murry had subsequently noted the difficulty of defining that term given the lack of a consensual orthodoxy against which it might be measured.[177] In a sense, this might be said to be the central difficulty in Eliot's criticism at this time—for while he was prepared to denigrate Murry's heresy, assuming the high ground of orthodoxy for the purpose, his critical writing was exhibiting a genuine difficulty in coming to an adequate formulation of the relationship between literary values and the complex of social values of which religious belief formed one part.

As has already been mentioned, Eliot had earlier experienced difficulty in describing the relation between his poetic practice and his religious belief, which had led him into the strange position of construing doubt as a form of belief. This paradox had resulted from his attempts to defend the scepticism of his poetry from the imputation that it represented 'a complete severance between his poetry and *all* beliefs'.[178] At that time he had refused to recognize an absolute gap between his poetry and religious belief, but had conspicuously avoided describing how that implied relation might be constituted. His reticence contrasted with Murry's unambiguous commitment to describing a common identity between poetic and religious experience. Critical of what he saw as Murry's facile elision of a complex set of problems in 'Towards a Synthesis', Eliot had reacted by describing an absolute separation of religious and artistic values: quoting Jacques Rivière's description of art as a pastime 'pour distraire les honnêtes gens'.[179]

Eliot had used this formula quite dogmatically in his attack on Murry. But when he attempted to use the same argument in his 1928 preface to the second edition of *The Sacred Wood*, describing literature as merely a 'superior amusement', he felt the need to qualify it: to describe poetry's relation to 'the spiritual and social life of its time and of other times'. This led him to a somewhat vague recognition of

---

[175] 'Art as Sacrament', *New Adelphi*, 1/2 (Dec. 1927), 100–2 (p. 101).
[176] 'Recent Books', *Monthly Criterion*, 6/2 (Aug. 1927), 177–9 (p. 179).
[177] See 'Platonism and the Spiritual Life', *Monthly Criterion*, 6/5 (Nov. 1927), 437–40.
[178] See 'A Note on Poetry and Belief', 15–17.
[179] 'Mr Middleton Murry's Synthesis', 344.

real, but indefinable, external influences operative on poetry: 'poetry as certainly has something to do with morals, and with religion, and even with politics perhaps, though we cannot say what'.[180] This kind of equivocation had been visible in 'The Idea of a Literary Review' and more recently in *Shakespeare and the Stoicism of Seneca*.

In the latter essay Eliot had tried to show how a literary work might encompass a meaning or a set of beliefs to which its author need not necessarily subscribe. Shakespeare, as an example, in adopting existing dramatic techniques, re-expresses the stoicism of Seneca without having accorded it either belief or intellectual assent. This approach is valuable for its description of the ways in which ideology can be unwittingly transmitted in the formal devices of a literary tradition, but it gets Eliot no nearer the centre of his problem: for while he recognizes a 'belief' inherent in the stylistic techniques and formal imperatives of drama and poetry, he also recognizes that the art in which they appear also has a source in an individual belief and emotional experience. This kind of problem again exercised Eliot in a lecture, 'Experiment in Criticism', given in the spring of 1929. Here he again lauded the seventeenth and eighteenth centuries for maintaining a criticism that 'recognised literature as literature, and not another thing'.[181] Acknowledging that such an absolute distinction is now invalid, that 'the process of time has obscured the frontiers between literature and everything else',[182] Eliot has to admit the impossibility of separating literature altogether from the knowledge and the beliefs of the ages in which it is both produced and read. He is unable to say, however, the extent to which those external factors impinge on literary considerations, describing such problems only as 'among the most interesting "experiments" of criticism in our time'.[183] Eliot's most positive suggestion is that criticism must clarify its centre: it must set about rigorously defining its central concepts. Even if Eliot was wholly committed to this analytical language (bearing in mind his earlier disparagement of purely 'technical' criticism) he would never come near to implementing it. By 1933 he was again emphasizing that the experience of poetry 'is only partially translatable into words', and acknowledging that 'even the most accomplished of critics can, in the end, only point to the poetry which seems

---

[180] *The Sacred Wood*, pp. vii–x.
[181] 'Experiment in Criticism', in *Tradition and Experiment in Present Day Literature*, 200.
[182] Ibid. 207.   [183] Ibid. 209.

to him to be the real thing'.[184] The same year finally saw him admitting to Virginia Woolf 'that he no longer felt quite so sure of a science of criticism'.[185] By 1956, when he had fully readmitted an intuitive component to the critical intellect (and the prevailing literary trend in criticism had swung from the impressionistic to the explanatory) he was warning that 'we are in danger even of pursuing criticism as if it was a science, which it never can be'.[186]

Perhaps Eliot's most honest, and penetrating, description of his critical difficulty in identifying personal belief in poetry came in a note appended to his *Dante* published in 1929. In that essay, he returned to Richards's imputation that he (Eliot) had effected 'a complete severance between his poetry and *all* beliefs'. Eliot again emphasized his opposition to this view, but in doing so could only employ the kind of vagueness for which he had condemned Murry. He attempted to refute Richards's argument by reference to his own experience: his personal responses to individual lines of Keats, Shakespeare, and Dante. From these experiences he concluded 'that I cannot, in practice, wholly separate my poetic appreciation from my personal beliefs'.[187] In 'Experiment in Criticism' Eliot had written that literary criticism was only valid 'so long as literature is literature', a begging of the question that he repeats in *Dante*: '*If* there is "literature", *if* there is "poetry", then it must be possible to have full literary or poetic appreciation without sharing the beliefs of the poet. That is as far as my thesis goes in the present essay.'[188] Eliot's sincerity here is refreshing: it represents the kind of openness he purported to show in *The Use of Poetry and the Use of Criticism*, in starting from the 'supposition that we do not know what poetry is', and in attempting to define 'a serious *via media*' between the extremes of Rivière and Maritain on the one hand and Arnold and Richards on the other.[189] His criticism of Murry, however, had shown much less of this kind of flexibility. In the latter part of their debate he had applied to Murry's criticism the precepts of an intellectualism derived from religious orthodoxy that he proved unable to apply to his own critical writing. During that debate Murry had warned that the activity of

---

[184] *The Use of Poetry and the Use of Criticism*, 17–18.
[185] *The Diary of Virginia Woolf*, ed. Anne Olivier Bell, iv: *1931–1935* (London, 1982), 10 Sept. 1933, p. 178.
[186] 'The Frontiers of Criticism', in *On Poetry and Poets*, 103–18 (p. 117).
[187] 'Dante', in *Selected Essays*, 237–77 (p. 271).   [188] Ibid. 269.
[189] *The Use of Poetry and the Use of Criticism*, 15, 137.

literary production could never be isolated from a complex web of external circumstances: that the beliefs of the man could never be separated from his poetic activity in the way that Eliot claimed was possible. To make such a claim, Murry argued, was to be in thrall to an ultimately sterile rationalism:

The *keeping* separate of things which are not separate, but have their real existence only in combination, is precisely that vicious and mistaken use of 'intelligence' against which my essay was directed. So long as the champions of 'intelligence' maintain at one and the same moment that this is the function of intelligence, and that intelligence is all a reasonable person needs, so long will they be confined to a sterile intellectualism: nor can they fall back on St Thomas, who declared quite plainly that a man needed faith as well, nor upon Aristotle who did not employ intelligence in this way. Intellectualism of this kind ceases even to strive for understanding reality, but degenerates into a device for scoring debating points.[190]

Away from that debate Eliot would acknowledge the contingency of his terms, and the impossibility of effecting an absolute separation between the man who suffers and the mind which creates. Impelled by the dictates of controversy, he had been forced into a kind of theoretical rigour that his own critical practice did not warrant.

Samuel Hynes has written that Eliot's espousal of a 'visible' religious conviction in his criticism only served to make that 'religion seem a way of being reactionary, ungenerous and cold'.[191] Eliot's dismissal of Murry provides an instance of that coldness, and the critical inflexibility from which it derived: the 'withered dogmatism' and 'monastic chill' of which Conrad Aiken would complain in 1929.[192] While never being exactly warm, personal relations between Eliot and Murry had always remained civil: during this later phase of their argument, for example, Eliot had written on Murry's behalf to Marianne Moore in the attempt to obtain some reviewing work for him. And even at the height of their disagreement Eliot continued to commission reviews from Murry, and would allow him the space to reply to criticism. It would also appear that he contemplated further debate with Murry late in 1927: the cover of the October issue of the

---

[190] 'Concerning Intelligence', 528.
[191] 'The Trials of a Christian Critic', in David Newton-de Molina (ed.), *The Literary Criticism of T. S. Eliot: New Essays* (London, 1977), 64–88 (p. 87).
[192] 'Retreat', *Dial*, 86 (July 1929), 628–30, repr. in *A Reviewer's ABC: Collected Criticism of Conrad Aiken from 1916 to the Present*, introd. Rufus A. Blanchard (London, 1961), 184–6 (p. 185).

Criterion carried an advertisement announcing the forthcoming publication of a conversation between the two men. But in spite of this seeming civility, and in spite of Eliot's avowal that he took Murry's ideas seriously, and that the *Adelphi* was one of only two journals in which Eliot could find 'a common ground for disagreement', the attack on Murry's 'Towards a Synthesis' is manifestly intended as a polemic rather than as a contribution to reasoned debate.[193] Eliot's notational comments on Murry's typescript of 'The Classical Revival' had shown evidence of an increasing exasperation with what he described, at one point, as Murry's 'intolerably specious' arguments, and in June 1926, just before the appearance of Murry's 'Reason and Criticism', he had published a facetious personal attack, in which 'Mr Muddleton Moral' was likened to a brilliant schoolboy become dull and stupid.[194] Eliot's publication of five essays in response to Murry's 'Towards a Synthesis' might be construed as an extension of that hostility: employing a broad frontal attack on Murry to which he would be unable to respond adequately.

Several years earlier Eliot had put Murry forward as what he had described as 'a sort of stalking horse' in order to solicit controversy in early issues of the *Criterion*.[195] In this later dispute it seems that Murry was to have fulfilled an analogous function in uniting *Criterion* contributors against his opinions. Murry had recently written, in a retrospective view of the early life of his journal, that '*The Adelphi*, when it began in 1923, did not know where it was going. But it knew, and knew very definitely, where it was not going.'[196] The *Monthly Criterion* similarly appeared to know very definitely where it was not going; and that was in the direction of Murry. Eliot had written to Herbert Read in 1924 of his desire to form a critical 'phalanx' at the *Criterion*; Murry, as a common enemy, appeared to offer an ideal opportunity for the formation and deployment of such a grouping.[197] Eliot had recently praised the polemicism of Poe's criticism in 'exterminating' the pests that were his inferior contemporaries, and it is perhaps not going too far to suggest that such a metaphorical extermination was planned for Murry.[198] In a letter

---

[193] 'A Commentary', *Monthly Criterion*, 6/3 (Sept. 1927), 194.

[194] 'FSF', 'Foreign Periodicals', *New Criterion*, 4/3 (June 1926), 625.

[195] See his correspondence with Thomas Sturge Moore, 3 and 10 Apr. 1922, *Letters*, 518, 520.

[196] Prospectus for the *New Adelphi* (Sept. 1927), [pp. 1–2].

[197] 'T. S. E.—A Memoir', in Tate (ed.), *T. S. Eliot: The Man and his Work*, 19–21.

[198] 'Israfel', *Nation and Athenaeum*, 41/7 (21 May 1927), 219.

quoted earlier Eliot had suggested that something 'conclusive' ought to be done to Murry.[199] As it turned out, Murry's career as a serious literary critic would effectively be concluded by this debate. That this was, in large measure, down to Murry himself is beyond question; but there is no doubt that Eliot exacerbated the situation, and chose to stress conflict and division when there might have been a real hope of reconciliation. That this is not entirely out of keeping with his character or practice was suggested by Conrad Aiken in his memoir, *Ushant*. In that book Aiken recalled 'a deliberate and Machiavellian practice of power-politics, of reputation-making and reputation-*un*making' at the *Criterion* and talked, in particular, of a literary 'assassination' that had been orchestrated by Eliot ('Tsetse'). Murry is not mentioned by name as the victim of this assassination, but the nature of the attack and its duration make it sound very like the one that concerned 'Towards a Synthesis':

a messy and unpleasant affair it had been, quite without credit to anyone present. The carefully picked quarrel had been public, prolonged, and pointless: and if it exhibited anything, it was that evident streak of sadism in the Tsetse's otherwise urbane and kindly character, which now and again . . . he enjoyed indulging.[200]

The full extent to which Murry's reputation had become unmade by 1927 was spelled out to Richard Rees by a member of the 'influential Cambridge and Bloomsbury set', who warned him 'of the unwisdom of associating with Murry: Virginia Woolf, who had once admired him greatly, apparently now spoke of him "as one might of a dear friend who had made a fool of himself and been obliged 'to retire to Boulogne'!" '[201] The deliberate isolationism of his critical position during a period in which the study of English was striving to become entrenched academically had made Murry something of an easy target. A. N. Whitehead, who ironically went on to inspire an American Process Theology movement, had in *Religion in the Making*, defined religion as 'what the individual does with his own solitariness'. Crucially, however, he had recognized the unwisdom of attempting to sustain any form of religious individualism in the consensual secular world.[202] It was this political sophistication that

[199] To Scofield Thayer, 20 Jan. 1922, *Letters*, 502.
[200] *Ushant: An Essay* (London, 1963), 232–3.
[201] Rees, *A Theory of My Time*, 57.
[202] See *Religion in the Making*, 16, 66.

Murry lacked, in failing to harness his literary and religious enthusiasm to a powerful secular organization. Eliot had both a Church and a phalanx—he had a secular organization that was axiomatically unavailable to Murry. It was ironic, but perhaps fitting, then, that in the political sphere of literary journalism it was precisely Murry's radical subjectivism that proved to be his undoing.

Eliot's critical sophistication belied the crudity of his literary scholasticism, and his critical position certainly contained a number of difficulties that he was not prepared to expose to Murry's criticism. Had he been faced with a more formidable, or perhaps credible, opponent than Murry he might more quickly have realized that the rigid definitions of scholasticism had little to offer the criticism of literature. But through a sometimes off-puttingly messianic individualism and a careless disregard for literary politics, Murry had allowed himself to become a marginal figure in the literary culture of the late 1920s. Eliot, who was reported to have described Murry leading his disciples into the wilderness 'to the accompaniment of a titter of derision from civilized Europe', could afford to dismiss out of hand the criticism that at one time had been valuable to him.[203] In disregarding it, however, he eschewed the dialogue out of which some of his own best criticism had issued. At one time, as had been the case with 'The Possibility of a Poetic Drama', he had been able to use Murry's work dialogically, as a prompt to his own meditations on the drama; by 1928, with 'A Dialogue on Dramatic Poetry', he found himself in the curious position of having to furnish all the parts of the dialogue himself.

Murry had not been the only critic of Eliot's increasing dogmatism. The *Calendar of Modern Letters*, which had helped to reinvigorate criticism in the mid-1920s, had, towards the end of its short life, become highly critical of Eliot. In spite of their acknowledged debt to his early critical writing, the *Calendar*'s young contributors began to repudiate the new turn that that writing had taken. In an editorial in April 1927, Bertram Higgins criticized the *Criterion*'s rigidity, describing it as the manifestation of a neoclassicism, derived from 'a reactionary Latin philosophy', that was acting as 'a repressive instrument of literary criticism'.[204] Eliot's somewhat condescending response was met by further criticism from Higgins, in which he

---

[203] Quoted by Murry in a letter to Eliot, 18 Mar. 1927. See Lea, *The Life of John Middleton Murry*, 132.

[204] 'Art and Knowledge', *Calendar of Modern Letters*, 4/1 (Apr. 1927), 56–61 (p. 58).

complained of Eliot's 'attempts to discredit that criticism without meeting it'. Higgins's reply was effective both in the serious points it made against Eliot's dogmatism (particularly its repression of 'certain modern developments of the theory of beauty') and its satire on Eliot's fogeyish pedantry (accusing Eliot of adopting 'the attitude of the coy judge who wanted to be told in Court the meaning of "cami-knickers" ').[205] Ironically, however, this exchange, with its more credible assault on Eliot's criticism, coincided with the demise of the *Calendar* in July 1927. The vacuum that this left was described by Edwin Muir when, in April 1928, he discussed the lack of a credible opponent for the *Criterion*. The *Criterion*, Muir argued, was in real need of 'a friendly but rigorous examination'.[206] He added: 'so far Mr Eliot and his collaborators have either received undivided allegiance or encountered unconditional opposition'. Muir described Murry as the most notable of the latter category, but argued that his polar opposition to Eliot had led to a disagreement from which no one had profited. Not recognizing Murry's initial advocacy of a critical 'reason', Muir pointed to the absurdity of a 'sham conflict' in which intuition and intelligence were construed as antitheses. 'Such a state of affairs', he argued, 'could only be brought about by partisanship; by holding the support of something to be more important than its practical advancement.'

Muir recognized that the lack of debate inhibited the exchange of opinions on which criticism thrived. This state of affairs had led to the stultification of Eliot's magazine and had placed Murry beyond the literary pale altogether. So that when a younger generation of critics emerged it was to neither writer's present critical writing they deferred but the criticism that had been written several years earlier. F. R. Leavis, for example, in a defence of Eliot published in 1929, acknowledged an early debt to Murry but repudiated 'the ardours of the private soul' into which his recent criticism had descended.[207] And although Leavis made an unequivocal commitment to Eliot's

---

[205] 'Correspondence', *Monthly Criterion*, 6/3 (Sept. 1927), 258–9. See also Eliot's 'Neo-Classicism', *Monthly Criterion*, 5/3 (June 1927), 284–5, and 'Neo-Classicism Again', *Monthly Criterion*, 6/3 (Sept. 1927), 193–4.

[206] 'Past and Present', *Nation and Athenaeum*, 43/2 (14 Apr. 1928), 49.

[207] 'T. S. Eliot—A Reply to the Condescending', *Cambridge Review*, 50/1230 (8 Feb. 1929), 254–6 (p. 255). Elsewhere Leavis wrote, of Murry's perceived decline, that in the 'notorious case of Mr Middleton Murry it is difficult not to lament a disaster. He was once a very fine critic'. 'This Age in Literary Criticism', *Bookman*, 83/493 (Oct. 1932), 8–9 (p. 9).

literary traditionalism, he was, in the same essay, already distancing himself from the new direction Eliot's criticism was taking: a direction that Jacob Bronowski had also deplored in writing chidingly of 'the moments when he is near becoming the intolerant cleric'.[208] Leavis continued to express his disapproval at the recent trends in Eliot's later criticism, writing in a review of *After Strange Gods*, 'that since the religious preoccupation has become insistent in them Mr Eliot's critical writings have been notable for showing less discipline of thought and emotion, less purity of interest, less power of sustained devotion and less courage than before'.[209] A further irony was supplied by W. H. Auden and Cecil Day Lewis when, in their introduction to *Oxford Poetry 1927*, they acclaimed Eliot's earlier poetry in something resembling Murry's critical style: calling for a poetic 'new synthesis' that would synchronize an emotional and intellectual prehension and an aesthetic youthfulness that 'should be a period of spiritual discipline, not a self-justifying dogma'.[210]

By the end of the 1920s Murry had cultivated the individuality of his critical response to such an extent that no one felt impelled to listen, especially the new generation of critics springing up throughout the academies of the Anglo-American world. Eliot had allowed his traditionalism to harden into an orthodoxy that would become at times (notably with *After Strange Gods*) equally repellent. The critics who rejected Murry would take Eliot as their model for a rigorous critical practice grounded in the values of a tradition and dedicated to detailed technical analysis. It was, however, to his earlier and not his current criticism that they turned: the criticism that had been written during the years of debate with Murry and with others. Murry and Eliot had been set on divergent courses from the start of the 1920s. The infusion of a religious content into this criticism only served to accelerate that divergence, making them not only alien to each other, but at times incomprehensible to their literary-critical successors.

---

[208] 'Criticism: *For Lancelot Andrewes*', *Cambridge Review*, 50/1226 (30 Nov. 1928), 176.

[209] 'Mr Eliot, Mr Wyndham Lewis and Lawrence', in *The Common Pursuit* (London, 1952), 240–7 (pp. 241–2).

[210] Preface, *Oxford Poetry 1927* (Oxford, 1927), p. vii.

Conclusion
Imperfect Orthodoxy

In the decade after the First World War the reputations of Eliot and Murry had undergone a gradual but complete reversal. By 1930, Murry, who ten years before had been the brightest prospect in literary criticism, had come to be perceived as an isolated, slightly embarrassing, figure on the margins of polite literary culture. His two books on Lawrence, *Son of Woman* (1931) and *Reminiscences of D. H. Lawrence* (1933), written shortly after that writer's death, only served to distance him even further from the literary mainstream: prompting, for example, Lawrence Durrell to write of 'that slimy little Jesus, Middleton Murry, croaking among the marshes'.[1] In contrast, Eliot, who had once been regarded as 'a wild man', now held a pre-eminent position in the literary world as, 'perhaps the most distinguished man of letters today in the British-speaking world'.[2] It was Murry who had been asked to give the Oxford lectures which would become *The Problem of Style* in 1921, and who was invited to give the prestigious Clark Lectures at Cambridge in 1924. Indeed, it was through Murry's exertions on his behalf that Eliot became the Clark lecturer in 1926. But by 1930 it was Eliot who was in demand as a lecturer, and it was in lecturing, rather than in the controversies of periodical criticism, that much of his later criticism would be conducted.

Through his creative writing and his lectures Eliot would achieve an immediately recognizable public identity as an authoritative voice in the intellectual culture of the mid-twentieth century; and his later

---

[1] To Henry Miller [early 1936], *The Durrell–Miller Letters, 1935–80*, ed. Ian S. MacNiven (London, 1988), 9.
[2] Paul Elmer More, in a review of Eliot's *Selected Essays* for the *Saturday Review of Literature* (1932), repr. in Leonard Unger (ed.), *T. S. Eliot: A Selected Critique* (New York, 1948), 24–9 (p. 2).

criticism would be marked with a solemn gravity characteristic of that status. Although his tone, as Roger Sharrock has shown, had developed during the period in which his criticism was at its most embattled—and had indeed been a useful weapon in that contention—it found its proper medium in the privileged, and unchallenged, monologue of the public lecture.[3] This legacy has, arguably, led certain commentators to regard his earlier criticism as similarly monological: as a particular kind of privileged *ex cathedra* pronouncement. It is this view that I have attempted to challenge, suggesting that Eliot's criticism, like Murry's, was dialogical in its growth: a negotiation through a particularly fraught time for literary criticism.

While several commentators have made valuable contributions in pointing to a number of philosophical traces present in Eliot's literary criticism, that criticism cannot be understood entirely by reference back to those sources. For what must also be taken into consideration are the practical needs to which that criticism was addressed, and the debates in which it was articulated. In concentrating on Eliot's debate with Murry, I have attempted to show just how important those contextual imperatives were, and how the resulting conflict helped shape each man's criticism.

In one sense the debate between them, hedged variously in the dichotomies of personality versus impersonality, romanticism versus classicism, and nonconformism versus Catholicism, can be seen as a particular manifestation of the perennial conflict between empiricism and rationalism, that is between a system of value that builds outward from personal experience and one that derives its authority from a value that is already given. In his attempts to institute a new experimental philosophy in *Reconstruction in Philosophy*, John Dewey, an older contemporary of Eliot and Murry, delineated two such competing elements in the history of the philosophy of the modern period. The empiricism of Bacon, Locke, Condillac, and Helvetius he described as having 'a critical purpose in mind' in undermining the status of traditional beliefs in a transcendental reason:

they made it their business to show that some current belief or institution that claimed the sanction of innate ideas or necessary conceptions, or an

---

[3] See Roger Sharrock, 'Eliot's "Tone" ', in Newton-de Molina (ed.), *The Literary Criticism of T. S. Eliot*, 160–83.

origin in an authoritative revelation of reason, had in fact proceeded from a lowly origin in experience, and had been confirmed by accident, by class interest or by biased authority.

In reaction to this intentionally disintegrative empiricism, Kant and his successors attempted to reconstitute a rationalistic idealism:

the rationalists employed the logic of sensationalistic-empiricism to show that experience, giving only a heap of chaotic and isolated particulars, is as fatal to science and to moral laws and obligations as to obnoxious institutions; and concluded that 'Reason' must be resorted to if experience was to be furnished with any binding and connecting principles.[4]

Where Dewey's reading deviates from other, more common, renderings of this history, and where it is of particular pertinence to this study, is in its insistence that these views are dialogical as well as antipodal: that each takes account of, and positions itself carefully in, its relation to the other. In historicizing these ideas, Dewey shows that the particular world-view espoused by each does not come about in a kind of ideational isolation, but is rather the product of particular historical and discursive factors: that, in fact, the demands of argument and of reaction are as important as substantive influences in the creation and transmission of philosophical ideas.

This study has suggested that a similar operation can been seen in the literary criticism of Eliot and Murry in the period discussed. In an unpublished article, 'Significant Persons', written towards the end of the 1920s, Murry had written of the post-war period that 'the traditional forms of human experience have dissolved. Each man who is committed to the burden of self-consciousness, has to reach his own conclusions.'[5] In this literary-critical void, Murry and Eliot were faced with their own reconstructive programmes. At first, their common concern with this reconstructive need saw them working in an unlikely partnership at the *Athenaeum*, doing what Richard Aldington has described as 'useful work in maintaining standards'.[6] But as the 1920s progressed, and as Eliot and Murry began to develop critical vocabularies in which their differences might become articulated, the trends that had been present in their criticism from an early stage

[4] John Dewey, *Reconstruction in Philosophy* (1920; enlarged edn. Boston, Mass., 1948), 82, 83.

[5] 'Significant Persons', undated holograph manuscript, Edinburgh, 13 pp. [p. 2]. Although the manuscript is undated, it shows evidence of having been written between the mid-1920s and the death of D. H. Lawrence in 1930.

[6] *Life for Life's Sake*, 218.

became more pronounced, beginning a process of divergence. The competition between the *Criterion* and the *Adelphi* only served to accentuate that divergence, and perhaps accelerate it; with the debates between the two writers forcing each to articulate a position that might otherwise have remained only implicit. Eliot would probably not have written 'The Function of Criticism' had it not been for the rise of the *Adelphi* and the provocation of Murry's 'On Fear; And on Romanticism'; which, as Eliot admitted, showed him the need for defined positions and that 'now and then one must actually reject something and select something else'.[7] Similarly, Murry would never have written 'Towards a Synthesis' had it not been for the assault on his romanticism by Eliot and Read. By the time that Eliot and Murry discovered a religious vocabulary into which they might translate the terms of their argument, their opposition had become entrenched. Eliot would, in *After Strange Gods*, attempt to recast the old classicism versus romanticism dichotomy into a more fundamental divide, between orthodoxy and heterodoxy.[8] But that movement, and indeed those terms, had been present in his dismissal of Murry's advocacy of a critical reason at the end of 1927.

Even at the height of this orthodoxy, however, Eliot's criticism betrayed a number of inconsistencies which made his claims to a coherent, autotelic theory of literary criticism seem little more than wishful thinking. This can be seen particularly in his difficulties in insisting upon literature's absolute separation from religious, and from wider social, discourses. The idiosyncratic interpretation of a kind of flexible orthodoxy, reminiscent of the mutable 'ideal order' of the monuments of the literary tradition in 'Tradition and the Individual Talent', only emphasizes the continuing failure of even religious terminology to secure a fixed literary-critical usage, especially when that orthodoxy is compared to the professions of doubt in *The Use of Poetry and the Use of Criticism*.

In his later criticism, Eliot would accept that literature might not be isolated from its wider social and religious contexts. During the later part of his debate with Murry, he had returned constantly to Murry's refusal to separate the functions of literature, ethics, and religion. By 1948, however, he was writing, that 'to judge a work of art by artistic or by religious standards, to judge a religion by

---

[7] 'The Function of Criticism', *Criterion*, 2/5 (Oct. 1923), 31–42 (p. 34).
[8] See *After Strange Gods*, 15–30.

religious or artistic standards should come in the end to the same thing'.⁹ That this was exactly Murry's contention in the later part of their disagreement is perhaps beside the point. What is of more interest is that it shows just how far Eliot's notion of orthodoxy might be stretched: from an initial Thomist concern to isolate literary from religious values, to a later emphasis on their integration. Similarly, Eliot's insistence that Murry provide a thoroughgoing verificationist defence of his belief in a meaningful literary intuition would perhaps be discredited by his own later concession that poets may be 'occupied with frontiers of consciousness beyond which words fail, though meanings still exist'.¹⁰

Eliot effectively stamped out Murry's oppositional force in branding him a heretic: resorting to an absolutist language to be rid of his constant qualifications. But the orthodoxy in whose name that heresy was expunged was little more consistent than the traditionalism it replaced. In *After Strange Gods* Eliot disparaged literary professors and historians for taking too seriously a romantic–classic dichotomy whose 'chief value is temporary and political'.¹¹ His replacement for classicism, orthodoxy, gives little evidence, however, of providing any more lasting or absolute standard for the evaluation of literature. Indeed, if anything, it is even more contingent and political than the earlier categorization; introducing the kind of extra-literary connotations over whose use he had admonished Murry. Just how far this process had come by the publication of *After Strange Gods*, can be seen in a review of that book by Sir Arthur Quiller-Couch in 1934. Quiller-Couch complains of Eliot's argument that,

what he means by 'Liberalism', except that it is something he dislikes, one must use patience to discern, so dextrously he shuffles religion into politics, politics into literature, tradition into dogma, to and fro, until the reader— let alone a listener—can scarcely tell out of what category the card (so to speak) is being dealt.¹²

Five or six years earlier it might have been Eliot criticizing his impressionistic elder in these terms; but now it is Quiller-Couch who, ironically but with some justification, points to the lack of rigour in Eliot's language of critical orthodoxy.

⁹ *Notes Towards the Definition of Culture* (London, 1948), 30.
¹⁰ *The Music of Poetry* (1942), in *On Poetry and Poets*, 26–38 (p. 30).
¹¹ *After Strange Gods*, 25.
¹² 'Tradition and Orthodoxy', in *The Poet as Citizen* (Cambridge, 1934), 44–65 (p. 61).

Eliot's own dissatisfaction with the conception of orthodoxy advanced in *After Strange Gods* was emphasized by his refusal to allow the book's subsequent republication. But if he had been more open to Murry's criticism, both he and several of the critics who have attempted either to discover an internal coherence running throughout his critical writing or to found a critical system on their perception of such a coherence, might have been less beguiled by the promise of an absolute, objective system within which literary criticism might discover a fixed set of principles. That he never would find such a system, or even a consistency, promised by his flirtation with Thomism and by his rejection of Murry would become clear in his later criticism, where he progressively backs down from, qualifies, or even revalues altogether his earlier, bolder statements.

Murry would come to recognize Eliot's position as one of the 'significant figures' of his literary generation, but he interpreted this significance as a personal trait, having little to do with the discovery of an objective critical method. Murry wrote that, in the wake of the First World War, 'even the modern apostles of authority write the word on the same *tabula rasa* as the individualist; they conclude that authority ought to be, they do not record its existence'.[13] That Eliot achieved a lasting authority, wrought out of such an unpromising context, is due, as Murry suggested, less to the objective truth or consistency of his contentions and rather more to his sensitivity as a critical reader and skill as a literary polemicist. A little like Murry, the authority that Eliot's critical work retains today rests firmly on his own discerning taste in literature: a quality that philosophy cannot teach. Where his philosophical training did benefit him, and this was a debt he acknowledged on several occasions, was in the defence of those tastes, and in their propagation in the dialogues of the competitive literary culture of the 1920s.

---

[13] 'Significant Persons', [p. 2].

Select Bibliography

UNPUBLISHED SOURCES

Manuscripts

The following documents, all by Murry, are contained in the John Middleton Murry Collection, Special Collections, Edinburgh University Library, MS 2506–MS 2519. As that collection has yet to be fully sorted and catalogued, I have included brief descriptions.

'Between Two Worlds', complete manuscript of the published work, quarto.
'The Classical Revival', copy of typescript with holograph additions by T. S. Eliot, 19 pp., quarto.
'The "Common-Sense" of Jesus', copy of typescript, 3 pp., quarto.
'The Detachment of Naturalism', holograph manuscript, 28 pp., quarto (Lilley, C.826).
'The Evolution of an Intellectual', typescript, 28 pp., quarto.
'God', complete holograph manuscript of the published work, quarto.
'Literary Criticism', typescript with holograph title, 6 pp., quarto.
'Man and the Supernatural', copy of typescript, 4 pp., quarto (Lilley, C.733).
'Matthew Arnold', copy of a typescript with holograph dating (29 Nov. 1923) and corrections, 9 pp., quarto.
'The Plays of T. S. Eliot', two typescripts, one with holograph corrections, 40 pp., quarto.
'Poetry and Philosophy', copy of typescript, 8 pp., quarto.
'Reason and Criticism', copy of typescript, 8 pp., quarto.
'Religion as Mystical Experience: 6 Lectures', copy of typescript, 76 pp., foolscap.
'Significant Persons', holograph manuscript, 13 pp., quarto.
'What is the Tradition?', typescript, 10 pp., quarto.
Untitled lecture (*c.*1940), holograph manuscript, 19 pp., quarto.
Untitled notebook, small foolscap.

Folio album of press cuttings with holograph additions.
Two boxes of assorted press cuttings.

Theses

Kereasky, M. R., 'The Classical and the Romantic Ideal in T. S. Eliot's Criticism' (Ph.D., London, 1988).
Noh, J. Y., 'T. S. Eliot and the Criterion' (D.Phil., Oxford, 1990).

PUBLISHED SOURCES

Primary Sources

Because of the extent of primary material by Eliot and Murry, I list only books published by them. Periodical and journal contributions have, when cited, been supplied with complete references at first citation in the footnotes. For a full list of these writings see the bibliographies of Bradshaw, Gallup, and Lilley listed in the Secondary Sources below.

T. S. Eliot

The Sacred Wood (1920; 2nd edn. London, 1928).
Homage to John Dryden: Three Essays on Poetry of the Seventeenth Century (London, 1924).
Shakespeare and the Stoicism of Seneca (London, 1927).
For Lancelot Andrewes: Essays on Style and Order (London, 1928).
Dante (London, 1929).
Thoughts after Lambeth (London, 1931).
The Use of Poetry and the Use of Criticism: Studies in the Relation of Criticism to Poetry in England (London, 1933).
After Strange Gods: A Primer of Modern Heresy (London, 1934).
The Idea of a Christian Society (London, 1939).
Notes Towards the Definition of Culture (London, 1948).
Selected Essays, 3rd, enlarged edn. (London, 1951).
The Frontiers of Criticism (Minneapolis, Minn., 1956).
On Poetry and Poets (London, 1957).
To Criticize the Critic and other Writings (London, 1965).
The Varieties of Metaphysical Poetry: The Clark Lectures at Trinity College, Cambridge, 1926 and the Turnbull Lectures, ed. and introd. Ronald Schuchard (London, 1993).
(trans. and ed.), *Anabasis: A Poem by St-John Perse* (1930; rev. edn. London, 1959).
The Letters of T. S. Eliot, i: *1898–1922*, ed. Valerie Eliot (London, 1988).

John Middleton Murry

Fyodor Dostoevsky: A Critical Study (London, 1916).
Aspects of Literature (London, 1920).
The Evolution of an Intellectual (London, 1920).
Countries of the Mind: Essays in Literary Criticism (London, 1922).
The Problem of Style (London, 1922).
Pencillings: Little Essays on Literature (London, 1923).
Discoveries: Essays in Literary Criticism (London, 1924).
To the Unknown God: Essays Towards a Religion (London, 1924).
Keats and Shakespeare: A Study of Keats' Poetic Life from 1816 to 1820 (London, 1925).
The Life of Jesus (London, 1926).
Things to Come: Essays (London, 1928).
God: Being an Introduction to the Science of Metabiology (London, 1929).
Countries of the Mind: Essays in Literary Criticism, 2nd series (London, 1931).
Son of Woman: The Story of D. H. Lawrence (London, 1931).
Reminiscences of D. H. Lawrence (London, 1933).
William Blake (London, 1933).
Between Two Worlds: An Autobiography (London, 1935).
The Challenge of Schweitzer (London, 1948).
Katherine Mansfield and other Literary Portraits (London, 1953).
Love, Freedom and Society (London, 1957).
Katherine Mansfield and other Literary Studies (London, 1959).
John Middleton Murry: Selected Criticism, 1916–1957, ed. Richard Rees (London, 1960).
Poets, Critics, Mystics: A Selection of Criticisms Written Between 1919 and 1955 by John Middleton Murry, ed. Richard Rees (London, 1970).
Defending Romanticism: Selected Criticism of John Middleton Murry, ed. Malcolm Woodfield (Bristol, 1989).
The Letters of John Middleton Murry to Katherine Mansfield, ed. C. A. Hankin (London, 1983).

Secondary Sources

ACKROYD, PETER, *T. S. Eliot* (London, 1984).
AIKEN, CONRAD, *A Reviewer's ABC: Collected Criticism of Conrad Aiken from 1916 to the Present*, introd. Rufus A. Blanchard (London, 1961).
—— *Ushant: An Essay* (London, 1963).
ALDINGTON, RICHARD, *Images of War* (London, 1919).
—— *Literary Studies and Reviews* (London, 1924).
—— *French Studies and Reviews* (London, 1926).
—— *Death of a Hero* (London, 1929).

ALDINGTON, RICHARD, *Stepping Heavenward: A Record* (Florence, 1931).

—— *Life for Life's Sake: A Book of Reminiscences* (New York, 1941).

—— *Ezra Pound and T. S. Eliot: A Lecture* (Hurst, Berks., 1954).

ALLAN, MOWBRAY, *T. S. Eliot's Impersonal Theory of Poetry* (Lewisburg, 1974).

ANGELL, NORMAN, *The Press and the Organisation of Society* (London, 1922).

AUBER, ROGER, 'The Modernist Crisis', in Roger Auber *et al.* (eds.), *The Church in the Industrial Age* (London, 1981), 420–83.

AUDEN, W. H., and LEWIS, CECIL DAY (eds.), *Oxford Poetry 1927* (Oxford, 1927).

AUSTEN, ALLEN, *T. S. Eliot: The Literary and Social Criticism* (London, 1971).

BABBITT, IRVING, *The New Laokoon: An Essay on the Confusion of the Arts* (London, 1910).

—— *The Masters of Modern French Criticism* (London, 1913).

—— *Rousseau and Romanticism* (Boston, Mass., 1919).

BALDICK, CHRIS, *The Social Mission of English Criticism, 1848–1932* (1983), corrected and enlarged edn. (Oxford, 1987).

—— *Criticism and Literary Theory: 1890 to the Present* (London, 1996).

BATESON, F. W., 'Dissociation of Sensibility', *EIC* 1/3 (July 1951), 302–12.

BEER, J. B., 'John Middleton Murry', *Critical Quarterly*, 3/1 (Spring 1961), 59–66.

BERGONZI, BERNARD, 'Before 1914: Writers and the Threat of War', *Critical Quarterly*, 6/2 (Summer 1964), 126–34.

—— *T. S. Eliot*, 2nd edn. (London, 1978).

BERGSON, HENRI, *Matter and Memory* (1896), trans. Nancy Margaret Paul and W. Scott Palmer (London, 1911).

—— *Le Rire* (1900), in *Comedy* ed. Wylie Sypher, rev. edn. (London, 1980), 51–190.

—— *An Introduction to Metaphysics* (1903), trans. T. E. Hulme (London, 1913).

—— *Creative Evolution* (1907), trans. Arthur Mitchell (London, 1911).

BRADSHAW, DAVID, 'John Middleton Murry and the "Times Literary Supplement": The Importance and Usage of a Modern Literary Archive', *Bulletin of Bibliography*, 48/4 (Dec. 1991), 199–212.

—— 'Eleven Reviews by T. S. Eliot, Hitherto Unnoted, from the *Times Literary Supplement*: A Conspectus', *Notes and Queries*, NS 42/2 (June 1995), 212–15.

—— 'The Best of Companions: J. W. N. Sullivan, Aldous Huxley, and the New Physics', *Review of English Studies*, NS 47/186 (1996), 188–206; NS 47/187 (1996), 352–68.

BRÉE, GERMAINE, *Twentieth-Century French Literature*, trans. Louise Guiney (London, 1983).

BRIDGES, ROBERT (ed.), *The Spirit of Man: An Anthology in English and French from the Philosophers and Poets, made by the Poet Laureate in 1915* (London, 1916).

BUITENHUIS, PETER, *The Great War of Words: Literature as Propaganda 1914–18 and After* (London, 1989).

BURNE, GLENN S., 'T. S. Eliot and Remy de Gourmont', *Bucknell Review*, 8/2 (Feb. 1959), 113–26.

—— *Remy de Gourmont: His Ideas and Influence in England and America* (Carbondale, Ill., 1963).

BUTLER, CHRISTOPHER, *Early Modernism: Literature, Music, and Painting in Europe, 1900–1916* (Oxford, 1994).

CARSWELL, JOHN, *Lives and Letters: A. R. Orage, Beatrice Hastings, Katherine Mansfield, John Middleton Murry, S. S. Koteliansky, 1906–1957* (London, 1978).

CASSAVANT, SHARRON GREER, *John Middleton Murry: The Critic as Moralist* (University of Alabama, 1982).

CHADWICK, OWEN, *The Victorian Church*, 2 vols. (London, 1966 and 1970), vol. ii: *1860–1901*.

CLARKE, I. F., *Voices Prophesying War, 1763–1984* (Oxford, 1966).

COLLINGWOOD, R. G., *Speculum Mentis: Or the Map of Knowledge* (Oxford, 1924).

COLLIS, J. S., *Farewell to Argument* (London, 1935).

COLLS, ROBERT, and DODD, PHILIP (eds.), *Englishness: Politics and Culture 1880–1920* (London, 1986).

COOK, SIR EDWARD, *Literary Recreations* (London, 1918).

—— *The Press in War-Time. With Some Account of the Official Press Bureau: An Essay* (London, 1920).

COPLESTONE, FREDERICK C., *Aquinas* (London, 1955).

—— *Friedrich Nietzsche: Philosopher of Culture* (1942; new edn. London, 1975).

CORKE, HILARY, 'John Middleton Murry', *Encounter*, 14/1 (Jan. 1960), 75–8.

COSSLETT, TESS (ed.), *Science and Religion in the Nineteenth Century* (Cambridge, 1984).

CRAIG, CAIRNS, *Yeats, Eliot, Pound and the Politics of Poetry* (London, 1982).

CRAWFORD, ROBERT, *The Savage and the City in the Work of T. S. Eliot* (Oxford, 1987).

DEWEY, JOHN, *Reconstruction in Philosophy* (1920; enlarged edn. Boston, Mass., 1948).

DOUGLASS, PAUL, *Bergson, Eliot and American Literature* (Lexington, Ky., 1986).

DOYLE, SIR ARTHUR CONAN, *To Arms!* (London, 1914).

—— *The German War* (London, 1914).

—— *A Visit to Three Fronts: June 1916* (London, 1916).

ECKSTEINS, MODRIS, *Rites of Spring: The Great War and the Birth of the Modern Age* (London, 1990).

ECO, UMBERTO, *Reflections on* The Name of the Rose, trans. William Weaver (London, 1985).

ELLIS, HAVELOCK, *The Dance of Life* (London, 1923).

ELLMANN, MAUD, *The Poetics of Impersonality: T. S. Eliot and Ezra Pound* (Brighton, 1987).

FERGUSON, JOHN, *The Arts in Britain in World War One* (London, 1980).

FOGLE, RICHARD HARTER, 'Beauty and Truth: John Middleton Murry on Keats', *D. H. Lawrence Review*, 2/1 (Spring 1969), 68–75.

FRANK, WALDO, *Salvos: An Informal Book about Books and Plays* (New York, 1924).

FREED, LEWIS, *T. S. Eliot: The Critic as Philosopher* (West Lafayette, Ind., 1979).

FULLER, J. G., *Troop Morale and Popular Culture in the British and Dominion Armies 1914–1918* (Oxford, 1990).

FUSSELL, PAUL, *The Great War and Modern Memory* (London, 1975).

GALLUP, DONALD, *T. S. Eliot: A Bibliography* (London, 1969).

GERRARD, THOMAS J., *Bergson: An Exposition and Criticism from the Point of View of St Thomas Aquinas* (London, 1913).

GILBERT, BENTLEY B., *British Social Policy, 1914–1939* (London, 1970).

GLOVER, T. R., *The Jesus of History* (London, 1917).

GORDON, LYNDALL, *Eliot's Early Years* (Oxford, 1977).

—— *Eliot's New Life* (Oxford, 1989).

GORE, CHARLES, *The Reconstruction of Belief: Belief in God, Belief in Christ, The Holy Spirit and the Church* (London, 1926).

GOULD, GERALD, *The English Novel of To-Day* (London, 1924).

GOURMONT, REMY DE, 'Tradition and Other Things', trans. Richard Aldington, *Egoist*, 1/14 (15 July 1914), 261–2.

—— *La Culture des idées* (1900; 15th edn. Paris, 1916).

—— *Le Problème du style: Questions d'art, de littérature et de grammaire*, 3rd edn., (Paris, 1902).

—— *Promenades littéraires I* (1903; 11th edn. Paris, 1922).

—— *Lettres à l'Amazone* (1914; 21st edn. Paris, 1924).

—— *Selections*, ed. and trans. Richard Aldington (London, 1932).

—— *Selected Writings*, ed. and trans. Glenn S. Burne (Ann Arbor, Mich., 1966).

GRAINGER, J. H., *Patriotisms: Britain, 1900–1939* (London, 1986).

GRAVES, ROBERT, and HODGE, ALAN, *The Long Week-End: A Social History of Great Britain, 1918–1939* (London, 1941).

GRAY, PIERS, *T. S. Eliot's Intellectual and Poetic Development, 1909–1922* (Brighton, 1982).

GREENE, EDWARD J. H., *T. S. Eliot et la France* (Paris, 1951).

GRIERSON, HERBERT J. C., *The Background of English Literature and Other Essays* (1925; new edn. Harmondsworth, 1962).

GRIFFIN, ERNEST G., *John Middleton Murry* (New York, 1969).

—— 'The Circular and the Linear: The Middleton Murry–D. H. Lawrence Affair', *D. H. Lawrence Review*, 2/1 (Spring, 1969), 76–92.

GROSS, JOHN, *The Rise and Fall of the Man of Letters: Aspects of English Literary Life since 1800* (London, 1969).

HAMMOND, M. B., *British Labour Conditions and Legislation During the War* (London, 1919).

HANNA, THOMAS (ed.), *The Bergsonian Heritage* (New York, 1962).

HASTE, CATE, *Keep the Home Fires Burning: Propaganda in the First World War* (London, 1977).

HEATH, WILLIAM W., 'The Literary Criticism of John Middleton Murry', *PMLA* 70/1 (Mar. 1955), 47–57.

HEPPENSTALL, RAYNER, *Middleton Murry: A Study in Excellent Normality* (London, 1934).

—— *Four Absentees* (London, 1960).

HOBSBAWM, ERIC J., and RANGER, TERENCE (eds.), *The Invention of Tradition* (Cambridge, 1983).

HOUGH, GRAHAM, *Image and Experience: Studies in a Literary Revolution* (London, 1960).

HOWARTH, HERBERT, *Notes on Some Figures Behind T. S. Eliot* (London, 1965).

HUGHES, H. STUART, *Consciousness and Society: The Reorientation of European Social Thought, 1890–1930* (Brighton, 1979).

HULME, T. E., *Speculations: Essays on Humanism and the Philosophy of Art*, ed. Herbert Read (1924; 2nd edn. London, 1936).

—— *Further Speculations of T. E. Hulme*, ed. Samuel Hynes (Minneapolis, Minn., 1955).

HYNES, SAMUEL, *A War Imagined: The First World War and English Culture* (London, 1990).

INGE, WILLIAM RALPH, *Outspoken Essays* (London, 1919).

—— *The Church in the World* (London, 1927).

ISER, WOLFGANG, *Walter Pater: The Aesthetic Moment*, trans. David Henry Wilson (Cambridge, 1987).

JACKSON, HOLBROOK, *The Eighteen Nineties: A Review of Art and Ideas at the Close of the Nineteenth Century* (1913; repr. London, 1988).

JAMES, WILLIAM, *The Varieties of Religious Experience: A Study in Human Nature* (London, 1902).

—— *Pragmatism: A New Name for Some Old Ways of Thinking* (New York, 1907).

—— *The Meaning of Truth: A Sequel to Pragmatism* (New York, 1909).

JOHNSON, PAUL BARTON, *Land Fit for Heroes: The Planning of British Reconstruction 1916–1919* (London, 1968).

JONES, GRANIA, 'Eliot and History', *Critical Quarterly*, 18/3 (Autumn 1976), 31–48.

JONES, JOHN, 'Murry Revaluated', *New Statesman*, 58 (12 Dec. 1959), 848.

KENNER, HUGH, *The Invisible Poet: T. S. Eliot* (London, 1960).

—— (ed.), *T. S. Eliot: A Collection of Critical Essays* (Englewood Cliffs, NJ, 1962).

KENNY, ANTHONY, (ed.), *Aquinas: A Collection of Critical Essays* (London, 1970).

—— *Aquinas* (Oxford, 1980).

KERMODE, FRANK, *Romantic Image* (1957; new edn. London, 1986).

KEYNES, JOHN MAYNARD, *The Economic Consequences of the Peace* (London, 1919).

KIPLING, RUDYARD, *Kipling's Message* (London, 1918).

KNIGHT, G. WILSON, 'J. Middleton Murry', in *Neglected Powers: Essays on Nineteenth and Twentieth Century Literature* (London, 1971), 352–67.

KOJECKY, ROGER, *T. S. Eliot's Social Criticism* (London, 1971).

KOLAKOWSKI, LESZEK, *Bergson* (Oxford, 1985).

KRAMER, JÜRGEN, 'T. S. Eliot's Concept of Tradition: A Revaluation', *New German Critique*, 6 (Fall 1975), 20–30.

KRETZMANN, NORMAN, KENNY, ANTHONY, and PINBORG, JAN (eds.), *The Cambridge History of Later Medieval Philosophy: From the Rediscovery of Aristotle to the Disintegration of Scholasticism, 1100–1600* (Cambridge, 1982).

KRIEGER, MURRAY, 'The Ambiguous Anti-Romanticism of T. E. Hulme', *ELH* 20 (1953), 300–14.

LAWRENCE, D. H., *Fantasia of the Unconscious* (1923), in *Fantasia of the Unconscious and Psychoanalysis and the Unconscious*, Phoenix edn. (London, 1961).

—— *Kangaroo* (1923; Phoenix edn. London, 1955).

—— *Phoenix: The Posthumous Papers of D. H. Lawrence*, ed. Edward D. McDonald (London, 1936).

LEA, F. A., *The Life of John Middleton Murry* (London, 1959).

—— 'Murry and Marriage', *D. H. Lawrence Review*, 2/1 (Spring 1969), 1–21.

—— *Lawrence and Murry: A Twofold Vision* (London, 1985).

LEAVIS, F. R., 'T. S. Eliot: A Reply to the Condescending', *Cambridge Review*, 50/1230 (8 Feb. 1929), 254–6.

—— 'This Age in Literary Criticism', *Bookman*, 83/493 (Oct. 1932), 8–9.

—— *New Bearings in English Poetry: A Study of the Contemporary Situation* (1932; 2nd edn. London, 1950).

—— *Revaluation: Tradition and Development in Modern Poetry* (London, 1936).

—— *The Common Pursuit* (London, 1952).

—— *D. H. Lawrence: Novelist* (London, 1955).

—— *Anna Karenina and other Essays* (London, 1967).

—— (ed.), *Towards Standards of Criticism: Selections from* The Calendar of Modern Letters, *1925–7* (1933; new edn. London, 1976).

—— and THOMPSON, DENYS, *Culture and Environment: The Training of Critical Awareness* (London, 1933).

LE BRUN, PHILIP, 'T. S. Eliot and Henri Bergson', *Review of English Studies*, 18/70 (1967), 49–61; 18/71 (1967), 274–86.

LEE, BRIAN, *Theory and Personality: The Significance of T. S. Eliot's Criticism* (London, 1979).

LEVENSON, MICHAEL H., *A Genealogy of Modernism: A Study of English Literary Doctrine 1908–1922* (Cambridge, 1984).

LEWIS, WYNDHAM, *Men Without Art* (London, 1934).

—— *Blasting and Bombardiering* (1937; rev. edn. London, 1982).

LILLEY, GEORGE P., *A Bibliography of John Middleton Murry, 1889–1957* (London, 1974).

LITZ, A. WALTON (ed.), *Eliot in his Time: Essays on the Occasion of the Fiftieth Anniversary of The Waste Land* (London, 1973).

LIVINGSTONE, R. W. (ed.), *The Legacy of Greece* (Oxford, 1921).

LLOYD, ROGER, *The Church of England, 1900–1965* (London, 1966).

LOBB, EDWARD, *T. S. Eliot and the Romantic Critical Tradition* (London, 1981).

LOWELL, AMY, *Six French Poets* (New York, 1916).

—— (ed.), *Some Imagist Poets* (Boston, Mass., 1915).

LUBBOCK, PERCY, *The Craft of Fiction* (London, 1921).

LUCY, SEÁN, *T. S. Eliot and the Idea of Tradition* (London, 1960).

McCALLUM, PAMELA, *Literature and Method: Towards a Critique of I. A. Richards, T. S. Eliot and F. R. Leavis* (Dublin, 1983).

MacKENDRICK, LOUIS K., 'T. S. Eliot and the *Egoist*: The Critical Preparation', *Dalhousie Review*, 55/1 (Spring 1975), 140–54.

MacNIVEN, IAN S. (ed.), *The Durrell–Miller Letters, 1935–80* (London, 1988).

MacQUARRIE, JOHN, *Twentieth-Century Religious Thought: The Frontiers of Philosophy and Theology, 1900–1960* (London, 1963).

MAIRET, PHILIP, *John Middleton Murry*, Writers and their Work 102 (London, 1958).

MAJOR, H. D. A., *English Modernism: Its Origins, Methods, Aims: Being the William Belden Noble Lectures Delivered in Harvard University, 1925–6* (London, 1927).

—— *Thirty Years After* (London, 1929).

MANSFIELD, KATHERINE, *Letters to John Middleton Murry, 1913–1922*, ed. John Middleton Murry (London, 1951).

MARGOLIS, JOHN D., *T. S. Eliot's Intellectual Development, 1922–1939* (London, 1972).

MARITAIN, JACQUES, *Art and Scholasticism, with Other Essays*, trans. J. F. Scanlan (London, 1933).

—— *Bergsonian Philosophy and Thomism*, trans. Mabelle L. Andison (New York, 1955).

MARTIN, GRAHAM (ed.), *Eliot in Perspective: A Symposium* (London, 1970).

MARWICK, ARTHUR, *The Deluge: British Society and the First World War* (1965; repr. London, 1973).

MASTERMAN, C. F. G., *England after War: A Study* (London, 1922).

MATTHIESON, F. O., *The Achievement of T. S. Eliot: An Essay on the Nature of Poetry*, 3rd edn. (New York, 1959).

MENAND, LOUIS, *Discovering Modernism: T. S. Eliot and his Context* (Oxford, 1987).

MESSINGER, GARY S., *British Propaganda and the State in the First World War* (Manchester, 1992).

MONTAGUE, CHARLES E., *Disenchantment* (London, 1922).

MOODY, A. D., *Thomas Stearns Eliot: Poet* (Cambridge, 1979).

MORGAN, KENNETH O., *Consensus and Disunity: The Lloyd George Coalition Government, 1918–1922* (Oxford, 1979).

MORSE, J. L., 'T. S. Eliot in 1921: Toward the Dissociation of Sensibility', *Western Humanities Review*, 30/1 (Winter 1976), 31–40.

MOSSOP, D., 'Un disciple de Gourmont: Richard Aldington', *Revue de littérature comparée*, 25/4 (Oct.–Dec. 1951), 403–35.

MOWAT, CHARLES LOCH, *Britain Between the Wars, 1918–1940*, corrected repr. (London, 1956).

MUIR, EDWIN, *Transitions: Essays in Contemporary Literature* (London, 1926).

—— *The Present Age From 1914* (London, 1939).

MURRAY, GILBERT, *How Can War Ever be Right?* (London, 1914).

—— *Thoughts on the War* (London, 1914).

MURRY, COLIN MIDDLETON, *One Hand Clapping* (London, 1975).

MURRY, KATHERINE MIDDLETON, *Beloved Quixote: The Unknown Life of John Middleton Murry* (London, 1986).

MURRY, MARY MIDDLETON, *To Keep Faith* (London, 1959).

NEEDHAM, JOSEPH (ed.), *Science, Religion, and Reality* (London, 1925).

NEWTON-DE MOLINA, DAVID (ed.), *The Literary Criticism of T. S. Eliot: New Essays* (London, 1977).

NICHOLS, ROBERT (ed.), *Anthology of War Poetry, 1914–1918* (London, 1943).

NIETZSCHE, FRIEDRICH, *The Will to Power*, trans. Walter Kaufmann and R. J. Hollingdale, ed. Walter Kaufmann (New York, 1968).

—— *Ecce Homo: How One Becomes What One Is*, trans. R. J. Hollingdale (London, 1988).

—— *Twilight of the Idols* and *The Anti-Christ*, trans. R. J. Hollingdale (London, 1990).

NOLTE, ERNST, *Three Faces of Fascism: Action Française, Italian Fascism, National Socialism*, trans. Leila Vennewitz (New York, 1966).

ORCHARD, W. E., 'Religion and Christianity: A Reply', *Adelphi*, 1/12 (May 1924), 1074–84.

ORWELL, GEORGE, *The Road to Wigan Pier* (1937; repr. Harmondsworth, 1962).

PATER, WALTER, *Appreciations: With an Essay on Style* (1889), library edn. (London, 1910).

—— *Miscellaneous Studies: A Series of Essays* (1895; library edn. London, 1910).

PICK, DANIEL, *Faces of Degeneration: A European Disorder, c.1848–c.1918* (Cambridge, 1989).

PICKERING, W. S. F., *Anglo-Catholicism: A Study in Religious Ambiguity* (London, 1989).

PILKINGTON, A. E., *Bergson and his Influence: A Reassessment* (Cambridge, 1976).

PONDROM, CYRENA N., *The Road from Paris: French Influence on English Poetry, 1900–1920* (Cambridge, 1974).

PONSONBY, ARTHUR, *Falsehood in Wartime* (London, 1928).

POUND, EZRA, *Literary Essays of Ezra Pound*, ed. T. S. Eliot (London, 1954).

—— *Selected Prose, 1909–1965*, ed. William Cookson (London, 1973).

QUILLER-COUCH, SIR ARTHUR, *On the Art of Writing: Lectures Delivered in the University of Cambridge, 1913–1914* (Cambridge, 1916).

—— *Studies in Literature* (Cambridge, 1918).

—— *On the Art of Reading: Lectures Delivered in the University of Cambridge, 1916–1917* (Cambridge, 1920).

—— *The Poet as Citizen and other Papers* (Cambridge, 1934).

RALEIGH, SIR WALTER, *Style* (London, 1897).

—— *Might is Right* (Oxford, 1914).

—— *The War of Ideas: An Address to the Royal Colonial Institute Delivered December 12, 1916* (Oxford, 1917).

—— *Some Gains of the War: An Address to the Royal Colonial Institute Delivered February 13, 1918* (Oxford, 1918).

—— *The War and the Press: A Paper Read March 14th 1918 to the Essay Society, Eton College* (Oxford, 1918).

RANCHETTI, MICHELE, *The Catholic Modernists: A Study of the Religious Reform Movement, 1864–1907*, trans. Isabel Quigly (London, 1969).

READ, SIR HERBERT, *Reason and Romanticism: Essays in Literary Criticism* (London, 1926).

—— *Collected Essays in Literary Criticism* (1935; 2nd edn. London, 1951).

—— *A Coat of Many Colours* (London, 1945).

REARDON, BERNARD M. G. (ed.), *Roman Catholic Modernism* (London, 1970).

REES, GARNET, 'A French Influence on T. S. Eliot: Remy de Gourmont', *Revue de littérature comparée*, 16/4 (Oct.–Dec. 1936), 764–7.

—— 'The Position of Remy de Gourmont', *French Studies*, 4/4 (Oct. 1950), 289–305.

REES, SIR RICHARD, *A Theory of My Time: An Essay in Didactic Reminiscence* (London, 1963).

—— 'Politics of a Mystic', *D. H. Lawrence Review*, 2/1 (Spring 1969), 24–31.

—— 'John Middleton Murry', *DNB, 1951–1960* (London, 1970), 761–2.

RICHARDS, I. A., *Principles of Literary Criticism* (London, 1924).

RICKS, CHRISTOPHER, *T. S. Eliot and Prejudice* (London, 1988).

RICKWORD, EDGELL (ed.), *Scrutinies* (London, 1928).

ROBERTS, MICHAEL, *T. E. Hulme* (1938; repr. Manchester, 1982).

RUSSELL, BERTRAND, *Principles of Social Reconstruction* (London, 1916).

SANDERS, M. L., and TAYLOR, PHILIP M., *British Propaganda During the First World War, 1914–18* (London, 1982).

SASSOON, SIEGFRIED, *Siegfried's Journey, 1916–1920* (London, 1945).

SCHUCHARD, RONALD, 'Eliot and Hulme in 1916', *PMLA* 88/5 (Oct. 1973), 1083–94.

—— 'T. S. Eliot as Extension Lecturer, 1916–1919', *Review of English Studies*, NS 25/98 (May 1974), 163–73; NS 25/99 (Aug. 1974), 292–304.

SHARMA, L. R., *The T. S. Eliot–Middleton Murry Debate: The Shaping of Literary Theory; Modernist to Post-Structuralist* (Allahabad, 1994).

SHUSTERMAN, RICHARD, *T. S. Eliot and the Philosophy of Criticism* (London, 1988).

SILLARS, STUART, *Art and Survival in First World War Britain* (New York, 1987).

SKAFF, WILLIAM, *The Philosophy of T. S. Eliot: From Skepticism to a Surrealist Poetic, 1909–1927* (Philadelphia, Pa., 1986).

SMIDT, KRISTIAN, *Poetry and Belief in the Work of T. S. Eliot*, rev. edn. (London, 1961).

SMITH, JAMES, 'Notes on the Criticism of T. S. Eliot', *EIC* 22/4 (Oct. 1972), 333–61.

SPENDER, STEPHEN, *The Struggle of the Modern* (Berkeley, Calif., 1965).

SPINKS, G. STEPHEN, with ALLEN, E. L., and PARKES, JAMES, *Religion in Britain since 1900* (London, 1952).

STALLMAN, ROBERT WOOSTER (ed.), *Critiques and Essays in Criticism, 1920–1948* (New York, 1949).

STANFORD, DEREK, 'Middleton Murry as Literary Critic', *EIC* 8/1 (Jan. 1958), 60–7.

STEAD, C. K., *The New Poetic: Yeats to Eliot* (London, 1964).

STEPHENSON, ALAN M. G., *The Rise and Decline of English Modernism: The Hulsean Lectures, 1979–80* (London, 1984).

STEVENSON, JOHN, *British Society, 1914–45*, Pelican Social History of Britain (Harmondsworth, 1984).

STREETER, BURNETT HILLMAN (ed.), *Foundations* (London, 1912).

—— *Reality: A New Correlation of Science and Religion* (London, 1926).

—— et al., *Adventure: The Faith of Science and the Science of Faith* (London, 1927).

SULLIVAN, J. W. N., *Aspects of Science* (London, 1923).

—— *Aspects of Science*, 2nd series (London, 1926).

SVARNY, ERIK, '*The Men of 1914*': T. S. Eliot and Early Modernism (Milton Keynes, 1988).

SYMONDS, JOHN ADDINGTON, *Essays Speculative and Suggestive* (1890; 3rd edn. London, 1907).

TATE, ALLEN (ed.), *T. S. Eliot: The Man and his Work* (London, 1967).

TAYLOR, A. J. P., *English History, 1914–1945* (1965; corrected repr. Oxford, 1976).

—— *The Teaching of English in England* (London, 1921).

THATCHER, DAVID S., *Nietzsche in England 1890–1914* (Toronto, 1970).

THOMPSON, ERIC, 'Dissociation of Sensibility', *EIC* 2/2 (Apr. 1952), 207–13.

—— *Tradition and Experiment in Present-Day Literature: Addresses Delivered at the City Literary Institute* (London, 1929).

UNGER, LEONARD (ed.), *T. S. Eliot: A Selected Critique* (New York, 1948).

VIDLER, ALEC R., *A Variety of Catholic Modernists* (Cambridge, 1970).

WALLACE, STUART, *War and the Image of Germany: British Academics, 1914–1918* (Edinburgh, 1988).

WATSON, GEORGE, *The Literary Critics: A Study of English Descriptive Criticism* (Harmondsworth, 1964).

WEINBLATT, ALAN, 'T. S. Eliot and the Historical Sense', *South Atlantic Quarterly*, 77/3 (Summer 1978), 282–95.

WELLEK, RENÉ, *A History of Modern Criticism: 1750–1950*, 7 vols. (London 1955–88).

WELLS, H. G., *War and Common Sense* (London, 1913).

—— *The War that Will End War* (London, 1914).

—— *The Elements of Reconstruction* (London, 1916).

—— *The War and Socialism* (London, 1918).

WHITEHEAD, ALFRED NORTH, *Science and the Modern World: Lowell Lectures, 1925* (Cambridge, 1926).

—— *Religion in the Making: Lowell Lectures, 1926* (Cambridge, 1926).

WHITING, CHARLES G., *Paul Valéry* (London, 1978).

WILKINSON, ALAN, *The Church of England in the First World War* (London, 1978).

WILLIS, IRENE COOPER, *How we Came out of the War* (London, 1921).

WINBOLT, S. E., 'The Reform of Classical Education', *Athenaeum*, 4625 (Jan. 1918), 25–7.

WOLLHEIM, RICHARD, 'Eliot, Bradley and Immediate Experience', *New Statesman*, 67/1722 (13 Mar. 1964), 401–2.

WOOLF, LEONARD, *An Autobiography*, ii: *1911–1969* (Oxford, 1980).

WOOLF, VIRGINIA, *Mr Bennett and Mrs Brown* (London, 1924).

—— *The Diary of Virginia Woolf*, ed. Anne Olivier Bell, 5 vols. (London, 1977–84).

WRIGHT, D. G., 'The Great War, Government Propaganda and English "Men of Letters" 1914–16', *Literature and History*, 7 (Spring 1978), 70–100.

Index